W9-BTM-209

"If you enjoy fine, minimalist prose and thoughtful, intelligent crime stories, you would be well advised to begin with the first in the series and read them all." —*Associated Press*

Praise for *Cypress Grove*

"*Cypress Grove* features another complex protagonist and a story brimming with Southern atmosphere . . . a mystery that demands to be savored . . . [It] should attract an even broader audience for the author's visually tantalizing, astute observations on crime and the human condition." —*Los Angeles Times*

"[A] masterly composed novel . . . Sallis, a poet in private eye's clothing, has found in Turner a rich new character to hang around with. Let's hope this isn't the last we see of him." —*Boston Globe*

"As Turner's memories are unlocked, so are his feelings—and his language . . . Although he went out to find a killer, Turner earns his redemption by finding his own lost voice."
—*New York Times Book Review*

"Sallis might be one of the best writers in America . . . Almost every page produces a sentence, phrase or paragraph so deliciously right that readers will want to reread it. Sallis fans will pounce on this one. If you're not acquainted with his work, this is a fine place to start." —*Cleveland Plain Dealer*

"As a construct, *Cypress Grove*, is virtuosic . . . very successful in many ways, least of all in making the reader ask himself some rather pointed questions." —*Newsday*

"Intriguing . . . Sallis's quirky sense of plot rhythms and careful prose make this an outstanding and unpredictable literary thriller."
—*Seattle Times*

"The setup sounds familiar . . . But Sallis pulls off the story with such panache that few will notice . . . fast and stylish."
—*Entertainment Weekly*

Praise for *Cripple Creek*

"The burned-out Memphis cop named Turner who sought refuge from his demons as a rural sheriff's deputy in *Cyprus Grove* is still a long way from being socialized in *Cripple Creek*. But he's now admitting visitors to his cabin in the woods, and when a mobster blows in from the city to spring a confederate from the local jail, Turner is mad enough to take his grievance straight back to Memphis. 'Figure they can do whatever they want out here on the edge, I'm thinking,' he says, in the spare but eloquent idiom that pegs him—along with this superior series—as a keeper."
—*New York Times Book Review*

"Sallis writes lean, sinewy prose, with a nice twang and rhythm, that grabs your attention from the start and holds it fast to the end . . . smooth as aged bourbon."
—*Philadelphia Inquirer*

"I can think of no other writer—especially a so-called crime writer—who ranges so freely in his work and makes social and racial concerns ('this unspoken apartheid we live with still,' as Sallis puts it) so central to his fictive worlds . . . Reading Sallis, we can't help but be aware of the intelligence behind the work, as well as how much reading he has done in his life. He's an erudite man, and this informs the work at the deepest level."
—*Los Angeles Times Book Review*

"Sallis is an artist who happens to write mysteries."
—*Sacramento Bee*

"Sallis's lyricism and power trump everything else, including a shock at the end of the book. This is one you absolutely don't want to miss."
—*Cleveland Plain Dealer*

"It's a crime that a writer this good isn't better known."
—*Chicago Sun-Times*

"A darkly moving mystery that is unlike anything else being written today."
—*Chicago Tribune*

Praise for *Salt River*

"A sweet song of the South from a crime novelist with the ear of a poet."
                                              —*Atlanta Journal-Constitution*

"A highly unusual, atmospherically unique mystery novel . . . fans of noir fiction will find much here to keep them turning its pages."
                                              —*Boston Globe*

"James Sallis might be the 'purest' writer of crime fiction in America today. Which means that, beyond whatever story he's telling, his books are worth reading solely for what rises from the inspired use of language . . . He assembles sentences like a virtuoso guitarist working the fret board, gracefully choosing each word (or more accurately, each note) and making it resonate. Scenes often read like prose-poems, but they are assembled with the rigor a mystery demands. The succession of chapters exert a rhythmic, almost tidal pull, leading to a conclusion that defies genre expectation—but satisfies something far deeper."
                                              —*San Francisco Chronicle*

"Haunting . . . Sallis writes poetic rings around the subject."
                                              —*New York Times Book Review*

"Sallis is a gifted polymath: poet, biographer, translator, essayist, musician and prolific (if criminally neglected) novelist. His Turner books are little gems, with their sharp descriptions and melancholy reflections."
                                              —*Seattle Times*

"Elegiac meditations on fate, grief, and how we persevere in spite of it all."
                                              —*Entertainment Weekly*

"Holds the power of simplicity and the musical ring of truth as only Sallis can deliver it—as he has done bravely, consistently, for the last few decades."
                                              —*Los Angeles Times Book Review*

BY THE SAME AUTHOR

Novels

The Long-Legged Fly
Moth
Black Hornet
Eye of the Cricket
Bluebottle
Ghost of a Flea
Death Will Have Your Eyes
Renderings
Cypress Grove
Drive
Cripple Creek
Salt River

Stories

A Few Last Words
Limits of the Sensible World
Time's Hammers: Collected Stories
A City Equal to My Desire
Potato Tree

Poems

Sorrow's Kitchen
My Tongue in Other Cheeks: Selected Translations

As editor

Ash of Stars: On the Writing of Samuel R. Delany
Jazz Guitars
The Guitar in Jazz

Other

The Guitar Players
Difficult Lives
Saint Glinglin by Raymond Queneau (translator)
Gently into the Land of the Meateaters
Chester Himes: A Life
A James Sallis Reader

WHAT YOU HAVE LEFT

THE TURNER TRILOGY

Cypress Grove

Cripple Creek

Salt River

JAMES SALLIS

WALKER & COMPANY
NEW YORK

Published by Walker Publishing Company, Inc., New York

All papers used by Walker & Company are natural, recyclable products made
from wood grown in well-managed forests. The manufacturing processes
conform to the environmental regulations of the country of origin.

LIBRARY OF CONGRESS CATALOGING-IN-PUBLICATION DATA IS AVAILABLE

ISBN-10: 0-8027-1687-3
ISBN-13: 978-0-8027-1687-3

Cypress Grove first published by Walker & Company in 2003

Cripple Creek first published by Walker & Company in 2006

Salt River first published by Walker & Company in 2007

Visit Walker & Company's Web site at www.walkerbooks.com

First U.S. edition 2009

1 3 5 7 9 10 8 6 4 2

Typeset by Westchester Book Group
Printed in the United States of America by Quebecor World Fairfield

WHAT YOU HAVE LEFT

Cypress Grove

To the memory of
DAMON KNIGHT

Great man,
great friend,
greatly missed

If your kneebone achin'
and your body cold . . .
You just gettin' ready, honey,
for the cypress grove.

—*Skip James, "Cypress Grove Blues"*

Chapter One

I HEARD THE JEEP a half mile off. It came up around the lake, and when it hit the bend, birds took flight. They boiled up out of the trees, straight up, then, as though heavy wind had caught them, veered abruptly, all at once, sharp right. Most of those trees had been standing forty or fifty years. Most of the birds had been around less than a year and wouldn't be around much longer. I was somewhere in between.

I watched the Jeep as it emerged from trees and the driver dropped into third for the glide down that long incline to the cabin. Afternoon light on the lake turned it to tinfoil. Not much sound. High-in-the-throat hum of the well-maintained engine. From time to time the rustle of dry leaves as wind struck them and they tried to ring like bells there on the trees.

He pulled up a few yards distant, under the pecan tree. Shells on its yield so hard you had to stomp them to get to half a spoonful of meat. I swore that squirrels left them lined up under tires for cracking and sat alongside waiting. He got out of the Jeep and stood beside it. Wearing gray work clothes from Sears, old-fashioned wide-top Wellingtons and what looked to be an expensive hat, though one that would have been more at home further south and west. He stood leaning back against the driver's door with arms crossed, looking around. Folks around here don't move fast. They grow up respecting other folks' homes, their land and privacy, whatever lines have been drawn, some of them invisible. Respecting the history of the place, too. They sidle up, as they say; ease into things. Maybe that's why I was here.

"Good afternoon," he said, final syllable turned up slightly in such a way that his utterance might be taken as observation, greeting, query.

"They all are."

He nodded. "There is that. Even the worst of them, here in God's country. . . . Not interrupting anything, I hope."

I shook my head.

"Good. That's good." He pushed himself off the door, turned to reach inside, came out with a paper sack. "Looks to be room for the both of us up there on that porch."

I waved him aboard. Settling into the other chair, like my own a straightback kitchen chair gone rickety and braced with crisscrosses of sisal twine, he passed across the sack.

"Brought this."

I skinned paper back to a bottle of Wild Turkey.

"Talk to Nathan, by some chance?"

My visitor nodded. "He said, as the two of us hadn't met

before, it might be a good idea to bring along a little something. Grease the wheels."

Nathan'd lived in a cabin up here for sixty years or
more. Step on his land, whoever you were, you'd get
greeted with a volley of buckshot; that's what everyone
said. But not long after I moved in, Nathan started turning
up with a bottle every few weeks and we'd sit out here on
the porch or, coolish days, inside by the fire, passing the
bottle wordlessly back and forth till it was gone.

I went in to get glasses. Poured us both tall soldiers and
handed his across. He held it up to the light, sipped, sighed.

"Been meaning to get up this way and say hello," he
said. "Things keep shouldering in, though. I figured it
could wait. Not like either of us was going anywhere."

That was it for some time. We sat watching squirrels
climb trees and leap between them. I'd nailed an old rusted
pan onto the pecan tree and kept it filled with pecans for
them. From time to time one or the other of us reached out
to pour a freshener. Nothing much else moved. Up here
you're never far away from knowing that time's an illusion,
a lie.

We were into the last couple of inches of the bottle
when he spoke again.

"Hunt?"

I shook my head. "Did my share of it as a boy. I think
that may have been the only thing my old man loved. Game
on the table most days. Deer, rabbit, squirrel, quail and
dove, be begging people to take some. He never used anything but a .22."

"Gone now?"

3

"When I was twelve."

"Mine too."

I went in and made coffee, heated up stew from a couple of days back. When I returned to the porch with two bowls, dark'd gone halfway up the trees and the sounds around us had changed. Insects throbbed and thrummed. Frogs down by the lake sang out with that hollow, aching sound they have.

"Coffee to follow," I told him. "Unless you want it now."

"After's fine."

We sat over our stew. I'd balanced a thick slab of bread on each bowl, for dunking. Since I'd baked the bread almost a week before and it was going hard on stale, that worked just fine. So for a time we spooned, slurped, dunked and licked. Dribbles ran down shirtfronts and chins. I took in the bowls, brought out coffee.

"Never been much inclined to pry into a man's business."

Steam from the cups rose about our faces.

"Why you're here, where you're from, all that. Folks do pay me to keep track of what's going on in these parts, though. Like a lot of things in life, striking a balance's the secret to it."

Frogs had given up. Paired by now. Shut out by darkness. Resigned to spending their evening or life alone. Time for mosquitoes to take over, and they swarmed about us. I went in to replenish our coffee and, returning, told him, "No great secret to it. I was a cop. Spent eleven years in prison. Spent a few more years as a productive citizen. Then retired and came here. No reason things have to get more complicated than that."

He nodded. "Always do, though. It's in our nature."

I watched as a mosquito lit on the back of my hand, squatted a moment and flew away. A machine, really. Uncomplicated. Designed and set in motion to perform its single function perfectly.

"Can I do something for you, Sheriff?"

He held up his cup. "Great coffee."

"Bring a pot of water to boil, take it off the fire and throw in coffee. Cover and let sit."

"That simple."

I nodded.

He took another sip and looked about. "Peaceful out here, isn't it?"

"Not really."

An owl flew by, feet and tail of its prey, a rodent of some sort, dangling.

"Tell the truth, I kind of hoped I might be able to persuade you to help me. With a murder."

Chapter Two

LIFE, SOMEONE SAID, is what happens while we're waiting around for other things to happen that never do.

Amen! as Brother Douglas would have said, hoisting his Bible like a sword and brandishing it there framed by stained-glass windows depicting the Parable of the Talents, Mary Magdalene at the tomb, the Assumption.

Back then and back home, there among kudzu in the westward cup of Crowley's Ridge and eastward levees built to keep the river out, I'd been a golden child, headed for greatness—greatness meaning only escape from that town and its mean horizons. I'd ridden the cockhorse of a scholarship down the river to New Orleans, then back up it to Chicago (following the course of jazz) where, once I had secured a fellowship, head and future pointed like twin bullets towards professordom. Then our president went surreptitiously to war and took me with him. Walking on elbows through green even greener than that I'd grown up among, I recited Chaucer, recalled Euclid, enumerated, as a means of staying awake and alert, principles of economy—and left them there behind me on the trail: spore, droppings.

No difficulty for *this* boy, rejoining society. I got off the plane on a Friday, in Memphis, stood outside the bus station for an hour or so without going inside, then left. Never made it home. Found a cheap hotel. Monday I walked halfway across the city to the PD and filled out an application. Why the PD? After all these years, I can't remember any particular train of thought that led me there. I'd spent two and a half years getting shot at. Maybe I figured that was qualification enough.

Weeks later, instead of walking on elbows, I was sitting in a Ford that swayed and bucked like a son of a bitch, cylinders banging the whole time. Still making my way through the wilderness, though. If anything, the city was a stranger, more alien place to me than the jungle had been. Officer Billy Nabors was driving. He had breath that would peel paint and paper off walls and singe the pinfeathers off chickens.

"What I need you to do," he said, "is just shut the fuck up and sit there and keep your eyes open. Till I tell you to do something else, that's *all* I need you to do."

He hauled the beast down Jefferson towards Washington Bottoms, over a spectacular collection of potholes and into what appeared to be either a long-abandoned warehouse district or the set for some postwar science fiction epic. We pulled up alongside the only visible life-forms hereabouts, all of them hovering about a Spur station advertising "Best Barbecue." A four-floor apartment house across the street had fallen into itself and a young woman sat on the curb outside staring at her shoes, strings of saliva snailing slowly down a black T-shirt reading ATEFUL DE D. A huge rotting wooden tooth hung outside the one-time dentist's office to the right. The empty lot to the left had grown a fine crop of treadbare auto tires, bags of garbage, bits and pieces of shopping carts, bicycles and plastic coolers, jagged chunks of brick and cinder block.

Nabors had the special on a kaiser roll, Fritos and a 20-ounce coffee. I copied the coffee, passed on the rest. Hell, I could live for a week off what he spilled down his shirt-front. But that day his shirt was destined to stay clean a while longer, because, once we'd settled back in the squad and he started unwrapping, we got a call. Disturbance of the peace, Magnolia Arms, apartment 24.

He drove us twelve blocks to a place that looked pretty much like the one we'd left.

"Gotta be your first DP, right?"

I nodded.

"Shit." He looked down at his wrapped barbeque. Grease crept out slowly onto the dash. "You sit here. Anything looks out of whack, you hear anything, you call in Officer Needs Assistance. Don't think about it, don't try to figure it out, just hit the fuckin' button. You got that?"

"Gee, I'm not sure, Cap'n. You know how I is."

Nabors rolled his eyes. "What the fuck'd I do? Just what the fuck'd I do?"

Opening the door, he pulled himself out and struggled up plank-and-pipe stairs. I watched him make his way along the second tier. Intent, focused. I reached over and got his fucking sandwich and threw it out the window. He knocked at 24. Stood there a moment talking, then went in. The door closed.

The door closed, and nothing else happened. There were lights on inside. Nothing else happened for a long time. I got out of the squad, went around to the back. Following some revisionist ordinance, a cheap, ill-fitting fire escape had been tacked on. I pulled at the rung, saw landings go swaying above, bolts about to let go. Started up, thinking about all those movies with suspension bridges.

I'd made it to the window of 24 and was reaching to try it when a gunshot brought me around. I kicked the window in and went after it.

Through the bathroom door I saw Nabors on the floor. No idea how badly he might have been hurt. Gun dangling, a young Hispanic stood over him. He looked up at me, nose running, eyes blank as two halves of a pecan shell. Like guys too long in country that had just shut down, because that was the only way they could make it.

I shot him.

It all happened in maybe twenty seconds, and for years afterward, in memory, I'd count it out, one thousand, two thousand. . . . At the time, it seemed to go on forever, especially that last moment, with him sitting there slumped against the wall and me standing with my S&W .38 still extended. Right hand only, not the officially taught and approved grip, never sighting but firing by instinct, how I'd learned to shoot back home and the only way that ever worked for me.

I'd hit him an inch or so off the center of his chest. For a moment as I bent above him, there was a whistling sound and frothy blood bubbling up out of the amazingly small wound, before everything stopped. He had three crucifixes looped around his neck, a tattoo of barbed wire beneath.

Nabors lay there lamenting the loss of his barbeque. Man like him, that's the note he should go out on. But he wasn't going out, not this time. I picked up the phone and called in Officer Down and location. Only then did it occur to me that I hadn't cleared the rest of the apartment.

Not much rest to clear, as it happened. A reeking bathroom, a hallway with indoor-outdoor carpeting frayed like buckskin at the edges. Boxes sat everywhere, most of them unpacked, others torn open and dug through, contents spilling half out. The girl was in the back bedroom, in a closet, arms lashed to the crossbar, feet looped about with clothesline threaded into stacked cinder blocks. Her breasts hung sadly, blood trickled down her thighs, and her eyes were bright. She was fourteen.

Chapter Three

"I'M IN OVER MY HEAD," Sheriff Bates said. "You came up around here, right?"

"Close enough."

"Then you know how it is."

We were in his Jeep, heading back towards town. Dirt roads pitted as a teenager's face. Now we turned out of the trees onto worn blacktop. The radio mounted beneath his dash crackled.

"Weekends, we break up bar fights, haul in drunk drivers. Maybe kids pay someone to buy them a case of beer and party till they get to be a nuisance, or some guy down on his luck climbs in a window and comes back out with a pillowcase full of flatware, prescription drugs, a laptop or TV. Not like there's much anywhere he can *go* with it. Once in a blue moon a husband slaps his wife down once too often, gets a butcher knife planted in his shoulder or a frypan laid up alongside his head."

The radio crackled again. Didn't sound to me any different from previous crackles, but Bates picked up the mike. "I'm on my way in."

"Ten-four." Guy at the other end loved those vowels, rolled them around in his mouth like marbles.

Bates hung the mike back on its stirrup.

"Don Lee. You'll be meeting him here shortly. Eager to get home to his six-pack and his new wife, most likely in that order. What time's it got to be, anyway?"

"Little after eight."

"My month to cover nights. Natural order of things, Don Lee'd be gone hours ago. Lisa'd have had his meat and potatoes on the table, he'd be on the couch and his second beer while she washed up. But long as I'm out of pocket, he's stuck there."

Bates hauled the Jeep hard right and we skidded out onto what passes for a highway around here, picking up speed. Almost immediately, though, he geared down, braked.

"You need help there, Ida?"

A saddle-oxford Buick, cream over blue, vintage circa '48, sat steaming in the right lane. An elderly woman all in white, vintage a couple of decades prior, stood alongside. She wore a hat that made you want to hide Easter eggs in it.

"Course not. Just have to let it cool down, same as always."

"I figured. You say hi to Karl for me, now."

"I'll say it. What he hears . . ."

A mile or so further along, the sheriff said, "Back in Memphis you had the highest clearance rate on homicides of anyone on the force."

"You've done your homework."

"I'm not in a habit of drafting help. Tend to be cautious about it."

"Then you know it wasn't me, it was us. What part wasn't plain luck owes mostly to my partner. I'd be jumping hoops of intuition, flying high. Meanwhile he was back down there on the ground thinking things methodically through."

"That would be Randy—right?"

I nodded.

"Like I said, I'm in over my head. Expertise, luck, intuition—we'll take whatever you've got."

We came in from the north, onto deserted streets. Pop. 1280, a sign said. Passed Jay's Diner with its scatter of cars and trucks outside, drugstore and hardware store gone dark, A&P, Dollar Store, Baptist church, Gulf station. Pulled in behind city hall. One-story prefab painted gray. Probably took them all of a week to put it up, and it'd be there forever, long as the glue held. The paint job was recent and hurried, with a light frosting of gray on bushes alongside. A single black-and-white sat nosed in close outside. Inside, a rangy man in polyester doing its best to look like khaki sat nosed close to the desk. On it were a radio, a ten-year-old Apple computer and a stack of magazines, one of which he was paging through. He looked up as we came in. Wet brown eyes that reminded me of spaniels, ruddy face narrow and shallow like a shovel, thin hair. Something electric about him, though. Sparks and small connections jumping around in there unremarked.

"Anything going on?" Bates said.

"'Bout what you'd expect. Couple of minor accidents at getting-off time. Old Lady Siler reported her purse stolen, then remembered she'd locked it in the trunk of her car. I ran the spare key out, as usual. Jimmy Allen showed up at his wife's house around dark and started pounding on the door. Then he tried to steal the car. When I got there, he had two wires pulled down out of the radio, trying to hotwire them."

"Been at it for an hour or more, if I know Jimmy."

"Prob'ly so."

"He in back?"

"Out flat."

"This goes on, Jimmy might as well just start having his mail delivered here."

Bates walked over and closed three of the four light switches on the panel by the door. Much of the room fell gray, leaving us and desk in a pool of dim light outside which shadows jumped and slid.

"Don Lee, this's Mr. Turner."

The deputy held out a hard, lean hand and I took it. A good handshake, no show to it, just what it was. Like the man, I suspected.

"Pleased to have you, Detective."

"Just Turner. I haven't been a detective for a long time."

"Hope you're not telling us you forget how," Bates said.

"No. What happens is, you stop believing it matters."

"And does it?" This from Don Lee.

"Does it matter, or does it stop?"

"There's a difference?"

In that instant I knew I liked him. Liked them both. All I'd wanted was to be left alone, and I'd taken giant steps to ensure that. Rarely strayed far from the cabin, had goods delivered monthly. The last thing I'd wanted was ever again to be part of an investigation, to have to go rummaging through other people's lives, messes and misdemeanors, other people's madnesses, other people's minds.

"Why don't you fill me in?" I said.

"You'n go on home," Bates told his deputy. "Appreciate your holding down the fort. Dinner must be getting colder by the minute."

"All the same to you, I'd as soon stay," Don Lee said.

Chapter Four

NABORS MADE IT, survived the shooting that is, but he never came back on active duty. Mondays, my day off, I visited him at the rehab facility out in Whitehaven. Sculptured, impossibly green lawns with sprinklers that went off like miniature Old Faithfuls, squat ugly buildings. Never did figure what those were made of, but they put me in mind of Legos. Soft-handed young doctors and platoons of coiffured, elegantly eyelashed young nurses manning the pressure locks, all of them with mouthfuls of comfort like mush for both visitors and patients, couldn't spit out those lumps of good advice fast enough.

Suddenly around the station house everyone knew who I was. Older cops who'd pointedly ignored me before, smelling as they often did of sweat socks, stale bourbon or beer, aftershave and last night's whore, now nodded to me in the locker room. Two shifts in a row I got put in a squad that didn't haul hard left or need new tires and assigned uptown. Really knew I was some kind of made man the day

Fishbelly Joe, the blind albino who'd run a hot dog stand outside the station house as long as anyone could remember, refused my money.

Then one Monday afternoon as I reported for the 3–11, word surfaced from the Captain. Come see him.

"I think it's a mistake, Turner," he said. "You're not ready for it. But you're bumped to detective."

I'd been a cop, what, two or three months at that point? Most of the men I worked with were ten, twenty years older, and most of them had packed their lives into the work. Little wonder they'd been reluctant to accept me, and only began to do so, haltingly, now.

Did I for even a moment recognize this as a repeat of what happened in the service? No. (But how could I not have?) There I'd passed from basic training to special forces in a matter of weeks, as in one of those TV shows where events stumble over one another trying to get past. I'm a quick study, have a quirky mind that gets on to things instantly. While others are still floundering and doing belly flops, I'm walking around, looking good—but my understanding never extends far beneath the surface.

At that time, remember, I had little enough training to speak of, and almost no experience. And the fact that Nabors and I had violated procedure was something I just couldn't get my head around. That went on every moment of every shift of every day, sure. No one did things by the book. You cut corners, jury-rigged, improvised, faked it, got by. But few of those shortcuts ended up with a fatal shooting and a seasoned officer going down. I kept ticking off the mistakes in my head.

We were supposed to stay together at all times. We should both have responded.

When I began to suspect that something had gone badly south, I'd started in without calling for backup.

I'd failed to follow my senior partner's orders.

Then, failing also to identify myself or fire a warning shot (which back then, before *Garner v. Tennessee*, remained policy), I'd shot a man dead.

Interestingly enough, few questions got asked outside my own head, and none of this ever came up for any sort of review. But right after gypsies and sailors, cops are the most superstitious folk alive, and while I was newly on the list of good guys, looked up to in some weird, abstract fashion, the whole thing stayed weird: no one wanted to partner with me.

So for a time, in direct violation of department policy, I rode by myself in the best cars the department had to offer. Ranked detective, I still spent most of my shift on routine calls.

What happened next I'm still not clear on, but somewhere (arbitrarily, I assume, from my experience with bureaucracies pre and post) a decision was made, and I started finding myself beside guys no one else would put up with. Likes attracting? Or maybe they were there as department brass's last, desperate effort to shake them out of the tree. We're talking rookies too dumb for Gilligan's island here, lawmen Andy wouldn't let have *one* bullet, bullies fresh off the schoolyard, lumbering southern gentlemen who stood when ladies and elders entered the room but had screenings of *Shane* and *The Ox-Bow Incident* playing continuously in their heads.

Then one morning I looked to the right, or so it seemed, and Gardner was sitting there. We'd just come off an unwarranted noise call, I'd let him handle it, and the boy'd done good.

What you got to do is put on their lives, way you do a robe or an old shirt, he told me. You stand outside looking, no way you can see in, no way they're gonna trust you.

That what they teach you these days?

Right after the choke hold, he said.

We'd been riding together three or four months by then. Why was he any different from the others? I'm not sure he was. Could have been me: maybe I'd just come around to the point where I was ready to start forging connections again. Or maybe it was just that the son of a bitch wouldn't give up. I'd done everything I could do to ignore him, frustrate him, demean him, and he just sat there sipping coffee and smiling, asking what I wanted for lunch. While I was busily turning into Nabors.

Like myself, Gardner came up from the backlands. But whereas I loved cities and needed them, or thought I did, he'd never caught on to city ways. Part of him would always be walking down some dirt road along train tracks, stopping by the bait shop for a cold drink. He was a good, simple man.

One morning over coffee Gardner told me he was quitting. His girl back home had written to tell him she was pregnant. He went, found out soon enough that she wasn't pregnant at all, only lonely, and shortly after turned up in Memphis again. Teamed with someone else now, but we kept in touch. After that, his heart never quite let him get back into the job. Riding alone one night, he answered a disturbance call at a motel, an altercation between a prostitute name L'il Sal and her client. All of us knew L'il Sal. She'd turn black to white and charm the sun down if it gave her points. Either Gardner had forgotten L'il Sal or didn't care. He was listening to her story when the john came up behind and slit his throat with a buck knife.

Chapter Five

"ORDINARILY, the way we'd work this is, State would send someone over. Highway Patrol. But they're too short-handed, couple of guys out on short-term disability, another off in Virginia for training. Not to mention the backup in their own cases. Someone'll be there, the barracks commander told me, but *when* he'll be there . . ." Bates grunted. "I also got the notion he might not be the barrack's best."

"That had to make you feel better."

"You bet it did. We still get breakfast, Thelma?" he said to the waitress who'd dropped off coffees, gone about her business and now ambled back around to us. She wore badly pilled gray polyester slacks, a black sweater hanging down almost to her knees in front and hiked over her butt behind. Hair pinned up in a loose swirl from which strands had escaped and hung out like insect legs.

"You see there on the menu where it says breakfast twenty-four hours a day, Lonnie?"

"You're not open twenty-four hours a day, Thelma."

"Not much gets by you, does it? Must be what keeps down the criminal element hereabouts, why the good people of this town keep reelecting you."

"What's good?"

"Nothing. But you can eat most of it."

I found myself wondering how many times they'd been through this routine.

"What are you doing asking me anyway? We both know what you're gonna have. Three eggs over easy, grits, ham. You're done, some of these other folk might appreciate getting the chance to order."

"Got it by yourself, huh?"

"Yeah. You want anything besides coffee, Don Lee?"

"Coffee'll do me," he said.

"New girl supposed to be here, worked half a shift yesterday. Guess she decided maybe this wasn't what she wanted to do with her life after all. Her loss. God knows there's rewards. Toast?"

Sheriff Bates nodded.

"You know what, I'll have an order of toast, too," Don Lee said.

"Been most of an hour since the boy ate," Bates said.

"And what can I get you, sir?"

I ordered a club sandwich on wheat without mayo and a salad, no dressing. The coffee was actually very good. For a long time I'd never order coffee in restaurants. I liked it the way we used to fix it back home, throwing a handful of coffee into boiling water. Nothing else ever seemed worth bothering with. Then coffeehouses started sprouting everywhere. I didn't much care for their little ribbon-tied bundles of gourmet this and that, trinkets and dumb posters, but they brought coffee in America to a new level.

"What do you want to know?" Bates said.

"Usually I find it doesn't much matter what I want to know, I just get what people want to tell me. So I go with that." I looked around. A dozen or so people were in the diner, most of them sitting alone over plates of chicken-fried steaks, burgers, spaghetti. Three middle-aged women at a back table laughing too loudly and looking about furtively to see if anyone noticed. "It's been a while, as I said. But as I recall, we generally started with a body."

"And while we do things our own way up here, we don't do them *that* differently." Bates smiled. "Don Lee was on duty that night."

Caught by surprise, the deputy said, "Right," then took a sip of coffee to gather himself. "Call came in a little after twelve, which is when the bars close 'round here—"

"What day was it?"

"Beg pardon?"

"I'm assuming it had to be a weekday, that bars don't close at twelve on weekends even 'round here."

"Right. It was a Monday."

"Back in Memphis everyone called Monday the day nothing ever happens."

"Hard to tell it from any other day 'round here."

"You were on by yourself, right? There're only the two of you?"

"Lonnie and me, right. We have someone on dispatch, on the radio that is, eight to four every day. Lonnie's daughter, mostly, or else Danny Lambert. He was sheriff close to twenty years before retiring. And we get lots of part-time help with answering phones, filing, all that, from Smith High. Secretarial classes looking for . . . what do they call them?"

"Practicums," Bates said.

"Right."

"Look," I said. "I don't want to come on like some kind of asshole here." Maybe I was bearing down too hard. "You two've worked together a while, you have a pace of your own. So does the town. Out of habit, experience, just because I'm who I am, I'm inclined to go about this a certain way. But it's your investigation—yours all the way. I'm a ride-along."

"Appreciate your saying that," Bates said. "But we'd be more than one kind of fool not to accept the very assistance we asked for."

"Okay. . . . So how'd the call come?" I asked.

Don Lee answered. "Kids phoned it in, out there looking for a place to park. They'll go out to a block of new houses—every few years developers put these up, but no one ever seems to move into them—and they'll back in a driveway like they belong there. Girl stops with bra at half-mast. What's wrong? Seth says. Seth McEvoy. Quarterback with the high school team, plays clarinet, honor student. What *is* that? Sarah says. Sarah Perkins, her family runs the local dollar store. Sarah herself's a few steps off to the side of most of us, I guess. At any rate, she points."

Our food came. Thelma dealt plates off an extended arm, stepped away and came back with a tray holding A-1 steak sauce, Tabasco, ketchup, Worcestershire. Seeing it,

I had a rush of recognition. If we ordered iced tea, she'd ask sweetened or unsweetened.

"Y'all set, then?"

"Looks great, Thelma. Thanks."

"What she was pointing to was what looked like a scarecrow standing there at the side of the carport. Sarah says it moved—that was why she noticed. Doc Oldham says no way, the body'd been dead four, five days. So we figure something else moved."

"Field mice, most likely," Bates said. "We build subdivisions where they used to live, the mice don't know they're supposed to leave."

"Especially if provisions keep getting shipped in," I said.

"Right. Seth gets out of the car and goes over to look. Male, mid- to late forties, Doc figures. He's wearing two or three shirts, a pair of Wranglers so old the rivets are worn away. Been homesteading under the carport for a while from the look of it. Had a bedroll there, couple of sacks of belongings, an old backpack with one strap."

"He'd been chewed on some. Eyes and tongue, mostly."

"Postmortem?"

Don Lee nodded.

"Cause of death?"

"The developer had finished up the subdivision in a hurry and moved on. Yards still had these stakes set out in them, eighteen inches long, sharpened at one end. Someone pulled up one of those and drove it into his chest. Someone's seen one too many vampire movies, Doc said."

"That's not gonna be easy," Bates said. "Takes some industry."

"Broken fingernails," Don Lee went on, "maybe from the struggle, maybe from before, hard to say. Splinters in his palms. Tried to pull the stake out, we figure."

"Or keep it from going in."

"We found him pinned against some latticework, trellis kind of thing. Arms crossed above his head, wrists turned out. He'd been fastened up there with picture wire."

"So the body was repositioned once he was dead."

"Way it looks. Doc said the stake missed his heart but nipped the vena cava."

"Meaning it took him a while to die. . . . Understand that I don't mean any disrespect here, but what facilities do you have for processing a crime scene?"

"State issues us kits. Back when I started, I got sent up to the capital for a couple of months, passed along what I could remember. Don Lee's studied up some on his own. We did the best we could. But like I told you up front, we're in over our heads here."

"I went back through the manual, did it all by the numbers," Don Lee told me. "Multiple photographs of the scene and the body. Bagged clothes and belongings, including a notebook—kind of a diary, I guess. Cellotaped a half-footprint I found at the edge of the carport. Took scrapings, blood samples."

I looked at Bates. He shrugged. "What can I say? Me, I blundered into this. He's meant for it."

"Thing is," Don Lee said, "I can go on scraping, photographing and logging stuff in till kingdom come, but I still just have a bunch of bags with labels on them. All potatoes, no meat."

"Where's the forensics kit now?"

"Back at the station."

"You don't usually send them through to State?"

"No *usually* to it," Bates said. "Never had occasion to use one of the things before. Fact is, we weren't even sure where we'd put them."

"State said seal it, they'd pick it up when they got here."

"No identification on the body, I'm assuming."

Binaural nods.

"And when you canvassed, showing a photo, no one knew him, no one had seen him. Just another of America's invisible men."

Yep.

I'd finished my salad and sandwich and drunk three or four cups of coffee—Thelma kept creeping up and refilling. Altogether too fine a waitress. Don Lee's toast was crumbs on a plate and four empty jam containers with tops skinned back. Clots of yolk and a pool of runny ketchup competed on the sheriff's plate.

"What I have to ask is why you're pursuing this at all. You've got a good town here. Clean, self-contained. Obviously this guy's from outside, no one's visible father, no visible mother's son. Not a single city or PD I know, whatever size, would spend an hour on this. They'd write the report, skip it over the water into the files, move right along."

"Well, they'd be used to it, of course. We're not." Bates looked to the door, where an attractive, thirtyish woman in gray suit and lacy off-white blouse stood looking back. "Tell me that's not our State guy."

"That's not our State guy," Don Lee said.

"You know damn well it is."

As though to confirm, she strode towards us.

"We don't trip over bodies too often 'round here," Don Lee said.

"And when we do"—this from Bates—"they don't usually have the mayor's mail in their pocket."

Chapter Six

BASICALLY THEY DON'T get any more missing.

It wasn't a missing-persons case. In fact it was just about everything *but* a missing-persons case. Robbery, assault, murder. God knows what else. And that's the way it got passed out to us: they don't get any more missing.

The Captain himself took roll call that day. Gentlemen, he said. Officers. Has there been a misunderstanding? When I asked that you pool your efforts and give your collective best, I had expected that you would understand this was to the end of *finding* the suspect. Instead you seem collectively to have lost him.

There was laughter, uneasy laughter of a sort we all got used to over the next few months. Little by little the laughter subsided, till finally we sat stone silent through roll call. No jokes, no catcalls, none of the endless badgering that marks men thrown together in close quarters and shaky pursuits. We sat, we listened, some of us taking notes, then we rose, claimed cars, and went stolidly about our business.

It had begun long before that, of course, on a Saturday night almost two months before, when a scumbag by the name of Richards found his way into an apartment house just off campus of Memphis State where ten students lived. Most of them were out on dates. The three that weren't, he attacked. Tied them down with lamp wires and went from one to the other, back and forth. He'd come in with his member hard as a rock, one of them said, put it in her, and leave. Then after a while he'd come back. Never climaxed, or seemed to gain much pleasure from it. Lot of blood on it there at the end, one of the young women said. I kept wondering if it was my blood or someone else's, what he'd done to the others.

Richards spent his childhood in a series of foster homes, a social worker called in as consultant told us later, often shut into a room and ignored, brought food when they remembered, other times beaten or abused. My heart bled.

Anyhow, although Richards had been a busy boy, with a string of store robberies, B&Es of various sorts, auto theft and assault, rape was something new for him. But now, like a chicken-killing dog, he'd got the taste. And he liked it.

Over following weeks we got to know that campus well, spent more time there than its students did. Ants at a picnic, and just about as inconspicuous. But the next time Richards struck, it was across town, at a dorm next to Samaritan Hospital where nurses in training lived. The hospital put them up free, they attended classes half a day and helped take care of patients the rest, and after a year or so they got certified as LPNs. Women with poor and no prospects came up from all over the South. Richards went in there on a Friday evening about nine o'clock. Of the fifteen residents, eight were on duty, helping cover the evening shift as nurses although legally they weren't. Five more had gone out together for pizza and a movie. They're the ones who called it in when they got back home around midnight and found Mary Elizabeth Walker (Mobile, Alabama) and Sue Ann Simmons (Tupelo, Mississippi) strapped to their beds with duct tape. There was so much tape, one of them said, they looked like mummies, or cocoons. Mary Elizabeth stared at the wall and wouldn't respond when they spoke to her. Blood was running from both vagina and anus. Sue Simmons didn't respond either. She was dead.

We got on to Richards the usual way, through an informer. This informer lived in the neighborhood, often wound up in some of the same diners, poolrooms and bars as Richards, and almost certainly carried some grudge against him. Once we had this, still with nothing but hearsay and suspicion to take to market, we bird-dogged Richards in solid shifts, staking out his apartment from unmarked cars. For two days nothing happened. We learned a lot: that he kept unpredictable hours, had no visitors, and thrived exclusively on carry-out hamburgers. On the third day, he disappeared.

We went in with a judge's order on the fourth day and everything was just as it had been the times we'd gone in without, clothes scattered about, toiletries in place, bottle or two of prescription drugs in the bathroom, piles of mustard, salt and pepper packets on the kitchenette counter by a pool of loose change. He was gone, purely gone. Evaporated. Vanished. No one ever heard from or of him again.

That was the first one.

"A vigilante," someone said at roll call.

"The position of this department," the Captain said, "is that it's an isolated incident. That is also your position."

I'd have to pull records to check, and of course I can't, but it seems maybe two, three months went by before the next one.

These shitheads were hitting mom-and-pop stores all over the city, pistol-whipping whoever was behind the counter, mom, pop or one of numerous kids, when they objected or proved too slow at scooping up money. The perps were easy to mark. There were always three. One never spoke. He lurked on the fringes, carried a steel baseball bat over his shoulder, and moved in only when the others had got the goods and left. Then he'd swing his bat, smashing hips, knees, wrists and ankles.

Again and as usual, confidential information came up the line from one of the city's bottom feeders. Three guys who'd always had trouble putting together the price of a draft beer of late had been seen with hands wrapped around the dewy necks of imports. One of them, the informant said, was truly spooky. Never spoke, smiled a lot, sat perfectly still. Always wore a baseball cap, Yankees one day, Dodgers the next, Orioles, Rangers. Must have one hell of a collection.

Like a lot of their breed, these guys started out doing occasional hits, then, when they got away with it repeatedly, and got used to the benefits as well, started making it a regular thing. That, along with informants, is what broke most of these cases for us. Soon these guys were surfacing every Friday night.

We knew where they were staying, in a swayback, half-abandoned apartment complex out in south Memphis, near Crump and Mississippi, kind of place where plywood's been nailed up to make small rooms out of large and where to sit on the toilet you have to draw up your knees to fit them jigsawlike into the space between sink and door. But we still had to catch these guys with pants down. Every squad car went out with a list of mom-and-pop convenience stores in central Memphis that *hadn't* been hit. We circled them like sharks.

One Friday, then another, went by without these guys showing at the crib. Hadn't been around the bars either, our informant said when his contact tracked him down. No one had seen them. No one ever saw them again.

"Comes from inside the department," scuttlebutt had it in locker rooms and lounges, "who else would know."

Couple more, at least.

Someone who was offing cabdrivers. He'd hit late at night when drivers were inclined to take just about any fare they could get, he'd direct them to the city's fringes and leave them there with their heads bashed in. The department pulled hundreds of pages of copies of log sheets and dispatcher's records. We'd just begun heavy cruising of areas from which calls had come in the past when, abruptly, the killings stopped.

Next, a series of suspected arsons in upscale housing developments under construction. Two of those developments, then three, went up in flame. At the third, an elderly couple had moved in prematurely, before construction was completed. They went up in flame, too. Then it all stopped.

What the hell, the Captain said, sentiments echoed by many others, by the press, for instance, repetitively and at great length, is going on here?

We never really knew. But almost a year later, on an anonymous tip, in the woods just across the Mississippi line we found six shallow graves side by side, each topped by a wooden plaque into which had been burned a smiling skull and crossbones.

Chapter Seven.

"GET YOU SOMETHING? Coffee? Pie?"

"No thanks, Sheriff."

Introducing herself, spelling the last name, Valerie Bjorn had settled in beside Don Lee.

"You new up at State?"

"Over a year now."

"Can't help noticing you're out of uniform."

"Out of—oh. I'm not a trooper, Sheriff. I'm attorney for the barracks. Commander Bailey asked if I'd mind picking up the evidence kit."

"State's paying top dollar for messengers these days, then."

She smiled. "I live here, Sheriff. Well, not here exactly. Not far out of town, though."

"The old Ames place."

"I moved in two months ago."

"Heard someone bought it. That house's been empty a

long time. Few rungs down from fixer-up would be my guess."

"I'm doing most of the work myself. My grandfather was a builder, the kind that back in his day handled everything himself, plumbing, electric, carpentry. He raised me. I started crawling under houses when I was eight or nine."

"And haven't quit yet," I said.

"I thought I had. But we're so often wrong about such things, aren't we? Not that I get much chance to crawl and so on, between my own work and what I do for the barracks. Hope you don't mind my tracking you down, Sheriff. I saw your Jeep outside."

"Not at all, Miss Bjorn."

"Val. Please."

Suddenly Thelma was at the booth, saying "Here, let me clear some room," scooping up plates and laying them along her left arm. "Get you anything else, boys? Ma'am?" Their eyes met briefly. "Some more coffee? Just made a fresh pot."

"Gettin' too late for this old man," Bates said. "Prob'ly be up through Tuesday or so, as it is."

Don Lee and I also declined.

"I'm fine," Val said. "But thank you."

"We have the check?" Bates said. Thelma turned back and shook her head. He shook his.

"How long we been doing this, Thelma? Four, five years now?"

"Sonny says I don't give you a bill. You know that."

"And you know—"

"He's my boss, Lonnie. I got to do what he tells me.

That's how most of us live. What, this job isn't hard enough already?"

"Okay, okay. Anyway, your shift's almost over now."

"Life's just chockful of almosts, ain't it."

Waiting till she was gone, Bates pulled out his wallet, extracted a twenty and a five, and tucked them under the sugar bowl. Easily twice what the bill came to.

"She's dying to know who you are," he told Val.

"I got that."

"You want to come on back with me to the station, pick up that kit?"

"Would you mind if I waited and came by on my way in to work tomorrow, Sheriff? I'd dearly love to go on home now, get some rest."

"Wouldn't we all." He nodded. "What time you figure to be swinging by?"

"Seven, seven-thirty?"

"Good enough. I'm not still there, Don Lee will be."

We stood and made our way to the door.

"Goodnight, then," Val told us outside. Her eyes met each of ours in turn. She shook hands with Bates.

"Lisa's gonna hang me out to dry," Don Lee said.

"Reckon she will. Not to mention having fed your dinner to the pigs." Bates turned to me: "You'll be needing a ride back."

"You don't live in town?" Val said.

I shook my head. "Cabin up by the lake."

"Nice up there."

"It is that."

"Awfully late, though. He's one of yours, Sheriff, right?"

"Well . . ."

"Look, the lake's a long way. I have a spare room. Not much in there yet, an old bunk bed with a futon thrown across it, some plastic cubes, a table lamp without a table. But all that could be yours for the night."

"A kingdom."

We drove out of town in the opposite direction from the lake, past Pappa Totzske's sprawling apple orchard and spread of seventy-five-foot chicken houses. The back seat of Val's six-year-old yellow Volvo was piled with boxes, portable files, clothing, a stack of newspapers. When she hit the key, old-time music started up at full blast. Gid Tanner, maybe. She punched the reject button on the cassette player.

"Sorry, I usually have *this* world to myself."

"Trying to assimilate?"

She laughed. "Hardly. I grew up with this, been listening to it, playing it, since I was ten years old."

"Right after you began your carpentry career."

"Exactly. Hammer, screwdriver, mandolin. Lot better with the hammer, though."

The old Ames place was six or seven miles outside town, at the end of a dirt road so deeply pitted that it could have been passed off as a child's projection map of the Grand Canyon. Papershell pecan trees and a huge, utterly wild and unkempt weeping willow stood by the house. Whole tribes could be living in the thing unbeknownst.

Val pulled up under one of the pecan trees and we climbed out. I had to hit the car door hard with the heel of my hand to get it open. She'd warned me it stuck sometimes. From the trunk she took a canvas book bag that looked to serve as briefcase. A squirrel sat on a limb just above, fussily chattering at us.

"I've only got two of the rooms really habitable so far," Val said as we entered, through the entryway into a small living room that, when the house was built, would have been used only on holidays and formal occasions. Now it sported a narrow bed, a rocking chair, a table doing triple work as desk, eating space and storage area. An antique wardrobe sat in one corner, drawers on the left in use even as the right side went on being stripped of multiple layers of varnish and paint, down to fine wood beneath. Sandpaper, a shallow dish and rags lay atop it.

On the wall by the table hung a gourd banjo. I ran my thumb across the strings, surprised to find they weren't steel but soft, like a classical guitar's.

"You really are into this."

"I guess I am."

She lifted down the banjo and, sitting, balanced it on her lap. Plucked a string or two, twisted pegs. Then started playing, back of the nail on her second finger striking a melody note then brushing other strings as the thumb popped on and off that short fifth string. "Soldier's Joy." Abruptly she stopped, putting the instrument back in place.

"Would you like tea?"

"Love it."

We went through a double doorway without doors into the kitchen.

"Here's my real bona fide as a southerner," she said.

While even the living room had about it an element of improvisation, camping out or making do, the kitchen was fully equipped, pots and provisions set out on shelves, towels on drying racks, dishes stacked in cupboards, knife block on the counter by the stove. We sat at a battered wooden table waiting for water to boil.

"Funny thing is," Val said, "I *wasn't* into this, not at all, not for a long time. As a kid I couldn't wait to get away."

"You grow up around here?"

"Kentucky. Not a spit's worth of difference. When I left for college, I swore that was it, I'd never look back. And I'd absolutely never ever *go* back. Took the two JCPenney dresses I'd worked as a waitress to buy, and some books I'd kind of forgotten to return to the library, and settled into a dorm room at Tulane. It was 1975. My Texas roommate's debut had been attended by hundreds of people. She used most of my closet space in addition to her own—I didn't need it. And those dresses looked as out of place, as anachronistic, as a gardenia in my hair."

Val poured water into a round teapot.

"I was smart. That was one of two or three ways out of there. Tulane was full of rich East Coast kids who couldn't get into Ivy League schools and poor southerners on scholarship. I lost the dresses first, the accent not long after. Most any social situation, I discovered, all you had to do was keep quiet and watch those around you. Sugar? Lemon or milk?"

I shook my head.

"By the second year you couldn't pick me out of the crowd. 'Wearing camo,' as a friend of mine put it. I finished near the top of my class, went to Baltimore as a junior partner, very junior, in a group practice."

She set a mug before me, thoughtfully turned so the chip on its lip faced away.

"I don't usually prattle on like this."

"Not a problem."

"Good." Settling back at the table, she sipped her tea. "I was up there for four years—dancing with the one who brung me, as my father would say. I liked Baltimore, the firm, liked the work. And I was good at it."

"What changed?"

"Nothing. Something. Me?" She smiled. "I wanted to, anyway. Do we ever, really?"

"Change?"

Nodding.

"If we don't—if we can't—nothing else makes much sense, does it?"

She half-stood to pour us more tea. Close by, just past the window, an owl hooted.

"You're not a cop, are you?"

"Not for a long time. I was."

She waited, and after a moment I told her the basics.

"Another Cliff Notes life."

"What?"

"Those pamphlets on great books that students read instead of the books themselves. A lot of us experience our lives that way. Sum up who we are and what we're about as a few broad strokes, then do our best to cleave to it. All the good stuff, the small things and distinctions that make the rest worthwhile—Sunday mornings sitting over coffee and the paper, taste of bread fresh from the oven, the feel of wind on your skin, sensing the one you love there beside you—all these get pushed aside. Unnoticed, lost."

"If we let them."

"If we let them, right. And as much as anything else, that's why I'm here."

Dark had become absolute. Far off, frogs called. Their cries bounced across the pond behind the house, amplified by the water as though it were in fact the metal dish that moonlight made it appear. Moths beat at the window beside us, and at the kitchen's screen door.

"I drew my weapon three times," I said. God knows why I told her this. "And each time someone died. The second time, it was raining, I remember. His blood was running down the street. I was in the street too, with his head in my lap. And all the time I kept thinking: My kids are home waiting for me."

"Kids?"

"A boy and a girl. They grew up without me, have their own lives now. Probably for the best. . . . Thing is, there in the street, in some strange way I was closer to that stranger as he died, this man I'd shot, than I've ever been to anyone else my whole life."

For some time she was silent. We both were.

"I don't know what to say."

"You don't have to say anything."

"Suddenly everything in my life seems so small."

"Our lives *are* small."

She nodded. "They are, aren't they?"

I followed her outside, onto the porch.

"Don't suppose you're hungry?"

"Not really."

"Seems I always am. Buy popcorn by the case, eat carrot sticks till I start turning orange myself and have to stop, chew celery till my teeth hurt."

We stood looking up at the sky.

"What about the third time?" she said.

"That I drew my weapon."

"Yes."

"That time, it was my own partner."

"Oh."

"There's a lot more to it," I said.

"There would be." She looked off into the trees. "Listen."

I did, and for this one perfect moment silence enveloped us, absolute silence, silence of a kind most of the world and its people have forgotten. Then the frogs started up again and from miles away the hum of cars and trucks on an interstate reached us.

Chapter Eight

A YEAR OR SO into playing detective, I pulled the chit on a missing-persons case. Rightfully it should have gone to Banks, who was senior and next up. But Banks was actively pursuing leads, the Lieutenant told me, on a series of abductions and rapes at local private schools. Would I mind.

A patient had disappeared from an extended-care facility. Patricia Pope, nineteen years old. She'd been out with friends celebrating her birthday with slabs of pizza and pitchers of Co'Cola. As they ferried home around eight in the evening, a drunk driver smashed head-on into their car. He'd been drinking since he got off work at five and somehow had entered the new interstate by an exit ramp. The other four in the car were killed. Patricia, riding in the front passenger seat, went through the windshield and onto the hood of the drunk's F-150. She'd received acute care in Baptist Hospital's ER, from there had been moved up to neuro ICU for several days where a shunt in her head dripped fluid into a graduated cylinder, then onto a general ward, finally to a separate, step-down facility. She made no acknowledgment when spoken to, reacted but slightly to pain. (In ER they pinched nipples and twisted. Upstairs, kinder and gentler, they poked pins about feet, ankles, forearms, torso.) Her hands had begun curling in upon themselves, first in a series of contractures pitching muscle against bone. Eyes rolled left to right continually. She was incontinent, provided nutrients through a tube that had to be reintroduced with each feeding. Caretakers threaded these tubes down her nose, blew in air through a syringe and listened with a stethoscope to be certain the tube was in her stomach.

The incident occurred on April 3. Patricia had been relocated to the EC facility on April 20. When oncoming nurses went in to check patients early in their shift on the morning of June 17, Patricia was absent from her bed. That was the way the administrator put it when he called. Absent from her bed. Like it was summer camp. The call came in at 7:06. Half an hour later, 7:38 by the brass-and-walnut clock on the wall, I was sitting in the administrator's office with a cup of venomous coffee in hand watching said administrator, Daniel Covici, MBA, CEO, rub a thumb against the burnished surface of his desk. It was the facility's desk, of course, but I had no doubt he thought of it as his own.

Most investigations are little more than paint by the numbers. You ask a string of questions in the proper order, when they don't get answered you ask them again, sooner or later you find your way to the husband or wife, spurned boy- or girlfriend, business partner, parent, younger brother, gardener, eccentric uncle, jealous neighbor. This was no different. Within the hour, down in the Human Resources basement office looking over a list of recent terminations, I came across the name of an orderly who had quit without prior notice at the end of his shift on June 16, saying simply that he was going on to another, better job. He'd been with the hospital sixteen years. Douglas Lynds. Address out by what was at that time Southwestern, a tiny freestanding wooden house.

From the street I caught glimpses of the university's Gothic spires and buttresses among the trees. The house sat ten or twelve yards back, though the frontage could scarcely be called a yard. Traces of old foundation showed, like teeth rotted to gum level. Probably there had once been a stand of such structures, housing for graduate students maybe, of which only the one remained. It was in immaculate condition, however, freshly painted pristine white, window frames and trim a light, minty green.

Things were a lot looser those days. When I didn't get a response to my knock, I went around back, knocked again there, then shimmed the kitchen door. If it ever came to it, I'd just say the door was ajar, I heard sounds inside, suspected intruders.

Three rooms. Kitchen with counters and stove immaculate, bath just off it to the right, living room straight ahead, bedroom to the left. That's where I found her. She was propped up with pillows, dressed in a pale pink nightgown with small blue flowers at neck and hem and larger blue flowers for buttons. Her hair, clean and bright, lay on the pillow, framing a face wherein eyes rolled left, right, left. Mucus ran out of one nostril and snailed towards the slack mouth.

"Please don't hurt her," a voice said behind me.

I told him I wouldn't, told him who I was.

"I've been out shopping. I never leave her alone any more than I have to." He put the bag of groceries on the floor by the door. "She needs changing. All right if I do that?"

Yes.

Going to the bed, he unbuttoned the nightgown and unpinned the towel doing service as diaper. The strong chemical smell of her feces spilled into the room. He took the diaper into the bathroom, to a covered pail there. He ran water till it was warm, and wet a facecloth. Brought it out and, holding her up effortlessly with the flat of one arm, wiped her clean. He took the facecloth back into the bathroom, rinsed and hung it on a rack there, washed his hands. He replaced the diaper, buttoned her gown and smoothed it. Then reached up to snap a fingernail against the IV feed, checking patency, drip rate, level.

"I thought I'd have longer with her. Just the two of us."

"I'm sorry."

He hadn't meant for this to happen, he told me, standing there looking down at her, into her face; hadn't intended to cause any trouble. He only wanted to take care of her. That's what he'd been doing at Parkview, for a long time now. Cleaning and bathing her, seeing after her feeds. But there was always too much else to do, too many others needing attention. She deserved better than that.

"What will happen to her now?"

"She'll go back to the hospital."

"Parkview, you mean."

"Right."

"And I'll be going to jail."

"For a while."

"Any notion how long?"

"Hard to say." God knows what they'd charge him with. Kidnapping, endangerment? Excessive kindness? "A year, eighteen months, something like that. After that you'd be on probation."

He nodded.

"Once I'm out, I'll be able to visit her."

Chapter Nine

BREAKFAST WAS STRONG coffee and bagels. There were five kinds of bagels in a paper bag in the freezer (shipped in from Memphis? Little Rock?), butter, homemade fig preserves and cream cheese with chives below. Also a package of lox we both agreed should be put to rest. I washed my face and did what I could by way of brushing teeth while Val assembled it all; then, once we'd eaten, took care of the kitchen while she showered and dressed.

In the yellow Volvo on the way into town I thanked her.

She smiled. "Any time. It's a pleasure to have someone to talk to. You like my house?"

"I like your house a lot."

At the office she signed out the forensics kit and told us she'd be in touch when word came down. I walked her to the car.

"You get caught in town again, there's always my spare room," she said.

"I'll keep that in mind. Thanks."

"Take care of yourself, Turner."

I watched till the Volvo was out of sight. Eyes swiveled towards me when I went back in the office.

"Guess you two hit it off," Don Lee said.

"Guess we did."

"House look good?" This from Sheriff Bates.

You'd better believe it, I said, and filled him in on what I'd seen. Floors taken down to bare wood, missing pieces of banisters and mouldings pieced in, layers of paint painstakingly rubbed away.

"Wish there were more like her," Bates said. "Most of those old places have been torn down by now. Or fallen down. We won't ever see their like again. Coffee?"

"Sure thing." I chewed my way through half a cup of it. Busy day in town. Every four or five minutes a car passed outside. The phone rang and went on ringing in the real estate office next door.

"The mayor's mail?"

"Beg pardon?" Don Lee.

"What you found on the body. Outgoing mail or incoming? Circulars? Bills? Bank statements? Personal letters?"

"Bills, mostly. That's what he put out for pickup. Clipped them to the front of his mailbox with a clothespin. Same clothespin's been out there eight or ten years."

"His mailbox at home."

"Right."

"On the porch or streetside?"

"These parts, they're all by the street."

As Bates was pouring more coffee, a fortyish woman

pulled the door open and stepped in. She stopped just inside, blinking. Ankle-length pants that had started off black and with repeated washings gone purplish gray, red-and-blue flannel shirt over maroonish T-shirt. She was tall. The shirt's sleeves, left unbuttoned, came halfway up her forearms.

"Billie," Don Lee said. "How you doing?"

"C. R.'s left again."

"Honey, he'll be back. He always comes back. You know that."

"Not this time."

"Course he will."

"You think so?"

Bates walked over to her. For a moment before she looked off, their eyes met.

"Thought he liked the new job."

"Job was okay, Sheriff. What he didn't like was me."

Steering her to the desk, Bates said, "You had any break-fast? I could call across, have something sent over."

"Kids ate good this morning."

"They always do."

"Pancakes."

"Billie does great pancakes," Don Lee told me.

"Put pecans in, the way they like them." Her eyes swept the ceiling. "Woodie has to turn in his geography project today. I made sure he packed it up safe."

"You get any sleep, sweetheart?" Bates asked.

"I don't think so. I made brownies, for the kids. C. R. likes them too. It was dark outside. I think maybe I burned them."

"Don Lee, why don't you take Billie on home, see she gets settled in. That be okay with you, Billie?"

She looked wildly about for a moment at the door, window and floor, then nodded.

"He'll take her out by the ballpark," Bates said once they'd left. "They'll sit in the bleachers a while. Don't know why, but that always seems to calm her down."

"Is she okay?"

"Basically. You couldn't ask for a better person. Just sometimes, every six or eight weeks, things get too much for her. Get too much for all of us sometimes, don't they?"

I nodded.

"Been going on for three or four months, we figure—the missing mail. That's how far in arrears the mayor's bills had fallen. Gas, water, electric. Near as we can tell, he didn't know."

"Which tells us he doesn't bother balancing his checkbook."

"Mm-hm."

"And service was still being provided?"

"Things don't get shut off much 'round here. Just not the way we do it. And he's the mayor, after all."

"What about credit cards?"

"Looks like he paid those from the office. Those and the phone bill."

"He works at home?"

"Town this size, there's not a lot of mayoring needs doing. Not much call for regular office hours."

"So why would he pay the phone bill at the office? Some

reason he doesn't want his wife seeing the bill, maybe? I assume there's a wife."

"Oh," Bates said, "there's a wife sure enough."

"Can we get a warrant for his phone bills? Home and at the office? See who he called, who called him?"

"No need for all that." He grabbed the phone and dialed, spoke a minute or two and hung up. "Faxing it over. Give her half an hour, Miss Jean says."

"That simple."

"Seems simple to you, does it?"

I understood. As a cop on city streets you learn to dodge, duck, go along, feint. You find out what works and you use it. Same here, just that different things worked.

"Where's the mayor live?"

"Out on Sycamore. Far end of town."

"Anyone else on that route have mail missing?"

"There's only the one route. And if so, they didn't notice."

"Or didn't report it."

Mug cradled in both hands, Bates swung his chair several degrees right, right knee rising to a point northeast, then a few degrees left, right knee dipping as the left V'ed northwest. "Hard as this may be for you to believe, Detective, we did get around to asking after that. Took us a few days to think of it, most likely. Probably have it written down somewhere."

"I don't mean any disrespect, Sheriff. I'm only here because you asked me, doing the job you asked me to do the only way I know how."

Our eyes met.

"All right," he said at length.

"So you found the mayor's mail in this guy's pocket."

"Right."

"But no wallet, no identification."

He shook his head.

"Don Lee mentioned a notebook."

"Nothing much there, far as we could tell."

"And he'd been holding some of this mail for what? Three, four months?"

"Right."

"Thought he was some kind of postman," I said.

"Undelivering mail."

Chapter Ten

I'D KNOWN SALLY GENE for two or three years. She'd done a couple of ride-alongs back when she started with Child and Family. I remember giving her a hard time, claiming she couldn't be much older than the children she was investigating, and her saying, "You're *kid*ding me, right," my partner not getting it at all. Sally Gene and I had crossed paths professionally five, six times since. What she did was to her the most important thing in the world. I think deep down it may have been the only thing she really cared about. A lot of people who are outstanding at what they do seem to be like that. The rest of us look on, at once admiring and critical; vaguely ashamed of ourselves and our wayward lives.

That Sunday, she was waiting for me outside the station house.

"Think I might get a ride, Detective?"

"Sure thing, little girl."

She'd already cleared it with brass. Bill took one look at

us coming out together, chucked me the keys, and got in back. "What the hell. So we give up an hour or two of knock-on-doors-and-ask-questions excitement."

Recently the department had bolstered the auto pool with half a dozen new blue Plymouths. We pretended we were being sly, but two guys that looked like Joe Friday driving around in a plain car with no chrome trim, black tires and no radio were pretty obvious.

"And what lovely suburb of the city might the three of us be touring today?" Bill said.

Round about the airport, as it turned out, in those years an undeveloped region of cheap motels and eateries. We nosed down the highway that led into Mississippi and turned off into a subdivison of tiny, plain houses once part of the army base. Trucks sold pecans, watermelons and peaches at the side of the road. The smell of figs and honeysuckle was everywhere.

I stood a few paces back as Sally Gene knocked. We weren't supposed to have much of a presence on these calls. Bill stayed by the car. I'd already had a look around. A vegetable patch ran alongside the west side beneath a double clothesline, okra, tomatoes and green peppers, all of it pretty much gone from lack of care. No car in the driveway, and what oil spills there were, were old ones. Four or five *Press-Scimitar*s lay unrolled and unread at the back of the driveway, one near the front door, another halfway into the front yard.

The door opened. Flat, uninflected sound of TV from within. Cartoons, maybe, or a sitcom. But then I heard "Willa Cather tried in her own inimitable way . . ." I watched Sally Gene's head tilt forward and down as the door came open. A child's face stared up at us. Twelve, maybe. Wearing a yellow nylon shirt he'd grow into in another four or five years and a serious expression.

"Daddy says not to let anyone in."

Sally Gene introduced herself.

"Daddy says not to let anyone in."

"I told you my name. What's yours?"

"William."

"William. I'm sorry, I know this is confusing, and I'm not saying your daddy was wrong, he wasn't. But I have to come in. Hey: I'd rather be home watching TV, too. But the people I work for tell me I have to come in and look around. They're kind of like your parents, you know? Always telling me what I have to do?"

The merest flicker as his eyes strayed to me, but I caught it. He was looking for a way out.

"How you doing, William?" I said. "Friends ever call you Bill?"

After a moment he shook his head.

"You hungry, William?"

Again the head went right, left, right. "I fixed breakfast. I know how to cook. I have a load of clothes in the dryer. Oughta get them out."

"Are your parents home, William?"

"They'll be back soon."

"How long have they been gone, William?"

He just looked at me. More than he could handle, I guess. Like so many things in his life.

"Miss Sally Gene and I need to come inside. Look:

here's my badge. You hold on to it till I'm ready to leave. That should be okay, shouldn't it?"

After a moment he nodded and undid the chain.

In one bedroom we found a four-year-old girl locked in a closet. She'd very carefully defecated only in the rear corner by boots and old shoes, but urine had gone its own way, she'd had no control over that. A plate near the front held frankfurters and slices of American cheese.

In the bathroom a younger child with severe diarrhea, maybe two or three, was lashed by brown twine to the bathtub faucets. A Boy Scout manual on the back of the toilet bore a folded square of toilet paper at a section on knots. Jars of applesauce and peanut butter and plastic spoons sat within reach.

In a rear bedroom with bunk beds stacked north, south and east, children of various ages, six of them, sat straight-backed as army recruits. Their eyes swiveled to us as we came in. Plates of cold cuts and Oreo cookies sat on windowsills.

"I had no idea," Sally Gene told me.

"You must have."

"Oh, I knew something was wrong. But this . . ."

"Foster home?"

"One of the few we've never had complaints about. No trouble at all."

"I found a credit card in the desk drawer." William stood in the doorway behind us. "We haven't had real food for a long time."

"A Visa," Sally Gene told me, "and well past its limit. Two days ago someone tried to use its mate down in Vicksburg to settle a hotel bill that included an impressive bar tab. The card got confiscated."

"Foster parents?"

"Their card, anyway."

"I'm sorry," William said. "I know it was wrong."

"You did okay, son."

"You did great," Sally Gene said.

"Daddy put me in charge. I was just trying—"

"Who the fuck are you people?"

We both turned. He held a 12-gauge shotgun.

"Daddy!" The boy had moved on into the room beside us.

"And what are you doing in my house?"

I looked at Sally Gene, who fed me the name: "Sammy Lee Davis."

"Just stay cool, Mr. Davis, okay? I'm Detective Turner, Miss Lawson here's from city social services. We need to talk to you, that's all, just talk. Why don't you start by putting the gun down. There's a lot of kids in here, man. No one wants to see the kids get hurt. William: show your father my badge?"

The boy held it out.

"You're trespassing."

Thinking this wasn't the best time to discuss probable cause and his being at any time open to public inspection as a foster parent, I said, "Well, yes sir, truth is, we are. I can appreciate that's how it must look to you."

"You're the son of a bitch ran off with my wife, aren't you?"

The 12-gauge went to his shoulder. I have to give it to Sally Gene. She never once blinked, flinched or cut her eyes. He saw it in the boy's face, though, and turned just in time to take Bill's riot stick square on the forehead.

"You guys through with your business yet?" Bill said. "It's getting hot out there and I'm getting hungry. And that goddamn magnolia smells to high heaven."

Chapter Eleven

SETH MCEVOY played quarterback, was a top band member, and had a four-point average. He also, judging from the photo on his computer desk, went with the prettiest girl in town. Kind of kid you hated when you were back in school, couldn't do anything wrong.

Don Lee came with me. We'd spoken with the boy's mother downstairs. Seth was busy filling out college applications. All the pictures on his walls hung perfectly straight. The spines of the books in the bookcase behind the door were all flush.

"How come you're so much older than the sheriff and Don Lee?"

"Mr. Turner's retired, Seth. He's agreed to help us out, more or less as a consultant."

You could see the intelligence in his eyes, the interest. He'd rather ask questions than answer them. He knew about his world. Knew it too well, perhaps. Now he wanted to know about other people's.

"So what can I do for you?"

"I was hoping you could tell me again what happened."

"I don't think there's anything I can add to what I told the sheriff." But he went along, forever the good kid, reciting all but verbatim what was in the official report. With time and retelling the story had baked to hard clay; nothing new or surprising was likely to peer out of doorways or corners.

"Sarah stopped because she saw something move."

"Said she did. You're gonna talk to her, too, though—right?"

I nodded. "She didn't scream, anything like that."

"Unh-unh. She just pushed herself up in the seat and said, 'Seth, what is that?' I didn't see anything, but I got out of the car and went to look. After a minute she came up behind me."

"Was there blood?"

"Not near as much as you'd expect. I remember thinking then how that made it all seem so much stranger. Just that hunk of wood sticking up out of him, and everything arranged so neatly there by him like he was, I don't know, in his room at home."

"Were there field mice around, rats, anything like that?"

"If there were, we didn't see them." He looked full at me. "Why would you ask that?"

"No real reason. What you do is, you go ahead and ask whatever comes to mind, never mind if it makes sense or not, just trying to get the shape of the thing, hoping it might shake something loose."

"For you, or for me?"

"I'd settle for either."

"Interesting." He jotted something down on a notepad beside him.

"How long have you and Sarah been dating?"

"Sarah and I aren't dating. We just hang out together."

"In the driveways of unoccupied houses."

He started to say more, then shrugged.

I glanced pointedly at the photograph on his desk. "What does *she* have to say about that?"

"A lot. Pretty much nonstop. But Sarah . . . Sarah and I have been friends a long time. A lot of the others don't like her, think she's weird. But there aren't many people around you can have a conversation with, talk about the things you think are important. Look, you're from the city, right?"

"Yeah. But the place I came from's a lot like this one."

He nodded. "Then maybe you know how it is."

⁂

I HAD NO IDEA what was playing on her CD. I wouldn't even have known what to call it. It wasn't like any rock and roll I'd ever heard. And it wasn't on her CD player at all, as it turned out, but coming directly off her computer.

Music's the first handhold you lose in growing old, I thought as we made our way down narrow wood stairs to the basement Sarah Perkins had claimed as her own. The stairs were plain, untreated planks set into notches in doubled two-by-fours, heads of ten-penny nails dark against them. Sarah sat below in a pool of light. The music washed up from below, too, a drain in reverse. To me, it sounded like a slurry of things recorded from nature—cricket calls, footsteps over gravel, apples falling—then tweaked beyond recognition.

Sarah turned in her chair as we stepped onto the cement floor. Years ago, someone had laid in a frame of two-by-fours, started putting up Sheetrock, even tacked up one wall of cheap woodgrain paneling before abandoning the project. Sarah had covered the spaces with old album covers (mostly 1950s jazz), movie posters (a decided taste for horror films) and a hodgepodge of pieces of dark fabric of every conceivable size, shape and texture. Books were stacked against every wall. But mostly the room took its form from the U-shaped desk within which Sarah sat in the midst of three or four computers and as many monitors, along with various cross-connected black boxes, scanners and the like. The huge half-dark, half-bright room was the inside of her head, this the cockpit from which she kept it on course.

Almost instantly, she broke into Don Lee's introduction. "How's Seth?"

"He's fine," I said. "You two haven't seen one another?"

"Our parents won't let us. Here." She handed across one of those clear folders with a plastic piece that slips over the edge to bind it. "This should help. *And* save time."

Don Lee looked at it a moment and handed it to me. The cover read, in small capitals: INCIDENT OF THE NIGHT OF MAY 14. Then, following a two-line space: AS AVERRED BY SARAH PERKINS. Below that, her address, phone number, two e-mail addresses and a signature.

Inside, with approximate times, was a step-by-step listing of her and Seth McEvoy's arrival at the subdivision, their pulling into the driveway, her first sight of what she believed to be movement, their investigation of same and subsequent call to the police. She had fixed the times by checking her memory of the music being played against the radio station's log.

"I have a good ear for music, and excellent recall," she said.

Oh?

The second page of her report recounted what she and Seth had said to one another, beginning with "Seth, what is that?" and ending only with them saying good-bye when her parents (her mother, actually) picked her up at the police station. The third and fourth pages held computer-generated diagrams of relative positions: car, body, moon-light, the man's belongings, the stake.

"Thank you," I said.

"You're welcome, Mr. Turner. Is there anything else?"

"Tell you the truth, I don't know. I'm kind of over-whelmed here." I had another look. "This is great." After a moment I said, "Seth told me you and he aren't dating."

"Seth and I are friends."

"Friends. That's one of those words that can mean different things to different people."

"Words are like that." She smiled at me. "Aren't they?"

"He also told me his girlfriend—what's her name, again?"

"Emily."

"That Emily isn't too happy about you and Seth spending so much time together."

"Imagine that." A couple of bells sounded somewhere in her instrument panel. She glanced briefly down. "Do you know what a truffle is, Mr. Turner?"

"More or less, I think."

"They're tubers. They grow underground, on the roots of trees that have spent years earning their place, struggling for it, working their way up into the light. The tuber lives off the tree and gives nothing back."

"Okay."

"Emily is a truffle."

*   *   *

"DOC OLDHAM takes care of most ever'thing medical 'round here."

"Even had a look at Danny Bartlett's cows last year when they came up frothing at the mouth," Don Lee said. "Been known to pull a tooth or two, need be."

"He had a few choice words to say about my bothering him, but he's on his way."

"I could have gone to see him."

"I offered. Said he had to come into goddamn town anyway, he just hadn't goddamn it planned on it being so goddamn early."

"Barks a lot, does he?"

The sheriff nodded as the door opened and, borne on a flood of badinage, Doc Oldham entered. "Goddamn it, Bates, what's the matter with you, you can't handle a simple thing like this without hollering for help. This here your city boy?"

Boy—though we were much of an age. I nodded, which seemed the safest way to go at the time.

The sheriff introduced us.

"Don't talk much, does he?"

"You looked like you had more to say. I figured I'd best just wait till you wound down."

"I don't wind down. I ain't wound down in sixty-some years now and I don't aim to start. What the hell, you got coffee here to offer a man or not?" Don Lee was already pouring one, and handed it over. "Worked up to Memphis, I'm told."

"Yes, sir."

"You like it?"

"The city, or the work?"

"Both."

"I liked the work. The city, I got to liking less and less."

"'Spect you did. Saw things from the other side for a spell too, I hear."

"Didn't much like that either."

"Make the city look right tame?"

"Most ways it *was* the city—just a smaller version. Same tedium, same hierarchies, same violence and rage."

"Goddamn it, Bates, I will say one thing for you. You send for help, at least you got the decent good sense to bring in someone able to find his own head in the dark."

The sheriff nodded.

"And he ain't talkin' all the time like some others. Momma brought him up right."

"Actually, sir, it was my sister. Our mother passed when I was five."

"How much older was your sister?"

"She was sixteen."

"Good woman?"

"The best. Lives out in Arizona now, has three kids."

"Bringing up her *second* family."

I nodded.

"My folks disappeared when I was fifteen," Doc said. "We never did find out what became of them. There were two kids younger than me, one older. I was the one took care of us. It's a miracle, but we all turned out all right."

"That's what families are all about."

"Used to be, anyhow." He finished his coffee, put the mug down on the desk, and slid it towards Don Lee, who went to refill it. "You wanna put some goddamn sugar in this one to kill the taste?" Doc said. Then to me: "What'd you need?"

"Considering what I have, just about anything would be welcome."

"You read the file?"

"Sheriff Bates showed it to me."

"Don't know as I can add much to what's there."

"You didn't do the autopsy yourself, right?"

"Just the preliminary. Autopsy gets done up to the capital. Technically speaking I'm just coroner. Hereabouts that's an elected position, doesn't even require medical training."

Don Lee began, "It's an important—"

"It's political bullshit's what it is. Nobody else would take it, and for damn good reason."

"The body had been there a while, you said."

"Been there alive for some time before he was there dead, and that was three, four days."

"The stake had been driven in there?"

"No way. Where he lay'd be my guess. Someone mopped up as best he could. Lot of blood trace still. The bedding was rolled. Makes me think maybe he'd come back, laid down to rest thinking he'd go back out."

"So the body got moved."

"Absolutely. Some point after the stake went in—dead or almost, really no way to tell—he got wired to that trellis."

"Blood and skin under his nails?"

"Looked to be. Could just be dirt, grease."

"Maybe that'll give us something. I assume State'll do blood typing, run the DNA?"

"Blood, yes. Anything heavier'n that gets shipped out to Little Rock or Memphis, one of the big labs."

"You're saying be patient."

"Be very patient."

"Nothing else?"

I looked around the room in turn. Bates shook his head, as did Don Lee.

"One thing I have been thinking on," Doc said.

"Okay."

"This man's been out there, on the street, a while."

"Three, four months at least. Probably a lot longer."

"So how's it come about he has soft hands?"

Chapter Twelve

FOR YEARS IT WAS KNOWN around the department as the Monkey Ward caper.

We got tagged midday one Saturday. Dispatch was sending out a black-and-white, but the Lieutenant wanted detectives to rendezvous. Half a dozen calls had come in about whatever the hell was going on out there.

It was one of those new developments north of Poplar near East High School, reclaimed land where long-boarded-up storefronts, restaurants and thrift shops were being leveled to create inner-city suburbs, row upon row of sweet little perfect houses each with its own sweet front and rear lawn.

When we pulled up, one of the guys had a hedge trimmer, the other one a posthole digger. Took us some time to sort out they were in each other's yards. They'd gone from insults across the fence to a swinging match, and when that did neither of them much good, they'd opted for technical support. One was busily defoliating every bush and small tree on his neighbor's lawn, including plants in window boxes. The other was busily making the next yard look like a convention of moles had just let out.

The uniforms had just about talked them down by the time we got there. These guys had been riding together for fifteen, sixteen years; everyone in the department knew them. Tall one was Greaser, named for the hair tonic he must have bought in quart jars. Short one was Boots, for the zip-up imported footwear always polished to a high shine. Light reflected off Greaser's hair or Boots's boots could blind you.

Boots had Mr. Ditch Witch, Greaser had Hedge Man. They'd persuaded them to lay down the appliances and were bringing them together as we arrived. Close-up disputes like that, it's always a kind of square dance, swing them apart, bring them together, open it up again. As we climbed out of the car, the two had just shaken hands and were talking. Next thing we knew, they'd grabbed up a garden hoe and a leaf rake and were going after one another again, Robin and Little John with quarterstaffs on that narrow bridge. Should have been on riding mowers, galloping towards one another, lances at ready.

Randy looked across the top of the car shaking his head and said he knew all along it was gonna be one of those days. About that time the hoe caught Greaser hard on the side of the head. He'd moved in to intercede, baton high to protect himself, then half-turned to check on the other guy's position. Went down like a burnt match.

"You see that?" Randy said later. "Hair didn't move at all. What *is* that shit he puts on it?"

The citizen let the blade of the hoe fall to the ground, handle in his hand. Jesus, what had he done. But the one with the rake was still charging toward him, teeth aloft like a giant bird claw. Then his left foot stepped over a garden hose, we saw Boots run between them, suddenly Boots was behind the guy, still had hold of the hose, now he was pulling it tight—and the guy slammed to the ground.

Randy stood shaking his head. "Sure hope he don't aim to hog-tie him, too."

"I'll call it in," I said.

Doctors stitched it as best they could, but the hoe had opened it up even better, and Greaser wound up with a scar that ran an inch and a half or so down his forehead over the left eye. He took to pasting a lock of hair in place over it.

"Missiles take out civilization as we know it," Randy said, "that hair of his'll still be perfect."

Chapter Thirteen

WEDNESDAY HAD GONE BY, that was the day Bates came and collected me and the night I stayed at Val's, then Thursday, when I'd interviewed the two kids and Doc Old-ham. Now it was Friday. I'd slept on the office couch, awake at 10:35, 11:13, 2:09, 3:30, 5:18, 6:10. (Ah, the digital life. Never any doubt where you stand.) From time to time the radio crackled. The faucet in the bathroom had an on-again, off-again drip. Now someone was hammering boards in place over the windows.

No, someone's knocking at the door. And Don Lee is heading that way. Coffee burps and burbles in the maker, aroma spreading insidiously through the room like an oil spill. I'm fascinated by the fact that the door to the sheriff's office is locked. One of those weird things in life that seems to be the setup for a punch line you never quite get to.

A woman came in as I struggled up from the couch. She wore a tailored, narrow-waisted business suit the like of which don't seem to be around much anymore. The suit was green. So were her eyes. They went from Don Lee to me and back. Obviously she wondered if I shouldn't be in one of the cells, instead of out here.

"Sheriff Bates?"

Behind her soft urban lilt was a hill-country accent, East Virginia maybe. Getting along in years, and it hadn't stuck its head up to look around for a time, but it was still there. Don Lee said who he was and asked if he could help her.

"Sarah Hazelwood." She held out her hand to shake his, not something you saw a lot with women in this part of the country even now. "From St. Louis."

"Not originally, though," I put in, God knows why. I'd escaped the couch's hold by then. Her eyes met mine at a level. That was a harder hold.

"We're from where we choose to be. And what we choose to be."

Turning back to Don Lee, she went on.

"I'm looking for my brother. He . . . dropped out, I suppose is the right word—disappeared—almost a year ago."

"From St. Louis."

"Fort Smith. He lives . . . lived . . . at home, with our father. And this isn't the first time he managed to go missing, by any means. But always, before, he'd turn up again in a week or two. We'd get a call from an ER in Clarksdale or West Memphis, or from the police down in Vicksburg, and go fetch him."

"And now you think he's here?" Me again.

Again, those eyes level with my own: "You are . . . ?"

Don Lee introduced us, explaining my function as consultant. That word just kind of hung there in midair, letters malformed, dripping paint.

"We've reason to believe he may be."

Don Lee had poured his own and was adding in sugar before it occurred to him. "Like some coffee, Miss Hazelwood?"

"No, but thank you."

"And your reason is?" I said. "For believing he's here, I mean."

"I work as a paralegal, for the firm of Scott and Waldrop. We handle estates, trust funds, endowments. That sort of thing."

"Good work if you can get it," I said, with little idea why I was baiting this woman.

"The firm has nine attorneys, Mr. Turner. Two by choice work full-time at immigration, wrongful termination, civil-rights issues. Mostly pro bono."

"I apologize. Sometimes I get up in the morning and find I've gone to bed with this absolute jerk."

"How does the jerk feel about it?" After a moment she added: "I accept your apology."

Don Lee cleared his throat. "You've come all the way from St. Louis?"

"I flew into Memphis yesterday afternoon. We drove up from Fort Smith this morning."

"We?"

A black woman wearing a full-length dress slit on both sides to the upper thigh stepped through the door and stood there blinking. Earth colors, print, vaguely African. "Sorry to interrupt, but Dad's not doing so well out here."

Clipped short, her hair directed attention to the long, graceful curve of her neck, high cheekbones, shapely head. The dress was sleeveless, showing well-developed shoulders and biceps.

Moments later, the second woman—Adrienne, as I was soon to learn—pushed a wheelchair through the door Miss Hazelwood held open. In it sat a man with what looked to be a military brush cut. Ever seen a porch whose supports on one side have been kicked out? That's what he reminded me of. Everything on the right side, from forehead down through mouth to foot, sagged. That much closer to the earth we all wind up in.

"Daddy, this is Deputy Sheriff Don Lee. And Mr. Turner. Memphis police, I think."

Adrienne rolled the chair into a corner away from the heat of morning light.

"This okay, Mr. H?"

He turned his head to nod and smile at her. The right side of his face gave the impression of trying to stay in place, moving half a beat behind, even as the left side turned. Same with the smile. Left side voted yes, right side abstained.

Adrienne and Sarah Hazelwood exchanged gazes filled with wordless information.

"In St. Louis," Miss Hazelwood said, "at Scott and Waldrop, we handle a lot of legal work for the county. Mostly it's clerical, routine. Getting papers filed on time, filling in forms. But we also represented Sheriff Lansdale in a wrongful-death suit last year when a sixteen-year-old died of asthma while being held in his jail."

"Black?" I glanced at Adrienne. No reaction.

Miss Hazelwood nodded. "We've maintained something of a special relationship since then. Dave Strong heads up Information Services. Created and pretty much runs the computer system and database single-handed. He's my contact there."

"You hitched a ride on the information superhighway," I said.

This time she almost smiled.

"Two days ago, according to parameters he'd set, his computer flagged a bulletin. An unidentified murder victim whose description matched my brother's. Dave pulled down prints, and they matched too."

"I sent the bulletin," Don Lee said. "We put prints out on the wire, too, but nothing came back."

"We have a set taken on one of Carl's admissions to a psychiatric hospital, expressly for the hospital's own use, never broadcast. Sheriff Lansdale's people compared them for us."

Later, in the back room of Dunne's Funeral Parlor, which doubled as morgue, standing beside her father with one hand lightly on his shoulder, Sarah Hazelwood said, "Yes. That's Carl," and looked—not quickly or nervously but cautiously—from Adrienne to her father. Everyone bearing up as well as could be expected. Better, actually, given the circumstances.

"So there's one of us poor bastards put to rest, at least," Doc Oldham said. He sipped coffee, then, frowning, sniffed the mug. It bore the photo of a man's face that, when hot liquid got poured in, by degrees became a skull. "Damn milk went south at least a day ago. I wanted buttermilk, I'd of ordered up cornbread to go with it."

"They said back home he'd sit out on the porch half the morning waiting for the mail to come."

"So you were right," Bates said. "About him thinking he was a postman. Wouldn't think he'd be likely to be getting much mail."

"But he *could* have. That's what it was all about. Anticipation, promise. Like the world's holding its breath, and for just that one moment anything can happen, anything's possible."

"Doesn't sound like his life was exactly awash with possible."

"Okay, okay. Business you had here is over," Doc Oldham suddenly announced. "Anybody alive, able to move, you're out of here—now. Dead folk and me've got work to do."

Chapter Fourteen

RANDY WAS the funniest man I ever knew. Back there at first, all those "hair'll last long as roaches and cigarette butts" remarks, I tried to keep up with him, even managed to do so for a while, but it flat wore me out. Before Randy came along, I'd had a clutch of temporary partners, among them Gardner, who died in a cheap motel listening to a prostitute's sad tale, and Bill, who I think may have said thirty words to me the whole time, twenty of those the day he cold-cocked Sammy Lee Davis when we found all those kids left alone; then I'd worked by myself again for a while. Randy was supposed to be temporary, too. Maybe the desk jockeys forgot where they put him, or maybe after Randy and I'd been together a few weeks they just up and decided what the hell, it ain't broke. . . .

Boy was Jewish, God help him, problematic those days outside the shelter of owning, say, a jewelry or furniture store, but not even God proved much help to other cops who decided to make it an issue. They'd find themselves with new nicknames they couldn't shake off, enough jokes at their expense to bury them alive.

From the first, though, for reasons I never understood and still don't, I was somehow exempt.

"Pawnshop's right around this corner," I told him the first night we rolled out together. Following up on a double murder, possibly a murder-suicide, we had a long night of knocking-on-doors-and-asking-questions to look forward to. Car had the rearview mirror duct-taped to the side, and the seat jumped track whenever I hit the brakes. He made no secret of his heritage. Nor was I what you'd call a beacon of charity those days—and already he was wearing me down. "Want I should drop you?"

After a moment he said in perfect black dialect, "Nawsir. I be trying to 'similate."

Fact is, we got along great. The standing joke between us got to be if we didn't know better we might have thought the Captains knew what they were up to when they put us together. Guaranteed a laugh anywhere cops were.

And cops were most everywhere we went. Dinner at Nick's before going in on second watch, D-D's Diner noon-time days, breakfast at Sambo's coming off long late nights, bars in the Overton Square area Randy and I went to afterwards to wind down. After a while it started getting to me. We don't see anyone *but* cops anymore, I told him one night.

"They're our family."

"You *have* a family."

His expression, in the moment before he checked its green card and deported it, told me more than I wanted to know. How much of recent behavior did that expression explain?

We'd have got into it then but got tagged. No patrols available, could we take it? Speak to the lady at 341 E. Oakside, she'd be standing by the weeping willow out front. And she was, demanding to know before Randy and I even had the squad doors open what could be done about her son, could we please help her, no one should have to put up with this, she couldn't stand it any longer. The tree was huge, a wild green bouffant mimicking her blondish one, clay irrigation ports at its base. Near as I could tell, she didn't have those.

Her son, she told us, kept breaking into her house. Twenty-six years old and he wouldn't work, wouldn't do much of anything but hold down the couch, watch TV and eat. Whenever she brought it up he'd say he was going to do better, he knew all that, he was sorry, she had every right and so on, and she'd put up with it a while, but then he'd never follow through, so she'd toss him out again. Change locks, the whole works. But he'd just break in, be there on the couch like nothing happened when she got home. She'd had enough. She'd had it this time. She wanted his fat useless butt off her couch and out of her apartment and she wanted him to know that's how it was going to be from now on.

She couldn't get away right now, everybody else was out of the office, showing houses. Must she go along? Could we . . . ? Old Miss Santesson from across the alley had called to let her know that, after she left for work, Bobbie had gone over the back fence, kicked out the bathroom window and climbed through.

Some miles of heavy traffic to go. Randy called it in as we pulled away from the willow's shade. Still holding the mike, he looked out his window and said, "Things haven't been going real well between Dorey and me."

"So I figured."

He looked over at me.

"Kinda lost that sartorial edge you used to have," I said. "I'd of sworn I actually saw a spot on your coat one time last week."

"A spot."

"Try club soda."

"Club soda, right." He leaned forward to cradle the mike. "Couple starts having trouble, everyone says they're not spending enough time together. But it seems like the more we're together, the worse it gets."

"I'm sorry, man."

"Me too. So is Dorey. So are our folks. Everyone's sorry. Betty most of all." His daughter, what, fourteen now? "She doesn't say anything, pretends she doesn't know. But it's there in her eyes."

"Has to be hard."

"Scary thing's how easy it is, some ways."

Bobbie put up no struggle. He met us at the front door when we rang (one of the chimes then popular) and told us he knew, he knew, but she had no right, it was his house too. He went on saying that all the way downtown, eyes making contact in the rearview mirror above a stained orange sweatshirt. He was still saying it when we dropped him off at John Gaston ER on his way to the psych ward. By that time it was nearing shift's end and the station house loomed before us, this sudden cliff of bright lights, as we pulled up in our little hiccoughing skiff with side mirror flapping like a tiny, useless wing. Randy told me he'd do the paperwork.

"No way in hell."

"Hey—"

"Go home, Randy. Go home and hug your daughter, fix breakfast for your wife. Talk to them."

He didn't, of course. But at the time I wanted to think he might.

He called in the next day and again the one following. Captain pulled me over the third morning to see if I'd say anything about what was going on. He didn't ask outright or push, just told me he hoped Randy'd be back on his feet soon, that he'd never missed a single day before.

That night, I called.

Hey. Turner. Good to hear your voice, Randy said. Just I'm spending some time at home, he told me. Taking your advice. Taking it easy.

"You doing okay, then?"

"Better than that. Home-cooked meals every night. Meat loaf, mashed potatoes, gravy. Have the leftovers with biscuits next morning. Sorry to cut out on you like this, though. How's the bad guys?"

"Still winning. Don't stay out too long or we'll never catch up."

"I won't, then. See you soon, partner."

Two days later I went over there. It was twilight, color

draining visibly from the world, leaves blurring on trees, shadows stepping in everywhere. Through a window set high in the front door I could see over the back of the couch to a coffee table piled with plates, glasses, hamburger wrappers and potato-chip bags. The TV was on, some local talent show for kids, picture rolling like clockwork every three seconds.

I rang the bell twice more, then opened the screen and banged on the door. Maybe try around back? Check with neighbors? I looked to the right, where a window curtain in the house next door fell closed, and looked back just as Randy's face came up over the couch. Kilroy. Just this half a face and the fingers of two hands. When I waved, one of the hands lifted to answer. Randy glanced at it in surprise. I expected him to get up and come around the couch, but instead he clambered over the back and, hitting the floor, did a little off-balance shuffle and recovery, Dick Van Dyke on a bad day. Closer to the door he stumbled for real.

"Hey," he said, "you want some coffee?" and without waiting for a reply went off opening drawers and closet doors and looking under chairs. "Got some here somewhere."

I went out to the kitchen. Sure enough, there it was. In a Corningware pot with blue flowers on it. The pot was full, and it had been sitting there for some time. But Randy wasn't drunk, as I first thought. It was worse.

When I walked by him, he'd followed me like a lost kitten. Now he went eye-to-eye with the little red light atop the handle.

"*There* it is!"

Took me over an hour to start getting any sense out of him. I poured Randy's vintage coffee down the drain, made more, and we sat at the kitchen table knocking it back. He was like a child. Like a boat cut loose, drifting wherever wind and current took it. I don't think he had any idea whether it was day or night, how long he'd been here like this, even that something might be wrong. Alone in the house with the world shut out, without landmark, limit or margin, he had drifted free.

Momentarily, intermittently, Randy came into focus and was able to tell me what happened.

Dorey had moved out a month ago. We'd been on second-shift rotation then, and he'd come home just after midnight to find the house dark, a single lamp burning in the living room on the long table inside the door where they always dropped mail. At the table's far end was a stack of freshly ironed shirts. Beside that, Dorey had laid out bills in the order they would come due, with postdated checks attached. Her note was leaning against the lamp.

*I love you but I won't be back. I'll send
an address when I have one. You'll be
welcome to see Betty any time, of course.
Please take care of yourself.*

It was signed, rather formally, "Doreen." Randy took the note out of his shirt pocket and handed it to me. It was broken-backed at the creases from much folding and unfolding. There were stains.

"I did all right at first," he said. "I'd come home, eat something, have a beer, and be okay. Start thinking: I'm gonna get through this."

"You should have told me."

"Yeah, well . . . Lots of things I should have done."

We talked a while longer, much of our dialogue making little sense, some of it making none, connectives torn away, grammarless sentences left dangling for the listener to punctuate or parse as he would. Eventually I left Randy at the kitchen table and went out to the phone in the hall. He was still in there talking to me.

I didn't bother calling Sally Gene at home, but after a number of tries tagged her at the Baptist psych unit. When a nurse handed the phone over, Sally Gene took it and said "I'm busy."

"You always are. I'm looking for my favorite social worker."

"Turner?"

"Your favorite driver. But this time, I'm the one who needs a ride-along."

I told her about Randy.

"Is he oriented?" Sally Gene asked.

"Comes and goes. Rest of the time, it's hard to tell."

"He knows you?"

"Yes."

"And once you started talking to him, he was able to lay out a sequence of events?"

"More or less."

"Has he been eating?"

Yes again. I'd looked in the refrigerator and found stacks of TV dinners.

"Alcohol?"

"Not that I know. I'd be surprised. Never much of a drinker, two or three beers'd be his limit. And I think he only did that to fit in."

"So what are we looking for here?"

"I don't know. We're on your ship, with this. You're the skipper."

"Little outside what I'm used to, what I do day to day. And it's been a while since I trained. We want to get him some help, obviously. Observation, at the very least. . . . Any sign he's a danger to himself?"

"Not that I can see."

"We don't want to jam him up on the job, so we'll be wanting to keep it off the public record."

"If that's possible, great. But the most important thing's to help him dig out of this, whatever it takes."

"Okay, listen. Let me make a few calls. I'll get back to you. What's the number there?"

I gave it to her and went out to the kitchen, where Randy, quiet at last, had fallen asleep with his head on the table. On the refrigerator, magnets shaped and painted as miniature vegetables held up sheaves of coupons and grocery receipts. A drawing his daughter Betty had done years ago hung under another magnet that first looked to be an angel or cherub but on closer inspection turned out to be a pig with wings.

"Hey, you're here!" Randy said.

Within the hour, we were checking him in at Southside Clinic. Set up to care for the indigent, Sally Gene told me when she called back, by a young doctor from up east, an idealistic sort, but damned good from all she heard. She'd made inquiries of colleagues, pretending she needed the information for one of her clients. Southside was expecting us. She'd meet us there.

Chapter Fifteen

"THE THING WE CAN'T understand is who could possibly want to kill Carl. He was harmless, sweet. It would be like crushing a kitten. Nor do we have any idea what he was doing here, or how he got here in the first place, or why."

Sarah Hazelwood and I were sitting on the bench outside Manny's Dollar $tore. Adrienne and Mr. Hazelwood had driven off to find rooms. I'd directed them to Ko-Z Kabins out by the highway. A longish drive, and the sort of place you apologize ahead of time for recommending, but what else was there.

"I take it you're all a family."

"Just like choosing where to be from, Mr. Turner. Families can be chosen too." She smiled. "I don't mean to be confrontational."

"I understand."

"Dad's not Adrienne's father, but she never treats him as if he's anything else. In some ways, she's closer to him than I am."

"You and Adrienne—"

"Half sisters. Mother had her before she married Dad, when she wasn't much more than a girl herself. Adrienne was raised by grandparents. Then, not long after Mother died, Adrienne came looking for her. This wasn't supposed to be possible, with all kinds of blinds set up, but Hazelwoods are a resourceful lot. Adrienne and Dad got along famously from the first. She stayed with us for a few days, days became a week, eventually we all understood she wasn't going to leave. The rest developed slowly."

Whether to assess my reaction or judge if I needed further explanation of "the rest," Sarah Hazelwood regarded me steadily.

A huge grasshopper came out of nowhere and landed in the middle of the street. It sat there a moment then leapt on, heading out of town, glider-wings thrumming. Thing looked to be the size of a frog.

"Where does Carl fit in?"

"Mother was along in years when she had me. Her health was never good after. As I said before, where we belong, our families, we're able to choose those. Mother always said they pulled me out and pulled her plumbing right after."

A mockingbird swooped down at the grasshopper from behind, realized it didn't have time to clear Ben McAllister's truck coming towards them, bed crisscrossed with feed sacks, and flew back up. I waved at Ben, who nodded his usual quarter-inch. The grasshopper emerged from underneath and hopped on.

"One day Dad was out hunting. He happened to pass

close by the neighbor's house a mile or so up the hill and heard a baby crying. He knocked, got no answer, and went on in. The house wasn't much more than a shack. A man named Amos Wright had been living there for as long as anyone could remember. Then a year or so back he'd suddenly turned up with a wife. No one knew where she came from, or how the two of them ever met. Amos had always kept to himself.

"Dad said he could smell the stench before he set foot on the porch. And when he went in there, the place was full of flies. They were buzzing all around the baby laying in its crib. The baby's mother was on the floor by the bed. Flies had laid eggs in her wounds and maggots were boiling up out of them."

"The baby—"

"The baby was Carl. Amos didn't have family that anyone knew of, and no one knew anything at all about the mother, so my folks took the boy in and raised him, the way country people will. Amos wasn't ever seen again, and they never did find out anything more about what happened. Some said it was an accident, others claimed someone must have broken in and beat the woman to death, maybe even a relative. A lot of people assumed Amos just up and killed her, of course, then ran."

"Carl knew about this?"

"Most of it. It was never easy to be sure how much or what Carl understood. Sometimes you'd be sitting there talking to him and you could all but see what you were telling him get . . . bent. You'd watch it start turning to something else inside him."

"Troubles came early, then."

"He seemed all right at first, Dad said. And for a while they shrugged it off. Hill folk have a high tolerance for peculiarities. Later, doctors told them it could have been from those days he was alone there in the cabin without food or water, no one knew for how long."

"Brain damage."

She nodded. "Possibly. But he'd had no prenatal care—or postnatal, for that matter. He'd been born right there in the cabin to all appearances. Easily could have suffered insult during birth, deprived of oxygen, too much pressure on the head, causing a bleed. Or he could have picked up an infection, either then or later on, passed on from his mother, carried by insects. Simple heredity? The mother never looked healthy or quite right herself, most said. For all that, my folks brought Carl up the same as me. They tried to, anyway. Not much about it was easy for them."

"Or for you, would be my guess."

"I liked having a brother. And it's not as though he was ever violent, anything like that. He just wasn't always *there*. I did have a few fights back when he started school. You know, taking up for him. But pretty soon the others left us alone."

"He finished school?"

"And got a job, working at Nelson Ranch. We'd moved by then, to the closest town. Called it a ranch, but what they raised was chickens."

"Takes a small lariat."

She looked at me oddly a moment, then laughed.

"Carl had been getting worse the past year or so. His mind would wander off and he'd go looking for it, Dad said.

He got fired after a month or so. Mrs. Nelson came over herself to talk to Dad and tell him how bad they all felt. After that, he just hung around the house, I guess. I was off at college. At first I wrote to him, but he never answered, and we soon lost touch. We never had much of anything to say to one another the few times I came home."

"You didn't get home regularly?"

"I was paying my own way. I had a half-scholarship, but that didn't go near far enough. Every weekend, most breaks and holidays, most days after class, I was working."

"Good grades?"

"Good enough that I got my degree in three and a half years. I wanted to go on to law school, but there was no way I could afford it. The cupboards were bare."

"You're still young. You could go back."

She shook her head. "It's a question of confidence—confidence and momentum. Back then it never occurred to me that anything could stop me. I know too many things that can stop me now."

For reasons known only to himself (turndown on a date? bad test grade? failure to make the football squad?) a teenager leaning from a passing car shouted "I'm soooo disappointed."

Sarah Hazelwood smiled. "Well. There it is. What more need be said? For any of us."

Chapter Sixteen

DOORS SLAMMING SHUT and locks falling: you never forget that sound, the way it makes you feel. That was something waiting in my own future, something I'd get used to, inasmuch as one ever does. Looking back even now, a familiar horror clutches at my throat, squeezes my heart in its fist.

When the buzzer sounded, I pushed through double doors into Wonderland. Here's another hall, another birth passage. Up two levels in an elevator crowded with bodies, down a cluttered hall—linen carts, food carriers, house-cleaning trucks—to the tollbooth. Nurses in a patchwork of whites, scrubs, Ban-Lon and T-shirts, jeans, slacks. One of them showed me into a double room where Randy, dressed in a jogging suit I'd packed for him, sat on one of the beds. Everything in the room, bedspread, curtains, towel folded neatly on the bedside table, was pastel. Randy's jogging suit was sky blue.

He looked up at me. "Stupid, huh?"

I had no idea how much he remembered, and asked him.

"All of it. But it's like a TV show I saw, or a movie. Like it's not me, I'm standing off somewhere watching: who *is* this asshole? Beats all, doesn't it?"

"I spoke with the Captain this morning. He's the only one back at the station house who knows what's going on. Wants me to tell you don't worry, he's got you covered."

Neither of us said anything else for a time.

"I appreciate this, buddy," Randy said finally.

"Hey. Don't get me wrong, you're no prize. But with you gone, either I head out alone or wind up having to take care of some half-assed retard no one else'll have. At least I'm used to you."

We both let the silence have its way again. After a while he said: "She's gone, isn't she?"

"Looks like it."

"I don't know what I'm going to do."

"Besides get your shit together and get back on the job, you mean."

"Yeah . . . besides that."

A nurse came in with a tray. He held out his hand. She upended a fez-shaped container of pills onto it, handed him a small waxed cup of water. He drank and swallowed. She went away.

Anything I can get for you? I said. Anything I need to take care of?

He shook his head.

"Bills are all paid up. Plenty of food in the house. . . . Unless you want to try to get in touch with Dorey, find out where she is."

I'd already done that, but I wasn't going to tell him. I said I'd look into it.

"I can't, I just can't," Dorey had told me. She was staying with a friend on Clark Place, in an old red-brick house behind a screen of fig trees. We sat in wicker chairs on the enclosed front porch, behind a checkerboard of glass, struts and putty. Full of imperfections, each pane warped the world in a different way, reducing, enlarging, folding edges into centers, bending right angles to curves. Mockingbirds thrashed and sang in the fig trees. "Will you let me know how he is?" Dorey asked. I said I would.

"Gotta get back on the horse," I told Randy. "Anything you need, you'll call me, right?"

He promised he would.

"I'm so sorry," Marsha said that night over Mexican food. We'd been together six or eight weeks. A band looking like something from *The Cisco Kid* or a Roy Rogers movie, guitar, *bajo sexto* and trumpet, emerged from the kitchen playing "Happy Birthday" and stepped up to a table nearby. Our enchilada plates emerged moments later, pedestrian by comparison.

Marsha was a librarian. We'd met when a drunk fell asleep at one of the reading tables, she'd been unable to wake him at closing time, and, being right around the corner, I took the call. She was strikingly attractive, all the more so for never giving her appearance a thought one way or the other. Her mind was agile, the angle it might take at any given time unpredictable; good conversation sprang up spontaneously whenever she was around. Ten minutes after meeting someone, she'd be winnowing her way to the very best that person had. Despite my protests that it was important work I was good at, she kept insisting I was wasting my time as a detective.

"You remind me of my sister," I told her when she first brought it up. "Always going on about how when I was young I'd been a natural leader, and she wondered why that changed."

"Did it?"

I shoveled about half a cup of salsa onto a chip and threw it back, washed it down with a long sip of Miller's.

"What happened, I think, was we grew apart."

"You and your sister?"

"Me and the other kids. We had everything in common at first. They weren't a particularly vocal or imaginative lot, and I'd just step up there, speak for them, pull them together. But as time went on, as we became individuals, our interests diverged. They took to sports, which I couldn't care about. I just never got it, you know? Still don't. Then I gravitated to books—every bit as mysterious to them, or more so."

Marsha reached over and got my beer, took a swig. Things liberated always taste better. "Just listen to yourself," she said. "Exactly what I mean."

Flagging down the waitress, I ordered another beer.

"Don't suppose you want one?" I asked Marsha.

"Me? A beer? Why on earth would I?"

"Just as I thought."

She forged ahead into enchiladas, refried beans and soggy pimiento-shot rice, bolstering same with occasional forkful from my plate, though it was identical with hers.

Neither of us did well, finally, by the challenge. Fully half the food remained heaped on our plates when we were done, foil-wrapped tortillas untouched. I had another beer. We declined offers of take-home containers.

Out, then, into a typically fine southern evening, cicadae singing, moths beating at screens, quarter-moon above. My car waited. Beneath artificial lights its shiny, hard, blue-green body resembled nothing so much as the carapace of another insect.

"Randy doesn't have much to look forward to, does he?"

"Not right now."

"Without you, he'd have far less." She laid her head back against the seat. "It's so beautiful, you almost forget."

Years later in similar circumstances, in what might have been the same night inhabited by the great-great-grand-children of those same cicadae, Val Bjorn turned her head to me and said, "A real Hank Williams night." As she hummed softly, the words came to me. A night so long . . . Time goes slowly by . . . His heart's as lonesome as mine.

Chapter Seventeen

MUCH PRISON CONVERSATION consists of homilies, catchphrases, familiar incantations passed back and forth without thought. Someone gave voice to one of them, others within hearing would nod, that was an entire conversation. A particular favorite was: You don't use your time, it'll sure use you.

From every indication Carl Hazelwood had been well used by time, long before he wound up pinned like a specimen moth to a carport wall.

I'd barely got back to the office from talking to Sarah, who'd been picked up by Adrienne after she put their exhausted father to bed, when Don Lee answered the phone and handed it over.

Val Bjorn jumped right in. "Hey, I have your man. Had to hold my head right, figure out which way to look. His fingerprints . . ." She trailed off. Because I'd not responded? "You had it already, didn't you?"

"Just."

"Day late and a dollar short."

I filled her in on the Hazelwood family's arrival. "Not that this in any way lessens my appreciation of your efforts, you know."

"You have no idea how hard I humped to get this."

"Maybe I can make it up to you."

"How *are* they? The family. They have any idea what might have gone down?"

"Mostly they're still trying to figure out what he was doing here."

"Aren't we all." She paused to sip at something. "What'd you have in mind with that making-up thing?"

"Dinner, maybe? I'm open to suggestion."

"You cook?"

"I buy."

"That could be a problem 'round here."

"So could my cooking."

"Hmmm. Then maybe I should cook. Lesser of two evils. Not a lot lesser, I'll admit."

"Or we could throw that whole food business overboard—"

"Quick footwork there, Turner. Look out below!"

"—and just have a drink."

"Done."

"There has to be a bar somewhere around here. I'll ask."

"Don't bother. I know just the place."

"Have a date, do we?" Don Lee said when I hung up.

We spent the day updating files on the murder, sorting medical reports and bits of information that had come in by e-mail and fax, reading back through it all, sifting, sorting, making lists. Like much of life, a murder investigation consists mainly of plodding along, circling back and waiting, considerably more low cleric than high adventure. Don Lee brought the sheriff up to speed on our visitors. Bates had called in a couple of times, around noon and again at three or so when we'd gone down to the diner for coffee, to see how we were doing, then showed up to take over not long after, just before daughter June went off duty at the desk. Father and daughter hugged, Bates and Don Lee did a quick shift report, most of it already covered by phone, and Don Lee headed home. I stayed around a while to talk things over. Then the sheriff dropped me off for my rendezvous with Val.

Just the Place turned out to be not a description but a proper name. Surrounded by a gravel parking lot, it sat in a clearing on a blacktop road three or four miles out of town. Just the Place was what folks back home called a beer joint, and most of them would have tipped over stone dead rather than get caught near one. Beer joints were for drunks—dagos and winos, people in blue jeans or greasy work clothes who drank up paychecks, beat wives, let kids go hungry and wild.

The inside looked pretty much what the outside, and old prejudices, promised. Val was sitting at the bar with a beer at half mast.

"I was gonna be a lady and wait—"

"Must have been a struggle."

"—but then I figured, what the hell."

"Objection sustained."

She raised her bottle in agreement. Moments later I managed to extract one of my own from the bartender, a woman with a western shirt straining at the snaps and big hair of the kind one rarely sees outside Texas. I expanded on what I'd already passed along about Carl and the rest of the Hazelwood clan. Their identification of the body, what they'd told me of his background, what I'd learned about them. Val said we'd be getting initial results on the forensics kit first thing in the morning by fax once the medical officer had had a look and signed off on it. Don't think it's gonna help much, though. Got some blood types and so on for you, but it's all generic.

Then she was telling me about a current case. She'd been in court from nine that morning till just before we met.

"Mostly I do family law. Almost a year ago, my client's husband got upset because she'd gone out to dinner with an old friend from high school. He went into their daughter's room, she was four at the time, and began beating her. The mother came home and found her there in the crib, eyes filmed over, slicks of mucus and blood on sheets printed with blue angels and pink rocking horses. The husband said he didn't know anything about it, the kid was fine the last time he looked in. My client moved out immediately, of course. But the girl had sustained significant brain damage. She's never recovered, she'll never develop mentally, even as her body continues to grow. Medical bills and maintenance costs are staggering. The husband's not paid a cent of child support."

"So you're going after him."

"Hardly. I represent the mother, but we're the defense. He's petitioning for full custody."

What could I say to that?

"No way he wants the child. Susie's a symbol, a posses-sion. Like a couch or a painting, the contents of a lockbox."

"He has to hurt his wife once and for all, worse than ever before."

Val nodded.

I became aware that for some time there'd been activity behind us, against the far wall. Now someone blew into a microphone and music started up. A simple riff on guitar, then a steel swelling behind, a long bass glide, drums. I turned on my bar stool, as did Val. We glanced at one another and moved to a table ringside.

"These guys are amazing," she said. "Just wait."

Interestingly, the band's front man and singer was black—the first black face I remembered seeing since moving back here. Save Adrienne's, of course, but she was an import. After a couple of Hank Williams songs and a creditable cover of "San Antonio Rose," the band locked onto Sonny Boy Williamson's "Gone So Long," taking it down home the same way early Texas string and swing bands had liberated "Sittin' on Top of the World" or "Milk Cow Blues," making it their own.

Fine stuff, followed by more. All of it purest amalgam country, voice calling, guitar responding, steel and bass lay-ing a foundation, cellar, stairs. Chunks of Appalachian bal-lads, Delta blues, early jazz and Hawaiian floating about in there like vegetables in a rich stew.

"I once fell in love with a man because he had nothing but George Jones tapes in his apartment," Val said during an intermission.

"Is this something I need to know?"

"Think about it. It's a better reason than most others. I figured any man that devoted to Jones had to have something to him. Your lover's going to lose jobs, hair and interest in you, get fat, sit on the couch farting. Those tapes will still be there, still be the same, old George pouring his heart into every note. Always sounds like he's wrestling himself, squeezing notes out past some kind of emotional or physical obstruction. His voice stumbles, crawls and soars, always somehow at the very edge of what a voice is, what a man can feel." Dregs of a fourth beer went down her throat. She waved off another. "Sorry. I take this music seriously. Not many people do anymore. For a long time it was all that remained of our folk music. Now it's gone, or almost. Become just another part of the commercial blur."

By this time Eldon Brown, the band's singer, who, as it turned out, Val knew, had joined us. He sat with thin legs crossed, sipping from a cup the size of a goldfish bowl. Tea with honey and lemon, he said. For all his verisimilitudinous vocal renditions, not a trace of South or hill country in his speaking voice. Hoboken, New Jersey, he said when I asked.

"Family moved north during the war, looking for work. I grew up on local soul and gospel radio and this monster country station over in Carlyle, Pennsylvania. Came back south on tour with an R&B band, as guitarist, nine years ago, one of those last-minute pickup things. Third, fourth week into it, we're playing a bar in Clarksdale and the bass player takes after the singer with an oyster knife, to this day I don't know why. Not much left of the band at that point, but I stayed on. Been working steady ever since. Speaking of which . . ."

He excused himself to take his place on the bandstand, kicking off with a no-holds-barred "Lovesick Blues," yodels slapping at the room's walls like a tide.

Val and I left around nine, picking our way out through packed bodies and a full parking lot. At her place we pulled cold cuts, cheese, pickles, olives and apples from the refrigerator and took them, with beers, out onto the front porch. It was a gorgeous, clear night, stars like spots of ice. Wind worked fingers in the trees. An owl crossed the moon.

"It's good to have someone to talk to," Val said. She popped a bite of bologna into her mouth. The half-pound in her refrigerator (folks around here would call it an icebox) had come off the store's solid stick; we'd hacked it into cubes. "I'm not looking for anything more. I hope you know that."

Nor was I.

"You miss it?" she said.

"Someone to talk to—or something more?"

"Both, I guess." Her eyes met mine. "Either."

"Strange thing is, I don't. Not really."

Neither of us spoke for a time.

"I had a partner, back when I was a cop. His wife left him, took the kid, his whole life fell apart. One day I said to him it had to be hard. He looked across at me there in the squad car. Scary thing's how easy it is, he said."

After a moment she said, "I understand," and we sat silently in the wash of that amazing night, two people together alone under stars and pecan trees, personal histories tucked tight against our hearts as though to still or quieten them.

Chapter Eighteen

YOU DON'T USE YOUR TIME, it'll sure use you. Don't talk it, walk it. Putting money in the hat for those about to bail. Passing around meager, prized possessions—sheets, T-shirts, a transistor radio with extra batteries, Bob's Bodyshop calendar—as you leave. Homilies, slogans, customs. A world of things, objects. As though the narrowness and inaction of our days had excised verbs themselves from our lives. (And the pervasive violence an effort to reinvest them?) Everything ended a few yards past our eyes; it had to. That's what you did to get by, you drew everything in close to yourself, let short sight take over. Soon enough, imagination, too, started shutting down.

Homilies—and a lot of time staring at the join of cinder blocks. Counting them, tracking where at one end of the cell there's maybe a half-inch before the top line of mortar, at the other end almost two. Or where a previous tenant scraped away the mortar between blocks on the wall beside his bed and the toilet. Did he spend that much time on the toilet? Boredom, like blind faith, engenders strange errand lists.

Nine hundred and sixty-four cinder blocks, from where I sat.

Six weeks in, I wrote away to New Orleans and Chicago for transcripts. Nothing about this endeavor proved easy. While you were allowed two letters a month postage provided, sending money remained a tricky prospect, and both schools required five-dollar fees. The prison chaplain came to my aid. Reading those transcripts once I got them was like looking in the mirror and finding someone else's face. Could I ever have been that callow? Had I actually taken a course called Revolutionary Precepts, and what on earth might it have been about? Two semesters of medieval history? I hadn't a single concept, movement or date left over from that.

Who *was* this person?

Someone, apparently, who'd been on the express train, a dozen or so stops away from getting a master's degree. Strange how I'd managed to forget that. Stranger still to wonder where all of it—all those hours and years of burrowing, the knowledge issuing from them, the ambition that led to them—might have gone. None of it seemed to be in me anymore.

By this time I'd suffered through a cellmate in the bunk above murmuring words aloud as he read from his Bible and another given to Donald Goines's *Whoreson*, *Swamp Man* and Kenyatta novels. Then Adrian came along, by which time I myself sat nose sunk like a tomahawk in college catalogs and bulletins. Our gray, featureless submarine went on plowing its way through gray, featureless days. And I, it seemed, while still submerged could complete my degree courtesy of the state that held me in such cautious esteem.

Nowadays, of course, in the house Internet Jack built, there'd be nothing much to it. But back then the labors involved proved Herculean. Each month or so I'd receive a thick envelope of material. I was expected to read through it, write the papers required and complete a test at its end, then mail the whole thing back, whereupon another envelope would arrive.

That was the theory. But often two or three months would go by before I received a packet, at which time I might be handed three of them, one, or a mostly empty envelope. Could have been inmates with a grudge working the mail room, some guard's petty meddling or arrogant notion of control, or it could have been just plain workaday pilferage. Never an explanation, of course, and you learned quickly, once those doors slammed shut behind you, never to question. Had it not been for the protection afforded me by fish-nor-fowl status and, later, by one teacher's taking an unwarranted interest, I'm sure the college soon would have scoured me from its pot. But it didn't. I'd gone into serious overdraft, but checks were still being cashed.

October of that second year, I received my M.A. The elaborate certificate, on heavy cream-colored bond replete with Gothic lettering and Latin, came rolled in a tube such as the ones in which other inmates received the *Barbarella*, Harley-Davidson and R. Crumb posters taped to the walls of their cells. University regents wished to inquire, an attached letter read, as to whether I would be continuing my education at their facility. Forever a quick study, having now survived inside and in addition found my way through thickets of university regulations, I felt as though I'd turned myself into some kind of facility veteran, slippery enough to slalom around raindrops, savvy enough to ride the system's thermals. Better the facility you know. You bet I will be, I told university regents.

If every year April comes down the hill like an idiot, babbling and strewing flowers, then October steps up to the plate glum and serious—never more than that one.

Lifting a pound or two of prison clothes off the counter, I'd picked up a ton of grief with them. That I'd been a cop was not supposed to get out. But guards knew, which meant everyone knew, and every one of them, inmates and guards alike, had good reason to despise the various shipwrecks that had cast them up here. They weren't able to slit society's neck or shove the handle of a plumber's helper up Warden Petit's rear end, but there *I* was. From the first, starting out small and escalating the way violence always does, I'd met with confrontations on the yard, at mealtime, in the showers, at workshop. Two months and half a dozen scrambles in, I received a rare invitation from Warden Petit himself—I hadn't been able to back off fast enough, and guards, looking away, had given me time to break the guy's jaw before moving in—who wanted to tell me how proud he was of the way I was handling myself.

"Thank you, Warden."

"Tremendous pressures on you out there. I appreciate that, you know. I see it. They never let up on a man, do they?" A triangular patch of hair had been left behind on his forehead as the rest withdrew. He made a show of consulting papers on the desk before him. "Like a cup of coffee?"

"No."

"Scotch?" His eyes came back up to mine. I'd been given a folding chair designed, apparently, for maximal discomfort. Reminded me of the bunk and toilet in my cell.

"You're dripping blood on my floor." He keyed the intercom. "Get Levison in here," he said, then to me: "Don't worry," as he smiled. "We're used to it. And it's not really my floor, is it?"

Petit was like those guys who as hospital administrators a decade or so later would start calling themselves CEOs, wanting to live just a little large. He wore a light gray suit that made him resemble nothing so much as a block of cement with a head balanced atop. The head kept nodding and bobbing about like it wasn't placed well and might topple off any minute. Hope springs eternal.

"Absolutely not mine. It's the taxpayers' floor."

His personal floors, I had no doubt, would be scoured clean. By inmates or trustees if not by his own scab-kneed wife.

"You'd best get on down there. Medic's waiting for you at the infirmary."

I was almost through the door when he said: "Turner?"

I stopped.

"You're on good road. What, two months more? Don't let 'em skid you out. Do it easy."

"Do my best."

As I left, Levison, seventy-plus if he was a day, shuffled past me carrying bucket and mop. Squirt bottles and rags hung on his pants like artillery.

Next morning, this guy steps up to me in the shower. I see him coming, the shank held down along his leg, see the fix in his eyes. At the last moment I shove out my hand and swing the heel up hard. The shank, a sharpened spoon, pierces his chin, pins his tongue. He opens his mouth trying to talk and I see the tongue flailing about in there, only the tip able to move as he slides down the shower wall.

Was that enough? Did I have to kill him? I don't know. At the time it seemed I'd been left no choice. Another homily, another of the commandments we live by, says once a man steps up to you, you have to put him down.

Neither did the courts feel *they* had much choice. In their hands my three-year sentence blossomed to twenty-five.

Chapter Nineteen

"I SERVED EIGHT MORE YEARS, got another degree, in psychology, a master's again, and began thinking maybe I could make some kind of life out of that. What else did I have to build on? By the time early release came around, I knew I wanted to work as a therapist. I set up in Memphis, made the rounds of school social workers, doctor's offices, community centers and so on to introduce myself and leave business cards, started picking up clients. Slowly at first, and anybody who walked in. But I had some kind of real feel, an instinct, for the acutely troubled ones—those at the edge of violence. Within a year that's mostly who I was seeing."

Sheriff Bates was nigh the perfect listener. His eyes had never left me as he leaned back in his chair, making himself comfortable, wordlessly inviting me to go on. Then he propped it up: "You found work you were good at. Damn few of us are ever lucky enough to do that."

"I know, believe me. Knew it then."

"But you quit."

"After six years, yes."

He waited.

"I'm not sure I *can* explain." Where's a movie-of-the-week plot when you need one?

A mockingbird lit on the sill and peered in at us, chiding.

"That the one Don Lee took to feeding?" Bates asked.

Daughter June nodded.

"And you wouldn't have anything to do with that."

In what was apparently a longtime private joke, she batted eyelashes at him.

"Time when that girl was eleven, twelve, every week she'd show up after school with some kind of orphan or another. A kitten, puppy, a hatchling she claimed fell out of a tree, not much to it but a skull, feet and hungry mouth. Once, a baby rabbit—they say once those have the stench of human on them, parents seek them out and kill them.

"You'd best go ahead and feed the thing," he said after a moment, "else we'll never hear the end of it." Then to me: "You've done some hard wading against the current."

"Off and on."

"More on than off, from the sound of things. Work like what you ended up doing, that has to be like police work, demands a lot of you. And the better you are at it, the more it takes."

"True enough. Just being on the job, on the streets, not anything in particular that happened, made a difference. Changed me, damaged me: the point could be argued. All those years tramping around in other people's heads was a kind of repeat."

"Not to mention prison."

We watched June, outside, scatter birdseed on the sill and back away from it as the mockingbird returned. Glancing up at us, she waved.

"One day ostensibly like all others, sitting there with my morning coffee and appointment book, I looked out the window and realized the floors were gone. They'd just dropped out from under me, they were gone. I knew I no longer trusted anyone or anything. That I could see around, through and behind every motive—my own no less than everyone else's."

"So you decided to be alone."

"I'm not sure it was a conscious decision. How much of what's most important in our lives ever is?"

June came in and pulled her purse from an open desk drawer, saying she had to pick up Mandy at school, she'd drop her off and be right back.

"That time already, is it?" Bates said. And I, once she was gone, that I hadn't known June had a child.

"No reason you would. But she doesn't—not yet, anyway. Friend of hers, Julie, works as a nurse, twelve-hour shifts twice a week. June helps out. The two of them went right through school together, kindergarten on up, you couldn't pry 'em apart with a crowbar."

"June and Julie."

"Cute, huh?"

"Other kids must have had fun with that."

"Only the first time or two. You haven't seen it yet, but that girl has a temper'd make a grizzly back off, go home and call out for food."

"Someone else takes care of the child once she drops it off?"

"Julie's brother. Clif's not old enough to have his license yet, but he goes over after school and stays with Mandy till Julie gets home. Has dinner waiting most nights, too, I hear."

The phone rang.

"Sheriff B—"

He looked at me, shook his head.

"Yes ma'am, I—"

His end of the conversation was like a motor turning over again and again, never catching.

"Yes ma'am. If—"

"Yes ma'am. Can I—"

"What—"

He tugged a notepad towards him and scribbled something on the top page.

"We'll get right on that, ma'am," he said, then, hanging up, "Surprise you?"

It took a beat or two for me to realize the last comment was addressed to me, that he was referring to what he'd told me about June and the friend's baby.

"A little, Sheriff."

What I'd truly been thinking was whether I was still in the United States. This couldn't be the same country I saw reflected in news, TV shows, current novels. Mind you, I didn't watch TV or read newspapers and hadn't read a novel since prison days, but it all filtered in. Thoreau, Zarathustra, Philip Wylie's superman alone and impotent on his mountaintop—in today's world they'd all be aware what shows were competing for the fall lineup, the new hot fashion designer, the latest manufactured teen star.

But people watching over friends' children as though their own? A teenage brother taking responsibility for his sibling's child?

Bates tore off the note he'd just made and tipped it into the wastebasket.

"Time you dropped that 'Sheriff' business, don't you think? Friends call me Lonnie."

Five or six responses came to mind.

"Friend's a tough concept for me," I finally said.

"It'll come back to you." He smiled. "You like chicken?"

* * *

THREE HOURS LATER I found myself seated at an ancient, much-abused walnut dining table. My new best friend Sheriff Bates aka Lonnie sat at the head of the table to my right, wife Shirley directly across, June at the other end, a couple of teenage sons, Simon with a brush cut and baggies, Billy with multiple piercings dressed all in black, in the remaining chairs. Plate heaped with mashed potatoes, fried chicken. Bowls of stewed okra and tomatoes, milk gravy and corn on the cob placed around a centerpiece of waxed fruit in a bowl. Shallow bowl of chow-chow, small white bowls with magnolia blossoms afloat in water scattered about. Anachronistic platter of commercial brown-and-serve rolls. The TV sat like a beacon, sound dialed down, angled in, just past the connecting doorway to the living room. The boys' eyes never left it as Fran Drescher's nanny gave way to *Fresh Prince*.

"We're pleased you could join us," Shirley Bates said.

"Thank you for having me. The food's wonderful."

"Nothing fancy, I'm afraid."

"I don't know, the magnolias add a certain festive touch."

"You like them?" Pleasure lit her face. "Lonnie thinks they're silly. It's something my mother used to do."

Mine too—I'd just remembered that.

Afterwards, the sheriff and I helped stack dishes and take them out to the kitchen through a door propped open with a rubber wedge of a kind I hadn't seen in years. Declining offers of further assistance, Shirley said "You go play good host, honey. God knows you can use the practice. I'll finish up here."

Bates poured coffee from a Corningware percolator into mugs with pictures of sheep and deer. A sliding door opened directly from the kitchen onto a patio. Four or five white plastic chairs sat about, the grid inside a grill was caked with char above white ghosts of charcoal, jonquils sprang brightly from a small plot by the house. A rake leaned against the wall nearby, tines clotted with dark, brittle leaves. We sat chatting about nothing of substance, sequence or consequence. When a knock came at the wooden gate to the driveway, Bates called out: "Come on in."

He wore a dark blue suit whose double-breasted coat

drained half an apparent foot or so off the actual height I encountered when I stood to shake hands. Around lower legs and cuffs were swaths of whitish-looking hair from a house pet, dog or cat. Leather loafers long neglected, a silk tie carefully knotted early that morning then forgotten.

"You must be Turner."

"Mayor Sims," Bates said as we shook hands.

"Henry Lee. Please. Thanks for having me by, Lonnie."

"Been way too long. And you'd best go in and pay respects to Shirley before you leave—if you know what's good for me."

"I will, I will."

"So why don't I go get drinks. Black Jack as usual, Henry Lee?"

"You have to ask?"

"Beer, if it's not too much trouble," I said.

"You've got it."

It took Bates a long while to get those drinks. A couple of times I saw him edging up to the kitchen window, looking out. I had little doubt he meant for me to see that.

"So," Mayor Sims said, sinking into a chair. "You going to be able to pull that layabout's butt out of the fire on this?"

"We'll see."

All about us, over by the house, near the gate, above a solitary fig tree, the cold chemical light of fireflies came and went.

"How's your mail delivery these days?" I asked.

"I have noticed a difference."

"Glad to hear it." I listened to mosquitoes spiraling in close by my ears. Whatever the reason, I'd never been much to their taste. They come in, do the research, apply elsewhere.

"I've been wondering how you were able to go three months without ever noticing no bills had been paid."

"Point taken." We watched a bat flap across moonlit sky. Scooping up gnats, mosquitoes and moths as it went, no doubt. *Joyful* is a human word, but it was hard to watch the bat's flight without its coming to mind. "My wife always took care of household bills, balanced the checkbook, all that. Anything needing my attention, something out of the ordinary, she'd let me know. Dorothy's in a nursing home. I put her there two weeks ago. Alzheimer's."

"I'm sorry."

"Took me a long time to admit to myself something was seriously wrong. A lot longer to admit it to others. Damn, I was getting forgetful myself, you know? Dorothy always hid it well. And when something did get past us and hit the wall, there I'd be, ready with an excuse for her. Besides, the way I was brought up—you too, would be my guess— whatever happens in the family, you handle it. You take care of your own."

Lonnie emerged with our drinks and the two of them made small talk for a few minutes, hunting seasons, local football, that sort of thing, before the mayor excused him-self, stood, downed the remainder of his drink in a single swallow, and went inside. Moments later the mayor came out, said good-bye to the two of us, strode through the gate and was gone.

* * *

"WHAT D'YOU THINK?" Lonnie said.

"Other than that you set me up?"

Full night now. Fewer mosquitoes, and the cicadae had quietened. Deepening silence everywhere. Stars brightened, intense white as though tiny holes had been punched in a black veil, letting through the merest suggestion of some blinding light that lurked just past, waiting.

"Get you another?"

I held up my half-full bottle.

"I live here," Lonnie said. "Sometimes—"

"I understand."

"Man's full of himself. And I don't approve of a lot of what he does. Few years back, the city council passed an ordinance that rental houses had to have internal plumbing, bathrooms. How they pushed that past him I don't know, since he owns almost every unit of cheap housing in the county—all those plywood, used-lumber and tarpaper shacks south of downtown?"

I'd seen them. Hell, I'd grown up with their like.

"Toilets went in wherever it was easiest. In kitchens, bedrooms, on the porch. Crew had it all done within the week. I'm going to freshen this up. Sure you don't want another?"

He was back in moments but instead of resuming his seat stood looking off at the dark silhouettes of trees.

"He doesn't need me or anyone else to approve of what he does. I don't need that, either. Don't have to approve of him, I mean."

"I understand, Lonnie. I really do."

"He told you about Miss Dorothy?"

I nodded.

"Been coming a long time. We all saw it, long before he did. Some ways, I think it's changed him as much as it has her. Never had children, there's just the two of them. Man has to be lonely."

He sat again.

"Beautiful night."

I agreed, and we sat quietly side by side, listening to gushes of water from the kitchen as Shirley rinsed dishes. Somewhere close by, a bullfrog called.

"You miss the city? I know I asked you that before."

"The city, yes. But I don't miss the person I became in the city."

"He really that much different?"

I nodded.

"Not a good man? Sort of person you saw him coming, you'd cross the street?"

"Right."

"So here you are, this beautiful evening, miles away from any city at all, with a handful of new friends. Still trying to get across the street to avoid that man."

Chapter Twenty

THE MOON HUNG ORANGE as Halloween candy in the sky, a perfect circle that made the city's spinal ridge—single-level convenience stores, three- or four-story apartment and office buildings and high-rises all in a jumble—look even more eccentric, more unnatural. No right angles in nature. I remembered that from some all-but-forgotten art class.

On the seat beside me, Randy tipped back his head to squirt saline up his nose. Bottle the size Merthiolate used to come in when I was a kid and everyone called it monkey blood. Stuff was like dye. Get it on you, it was there till the skin sluffed away. Not a lot of plastic around then, though. Monkey blood came in glass bottles. You painted it on with a glass stinger attached to the cap. Plastic dinnerware started showing up when I was in grade school.

"You okay?" I said.

"I'm fine. Look: you have problems with the squad you pull, you take it back in, right? It doesn't corner, scrapes its way over potholes or bottoms out, maybe the mirrors are gone permanently cockeyed, you take it back in." He tucked the saline bottle away, staring straight ahead. "No different with a partner."

Despite rank, we'd been put on the streets in an unmarked car responding to general calls. Other detectives were first call; we were backup. Brass didn't trust Randy.

We turned onto Maple. Outside a Piggly Wiggly there, a girl of sixteen or so sat slumped against a *Press-Scimitar* coin box, knees up, head down. She'd tucked the garbage bag that was her luggage and held everything she owned under her legs. As I got out of the squad, six yards off, the smell of her hit me. I walked towards the notch of wasted pale thighs.

"You okay, miss?"

Her eyes swam up, found me. "What?"

"Are you okay?"

"I don't know. I *look* okay?"

I helped her to her feet. Reflexively one hand shot out to grab hold of the bag, which came up with her. She tottered, then straightened, found the fulcrum. Near as tall as myself.

"Not many gentlemen left."

"You have some place to go, miss?"

She thought a moment, shook her head.

"Then—"

"A sister," she told me. "West Memphis. Just across the bridge."

"Best get moving that way. Stick around here, sooner or later you're gonna get hauled in, or worse."

She levered the bag over one shoulder. "Thank you, Officer."

"No need to thank me. Just take care of yourself, miss."

"You too."

"Five blocks from here she'll forget where she was heading," Randy said when I got back in the squad. "You know that."

"So—what? We take her in, she's back on the street tomorrow, nothing gained but a meal or two, some abuse if she's lucky, rape and a beating or two if she's not. We drop her off in ER, she gets a psych consult, who knows where that's going. Hard to imagine it'd be anyplace good."

We slowed to cruise a line of shopfronts, independent insurance companies, a travel agent, a used-clothing store, that sort of thing, then pulled around to the alley, an occasional favorite of local teenagers on the prowl, and ran that.

"It's the medication," Randy said as we pulled back into traffic. Cross streets ticked by. Walnut Street, left onto Vance across Orleans. "Dries you out something fierce."

Able north past Beale and Union.

All told, an uneventful shift. We pulled in at the station house with half an hour to spare, only routine paperwork outstanding, no mandatories to clear. Randy and I sat in the break room. He was filling out the shift report, I was drinking coffee. Sixth cup of the day? He pushed the form across the table for me to countersign. The rest of the shift's warriors had begun streaming in by then, clapping backs and telling new war stories, stowing uniforms in lockers (some of them, the uniforms, a little smelly, sure, but dry cleaning's expensive), splashing water on armpits, chest, neck and face at the bank of four narrow sinks in the communal washroom, smearing deodorant underarm, spritzing on cologne or nipping from flasks before heading out to rejoin the world as citizens.

As though they could.

I'd changed into jeans and a sweatshirt, my gray windbreaker. Pockets were long gone, the zipper was trying hard to follow, collar frayed half through. I went down the two steps the station house thought it needed to set itself apart from its surround, around the corner to the parking lot. I was just climbing into my truck, which looked a lot like the windbreaker, when Randy's head bobbed up alongside.

"Anywhere you need to be?"

"Not really."

"So maybe we could get a beer or two."

So we did, four in fact, in the lounge of a Holiday Inn nearby. Waitresses kept straying through from the restaurant to see if we wanted to order food. Out in the lobby a guy played piano, great rolling flourishes shaped with both hands like snowballs around rocks of five-, six-note melodies: tonic, dominant, subdominant, home. Barest kiss of the relative minor. In one back booth a man sat speaking intently with a woman half his age. His eyes never left hers. Hers never met his.

"Look, you know how the projectionist doesn't get the film focused just right, it's a blur?" Randy told me over the second beer. "You keep looking away and looking back, thinking it's gonna come clear. Like there's two pictures, two worlds, half an eyeblink apart. Then you take the meds and it all comes together, the blur goes away."

Maybe (I remember thinking even then) the blur is what it's all about.

We sat there quietly, glancing vaguely at clips from football games and wrestling on the TV above the bar as the doors from the lobby opened to admit a wheelchair. It came in backwards. Having no foot panels, it was propelled and directed by the occupant's swollen, bandaged feet. Watching in the rearview mirror mounted on one armrest, that occupant made his way into the lounge. Around his neck was what looked to be a twisted coat hanger. It held a kind of panpipe into which the occupant blew as he advanced, to warn of his passage. Possibly his arms, his upper body, were paralyzed?

But no, as he reached the bar and turned his chair about, the bartender handed across a glass of draft beer.

"How's it going, Sammy?"

The man took a long pull off the beer before answering. "Not bad. Could be worse. Has been, lots."

"Check came in on time, I see."

"Day late."

"Not a dollar short too, I hope."

Sammy's features drew together in what was obviously a laugh. His shoulders heaved. There was little sound to the laugh, and tears came out his eyes. After a moment he leaned forward to put the empty glass on the bar. The bartender had a replacement waiting. Sammy drank it almost at a gulp and put it on the bar beside the first. Shifting weight onto his right haunch, he tugged free a wallet.

The bartender waved away his effort. "This one's on me."

"You sure?"

"Sure I'm sure."

"Thanks, bud. 'Preciate it."

"Take care, friend."

Sailor Sammy tacked the wheelchair around and, puffing on his panpipe, started backwards towards the door.

"Wet his whistle," Randy said to the bartender as he came back from opening the door.

"He did that all right. Get you another?"

"Why the hell not."

I nodded.

He brought them.

"Boy comes in every week, sometimes Monday, sometimes Tuesday. Has two beers like you just seen. Flat downs them, then he's gone. Don't have any idea what this check is he's always talking about—welfare, some kinda government thing—but he flat won't come in till it gets there. Not that I've ever taken his money."

"You know him?" Randy asked.

"Not really. Lives in a garage out behind someone's house, I think. Maybe up Fannin Street way, just off Pioneer? Somewhere in there."

"What happened to him?" Randy asked.

The bartender shrugged, shoulders rising momentarily from a tier of low-end vodkas and gins to one of call Scotches and subsiding.

"You've done a mitzvah," I said.

The bartender looked at me as Randy grinned. 'Round those parts, those days, Judaism was as exotic as artichokes. I may as well have brought up Masonic rites, alchemy, the pleasures of goat cheese.

Doors from the lobby again swung open, this time to admit a party of office workers, six of them, in ill-fitting dresses and suitcoats with something of the oxbow about them, stiff plastic ties, costume jewelry, run-over shoes thick with bottled polish. From the back table where they settled, quickly their presence spilled out into the room, taking it over. As though in stop-time, suddenly the table was awash with empty bottles and glasses, cigarette packets, purses, ashtrays.

On TV, wrestlers Sputnik Malone and Billy Daniels took elaborate turns throwing one another about the ring. Memphis wrestling had been big for years and still drew huge crowds. It was televised locally; during the week, stars like Malone and Daniels toured the mid-South, wrestling in high-school gymnasiums, American Legion posts and Catholic clubs.

Sitting there, I noticed that while good paneling sheathed the walls and carpets shrouded floors, such refinements ended at the bar itself, undeveloped country with bare floors behind, sketchy shelves, squares of wood nailed to cabinets and drawers for pull handles. Bare wires hung from holes in the ceiling.

A basket of cheese cubes, cut-up pickles and bologna, all of them speared with toothpicks, appeared before us. I glanced over at the office workers' table. Three baskets there. Another half-dozen set out. Remains of the limb of a sizeable tree here in the room with us. Slivered. Julienned.

"Gentlemen?" the bartender asked.

Randy doubled him: "One for the road?"

I glanced at my watch—just as though I had somewhere to go.

"Sure."

For a time then, silently, we worked at the new drinks. Wrestling gave way to a local talent show, all but one of the contestants female and a fair divide among singers, baton twirlers and those offering dramatic recitations. The male tap-danced.

"You don't trust me," Randy said.

Falling back on the facile and hating myself for it: "I'm not sure you trust yourself."

"Two different things, though, aren't they?" His eyes found my face in the mirror behind the bar. "I love you, man. You know that."

I nodded.

I took that thought home with me and, half an hour later, soaking in a tub of hot water, nodded again. Country music drifted in softly from the bedroom, voices from next door came to visit through thin walls, and from the street through open windows, traffic swooshed and hooted beyond. In silent toast I held up my glass and watched the bathroom's light turn gold. I drank then, eyes shut, eyes behind which, perhaps in their own quiet way growing impatient, dreams waited.

Grace be with us all, who are so alone and lost.

Chapter Twenty-One

GRACE IS TOUGH GAME to bring down. Sputnik Malone or Plato, either would be hard put to pin it. Most of us are lucky if we so much as catch a glimpse of the thing our whole lives—its back, maybe, as it hurries away through the crowd. I remembered the prodigy Raymond Radiguet. *In three days' time I will be shot to death by the soldiers of God.*

Val had brought Carl Hazelwood's notebook back to us two days before. Nothing much of forensic interest, she said. Techs had what they needed, manufacturer, item, batch numbers, all that, they'd be following up. Our own files contained photocopies of notebook pages, and I'd been through them a dozen times at least. We all had. But something about having in my hands the actual, much-abused, saddle-worn artifact drew me to it, and I sank in again. Not that anything had changed. Not that I had new information, new understanding or insight. Or the paltriest clue as to what might be going on.

It was one of those huge five-subject notebooks, sections

divided by heavy inserts, doubled coils of wire at the spine. Two lines of obsessively neat script ran right up to page edge on either side between scored blue lines. A thousand words per page, at least. Most early entries had faded away, now only blurred cuneiform, ranks of diminutive Rorschachs, make of it what you will or can. Elsewhere ink had given up the ghost entirely, dissolving into pools of wash, like watercolor.

Dad told me the stew was good. I had it waiting when he got home. We talked a little bit afterward, then It Came from Outer Space was on TV. When dad came in I was wiping up spills off the floor with one of his shirts. It was dirty already so I don't understand why he got so mad. Maybe I ought to put more celery in next time. He looks like my uncle, sure he does, but he's not. That's from the movie.

I was sitting outside this morning and a cat came up to me, orange all over, even its eyes. It came up and rubbed against the step where I was, kind of half falling down, but every time I tried to touch it it ran off. Then a minute or two later it'd come back. I pinched off a piece of bologna and held it out. Mr. Cat liked that. He'd dodge in and grab hold, then go off under some bushes to eat. Mr. Cat ate most of a sandwich that way. Finished off the bread myself.

Found a cache of magazines in the basement in a box under some empty suitcases. Since the top of the box was filled with old newspapers I almost didn't look any further, but there they were underneath. A stack of Popular Mechanics, two years of Scientific Americans, a bunch of Astoundings and Fantastics crumbling at the bottom. Guess bugs must like those. One of the Popular Mechanics had a piece on building your own electric car, diagrams, specs, the whole works, even where you could order parts. Read most of a story by Fredric Brown, but the last two pages were missing.

———

Wrote a long letter to Sydney. I really miss her. I'd copy it down here, but my hand hurts. Anyway, it's already in the mail and gone. I looked up Minnesota in the encyclopedia. They put electric blankets inside their car hoods. There are lakes everywhere. Cissie says she checked and where Sydney went is a good place. They'll take good care of her there, Cissie says. Someone will read your letter to her. I hope she remembers me. It's been a long time. You do understand, don't you, Cissie said. She just got so she needed more taking care of than her mom and dad and her family could handle. Sure I did. I watched it happen. I even remember wondering if that could happen to me, if maybe someday I'd get like that, get lost the way Sydney did and have to go away.

———

Oatmeal for breakfast. Bacon, lettuce and tomato with lots of mayonnaise for lunch. The rest of the meat loaf, turnip greens, roasted sweet potatoes and ice tea for dinner. A good day. I even got a letter! From a pen pal in Finland. I found his name and address in the back of an old magazine. He was fourteen when he placed the ad, he wrote, and he's amazed that my letter found him. It had been forwarded through three addresses. Now he's a history professor at a university, has a wife and two daughters. Finland sounds a lot like Minnesota.

―――――――

The social worker we'd been waiting for came this morning, just like in A Thousand Clowns. There was white stuff all over the front of her blue sweater and long hairs on the back, her own and a cat's I think, and she smelled like sour milk. Afterwards she and Dad talked out in the kitchen. I got the door for her and watched as she hobbled off down the hall, thinking how much she looked like Piper Laurie in The Hustler, right up to the limp. The limp's a kind of badge, I guess. Maybe they even teach it in social worker school. I'M ONE OF YOU.

―――――――

Jack Finney's book was a disappointment after Invasion of the Body Snatchers. On the other hand, Evan Hunter's novel of Blackboard Jungle was much better—no contest, really. Right next to it on the shelf was Streets of Gold, so I picked that one up too, and it's my new favorite. I've read it half a dozen times by now. The writer publishes as Hunter and as Ed McBain, neither of which is his real name, which is Salvatore Lombino. He also wrote the screenplay for The Birds. I couldn't make much more sense out of O'Hara's novel of Butterfield 8 than I did the movie.

Whole pages were filled with pasted-in receipts for magazines and paperbacks, lunches at McDonald's, Good Eats cafeteria and Poncho's, city bus transfers, cash tickets listing writing tablets, athletic socks, hard candy and break-fast cereals, verses and scrawled signatures scissored from greeting cards, ragged entries torn from *TV Guide*s.

"Come across something there?" Don Lee asked, dredging me back, salvaged. I'd been quite literally out of this world, feet planted squarely in Carl Hazelwood's, a world that made a lot more sense than our own. I was a visitor there, of course, a tourist, nothing more. Rare enough for any of us to be able to manage even that. But I'd become an old hand at looking through others' windows from inside. In a way that's how I survived prison. More to the point, it's what made me effective as a therapist. And why I'd stopped.

I got up, dumped last night's leftovers from the coffeemaker, scrubbed cone and carafe, found a filter, put on a fresh pot.

"Ever consider coming on full-time, you've got my vote," Don Lee said.

"I do a mean grilled cheese, too."

He sighed dramatically.

Adrienne picked up on the fourth ring, breathing hard.

"Turner," I said. "Not calling too early, I hope."

"Not at all. We're used to short nights. Dad always tries to hold still as long as he can so as not to disturb us, but he doesn't sleep much. Two or three hours at the most. Good days, he's able to fall back asleep around dawn."

The coffeemaker burbled. A raked pickup with glass packs and booming bass blew past outside. When the phone rang, Don Lee punched in the other line and picked up, from old habit pulling a pad of paper close. June would be in soon. For a half-hour or so the street would be busy. If

I stepped outside now, I'd emerge into congeries of smells: toast and bacon and coffee from the diner, car exhaust and unburned gasoline, cheap unbottled perfume of magnolia, newly watered front yards.

"Sarah's out running," Adrienne said. "I'd had enough, but she thought she'd go on a bit, should be back soon. Shall I have her call you?"

As one ages, signs that the world has changed at first appearance are subtle. One day you realize you've lost touch with music, don't have a clue what this new stuff's all about. Then the cops start looking like teenagers. You sleep again and wake to a world you scarcely recognize. Running, for instance. Suddenly everyone's doing it. Everyone's working out at Bally's or L.A. Fitness, clinging to the sides of cliffs in day-long climbs, stoking yogurt, power shakes and smoothies like firemen in ancient railroad engines. What the hell's happened?

"You may be able to help," I told Adrienne.

"All right."

Across the room Don Lee said, "We'll look into it, Bonnie. . . . Right. . . . I've got it all written down here. . . . Right. . . ."

"You all getting along okay out there?" I asked.

"We're adaptable, Mr. Turner, always have been. Making do is where we live." Upturning a bottle of water, she drank. I heard each segment of the process, from unscrewed cap through glugs to the bottle coming back upright. "What was it you wanted?"

Don Lee said: "Any questions, anything comes up, I'll give you a call."

"Who's BR?"

"Beg your pardon?"

"BR. It keeps coming up in Carl's notebook, more and more as time goes on."

"A friend, maybe?"

"His barber, for all I know. A pen pal, maybe?"

"I don't think I—hold on."

Voices off, as the phone changed hands.

"You come up against any more trouble like that, you give us a call right away," Don Lee said, disentangling with a sigh and setting the phone down.

"Mr. Turner?"

"Have a good run?"

"Remember what Woody Allen said about sex? The worst he ever had was wonderful?"

"Chasing endorphins."

"I'm sorry?"

"Supposedly they come to you when you push yourself to the limit. I ran for years, smacked up against my limit more than a few times. But I never so much as caught sight of the back end of one single endorphin."

Don Lee poured coffee for us both, set mine before me. I nodded thanks. He sat back down. Attending to his cross-word-puzzle book from the look of it.

"Did you have something for me, Mr. Turner?"

"Only a question, I'm afraid. . . . Carl seems to have felt the same way about movies that you feel about running. Or Woody Allen about sex."

She laughed. "He did! And he loved the bad ones best of all. Like those old science fiction and horror movies he grew up on, godawful stuff. Herschell Gordon Lewis, Jack Arnold, Larry Cohen. *Basket Case, Spider Baby, The Incredibly Strange Creatures.* A lot of them had something about them, though, awful as they were. Some basic integrity, a personal vision."

"He talked about them a lot?"

"All the time. At least one of his therapists became exasperated. Said the kind of movies Carl was drawn to merely objectified his paranoia."

"So would the *Congressional Record.*"

Laughter again. "Creatures from lagoons, lost worlds and outer space are a lot more fun."

"Not to mention every bit as believable."

The door opened to let June slip through smiling. I noticed she kept her face turned away, and when she took her place at the front desk I understood why. That left eye was a prize of a shiner.

"Did Carl have particular favorites? Movies, actors, directors?"

"You know he was kind of a savant, right? Wherever his attention fell, it set down hard. He was like a sponge that would only soak up certain liquids. I remember one day we were talking in the kitchen and this song came on the radio, 'You Better Move On.' A week later he was telling me all about this obscure singer Arthur Alexander, his handful of hits, his comeback attempt with an album of autobiographical songs. God knows how or where he found out about all this stuff."

"Same with movies, I take it."

"Exactly. He could go on for hours about what studio

put them out, where they were shot, who wrote the stories and scripts, how they set up this or that scene. He'd quote whole chunks of what Robert Mitchum or Brian Keith had said in *Thunder Road* or whatever. 'Bullet through the chest, ma'am, just routine'—that was one of his favorites. He absolutely worshiped Richard Carlson."

She paused, said, presumably to Adrienne, "*Please*," then to me: "Here's a man who wouldn't use newfangled things like coffeepots, walked on the other side of the room to avoid microwaves, slept on the floor often as not, wore clothes till they dissolved around him, ran in terror from ringing telephones. But movies, he couldn't give up. When he left this last time, looking for any clue what might have happened, where he'd gone, we came across stacks of books out in the garage, had to be close to a hundred of them, behind cans of Valvoline and hand cleaner that looked like gray putty. Books with titles like *Forgotten Horrors, Truly Strange Movies, Grindhouse Fare*. They'd been taken from libraries all over the Midwest. Cedar Rapids and Iowa City, Dubuque, Chicago, Minneapolis, Cincinnati."

"Checked out?"

"Liberated. He didn't have cards, couldn't have got them."

"So he hadn't just wandered off, all those times. Some of them, anyway. He'd gone out there purposefully, into the wide world, to find and bring back those books."

"His treasure. Excuse me a moment, Mr. Turner."

The receiver clunked hollowly onto what I assumed to be a pressboard desktop. Briefly I heard footsteps receding; for a while, nothing at all; then she was back.

"I apologize. Dad's doing poorly this morning, I'm afraid. Can you tell me: should it become necessary, to what hospital should we take him?"

Expressing my concern, I told her there was a county hospital a bit less than an hour away on the interstate. But for anything serious she'd probably want to head to Memphis or Little Rock.

"Just in case," Miss Hazelwood said. "We're not there yet. . . . What?" Words off. "Nor do we expect to be, Adrienne says I should tell you."

"That's good."

Don Lee held up his cup. More? I shook my head. Momentarily June's eyes met mine. She looked down.

"But who or what," I asked Sarah Hazelwood, "is BR?"

"Not a clue, I'm afraid."

"Okay. Thank you for your time. And listen, if your father—"

"Should we need anything, I promise I'll call."

Downing one last swallow of coffee, Don Lee stood, stretched, and headed out for afternoon patrol. June and I sat looking at one another. We heard the unit's door slam, heard the motor start and catch. Then the low whine of gears as Don Lee backed away. The radio crackled.

"You want to tell me about it?" I asked her.

"Not really," she said.

Chapter Twenty-Two

SO GODDAMN ALONE and lost. Not my words but those of my final cellmate, Adrian.

Years later, Lonnie Bates would accuse me of expending too much energy distancing myself from the man I'd been. Maybe he was right, maybe I'd always be trying to get away from that man. Just like a part of me would always be in that prison cell, or another part sitting with a man's head in my lap, leaning over him as bright blood ran down the street in the rain. Just as a part of me would forever be standing there over the partner I'd just shot.

Amazing how static memory is, most of our lives gathered around a handful of tableaux.

Adrian once told me about African musicians he used to play with. When things became too predictable, too worked out, too repetitious, they'd exhort their fellows to "put some confusion in it."

I've never been able to describe what it was like to kill a

man. Remembering the act itself is easy. There he is three showerheads down, makeshift knife held along his leg, now he's walking up to me, now he's stepping back, trying to talk with tongue pinned to the roof of his mouth, but what come out are animal sounds. All this is vivid. Vivid for him too, I'm sure, momentarily, these last few moments of his life. There has to be something of weight and substance here, some revelation, you think, there just *has* to be. But there isn't. You watch the light drain away behind his eyes, you look around to see who's witnessed this, you get up and go on. You've learned nothing. Death makes no more sense than any of the rest of it. You're alive. He's not. *That's* what you know.

Cellmate Adrian was a fortyish man of ambiguous ethnicity, Caucasian, Negroid and Asian-Amerind features all boiled down together in the pot. He liked to refer to himself as octoroon. "Has to be lots more roons than that mixed up in me," he'd say, "but eight's high as they go, back home." Back home was New Orleans. Sexually, too, he was a puzzle: chocky, muscled frame and a hard, square stride, arms and hands moving fluidly when he spoke, an up-from-under glance. This had ceased being a topic of conversation his fifth week in. One of those who'd seen fit to remark it had a skull permanently deformed, soft as a melon rind, from the time Adrian came upon him with six batteries (taken from appliances and tools in the workshop) knotted into a pillowcase.

"Hear tell you're a cop," he said to me our first night together. I'd had a couple cellmates before him. Neither had lasted long.

"Not anymore. Not a lot of cops in here, I'd guess."

He laughed. "Not enough room for those that should be."

A guard walked the rows, dragging his baton lightly across bars to forewarn us of his coming.

"Man you killed, he was a friend?" Adrian said once the guard passed.

"Yes."

"Don't seem surprised I know that."

"I grew up in a small town."

"Small town. Yeah, that's what this is, all right."

Two or three cells down, a man sobbed.

"Poor son of a bitch," Adrian said. "Every goddamn night. Could be *you*'ll do all right in here, though. What's your name, boy?"

He had to know already, but I told him. Populated entirely by those unable to adapt to society's laws or societal norms, prisons have unspoken codes of etiquette such as to put tradition-bound southerners, Brits or Japanese to shame.

"Adrian," he said, "but most ever'one calls me Backbone. Tend to pick our name hereabouts, or if we don't, get 'em picked for us. In here, we're not what the world made us anymore. Long as you can back it up, you're what you say you are. Best get to sleep now. Sleep's just 'bout th'only friend you got here." Turning on his side, he breathed deeply. "'Cept me." And that quickly he was snoring.

There in the box that's become your home and second body, every small sound takes on unreasonable weight.

Rake of the guard's baton along bars, ragged breath of the man on the bunk below, conversations stealing in from adjacent cells or those across the block, coughs ricocheting from wall to wall.

With a sound like a novice's first attempt at notes on a French horn, someone farts, and someone else laughs. Voices zigzag along the block in response.

"Okay, who smuggled perfume aboard?"

"Hey, he just sendin' flowers to his honey is all."

"Big boo-kay a stinkweed, more like it."

"Some brothers *like* that brown perfume."

"Donchu be talking 'bout no brothers over there, boy."

"Yassuh!"

"I meant like big brothers."

"Sure you did."

"Why'n't you all just shut th'fuck up and go to sleep."

Which is what that same voice said every night, and what finally happened.

Three walls of the cell, then another wall. Imagine your way past one wall, there's another, then another. We live in them, in the hollows and crawl spaces, like rats. The walls are what's important. We're what's not, though the walls are here because of us.

"Might dole up s'more roughage for my man here," Adrian said the next day in lunch line, "boy's new to the game." Another gloppy spoonful of cabbage hit my tray. "Good man," he told the inmate serving. "You'll be remembered."

"Move along," the server said. "Fuck off and die too, while you're at it." Hair buzzed to an eighth-inch, sleeves rolled above cable-like biceps, some kind of home-cooked tattoo there, a scorpion, maybe.

That's when I saw it for the first time. Adrian went dead still, face blank as the walls about us.

"You got somethin' to say to me back there, tattoo man?"

Briefly the server's eyes met Adrian's. Then he cast them about like a fisherman's net. Being in control of mashed potatoes and lima beans wasn't going to help him much. Nothing was. Not even his tattoo.

"Sorry," the server said. "Been a bad day. You know."

"Ain't they all?"

We moved along the line.

"Motherfuckers call themselves a brotherhood."

"White supremacists, you mean."

He nodded. "They be getting in touch witchu soon enough, I reckon."

"Damn," I said, trying my best to sound like Adrian. "All *kind* of scum in here, ain'there?"

He laughed. "There is, for sure."

It was a couple of weeks later that they came for me, two of them edging out around the massive dryers on a day I'd been assigned laundry duty.

"You and big nigger been gettin' on all right?" one asked. He had to shout to be heard above the dryers. From talk on the yard I knew him as Billy D. Barely topping five feet, he looked like steel wire braided into human form. Sleeves split to give biceps room.

Anything you say in these situations usually serves only to make it worse, so I didn't answer, just stood waiting. See how it comes down. Four or five more of what I assumed to be sworn members of the brotherhood shuffled into place. Two behind Billy D, two or three behind me.

"You're a white man, Turner. One of us."

I watched him, waiting for the body shift, the change in posture or expression that would signal we were taking it up a notch.

"Maybe you like that big dick of his so much, you just plain forgot that."

Then: "Not much for talking, are you?"

Inmates were expected to cringe in fear at Billy D's approach. That I hadn't, that in fact I'd shown nothing at all, unsettled his lackeys. Seeing that, he knew he had to lean in hard.

"You join us, Turner," he said. "Here. Today."

"No thanks."

Above and all about us, dryers rumbled. They were the size of the tumblers on cement trucks.

"What, you think you have some kinda choice?"

"Like you say, he's not much for talking."

All heads turned as the speaker stepped into the space between Billy D and myself. I knew him from talk on the yard. Angel. Looking around, I saw that each of Billy's lackeys by the wall had been flanked as well, two by blacks, one by an elegant Thai called Soon, three others by the 300-pound Samoan whose name seemed to be composed entirely of L's and gulps.

"We all got choices, white bread," Angel said. "How yours lookin' to you right now?"

Currents of fire and ice slammed back and forth. Ice won. Nodding, Billy D backed off a few steps, turned and left. As he did so, his men faded away too, then Angel's. Within moments I stood there alone.

"It's not over," Adrian said later when I tried to thank him. "You know that. May take a while, but they'll be back."

The day the guy came at me in the shower with the knife, I knew he was right.

Chapter Twenty-Three

"I TOLD DADDY I got it playing softball."

"And he believed you."

"Probably not. He did ask when I'd started playing soft-ball. He . . . Well, you've gotten to know my father, you know it would take a lot for him to—what's the word I'm looking for?"

"Trespass?"

"I guess." For the first time, her face met mine straight on. "How bad does it look?"

"Purple's on your color chart, right?"

"I feel so . . ."

"Ashamed?"

"Stupid."

"You know you shouldn't."

"Of course I do."

A kid's face appeared in the window. Pushing against the glass, the boy pugged his nose, stuck out his tongue so that it too flattened, and crossed his eyes. Without benefit of the window, June returned a remarkable likeness of his caricature. He grinned and, mounting his skateboard like the Silver Surfer, sped away. I had the sense they'd done this before.

"Anyhow, he's gone," June said.

"This is someone you cared for?"

She nodded.

"I'm sorry."

"Me too."

I fought your impossible war, America. I came back from it and for eight years as a cop, day in and day out, I witnessed the worst you and your citizens could do to one another. Then for almost as long I lived in the heads of some of those we—you and I—had most damaged. When I say her smile would break your heart, I mean it.

"I miss him," June said.

The phone rang.

"Sheriff's. . . . Yes, ma'am. . . . That's out by the Zorik place, right? . . . Right. . . . We'll send a deputy right out."

Putting the phone down with a shrug of apology, she picked up the radio mike and keyed it on.

"Don Lee, you there?"

Ten-four.

"See the woman, third house off the gravel road half a mile past Fifty-one and Ledbetter."

Near the old Zorik farm. Pecan orchard?

"Right."

Complaint?

"Says her boy's back. Been snaring and killing her chickens for food but won't talk to her or let her get near him. ETA?"

I'm halfway there already, out by the town dump. Twenty minutes, tops.

"I'll call back, let her know."

"When I was a kid," I said once she'd done so, "my first real girlfriend, her family had a cousin living with them. From about twenty or so, life had turned into this steep downhill slide for him. Started out as assistant manager for one of the biggest clothing stores thereabouts and wound up doing janitor work at the elementary school—till he got fired from that. His own family threw him out once they found him in the baby's room standing over the crib. My girlfriend's mother took him in. Cissie and I'd be sitting watching TV, look up, and there he'd be, standing by the stove talking to it, or following the cat around the house from room to room for hours."

"Velma's boy hasn't been right since he turned twelve. Court keeps sending him away. Halfway houses, training schools, the state hospital. Sooner or later they let him go, or he runs off, and he shows up back here. Lives up in the hills mostly. Has to be all of thirty-five, forty now."

"None of us ever get too far from the cave."

"What happened?" June asked after a moment.

"Just what's supposed to happen. I went off to college, wrote long, passionate letters back almost daily. By the second semester I noticed I was getting fewer and fewer, ever briefer responses."

"I meant with the cousin."

"Oh. . . . Well, one night, Ben was his name, one night Ben managed to get the latch off the porch door and wandered away. Next morning my girlfriend's mother was backing out of the drive, looking around hoping to see Ben or some sign of him, and ran over her infant son, my girlfriend's little brother."

"He make it?"

"Depends on your definition. He lived."

"Are you always so upbeat, Mr. Turner?"

"You caught me on a good day."

"Lucky me." She leaned forward to turn the radio on. Something ostensibly country, but worlds away from Riley Puckett or Ralph Stanley. "Get many dates, do you?"

"Enough."

"Out on the limb here, I'm gonna guess they're mostly first dates."

We sat together quietly. The phone rang. June answered, listened a moment and hung up. *I've looked and looked in all the bars, all the old places*—from the radio, spearchucker guitar behind.

"Sarah's a fine-looking woman."

"She is."

"You see anything happening there?"

"Happening?"

"Between the two of you."

"A little late in the game for that. When you're young, every chance encounter holds a bounty of possibilities. Pay for a six-pack at the 7-Eleven and this spark jumps up between you and the woman behind the counter. You think that'll go on happening forever."

June nodded.

"It doesn't. Before you know it, that's become the fantasy it always was, really. Someone's pulled the drawstring on the big grab bag. Everything's turned to wallpaper."

"I'm no expert, but you look to have, oh, I don't know, at least a good year or two left in you."

Both of us laughed.

"You worked as a therapist, Daddy says. Helping people figure out things like that for themselves."

"There never was a lot to figure out. Ninety-nine times out of a hundred, people understand perfectly well what's going on. They know what's right, what they need, why they do things the way they do."

Hard as I looked, no one looked like you.

"The majority of my clients went dutifully about lives and jobs. Many were exceptional at what they did. But, to the man, inside they were twisted, contorted, in pain—a chorus line of Quasimodos. Whether the wounds were real or not finally didn't matter, only their belief in those wounds. I'd kick back and listen. Sometimes I'd tell them how when you hear a good jazz guitarist you think he knows something the rest of us don't, that he understands how things connect, but he doesn't, it's just that he's honed this one small, special skill he has. He's got a hundred ways to get from here to there, sure. But the single most important thing he knows is simply to keep fingers and mind moving."

All around us, the town's gone still. From time to time the phone rings or the radio crackles into life.

"Your father tell you anything else?"

June shook her head. "Not really. I know you were a detective, of course."

So, with no real reason to do so, just that it seemed right at the time, I told her everything. My undeclared war, Memphis streets, Randy, prison and Backbone—all of it. Amazing how little space a life takes up, finally. That it should fit in so small an envelope.

When I was done, she sat silently a moment before saying, "This calls for *good* coffee, for a change." Minutes later, a kid's delivered from the diner and we're sipping the result. "We have an arrangement," June told me when I tried to pay.

"Your father know about this?"

"Sheriff Lonnie? That's what people call him around here, you know. Buy him a tank for his birthday if they thought he wanted one. Sure he knows. Sheriff Lonnie knows everything. He just doesn't approve of much of it."

"You included?"

June peered over the rim of her mug. "I'm bad," it read. She shrugged. The phone rang and, as though continuing the shrug, a single, extended motion, she picked up.

"Hi, Daddy. . . . Quiet so far. Velma's boy's back again. . . . Usual, sounds like. Don Lee's on his way out there. . . . I'm fine. . . . No. . . . No."

"What the hell," I said, staring out the window.

A caravan of ancient trucks, cars and station wagons paraded down Main Street. As with covered wagons in westerns, belongings—furniture, housewares, pots and pans, boxes, what looked to be bedrolls—were lashed onto truck beds and the tops of vans and peeked from beneath car trunks lashed shut with rope.

"Gypsies just got here, Daddy. . . . You said they'd be early this year, guess you were right. . . . Old Meador place again? . . . They'll leave it clean, at least. . . ."

"They used to come with the carnival," June told me, hanging up. "They'd have rides that went up like Erector sets, games of skill, food stalls, maybe a freak tent, belly dancers, muscle men. Afternoons they'd descend on the town. Go into stores and while one of them paid for twine or a washboard at the front counter, others helped themselves to merchandise. They'd move door to door selling jewelry and hand-dyed cotton skirts and meat pies and when they were gone folks would find things missing, a gilded statue here, a humidor or crystal goblet there.

"Once the carnivals petered out, the gypsies kept coming, year after year, like robins and hummingbirds. But the carney mentality—the excuse of it?—passed with the carnivals. Now they kept to themselves, wouldn't think of going into homes. Two or three of them would show up in town, shop for staples at local stores, pay cash and hurry off."

"The code had changed."

"Right."

"If they're anything, gypsies are testaments to the adaptability of tradition, how you change to stay the same."

"You think about that a lot? The way things were, how you've changed to go along?"

She had something of her father's knack for staying quiet and waiting, like men on deer stands. Maybe she'd learned it from him. Or maybe she was just naturally a good listener. That very quality in her could attract men with baggage, the kind of men whose shrouded pain gradually congealed to abuse of one kind or another, emotional, physical. I'd seen it often enough before.

Though maybe I should stop reading so much into simple things.

I remembered all too well the smugness of therapists to whom I'd been subjected and others whom, later, I understudied. So many of them proceeded as though personalities were like Chinese menus, one from column A, one from column B, same few sauces for dish after dish, just different additives, give us ten minutes, no secret here. Early along I swore to myself—one of the few covenants I've kept—that I'd resist such an approach with every resource I possessed. Upon occasion this decision made me effective. Just as often, I fear, it rendered me worthless. But instinctively I swerved from that cocksure, mechanistic, reductive attitude whenever I saw it coming: knew it would diminish me as surely as it did my clients.

"I don't mean to pry, Mr. Turner," June said.

Don Lee's voice interposed itself, foot in the door, between radio crackles.

June, you there?

"Ten-four, Don Lee."

Heard from the sheriff?

"Just."

Need him out here, now.

"You still at Velma's?"

Affirmative.

"He'll be asking me why."

Tell him I found Velma's boy trussed up in the shed back of the house. The chickens have been at him. They've done a good job. Got most of the good parts.

Chapter Twenty-Four

"WORD IS, your ticket's getting punched," Backbone said.

I was up for a hearing the next morning.

"Maybe."

"No maybe to it. Done deal."

His hand came over the edge of the bed. I took and unfolded the sheet of paper it held.

"Two, three days' work there at the most, way I figure. You're not bound, you know. To any of it."

I looked. Messages I was asked to convey to wives, children, parents, companions, friends. A locker key to be picked up and passed along. Two or three other minor errands. Not at all unusual for departing inmates to carry wish lists like this out into the world with them. I told him it was all okay.

"No problem with that last one?"

A classic hat job. And for Billy D no less, the man who'd first marshaled his cronies against me in the laundry room. Now he was asking me to reach out to the partner who'd betrayed him, a partner who'd made it safely away from the job that put Billy inside and who'd stowed the take for later retrieval, Billy's share included, before turning stoolie and state's evidence and claiming he had no idea where the money'd gone. Billy D wanted him to know he was remembered, wanted to "send a birthday card," as he said when we got together later that day in the mess hall. Fried Spam the color of new skin that grows in after severe burns lay across the top half of our aluminum plate-trays, limp greens in the compartment lower right, watery mashed potatoes beside them.

"Just so he knows who the message is from," Billy told me. "The message itself, the form it takes—that's up to you. You're an imaginative guy, right? Things stay on track, I walk in four, five years. No way Roy's not countin' down. I just want to help him along some, get him to thinking what he has to look forward to?"

"I'll give him your best regards."

Though it had the texture of soggy bread, Billy used knife and fork to cut his Spam into small, precise squares. He'd stoke a bite of Spam into his mouth, follow it with half a forkful of mashed potatoes, then another of greens from which a pale, vaguely green, vaguely greasy liquid dripped onto his denim shirt.

"Roy ain't near as nice as me."

"Then maybe I'll give him more than just your regards."

Billy smiled, showing narrow brown teeth, Spam, and a stalklike strand of greens.

At the next table a con scooped food towards his mouth with two bent fingers. Weighing all of ninety-eight pounds, he was built, nonetheless, like a fat man: head seated directly on shoulders, biceps out from the body, thighs like repelling magnets, knees splayed, feet at a V. Billy watched a moment and shook his head.

"Man don't care for himself, respect himself, how's he expect anyone else to?"

"Wish it were that simple."

"Yeah. Yeah, that poor sorry bastard's every last one of us, ain't he? Like a goddamn fingerprint." Billy's attention shifted. "Look, I appreciate this, Turner. Goes to prove what I've said all along."

"All along, huh?"

He smiled again, Spamlessly this time. "Long enough."

And it was. We'd all washed up on the same shore, had to start from scratch here, build for ourselves whatever lives, whatever unlikely likenesses of civilization, we could. Know how people make shadow figures with their hands on the wall? That's what life inside is like, throwing up hard shadows with hands, mind and heart, pretending they're real.

Finished, Billy placed fork and knife side by side, perfectly aligned, handles an inch apart, in the upper portion of the tray.

"Where you from, anyway, Turner? Some world so far off we need a fuckin' telescope to see it. Old man went off to work every morning wearing Perma-Prest white dress shirts?"

"Matter of fact, most of his life, better than forty years—right up till it closed—he worked at the local sawmill. After that, he didn't do much of anything, including getting up from the kitchen table. Old-timey banjo players had a tuning called sawmill. Because that's where all the players worked, in the sawmills, and so many of them had fingers missing. Sawmill tuning, you could play just about anything with a finger or two."

Billy's eyes met mine. "Like I said, we misjudged you."

"It happens."

"Everyone knew you were a cop. But you sure as hell didn't act like one. First few guys that stepped up to you, and the last, they got put down hard. Then you turned into some kind of college boy. Now what the fuck's *that* about? Who *is* this guy?"

"One of you."

"We finally figured that out. About the same time you did."

"Let's move it," the guard called. "Got others waiting here." We stood on line to hand trays through an opening at one end of the mess. Beyond, new meat—fresh arrivals, who always drew KP—scraped leftovers into fifty-gallon bins, hosed trays down at stainless-steel sinks, and fitted them into open racks holding sixty at a time. Sweat pouring off the workers competed with output from the hoses.

We went out into a kind of cloister, cement walkway and overhang, moving two abreast back towards the block. Billy said, "You were in Nam."

"That was a long time ago. Another world. Another life."

"In here, everything's a long time ago. Everything's another life."

I nodded.

"How many worlds and lives you think we get?"

Out here the yard looked open, patches of grass and

weed sprouting off the walkway, walls far enough away that, if you kept your head down, you could almost imagine they weren't there, though never forget they were.

. . .

THE WORLD'S A TERRIFYING PLACE when you first come back to it. So much motion, so much noise, the whole of it barking and snapping about you, out of control. Just to get by, to cross a street, go for a walk, see a movie, requires dozens upon dozens of choices. Been a long time since you had to make choices, and the world just won't hold still, it keeps fidgeting, keeps demanding choices. Ordering a soft drink can paralyze you.

I took my free bus ride back to Memphis and, state-issue cardboard suitcase with its freight of books and diploma stowed beneath the bed, settled into a motel at city's edge, Paradise Courts, intending to stay only until my business was done but in fact remaining long afterwards, almost two months as it turned out, for lack of what my father doubtless would have called gumption. I was barely able to brave the day's wading pool of choices; no way I could face the sea of what to do next. Those first few days, I made promised contacts, delivered messages and keys, shuttled a package or three between stations, met up with Roy. All of it went smoothly enough that on the fourth day, Tuesday, I found myself emptied of short-term goals, sitting in a bar at eleven in the morning.

The sign out front of Paradise Courts was shaped like a painter's palette, powder-blue sky visible through the thumbhole, letters of the name in a fan of bright colors long since faded. Pure 1950s. The motel itself consisted of two levels of rooms, six on top, eight below, sketchy rail running along the upper tier, stairway at either end. Lower rooms opened directly onto parking lot, skinny moat of shrubs, interstate service road. Whenever anyone went up or down the stairway, walls shook and glasses fell off tables. Buffalo Nickel Diner, where daily I tested courage and fortitude, sat just past the edge of the motel's mostly unused parking lot; Junie's Bar, a concoction of cinder block and brown-painted wood, just past that.

You never get too far from the smell of the river and magnolia blossoms in Memphis. At Paradise Courts you were never far from the smell of the diner's Dumpsters, or from view of the swarm of derelicts, drunks and other dead-enders forever lurking behind Junie's.

Junie himself was a hunched, long-limbed man in his early sixties whose low brow and darting eyes underlined a monkeylike appearance. He always wore a blue dress shirt with button-down collar, sleeves folded back twice, and jeans. Jeans and shirt alike, including folded sleeves, were ironed; creases had gone white. Afternoons you'd find Junie sitting at the end of the bar reading old copies of *Popular Science* and *Saga* he bought in batches off a friend who had a used-book store. He'd look to the door as you came through, swing off his stool and be waiting behind the bar by the time you reached it. If you were a regular, your usual would be waiting.

I wasn't a regular. I'd been in a few times those past four days, including the night I shut the place down sitting three stools away from the bar's only other patron, a well-dressed woman a decade or so younger than myself. Her simple black dress hung loosely while somehow suggesting what lay beneath. When she lifted her glass, hooplike silver bracelets slid down her wrist and rings caught light. We'd spent the final hour lobbing verbal sallies back and forth, buying one another drinks, careful never to breach the three-stool safety zone.

Junie drew the beer I asked for and handed it across.

"Dollar-ten."

I put two singles on the bar and swung knees from beneath the overhang, north-northeast to south-southwest, to look out across the service road. Skimpy trees bowed in the spillage of wind from the interstate. Clouds crept slow as glaciers across the sky. Downing the beer in a couple of gulps, I asked for another. Junie brought it and stayed on. Eyes strayed to the TV propped up on old telephone books at the end of the bar, where a sexy older woman reminded her lover how passionate they'd once been, how much things had changed, and asked him, again and again, why. Leaving aside production values, you knew this couldn't be anything but a soap opera. Soap operas were the only place on TV where sexy older women happened.

"You're Turner, right? Over at Paradise?"

I admitted to it.

"Surprise you to hear the man's been poking around, asking questions?"

"Not really."

"Local, from the look of them. Already been up and had a check of your room too, would be my guess."

I put another couple of dollars between us. Magically they became a beer. Onscreen a young man with silver crosses for earrings, electric blue eyes and crow-black hair, radiating indolence and ambition in equal parts, spoke intensely into the camera.

"Just back on the street?" Junie asked.

"Coming up on a week."

"And seems a lot longer, I bet. You doing okay?"

"Know that much about it, do you?"

"Some. Most of my life, before I came upon these gracious surroundings you see about you"—his arm dipped and rose, pass of the bullfighter's cape—"I was a cop."

That night I closed the bar down again and then some, sitting not three stools away from Madam Mystery but across from, then beside, the bar's owner. I'd let on that I'd been a cop, too, so for better than an hour we swapped war stories. Then for a time we sat silently.

"Married?"

"Way back."

A coven of sirens screamed by outside. Fire truck, medics, a patrol car or two, from the sound of it. On the interstate, or closer by?

"People wonder why the hell I keep this place open," Junie told me. "Guys I was on the job with come in here, have a beer, look around and shake their heads."

Beers had been filing past as though on parade, each stepping proudly into the former's place. Then everyone else was gone, doors locked, single light still aloft above the bar, jukebox unplugged in favor of bluegrass from a cassette player by the cash register. Junie ferried out to the kitchen to fetch back a pizza. "Frozen," he said, "but I threw on real mushrooms and sausage before it went into the oven." I recalled a pizza I'd had years ago in one of Memphis's very first trendy restaurants, back when Beale Street was just starting to get dug out from under and Mud Island turned into a shrine: squirrel with feta cheese and artichokes. What's next, I'd wondered then—possum with pesto on a bed of grits?

Side by side, men of constant sorrow, Junie and I smacked lips, licked grease and molten cheese from fingers, went after runaway bits of sausage and mushroom.

"Time was, we'd get most anyone heading for Ozark retreats, Hot Springs or Nashville through here, plus a hearty tourist trade coming the other way, from Arkansas and Mississippi. They'd eat at local cafés, stay overnight at local motels, buy color postcards, carry home Kodaks of Aunt Sally trying to squeeze through Fat Man's Bluff. Then the interstate went in. Not to mention, not too long after, airlines with cheap fares. All of a sudden we look around and we're a watering hole, a gas stop. Not much reason even to keep the town open, much less the bar."

"But you do."

"Hey, I'd close in a minute, but then what'm I gonna do? Watch shit on TV all day long, get to be a god-awful nuisance to my neighbors, hang out at some senior center learning to drool?"

He brought a couple more beers. The collection was growing. Empty bottles upright on the table like gunnery, obelisks, small monuments.

"Back when I was young," Junie said, "new on the force

and married? I'd come home and find my wife just sitting there, looking out the window. Took a long time before I understood. You always wonder, afterwards, how you could ever have been so oblivious. But once I got so I could see the pain in her face, the pain at the center of her, I wasn't able to see much else."

Years to come, I'd spend much of my life sitting alongside other people's pain as I did that night, hearing it break, stammer, circle back on itself, duck, feint and run. I'd remember this moment.

"We'd been married almost four years when she died," Junie said. "I came home one morning and found her in the tub. She was leaning back, eyes closed. The water was cold. So was she. I've had a soft spot for junkies ever since."

He got up to shove in a new tape. Some early western swing group, Milton Brown maybe, doing "Milk Cow Blues." For a time Brown had this amazing steel guitar player, Bob Dunn, a natural on the order of Charlie Christian or Johnny Smith, played steel like it was a jazz trombone. His breaks gave you chills.

I got back to the room around three in the morning and, unable to sleep, lay watching lights from the interstate sweep the wall, radio on low beside me, both of them messages from a larger world beyond. Finally dawn's foot caught in the door. I hauled myself from bed, showered and went out to the diner for breakfast. When I returned, there was a lock over the doorknob of my room. Looked like a big clown's nose.

A young redhead with half a yard or so too little shirt

and half a dozen too many tattoos manned the office. He hooked his head as I came in, swiveled the phone up from his mouth and said he'd be with me in a minute.

"Can't get in my room," I said when he finished.

"Two-oh-three, right?"

"Yeah."

"Need you to pay up."

"I've been paying by the day, almost a week now. It's not due till noon."

"We're talking yesterday, not today."

"I brought money by around ten."

"No record of it."

"Short, fat guy, looked like his hair hadn't been washed for, I don't know, maybe ten years?"

"Danny."

I waited.

"Danny's gone. Checked out last night." He didn't think it was funny either, but hey. "With everything in the till, not to mention the office radio."

"And my money."

He shrugged. "Don't guess you have a receipt."

I did, as it happened. In prison you learn to hoard, you hang on to every single thing that comes your way.

Red studied the receipt, did everything but sniff it, and grunted. I paid him for the day. He grunted again.

"Be a lot easier if you paid by the week."

I just looked at him, the yard look, and watched his face go smooth. He pushed a receipt across the desk without meeting my eyes again. Then he got a bunch of keys and followed me up the staircase to unboot the door. The keys were hooked onto a giant steel safety pin and rang like tiny wind chimes as we climbed.

Inside, I switched on the TV to the rerun of an old cop show, some five-foot guy with a chip on his shoulder the size of a river barge and a taste in clothes running to big collars, slick fabrics and rips. All his shirts seemed to be missing the top three buttons. A gold medallion nestled in there among chest hair. I found myself wondering what it would be once it hatched.

Paired footsteps moved up the stairs.

Someone knocked at the door.

Cops and cons, you always know. Way they stand, way they walk, something in the eyes. The point man was there almost flush with the door, smiling, relaxed, but ready to push in or take me down if he sensed the need. He was one of the rare individuals whom off-the-rack fit perfectly; his dark JCPenney suit was immaculate, carefully pressed, but slick with wear. His partner (who'd be driving the Crown Vic pulled in at an angle below) stood off by the railing. Seersucker for him, spots baked into the tie.

"Mr. Turner?"

I nodded.

"Mind if we come in?"

I backed off and sat on the bed. Tugging up pantlegs to save the crease, Big Dog took the chair past the nightstand. B-side stayed on his feet just inside the door. He held a hand-carry radio unit. Every few moments it crackled.

"Can't help but notice you didn't ask to see badges. Situation like this, most people would."

"I'm not most people."

"True enough." He looked around, as though the limping dresser or precise angle of the bathroom door might divulge something crucial. "Nice place. Been here what? four, five days? Like it?"

"I've seen worse."

He nodded. B-side lifted the curtain to look out. "Hey! Get away from there!" he hollered. "Fuckin' kids." He stepped out onto the walkway and continued in the same vein, after a moment came back.

"You know a man named Roy Branning, Turner?"

"I could."

"Four-oh-four Commerce Parkway? You paid him a visit two nights ago."

"Carrying a message. Nothing more to it than that."

"And the message was?"

"Private."

"Sure it was." He got up and walked into the bathroom, came back holding my safety razor. "Private's a word you need to be careful around. You know?" Sitting again, he ran the razor along the edge of the nightstand, digging in. Veneer peeled off, thin shavings curled up behind. "Thing is, day after your visit, Branning turned up dead. We have to wonder what you know about that. Surprise you?"

"Not really. What I hear, he was pretty much the complete asshole."

"You heard right." This from B-side by the door.

"So there's nothing you can tell us? Now, when it could make a difference? Before this all goes any further?"

I shook my head.

He set the razor carefully on edge on the nightstand,

stood and ambled towards B-side, who shifted the radio between hands to open the door.

"We'll be in touch."

"Be careful out there, Detective."

"Thank you for your concern. So few care."

His smile put me in mind of a throat cut ear to ear.

Chapter Twenty-Five

CHICKENS MAY NOT have a lot on the ball, but once they start, they do go on. Velma's boy looked like what gets tossed off a butcher's block when everything remotely useful's been hacked away.

"Two violent deaths since you showed up here," Lonnie Bates said. "This sort of thing follow you around?"

"Could look that way, I guess." Did to me sometimes.

We stood over the cadaver with Doc Oldham. I was thinking how the words *cave* and *cad* were in there. I was thinking how frail our lives are, how thin the thread tethering us to this world. Go out for the Sunday paper and on the way back, half a block from home, you get hit by a delivery truck. Random viruses claim squatter's rights in our bodies and won't be evicted. Amazing any of us manage to stay alive.

"Lonnie, goddamn it, I got people to take care of. Live people. Not much I can do for this poor son-of-a-bitch, is there?"

"County pays you, Doc."

"Every village's gotta have an idiot." He wore good-quality clothes, Brooks Brothers tan suit, blue oxford-cloth shirt, carefully cinched tie—all so stained and body-sprung that Salvation Army sorters would have thrown them out. Half a mug of coffee disappeared at a single swallow. The mug had a nude woman on it. When you poured in hot liquid, her flesh disappeared and a skeleton emerged. As the contents cooled, flesh came back. Right now, she was about half formed. "Dozen more bodies, I might even be able to make my car payment this month, who knows?"

"What can you tell me?" Bates asked.

"Chickens ate him."

"Thank God we have you. All those years of study, all that expertise. Without that, where would we be?"

Doc Oldham shrugged. "If I wasn't here, why the hell would I care in the first place? Hell, I don't care now. Velma okay?"

"Don Lee's with her. Niece on the way up from Clarksdale. Only family she has."

"Igor!"

An elderly black man looking like a 1950s railroad porter appeared to claim stretcher and remains of body and wheel them away. Doc Oldham followed. Much-abused stainless steel doors swung to behind.

We walked out into stiffling heat, early-morning rain dripping from trees and eaves and steaming off the sidewalk.

"What's your day look like?" Bates asked.

"Assuming you don't have other plans for me, it looks like a drive into the city."

I'd spoken to Val and got the name of a guy who wrote about movies and taught film studies at the university. His books sported titles like *Biker Chicks and Fifty-Foot Women, Short on Clothes, Skateboard Cowboys*. He'd written an entire book, Val said, on the three versions of *Invasion of the Body Snatchers*. Kind of books Carl Hazelwood might have had out in the garage, from the sound of things. Guy's a little weird, Val added. What a surprise.

Just over two hours later I found myself on a block-long street a mile or so off campus where restaurants, cafés, coffee shops and bars still tilted their hats towards students. St. Martin's Lane didn't exist on any map; I'd had to stop and ask directions three times. Then, when I found the address, there was no house on the lot. Five-fourteen gave way directly to 518, with a spot between like a missing tooth. A structure stood back by the alley fence, though, a guest house or converted garage. I pulled into the ruins of a driveway and headed for that.

What at first glance I took to be a small, hunched man answered my knock. On closer notice I realized he wasn't small at all, only drawn into himself, so that he gave the appearance of such. He'd been wearing headphones that pulled away when, oblivious, he came to the door and, as it were, the end of his rope. He glanced back at them lying inert on the floor a yard or so behind. Two days' growth of beard, hair chronically unruly, scuffed loafers, baggy chinos with frayed cuffs, a black T-shirt. Over this, a many-pocketed hunter's vest.

Two rooms from what I could make out, possibly

another beyond? Shutters and curtains drawn. The whole of it seemed to be lit with a single 40-watt bulb.

"You're Turner? Come on in."

He showed me his back as he scuttled into, yes, a third room, and came back with a platter from which he peeled off plastic covering. Carrot sticks curled up like the toenails of old men, cheese cubes awash with sweat. I had the impression my host didn't entertain often and was into recycling.

Having delivered the goods, he bent to retrieve the headphones and put them on a table beside a rickety recliner.

"I was just having a beer," he told me, and picked up a can of Ballantine Ale. Tilting it back only to find it was empty, he looked puzzled, as with the headphones. "Maybe that was earlier, come to think of it. Have one with me?"

"Sure."

Again, back to me like a beetle, he exited. A hairless cat materialized at my feet, throwing itself to the floor in elaborate shoulder rolls. On a TV in one corner a black-and-white movie showed soundlessly. Long, back-projection shots of highway-patrol cars coursing down highways. Arizona? New Mexico?

My unaccustomed host stood in the doorway, beer in each hand. His name was Mel Goldman. He survived off novelizations of B-grade movies and TV series. Half a dozen paperbacks he'd written around a show concerning L.A. teenagers' crises (things are hell out there in the promised land!) did okay in the States but went gold in Germany. Publishers brought him over, major national magazines interviewed him. I almost shit my pants, he'd said of the experience upon return. Those people had to know I'm a Jew, right?

"Aliens have landed," Goldman told me. "The sheriff's kid saw them, but no one believes him. He's a dreamy sort. First reel's amazing—just kind of floats. Creates this whole town, this atmosphere of suspicion and dread. Then it all gets thrown away and the whole thing turns into one long, stupid chase. Kind of thing a man would eat his socks not to have to watch."

I tried hard not to look down at his feet.

He handed me a beer and asked what he could do for me. We sat watching a '52 Dodge with a green plastic screen like the brim of a card dealer's hat above the windshield careen off the road as a tall man, strangely stooped, stepped out before it.

"Something about a murder, you said on the phone. I don't see how I could possibly help you with something like that."

I gave him the abstract: my case and Carl Hazelwood's death in fifty words, dry as a science paper. Like notes you make about clients for your files. "I don't know what I'm looking for," I said. "But I read Carl's journal. Lot of it had to do with old films."

"Science fiction, gangster, prison stories—that sort of thing?"

"How'd you know?"

"What else would it be?" He watched as the tall, stooped man entered a cave hidden among trees. " 'Home. I have no home. Hunted, despised, living like an animal.' "

"Okay."

"*Bride of the Monster.*"

Onscreen, inside the cave, the tall, stooped man stood over a body laid out on a steel table.

"One of many he'll inhabit," Goldman said. "The bodies, recently dead, are imperfect and last but a short time. His supply is running out, his mission remains unfulfilled."

That had a ring of familiarity about it.

"Actor's name is Sammy Cash. No one knows much of anything about him, who he was. He came out of nowhere, starred in this string of movies—for a year or so there, he seemed to be in every cheap movie made—then he was gone."

"Carl's sister says films were realer than life to her brother, that he loved the bad ones best of all."

"Good man. There really is an inverse engine at work here. The cheaper the films are, the more they tell you what the society's *really* like, as opposed to what it claims for itself. Any particular names come up?"

I pulled out my notebook.

"Herschell Gordon Lewis, Larry Cohen, *Basket Case*, *Spider Baby*, *The Incredibly Strange Creatures.*"

"Mr. Hazelwood had good taste. Or bad. Depending." He laughed, and beer came out his nose. He wiped it, beer and whatever else, on his sleeve.

"Any idea who or what BR might be? It comes up on almost every page of his journal. An abbreviation, initials—"

"Just the two letters? No periods after?"

I nodded.

"Carl Hazelwood was murdered, you said?"

"You know something?"

"I might. You see the body?"

"Pictures."

"Like this?" Goldman brought his arms over his head in an acute V, wrists turned outward.

I nodded.

"Certain circles, that's a famous image. Couple of Web sites even have it as part of their logo. Branches with leaves breaking off. The leaves look like hands."

"Okay, I'm lost."

"You're supposed to be. Know much about cult films?"

"Nothing." Basic interview skills. Play dumb, admit to nothing. Interviewee's words rush in to fill the void. "Tell me?"

"I can do better than that. Hold on."

He stalked off to the corner of the room, rummaged in a stack of videocassettes there, then went to the desk for similar rifling. Came up with a CD. He ejected the resident cassette just as the tall, stooped man passed into a new body.

"This is all I have," he told me, "all anyone has, as far as I know. Downloaded it from an Austrian Internet site."

Long shots of suburban homes, tailored green lawns, billboards. Then suddenly, jarringly, the close-up of a man in agony. He stands or is propped against what may be a trellis, wooden lacework through which a white wall shows. His arms are pushed into a tight V above his head. There is a flurry of hands, four, then six, then eight, as they circle his, touch them, loop twine about wrists, tie them to the open weave. Left alone now, his hands droop to the sides. He smiles.

My host ejected the cassette as the screen filled with static.

"Sammy Cash again," he said, "though most people don't realize it. He'd been through a lot by then, he'd changed. This clip may be all that's left—all I've ever seen, at any rate. But the film's a legend. Any serious collector would trade his grandmother for a copy, throw in his first-born."

"Why?"

"You mean besides the fact that no one else has one."

"Right."

"Because it's the most elusive movie ever made. There are still a few people around that claim to have seen it, but just as many insist no such film ever existed—that the whole thing's a legend."

He replaced the former cassette. A nude young woman looked in the mirror and saw there the tall, stooped man she'd previously been. She reached out to touch the mirror but, unaccustomed to her new body, reached too hard. The mirror broke.

"*The Giving.* Interesting enough in itself, from what we know. But infinitely more interesting as the last legendary film of a legendary director. You need another beer?"

I told him I was fine. Sipped from my can to demonstrate.

"The director is almost as elusive. Supposedly started out as a studio salesman, flogging film bookings to small theatres all over the Southwest. In the only interview he ever gave, he said he made the mistake one day of actually watching one of the things he was selling and knew he could do a lot better. He sold his Cadillac, sank the money he got into putting together a movie. Friends and neighbors and his barely covered girlfriend served as actors in that first one. He shot it over a weekend, and when on Monday, driving a borrowed car, he went back out on the road, that was the one he worked hardest to sell.

"Took studio folk a time to cotton to what was going on, even with bookings starting to fall off all through Arizona, New Mexico and Texas. By then he'd put away enough money to make another movie. Four more actually. When studio folk finally caught up with him to fire him, he was coming off the plane from two weeks in Mexico with his girlfriend and actors he'd scrounged from local colleges and had those four new films in the can.

"He was like a lot of natural artists, told the same story over and over. Always a dance between this detective hero and his nemesis. At first the nemesis was nothing more than a cardboard character, a threat, a blank, a cipher. But as time went on, movie to movie, he began to become real. In some of the movies he had extraordinary powers. In others he was seen only as a shadow, or as a presence registered by others. Remember, the director was cranking these out in a week or less. Pouring them directly from his soul onto celluloid, as one critic put it.

"Then, suddenly, they stopped. A year went by. Finally— rumor or legend has it—his swan song: *The Giving*. This great mystery movie. There are half a dozen Web sites devoted to his work."

"Can't help but notice you've avoided the director's name."

"I haven't. No one knows it. The movies were all brought out as 'A BR Film.' No separate director's credit. Just the two letters, no periods after."

I stood, thanking him for his time.

"You want, I could skate around a bit on those Web sites, get e-mails off to my contacts, see what turns up."

"I'd appreciate that."

He tried drinking again from the empty can. "Done, then. I'll be in touch."

I almost stepped on the hairless cat who in lieu of giving up, had decided to outwait me and, when I moved, throw itself bodily in my path. As I tried to regain balance my hand went down hard on the couch. A floorboard near one leg cracked, descending like a ramp into darkness. Such was the unworldly ambience of that place, I wouldn't have been unduly surprised if a line of tiny men with backpacks had come hiking up the tilted floorboard.

"Mr. Turner?"

Yes?

"Sammy Cash, the actor? And whoever it was made the movies? Some think they're the same person."

Chapter Twenty-Six

ONE OF THE LAST CLIENTS I had was a man who had mutilated his eight-month-old son. He'd been two years in the state hospital, where things predictably enough had not gone well for him, and came to me on six years' probation, with weekly counseling sessions mandated by the court. I got calls from his PO every Friday afternoon.

Affable, relaxed and clear-eyed, he was never able to explain why he'd done it. Once or twice as we spoke, without warning he'd fall into a kind of chant: "Thursday, thumb. First finger, Friday. Second, Saturday. Third, Tuesday. Fourth, Friday." He seemed to me then like someone trying to express abstract concepts in a language he barely understood. He seemed, in fact, like another person entirely—not at all the quiet young man in chinos and T-shirt who weekly sat across from me chatting.

That's facile, of course. Though hardly more facile than much else I found myself saying again and again to clients back then in the guise of observation, advice, counsel, supposed compassion. Conversational psychiatry has a shamefully limited vocabulary, pitifully few conjugations.

"I just want to get in touch with my wife, my son," Brian would say. "I just want to tell them . . ."

"What do you want to tell them?" I'd finally ask.

"That . . ."

"What?"

". . . I don't know."

My apartment was across from a charter school. Through the window Brian's eyes tracked young women in plaid skirts, high white socks and Perma-Prest white shirts, young men in blazers, gray trousers, striped ties. Eventually I'd pour coffee, mine black, his with two sugars. We'd sit quietly then, comfortable in one another's company, two citizens of the world sidestepping it for a moment though both of us had important work to get back to, at rest and at leisure on time's front porch.

We'd been meeting for maybe three months, Brian having never missed a session, when one afternoon I got a call from him. Calls like that don't bode well. Generally they mean someone is cracking up, someone's found him- or herself in deep shit, someone needs a stronger crutch or more often a wrecker service. Brian just wanted to know if I'd be interested in taking in a movie, maybe grab some dinner after.

I couldn't think why not—aside from the covenant against therapists consorting with patients, that is.

I've no idea what movie we saw. I've since put in time at the library looking through files of that day's newspapers. None of those listed rings a bell.

Afterwards we passed on to an Italian restaurant. This part I do remember. Sort of family place where older kids waited table, all the younger kids and Mom were back in the kitchen, and Dad might come sidling up to your table any moment with an accordion or his vocal rendition of "Santa Lucia." Tonight, though, the villa was quiet. Baskets of bread, antipasto, soup, pasta, entrées, dessert and coffee arrived. Both of us turning aside repeated offers of wine.

I can't recall what we talked about any more than I remember the movie, but talk we did, before, during and after, more or less nonstop. Well past midnight outside a jazz bar on Beale I put Brian in a cab.

That was Tuesday. When Brian didn't show up for his Thursday session, I tried calling. When his PO checked in on Friday, I told him about the no-show. We sent a patrol around.

The PO called back a couple of hours later. I was home by then, changed into jeans and T-shirt, bottle of merlot recorked and in the fridge, fair portion of it in the deep-bellied glass before me. Hummingbirds jockeyed for position at the feeder out on my balcony.

Apparently Brian had gone directly home that night and hung himself. Was this what he'd intended all along? Responding officers said a Billie Holiday CD played over and over. He'd made a pot of coffee and drunk half of it as he undressed and got things together. Under his cup was a page torn from a stenographer's pad.

Wonderful evening, it said. *Thank you.*

Mild weather tomorrow, the radio promised. A beautiful day. High in the sixties, fair to partly cloudy. But when I woke, wind whistled at my windows and rain blew against them, forming new maps of the world as it dripped down.

Chapter Twenty-Seven

"I'M NOT SURE THAT'S POSSIBLE."

"Of course it is. I just need a bench warrant."

"To intercept the mayor's mail."

"Only to log it. I wouldn't be reading it."

"Judge Heslep's the one you'd have to see, then."

"Fair enough."

"Forget that. Man has a picture of Nixon and Hoover shaking hands in his office, no way he's going to issue the warrant. You consider just asking?"

"Asking?"

The sheriff shook his head, picked up the phone and dialed.

"Henry Lee? You playing hooky today or what? Taxpayers don't pay you to sit 'round watching *Matlock*. . . . Good point, we *don't* pay you, do we? And let me be the first to say you're worth every last damn penny. . . . Good, good. . . . Got a question for you. Any problem with our looking over your mail for, oh, say the last couple months? . . . Well, sure, but whatever you still have at hand. Anything like me, most of it's still in a pile somewhere. . . . Good man. . . . See you then.

"Clear your dance card. Five o'clock at the mayor's," Bates said, hanging up, "for cocktails." When had I last heard someone use the word *cocktails*? "He'll have copies of mail, payment records—whatever he's able to pull together. Said you should feel free to bring a friend."

"I assume you're coming with."

"I kind of got the impression he had Val Bjorn in mind."

"Not Sarah Hazelwood?"

"Hey. It's a small town. Sneeze, and someone down the road reaches for Kleenex."

"How's June?" I asked. She hadn't shown up for work.

"She's all right. Told me you know what's going on."

"Good that the two of you talked about it."

"She's out looking for the son of a bitch, Turner. You have any idea how hard it is for me to stay out of this?"

"I do, believe me."

"Our kids, what we want for them. . . . She's a smart girl. She'll work it out. By the way, Henry told me I should tell you you're a pain in the ass. He also says we're glad to have you here."

Framed in the parentheses of cupped hands, a face appeared at the window. One of the hands turned to a wave. That or its mate opened the door, and a short, stocky man clambered in. He wore dark, badly wrinkled slacks, white shirt with open collar, gray windbreaker. Somehow when he removed the canvas golf cap, you expected him to look inside to see if his hair might have gone along. Wasn't on his head anymore.

"They're at it again," he told the sheriff.

"What *they* we talking about this time, Jay?"

"Gypsies. Who else would I be talking about?"

"Well now, as I recall, last time you came by, it was a busload of Mexicans being trucked in to pick crops. Time before that, it was a carload of 'city kids.' "

"Gypsies," the man said.

"They haven't put a curse on you, I hope?"

"A curse? Don't play with me, Lonnie. Ain't no such thing as curses."

"So what are the gypsies up to, then? Stealing?"

"You bet they are."

"Which is what everyone says about them, same way they talk about curses. But the stealing's real?"

"Yep."

"You saw it?"

"Family of 'em came in to buy groceries. Afterwards, things turned up missing."

"What kind of things?"

"Couple of Tonka trucks, a doll."

"Family had children with them?"

"Course they did."

"You ever been known to pocket a thing or two you didn't pay for when you were little, Jay? Kids do that all the time. Hell, *I* did. . . . Tell you what. You bring me a list of what's missing, I'll go talk to them. Bet your goods'll be back on the shelf before the day's over."

"Well . . . okay, Lonnie. If you say so."

"I'll swing by and pick up that list on my way, say half an hour?"

"It'll be ready."

"Hard not to miss the excitement of law enforcement, huh, Turner?" the sheriff said once he was gone.

"Oh yeah."

"If you don't mind my asking, just what is it you do all day out there by the lake?"

"Not a lot. That's pretty much the idea. Read, put some food on the back of the stove for later, sit on the porch."

"What I hear, you earned it. Peace, I mean. Sorry we dragged you away, into all this."

"Some ways, I am too."

This, I thought—this was part of what I valued here, sitting quietly, no one afraid of silence.

"Just between the two of us," I said after a while, "I'm not sure I was coming into my own out there, not sure I ever would. Maybe all I was doing was fading away."

Bates nodded, then dropped his boots off the desk and stood.

"Let's go see the king," he said.

. . .

THE KING, who was all of twenty-one, wore a gold-colored shirt from the 1970s. Its panels showed great paintings, the *Mona Lisa*, a Rembrandt, a Monet. His palace was a battered silver Airstream trailer, one of those shaped like a loaf of bread, mounted behind a Ford pickup. Tea came to the table in a clear glass pot—started off clear, anyway. Hadn't been that for some time, from the look of it. Half a dozen children of assorted size and age sat against the wall watching TV.

"We have talked about this," he said. "Drink, drink. There's lamb stew if you're hungry. No? You are sure? Please let the proprietor know the articles will be returned. I will bring the children into town myself this afternoon and see to it that each of them apologizes to him. Some would say it's in their blood, I know that. But they are, after all, only children." He poured from the pot into a cup and drank, as though to prove it safe. "Thank you for coming to me with this."

"Your father and I always got along, Marek. I never knew him to do anything but what was right."

The king looked over at the kids, out the trailer window to where old women sat around a makeshift table chopping vegetables. "Maybe someone will say something like that about me one day."

"What I've seen this past couple of years, I suspect they'll be saying a lot more."

After finishing our tea, the sheriff and I climbed in the Jeep and headed back to town.

"You'll be wanting to pick up a necktie for the mayor's cocktail party," Bates said after a time, adding, once I'd made no response: "Joking, of course. Hell, you could wear a butcher's apron and waders in there and feel right at home."

A mile or so up the road we both stuck out our hands to wave at Ida chugging along in her cream-over-blue '48 Buick.

"Ask you something?"

I nodded.

"It's personal. None of my business, really."

I turned to look at him.

"You keep leaving things, quitting them, moving on."

"I'm not sure I ever had much of a choice."

"What would you have told a patient who said that?"

"That one way or another, we always make our own choices. Point taken." I watched a hawk launch itself off a utility pole and glide out across fields of soybean. "Much as anything, I think, that's why I quit. Couldn't listen to myself saying these really stupid things, repeating what I'd heard, what I'd read, one more time. It was all too pat—I knew that from the first. We're not windup toys, all you have to do is tighten a screw or two, rewind the spring, adjust tension, and we'll work again."

The hawk dove, and came up with what looked to be a small possum in its talons.

"The simple truth is, I *didn't* make those choices. Never chose to crawl around a jungle some place in the world so far away I hadn't even heard of it. Never chose to shoot my partner, or in prison to kill a man against whom I had nothing, a man I hardly even knew. And I sure as hell didn't call up my travel agent to arrange for an eleven-year holiday weekend in the joint."

True to form, Bates stayed silent.

"I never felt at home, never found a place I fit. Like you can use a wrench that slips, a screwdriver that's not quite right. They're close, you get the job done. But it makes things more difficult the next time. Threads are stripped, the screwhead's chewed all to hell."

Bates pulled hard right and bounced us and Jeep alike down a dirt path through trees. Bags of garbage had been dumped indiscriminately at roadside. Wildflowers and thick vines grew out of a forties-vintage pickup as though it were a window box. Bates pulled up at DAVE'S, a boathouse, bait shop and occasional barbeque joint built into a low hill alongside the lake and extending on stilts into it. DAVE'S didn't seem to be doing much business. Or any business at all. A lone truck not looking much better than the one sprouting vines back on the dirt path sat in the parking lot.

Bates climbed down and went inside. He was gone maybe five minutes.

"Everyone's okay. I don't get out this way all that often, always like to check on Dave and the family when I do. Been tough for them and people like them, these last few presidents we've had."

We made our way back onto the main road. A camel ride. Bates popped the top on a Coke, handed it over. I drank and sent it back. A couple of miles passed.

"Folks 'round here appreciate what you do for them?" I asked. "They even know?"

"Some do. Not that that has a lot to do with why I do it."

We were coming into town now. Serious traffic. Two, maybe even three cars at the intersection. We pulled up at city hall. Neither of us moved to climb down from the Jeep.

"Sometimes I think the first choice I ever made, my whole life, was when I packed all the rest of it in and came here."

"Hope it works out."

"Better than in the past, you mean."

"No, I just mean I hope it works out."

. . .

THE MAYOR'S HOUSEKEEPER, a black woman by the name of Mattie, had been with the family over fifty years.

"'Cept for the spell I got work up to the packing plant," Mattie said. "Always did like that job."

"Woman changed my diapers."

"Liked that job a *lot*."

She had glasses shaped like teardrops, permed hair that put me in mind of those flat plastic french curves we used in high-school geometry class.

"Mattie's part of the family," the mayor said. That peculiar, Faulknerian thing so many southerners espouse. It's always assumed you know what they mean. If you ask questions, they swallow their ears.

Mattie brought in platters of fried chicken and sweet corn dripping with butter, bowls of mashed potatoes, collard greens and sawmill gravy, a plate of fresh biscuits and cornbread. Two pitchers of sweet iced tea.

"You-all need anything else right now, Mister Henry?"

"How could we? Looks wonderful."

"Reckon I'll start in on the kitchen, then."

The mayor set his unfinished bourbon alongside his tea glass. We'd been having drinks on the patio when Mattie called us in to dinner. Mine was a sweet white wine from one of those boxes that fits in the refrigerator and has a noz-zle. You milk it like a cow.

Out on the patio the mayor had given me a thick manila envelope.

"Here's everything I could find. Won't claim it's com-plete."

"Okay if I give you a call once I've had a chance to look through it?"

"Don't know as I'd be able to add much, but sure."

Dinner-table conversation took in the high-school football team, how the mayor's wife was doing, a bevy of local issues ranging from vandalism at the city park and cemetery to the chance of a Wal-Mart, the latest scandal surrounding a long-time state congressman, the status of our investigation.

"Do the initials BR mean anything to you?" I asked.

The mayor, who a moment ago had been arguing pas-sionately that the town *had* to bring in new blood, leaned back in his chair. He'd been to the well for more bourbon and now sat sipping it. Dinner was a ruin, a shambles, on the table before us.

"Should they?"

"I don't know. . . . Maybe I'll take some of that bourbon after all, if you don't mind."

The mayor stood. "Lonnie?"

"Why not?"

He came back with two crystalline glasses maybe a quarter full. He'd replenished his own as well. We strayed back out onto the patio.

"Thing is," I said, "Carl Hazelwood's murder has . . . what university types would call resonance. The circumstances of his death match those of a movie called *The Giving*." I held my arms above my head, wrists turned out. "Man dies like that. Like Carl Hazelwood. Don't suppose you've seen it."

"Haven't even heard of it."

"Yeah, it's obscure, all right. What they call a cult movie these days. Actor playing the man who dies, his name was Sammy Cash. No one knows who the director was. Went just by his initials: BR."

I dropped it then. We cruised through another half-hour or so of pleasantries before the sheriff and I took our leave. Mattie waved from the front window.

"So?" Bates said.

"So, what?"

He glanced sideways, grinning.

"Okay, okay. I saw something, picked up on something, when I was talking about the film. I'm just not sure what."

"Mayor's gone out of his way to be of help on this. Not like Henry Lee to be so accommodating."

"What does that mean?"

"Jesus, man, is this what happens when you go to college—just like my parents said? You have to always be asking what everything means? I *said* what I meant."

Bouncing on ruts, we made our way towards the main road ahead. We'd reach it someday. Smooth sailing from there on out.

In the distance four loud cracks sounded.

"God, I hope that's someone setting off fireworks for a holiday I forgot."

His beeper sounded.

"There goes hope."

Chapter Twenty-Eight

BIG DOG AND B-SIDE turned up again a couple of days later, just after eight in the morning.

"Sure hope we didn't wake you."

"Nope. First thing I do every morning, get the day started right, is sit around without clothes on watching the news. Like to keep up."

"We brought some news about your friend Roy Branning."

"Hardly my friend."

"Hardly anybody's," B-side said.

"Seems he may have been put down by one of his . . . associates. Nothing to do with you. What do you think?"

"I don't, before noon."

"We got on to this the way we get on to most things. Guy we see regularly, what we call a CI, heard some loose talk in a bar, passed it on. But then, you know about CIs."

We were still standing in the doorway, where my clothes

weren't. When a young couple passed on the balcony, the girl did a double take. I felt my penis stiffen.

"Don't draw your weapon unless you're prepared to use it," B-side said.

Funny stuff.

Big Dog glared at him.

"We know about you, Turner. Word's come down to leave you alone, though. We don't much like that."

"Who would?"

"Right." He stepped back, forcing B-side to scramble out of his way. "Who *would* like that? Or for that matter, who'd give enough of a shit to pay attention to what some desk jockey wants, you know? Anyone wants this job can have it. Hell, I'll gift-wrap it for them, got a nice pink ribbon I've saved." He half-lifted one hand in mock benediction. "Be seeing you, Turner."

I went back to bed and was enjoying a luscious meal at a swank restaurant, accompanied by a woman every bit as luscious and swank, when a knock reached in and hauled me out of the dream.

"You Turner?" the small man asked. Something wrong with his spine, as though at some formative point he'd been gripped at head and hips and twisted. Dark hair grew low on his forehead, only a narrow verge of scaly skin separating it from the hedge of eyebrow. Cotton sweater with sleeves and waist rolled, cheap jeans with huge wide legs. "Something for you."

He handed me an envelope.

"Just out?" I said.

"Three days."

"Want to come in, have a drink?"

"Wouldn't say no." He pulled the door closed behind him. "Name's Hogg."

He kept watching me. After a moment I said, "What?"

"I was waiting for the jokes."

"Fresh out of them. Bottle's by the sink in the bathroom. Help yourself. Ice from the machine out by the landing if you want it."

"Ice. *Know* I'm back in the real world now."

He came out with two plastic glasses of brandy as I was reading the note.

Damn, man, you say you'll take a message out, you mean it! Guess Roy won't have to be worrying about my getting out no longer. RIP and all that crap. Now I'll have to come out and get right on finding that money. Thanks again for carrying for me. Good man. Good luck.

Billy D

"Not that I mind drinking alone," Hogg said, putting a cup down by me. "Alone. In a crowd. With camels." His eyes looked as though they'd been separated at birth and spent their independent lives searching for one another. I lifted the cup in salute or in thanks and drank.

"Got anything lined up?"

"Sure I do. Ninety percent of it'll fall apart before I even get there, way it usually does."

"How many years you pull?"

"Ten to fifteen on my head, little over four underfoot—

this time. Met some punk in a bar, both of us half drunk, heard all about his easy score, next thing I know I'm back on the boards. Damned embarrassing. Here I am, supposed to be a pro."

"How'd you find me?"

"I was told where to come."

"Billy D?"

He nodded and, downing what was left of the brandy, stood.

"You're welcome to stay."

"Thanks. But that'll do me." At the door he paused. "You're the cop, right?"

"I was."

"Couldn't have been easy for you inside."

"It's tough for everyone."

Hogg nodded. "I heard about you. You did okay. You helped a lot of people."

My hubris.

Though never in all the years before or since have I needed the excuse of it to make an absolute mess of things.

Chapter Twenty-Nine

"GODDAMN IT, Sue, just put the gun down."

She sat on the porch swing, shotgun cradled like a newborn in her arm.

"Where'd you get that thing anyway?"

"It's mine fair and square, Lonnie, don't you worry. I traded for it."

"Alban's hurt, Sue."

"Well I sure as hell do hope so."

"We need to get him help."

"Maybe his girlfriend could help. Why don't you go find her? She'll be hanging around the church somewhere."

The porch was bare boards, couple of feet off the ground, and ran across the whole front of the cabin. The steps were poured cement. They didn't quite match up with anything—ground or porch. Alban lay slumped against them.

"He's bleeding out, Sue."

"Good."

"Now you know I'm gonna have to come up there, put a stop to this."

She shook her head. Raised her left elbow half a foot or so to emphasize the shotgun.

"Wonder that thing didn't blow up when you first fired it. Crescent, maybe a Stevens, from the look of it. Hardware-store gun. Damn near as old as this town. No one else has to get hurt here, Sue. *Alban*," he called out. "You okay?"

Alban raised a hand, let it drop.

"Kids with your folks, Sue?"

She nodded.

"Freda's still bringing home those A's, I bet."

Bates stepped out from the shelter of the Jeep and began moving very slowly, hands held in plain sight, towards her.

"They're good kids, Sue. You don't want to leave them alone."

Noiselessly, Don Lee appeared on the porch behind her.

"We head down this road, take a few more steps along it, that's what it could come to."

Don Lee reached across the back of the swing with what I can only call infinite tenderness and took the gun. She offered no resistance, in fact seemed relieved.

Bates returned to the Jeep and picked up the mike.

"June, you there? Come back."

"Ten-four."

"Need an ambulance out to Alban McWhorter's."

"You have it. . . . What's going on out there?"

"I'll be home directly. Tell you about it then."

Don Lee came towards us with Sue in tow. "Alban looks

okay to me. Flesh wounds, mostly. My guess is she turned the barrel away at the last moment."

"I'm sorry, Lonnie," Sue said.

"We all are."

"I love him, you know."

"I know."

"He's gonna be okay?"

"You both are. Doc Oldham'll be in touch. We'll let you know what he has to say."

One hand under her shoulder, other at her head, Don Lee guided Sue into the back seat of the squad. She peered out from within, raccoonish.

"Lonnie, can someone call my parents?"

"I'll go by there myself."

They lived in a white house back towards town. It stood out among its peers: paint applied within the last few years, yard recently mowed, a conspicuous lack of abandoned appliances and cars. The curtains were open and, as I soon witnessed, the door unlocked. We could see inside. Past the back of the couch and two heads, animals gone biped strutted and spoke on the TV screen. When we rang the bell, two smaller heads popped up between the larger, facing our way. A handsome woman came to the door.

"Lonnie! How long's it been?"

"Too long as always, Mildred."

He introduced us. A beautiful smile, one eye (lazy? artificial?) that didn't track. You kept wanting to glance off to see what it was looking at.

"You boys come right on in. Horace, see who's here! What can I get you?"

"Nothing, thank you. Heading home to supper the minute I leave here."

Lonnie shook Horace's hand, then introduced me and it was my turn. Horace was a tall man, topped with a thicket of blond, haylike hair. He listed to the left, as though all his life a strong wind had been blowing from the east. Samplers and decoupage adorned every wall. Delicate figurines sat on shelves.

Mildred turned to the children.

"You know, I almost forgot to tell you, but when I went looking for liver in the freezer this afternoon—I couldn't find it, which you have to know, since we ate hamburgers—I saw someone had sneaked a gallon of ice cream in there. I don't know, but I was wondering if, once you're ready for bed, just maybe, you might be interested in trying some."

"It's Sue," Lonnie said once the kids were gone.

"We know what's been going on, Lonnie. Everyone does." This from Horace.

"She's okay. So is Alban."

Mildred: "God be praised."

"Sue somehow got hold of a shotgun. I don't think she meant to do much but scare him. Probably waited for him to come sneaking in—"

"He'd have talked back."

"Always did have a mouth on him."

"Don Lee thinks she turned the gun away at the last moment."

"As she was firing, you mean?" Horace said.

Bates nodded.

"Wouldn't have thought she had it in her."

Horace and Mildred exchanged glances.

"Alban's fine," Bates said. "He'll be out of the hospital in a day or two. There'll have to be a preliminary hearing, but that won't come to much. Sue should be back home about the same time."

"We want to keep our grandchildren, Lonnie."

"Sorry?"

"We don't want them to go back there."

"We love Sue—"

"—and Alban—"

"—but this has gone on long enough."

"You want to take Freda and Gerry away from their parents? Sure they have problems. Which of us don't? But you have to know how much they love those kids, what they mean to them. Take the kids away, their lives come to nothing."

"You think we *want* to do this? It's for their own good."

"It always is."

Afterwards I followed him out to the Jeep. Full dark now. Off the road to either side, frogs called forlornly. A moon white as blanched bone hung in the sky. It was some time before he spoke.

"I hate this shit," he said, "absolutely hate it. Everyone's right. And everyone loses."

"True enough." A mile or two further up the road I added, "But from what I see, you do good things here. You help people, bring them together, shore up their lives. Everything we think the job's about when we start."

"Then it changes on you?"

"Or you change. You listen to that hundred-and-tenth explanation and realize you just don't care anymore, you don't want to know. Helping people? Improving the community? Hey! you tell yourself, you're just the dog that keeps the cattle from straying."

Lonnie dropped me at the office. Few days back, he'd loaned me an old car he had sitting in the garage; now I figured to head back out to the cabin. I was looking down at the floorboard, thinking about a patient I'd had, Jimmie, who was convinced not only that he was a machine but also that he had less than a year left in his batteries, when someone rapped at the window. Startled, I turned. No one should ever be able to get that close without my knowing.

I tried rolling down the window, but it didn't, so I got out.

"Once again the true gentleman," Val said. "You hungry, by any chance? One of us owes the other one a dinner, I'm fairly sure."

"I had plans."

"Oh."

"Of course, those plans were only to go home and drink half a bottle of a really good cabernet."

"What, and let the other half go to waste?"

"Seems a shame, doesn't it? Want to see where I live?"

"Are you asking me out?"

"In, actually."

"Better than calling me out, I guess."

"I may even be able to scrounge up a handful of rice."

"Not brown, I hope. Never can be sure, with you monkish types." She walked around to the other side. "And I get to ride in this cool car, too! Lucky girl."

Between us, she pulling from without, me pushing from within, we managed to get the door open. Soon we were well out of town, exiled to the moon's province, in the company of owls. Neither of us said anything about how beautiful it was out here, though we both thought it.

"By the way," Val said, "did I mention I've just had the worst day of my life?"

"Not that I recall."

"No? Good. I was hoping I wouldn't bring that up."

The radio functioned on a single station: dim patter and songs from the twilight of the race. Val twirled the knob, found static, and spun it back. Herman's Hermits, girl groups, "Under the Boardwalk." She settled back, let her head rest, and moments later seemed asleep.

"I'm not," she said when I pulled in at the cabin. "Almost, but not quite. Drifting . . ." She turned towards me. Green eyes opened and found mine.

We went inside.

"Whoa, why do I feel I'm walking right into someone's head?"

"Things had gotten way too complicated. I wanted them as simple as they could get."

Old wooden kitchen table by the window, a single chair. Bed across from it—little more than a cot, really. Shirts and pants on hangers hanging from nails in the wall. Stacks of T-shirts, socks and underwear stowed under the cot. Basin and pitcher on the counter. (Pump just outside.) Toothbrush and razor laid out there. Books in undisturbed stacks along the back wall.

I popped the cork on the wine, one of those new plastic ones, and suggested we sit on the porch.

"Maybe I should hold out for jelly glasses."

"And potted meat on toast points."

The low, indefinable susurrus that's a part of living in the woods sounded around us. Always that or dead silence, it seemed. Far off, something screamed once, a spear thrown into the night. We watched a silhouette, possibly two some-things, cross the moon.

"The world's a shithole, isn't it?"

I reached for the bottle on the floor by my chair and freshened our drinks. An Australian wine, 1.5 liters. We would run out of conversation before we ran out of wine. Picture of a koala on the label, an endangered species. As though we all aren't.

"Except for music," she added.

Then, after a moment: "I don't know if it's myself or the job anymore. Seems whatever door I open, I don't like what's in there."

She held out her glass for more wine.

"You remember that night we sat out on my porch, hardly talking, with the night so quiet around us?"

I nodded.

"I think about that a lot," she said.

Chapter Thirty

NOT MANY SHIFTS GO that way. Most of them, you hit the street already behind, dance cards filling faster than you're able to keep track of. We spent the biggest part of that one rattling doors and doing slow drags down alleys. Had no calls for better than two hours, and when we finally got one it was a see-the-lady that turned out to be about a missing husband. We were twenty minutes into the call and halfway done taking a report when her response to a routine question stopped me in my tracks, follow-up questions eliciting the information that the man had died ten years ago.

Back in the squad, I sat shaking my head.

"What?" Randy asked.

"That one."

Randy glanced over as I pulled away from the curb.

"You notice the open kitchen window?" he said. "Saucer of milk on the sill?"

I admitted I hadn't.

"Woman's lonely, that's all. So lonely that everything in her life takes on the shape of her loneliness."

The next call was to a convenience store where the owner-proprietor supposedly had a shoplifter in custody. He'd taken a jump rope off one of the shelves and tied the shoplifter to it after a baseball bat to the thigh brought him down. But while he was on the phone, the shoplifter had chewed through the rope and gone hobbling out the door.

Nothing else, then, for some time. It was one of those clear, still nights that seem to have twice as many stars as ordinary, when sounds reach you from far away. We grabbed burgers at Lucky Jim's and ate at a picnic table outside East High, squad pulled up alongside with doors open, radio crackling. You didn't eat Lucky Jim burgers in the car. And you didn't need extra napkins, you needed bath towels.

Randy seemed to be doing okay. He'd moved out of the house, put it up for sale, found an apartment near downtown. He was hitting the gym at least three times a week, even talked about signing up for some classes. In what? I asked. Whatever fits with my work schedule, he said.

Three obviously stoned college-age kids were having their own meal, consisting mainly of bags of candy, potato chips, orange soda and Dr Pepper, nearby. They packed up and left not long after we arrived. Two people just as obviously on the street sat beneath a maple tree. The man wore a Confederate cap from which a bandanna depended, draping the back of his neck and bringing to mind all those movies about the Foreign Legion I watched in my youth. The woman had gone on trying gamely to look as good as possible. She'd hacked sleeves from a T-shirt whose logo and silkscreen photo had long since faded and cut it off just above the waistline. Rolled pant legs showed shapely if long- and much-abused calves. "You know that bugs me!" the man shouted towards the end of our stay. She sprang to her feet and started away. "Why you wanna be doing that?" he said, then after a moment got up and followed.

Though we were talking and continued to do so, Randy turned to watch the man go, I remember, and in that moment of inattention a compound of grease, grilled onion and mustard fell onto his uniform top, just south-southwest of his badge. We kept bottles of club soda in the squad for such situations, just as we kept half-gallons of Coke, useful for cleaning battery terminals and removing blood from accident scenes. But in this case the club soda lost, serving only to create concentric rings around the original stain.

We pulled out of the lot. Traffic was light.

"You give much thought to what we'll be when we grow up?" Randy said. "I mean, here we are, top detectives, still jumping patrol calls. That sound like a life to you?"

"We like patrol calls. It's our choice."

"Is it?"

When the radio sounded ten minutes later, we looked at one another and laughed. Randy was asking if I'd consider accompanying him to temple that Sabbath.

"You've been going to temple? When did that start?"

"You know when it started."

"And it's okay for me to be there?"

We pulled up at 102-A Birch Street, a duplex in a

recently fashionable part of town. Property values had rocketed here. Years later they'd coin a word for what was going on: gentrification. Bulldozers plowed the ground from first light to last, crunching homes, garage-size commercial shops and early strip malls underfoot, making way for new crops.

"You okay?" I remember asking Randy. He'd made no move to get out of the squad.

"Fine," he said. "Just not sure I can do this."

"Do what?"

"Never mind." He swung legs out and stood, with a two-handed maneuver I'd gotten to know well, smoothed down hair and put on his hat in a single sweep. "Forget I said anything."

Wary and watchful as always, we went up the walk to the front door. Several adjacent houses, though well cared for, seemed unoccupied, as did the other half of the duplex. Drapes behind a picture window at the house next door moved. Probably the person who'd called in, monitoring his or her tax dollars at work.

"Mind taking point on this one?" Randy said.

"Nottingham, huh?"

Police superstition. Back sometime in the 1950s, a squad answering a routine call according to procedure had eased up the walk just like us and knocked, only to be answered by a shotgun blast through the front door. The point man, Nottingham, went down, and died in the hospital six days later. His partner, a rookie, did all the right things. Checked pulse and respiration, went off to call in an Officer Down, came back to pack his partner's wounds.

Then he kicked in the door and took the perp down with his nightstick. After that, though, after that one perfect moment when he became, incarnate, what he was *supposed* to be, when the training flowed through him like a living force, the rookie was never again able to take to the streets. He tried once or twice, they said; then worked a few years more, filing, keeping track of office supplies, manning the evidence room, before he packed it in.

"I've got your back," Randy said.

"Not my back I'm worried about."

The door was answered by a half-dressed man whose eyes raked over uniform, badge, side arm and equipment belt before settling on my face. Then a secondary, dismissive glance at Randy behind me. From deep inside the house, echoing as in a cave, the sound of a TV. Something else as well?

"Sorry to bother you, sir," I said, "but we've had a report of a domestic disturbance at this address." Going on for hours, the caller said. "Mind if we come in?"

"Well . . ."

"I'm sure there's nothing to it. Do have to ask a few routine questions, though. Won't take more than three, four minutes of your time, I promise."

He rubbed his face. "I was asleep."

"Yes, sir. Most people are, this time of night. We understand that."

He backed out of the doorway. I followed into the room. Randy stayed just inside the door. He had yet to speak.

"Someone called, you said?"

"Yes, sir."

"Jeez, I'm sorry. Must have been the TV. My wife has trouble sleeping."

"Yeah, that's probably it."

"Your wife?" Randy said.

"Could we speak to her?" I asked.

"She just got to sleep, Officer. Sure would hate to have to wake her now."

"Please." This time I didn't smile.

He led us down three broad steps from the entryway, across a tiled living room the size of a skating rink, and along a narrow hallway into a small room adjoining the kitchen. Wood-paneled walls, single window set high, cotton rugs scattered about on a floor of bare concrete. Not much here but a couple of chairs and a console TV. A conical green TV lamp sat atop the console—these had just started showing up. The vacant chair was a recliner. The occupied one was an overstuffed armchair, ambiguously greenish brown, and nubbly, like period bedspreads.

The woman in that chair, wrapped in a tiger-pattern throw, makes no response when I speak to her.

"She's not well," the man says. "She's . . . disturbed. Look at her now. An hour ago she was screaming and beating at me. Walking through the house slamming doors."

"So it wasn't the TV after all."

He shook his head.

"Sounds like you need to get her some help, sir."

"She has plenty of help. I'm the one who doesn't." His eyes go from his wife to me. "Mostly she's up at the state hospital, has been for years now. Home on a pass."

Randy comes around me, sinking to one knee. Presses

two fingers against the woman's carotid. "Honey, you okay?" he says, but it doesn't register with me at the time what he's saying.

And afterwards it takes me a long time to understand what happened here.

The half-dressed guy steps forward, out of the shadow. His hand comes up. Something in it? Randy thinks so. He draws his side arm, stands, shouts at the man to drop the weapon and get down on the floor, hands behind his head. What the man has in his hand is a syringe. The woman's diabetic, we learn later. He walks towards her.

Glancing at Randy, shouting *No!* I see what is about to happen and I don't think about it, I react, just as trained.

"What—" Randy says, as I draw and fire. I intend only to stop him, take out the shoulder or arm, but you're taught to go for the trunk, the larger target, and I'm not in the driver's seat this time out, I'm on auto.

Randy goes down.

At first he's conscious, though rapidly heading into shock. I kick the S&W away from his hand, kneel beside him to check pulse and respiration. I'm sorry, I tell him. I go back out to the squad and call in an Officer Down, request a second response unit for the woman. When I get inside again, something's happened, something's gone even more wrong. Blood is pooling all around Randy and his breath comes in jagged bursts, like rags torn from a sheet. I slip out of my sportcoat, take off my shirt and fold it into a compress, hold it against the wound. Almost at once the shirt is saturated with blood. I push harder, hold on harder. My arms quiver and begin to cramp. The shirt darkens. His breathing quietens. Lots less blood now. I tell him again that I'm sorry.

Two or three minutes before the paramedics arrive, Randy dies.

As I said, it took me a long time to understand what had happened here. Turned out Randy knew the place. That's why he reacted the way he did when we first pulled up curbside. Doreen had worked with the guy who lived here, stayed with him for a while after she left Randy, had a brief affair. She'd long since moved on, but Randy was never convinced of that. All these months when I'd been thinking he was getting past Doreen, getting his life back together, he'd been spending much of his off time parked down the street.

The woman in the chair wasn't Doreen, of course. But she looked a lot like her. And to Randy's overloaded mind in that moment of crisis, I guess, in those final moments of his life, somehow she became Doreen. Lying there, looking up, it wasn't me but Doreen that he saw. He lifted a hand as though to caress her face. Then the hand fell.

I saw her, the actual Doreen, looking not much better than I felt, five days later at the funeral. She wore a blue dress. Bracelets jangled as she raised her arm to brush hair back from her face. We told each other how sorry we were, how much we missed him. We said we should keep in touch.

For her it was a promise. Twice a week in prison I'd receive chatty letters from her. They were penned in violet ink on four-by-six-inch lavender pages folded in half and filled with news of new neighbors, newborn children, new stores and malls. She persisted in this for almost a year, heroically, before giving up.

Chapter Thirty-One

THE OFFICE WAS EMPTY, though unlocked. Remembering all those hollow, echoing buildings and streets in *On the Beach*, which I'd seen at the impressionable age of fourteen (after which I'd read everything of Nevil Shute's the local library had), I found Lonnie and Don Lee at the diner.

"Out to lunch, huh? Maybe you should just move the sign over here. Sheriff's Office. Hang it up by the daily specials."

"More like breakfast for you, way it looks," Don Lee said. "Just get up?"

"Yeah. Nightlife around here's a killer."

"You get used to the pace."

Thelma materialized beside the booth. "What'll it be?"

I asked for coffee.

"You people come in at the same time, sure would make my life easier." She shrugged. "Lot you care." She slapped a check down by me. "And why the hell should you, for that matter? Rest of you want anything? Or you gonna wait, so's I have to make three trips instead of one?"

"We're fine," Lonnie said.

"For now."

Thelma walked off shaking her head.

"You're both on duty? Where's June?"

"We are," Don Lee said.

"And June's on her way down to Tupelo, best we know." Lonnie glanced out the window, voice like his gaze directed over my shoulder. "Looks like that's where he went once he cut out of here."

"Shit."

"Pretty much the way we feel about it, too," Don Lee said.

Thelma set a cup of coffee by the ticket she'd slapped down moments before. When I thanked her, she might as well have been stuck by a pin.

"I know I have to leave her alone, let her work this out on her own," Lonnie said. "We talked about that. Best I could do is make it worse."

Right.

"You get your message?"

I hadn't.

"Val Bjorn. Says for you to call her."

"Results of the forensics must be in."

"Probably not that. We got those late yesterday."

"And?"

"Not much there."

"There's a copy for you at the office."

I drank my coffee, called Val only to learn from her assistant Jamie (male? female? impossible to say) that she was in court. She bounced my call back around six P.M.

"Hungry?" Val said.

"I could be."

"Think you can find your way to my house?"

"I'll strap on bow and arrow now. Call for a mule."

"Thank God it's not prom night or they'd all be taken."

"Mostly surfing the Internet," I told her not long after, leaning against the kitchen table, nursing a glass of white wine so dry I might as well have bitten into a persimmon. She'd asked how I spent my afternoon. "You wouldn't believe how many Web sites are devoted to movies. Horror films, noir, science fiction. Someone made a movie about garbagemen who are really aliens and live off eating what they collect, which they consider a delicacy. There's a whole Web site about it."

Val tossed ears of corn into boiling water.

"This isn't cooking, mind you," she said.

"Okay."

"I'm not cooking for you."

"Your intentions are pure."

"I didn't cook the salad either."

"Wow. Tough crowd."

"You think I'm a crowd?"

"Aren't we all?"

"I guess."

"How'd court go?"

"Like a glacier." She bent to lower the flame under the

corn and cover the pot. "I'm representing a sixteen-year-old boy who's petitioning the court for emancipation. He's Mormon—parents are, anyway. The defense attorney has put every single member of his family and the local Mormon community, all two dozen of them, on the stand so far. And the judge goes on allowing it, in the face of all my objections of irrelevance. Courthouse looks like a bus stand."

"They love him."

"Damn right they do. You know anything at all about LDS, you know how important family is to them. They don't want to lose the boy—personally *or* spiritually."

"He has some way to support himself?"

"An Internet mail-order business he created. All Your Spiritual Needs—everything from menorahs to Islam prayer rugs. Netted a quarter million last year."

"Has different ideas, obviously."

"He's not a believer. Even in capitalism, as far as I can tell. It's all about pragmatism, I think. He wanted a way out, independence, and that looked good for it. Much of the profit from the company goes back to the very family he's trying to escape."

"Interesting contradiction."

"Is it? Contradictions imply we've embraced some overarching generality. They're the ash left over once those generalities burn down. Particular, individual lives are another thing entirely."

She was right, of course.

"He have much chance of getting the emancipation?"

Val shrugged. "I don't seem to have much idea how *anything's* going to go these days. This dinner, for instance."

"The one you're not cooking."

"Right."

Later, having smeared ears of corn with butter, salt and pepper and chins unintentionally with same, having stoked away, as well, quantities of iceberg lettuce, radish, fresh tomato and red onion dribbled upon by vinegar and olive oil, we sat on Val's porch in darkness relieved only by the wickerwork of light falling through trees from a high, pale moon.

"Back when you were on the streets, you thought you were doing good, right?"

"Sure I did."

"And as a therapist?"

I nodded.

"Still believe that?"

"Yes."

"But you stopped."

"I did. But not because of some existential crisis."

Sitting in the pecan tree, an owl lifted head off shoulders to rotate it a hundred and eighty degrees. Country musician Gid Tanner, with whom Riley Puckett played, was supposed to have been able to do that.

"When I was sixteen, my dad took me to buy my first car. We found a '48 Buick we both liked. Some awful purplish color, as I remember, and they'd put in plastic seats like something from a diner. Car itself was in pretty good shape. But the fenders were banged all to hell, you could see where they'd been hammered back out from underneath, more than once. I was looking for something bright and shiny, naturally, and those fenders bothered me. My father'd been a bit more thoroughgoing, actually checked out the engine and frame. 'It's a good car, J. C.,' he said. 'Just old—like me. Fenders are the first to go.'

"Later that's how I came to see people. The parts that are out there, between you and the world as you move into it, those parts sustain the most damage. Fenders wear out. Doesn't mean there's anything wrong, intrinsically, with the car. The engine may still be perfectly good—even the body."

"Tell me we're not out of wine."

I handed my glass across. Good half-inch left in there.

"We are, aren't we?" She finished it off, set the glass beside her own. "All day long I sat there looking at Aaron. Fans thwacking overhead. Was I helping him—or only further complicating a life that was complicated enough already?"

"You still want to fix things."

"Yes," she said. "I guess I do."

"You can't."

"I guess I know that, too."

"Ever tell you I was once half a step away from being an English professor?"

"One of your earlier nine lives, I take it."

"Exactly. I loved Chaucer, Old English, Elizabethan drama. Read them the way other people watch soap operas and sitcoms, or eat popcorn. Christopher Fry was a favorite.

"I expect they would tell us the soul can be as lost,
For loving-kindness as anything else.
Well, well, we must scramble for grace as best we can."

"That's what we're doing? Scrambling for grace?"

"For footholds, anyway. Definitely scrambling."

"And what does grace look like?"

"Hell if I know."

Chapter Thirty-Two

BUT I SUSPECTED it looked much like my face the morning I decided on exemption.

A sleepless night had filled with the gas of random, skittering thoughts and old memories. Around two A.M. I'd watched *The Incredible Shrinking Man* on TV. Went back to bed afterwards, tossed and turned to the accompaniment of Sibelius's First Symphony on the radio and the giant spider that chased me across roof- and tabletops and through a maze of high-school lockers, was up again at five with a cup of cooling, neglected coffee cradled like a Jacob's ladder in my hands, watching long-haul trucks take on cargo across the street. Soon they'd strike out for the new world.

Brian's last message (*Wonderful evening, thank you*) shimmered in my mind. Jimmie the Machine had been found lying on a bench in the park, eyes staring upward into bright sun, pigeons pecking at bare toes. No discernible cause of death revealed by autopsy. That very day a new patient told me how he'd killed a teacher he disliked. What I saw before me was a defeated fifty-year-old man with tonsure, strands of hair clinging limpetlike to his skull, tattoos like a carpet pattern long since faded. What I heard was a teenager who'd never got over being shut out.

Complex creatures fueled by knowledge, understanding and passion—that's how we like to see ourselves. Meanwhile, psychiatry insists we're little more than machines of a sort, broken toys to be mended. Some simple spring or swivel in the mind fails to work right, we jam, give up, misfire. Ask any child advocate. Nine times out of ten, the kid's been abused. Nothing recondite about it. Most of the rest is just smoke and mirrors.

Speaking of mirrors, that morning, looking into one, I saw something I'd not seen before. It didn't last, but for the moment it was there, I recognized it for what it was. Grace, of a sort. Wherever it was I had been heading all these years, I'd arrived. I had simply to off-load cargo now.

The divestment took most of a month. Clients, I passed along selectively to students from my seminars at Memphis State. These were working therapists, many with far more professional experience, if not more personal, than myself. Licensure requires continuing education credits. Bulwarked by such courses as Statistics for Health Care Providers and Personifications of the Other in Interpersonal Relationships, my own had long proved a popular choice.

Practical affairs—the apartment lease, notification of clients and service providers, packing—presented little difficulty. I possessed, still, the inmate's habit of simplicity;

had few ties and little of a material sort that couldn't be tucked under wing and taken along or freely abandoned.

That left Susan.

I had had my mind set against any relationship. Bad for me, worse for whoever sat at the other end of the teeter-totter, probably wouldn't do much good for the world at large. Likely to bring on biblical floods, eras of ice, swarms of locusts, for all I knew. Yet there I was, in a relationship, albeit a halting, tentative one. Coming off a horrendous fifteen-year marriage she'd barely survived psychologically, not to mention physically, Susan trod the eggshell court as lightly as did I.

"This prosciutto's amazing," Susan said.

Our favorite restaurant, just around the corner from her studio apartment, restaurant and apartment much of a size. Waitress a six-footer in miniskirt, tube top and platform sandals stumbling from table to table, dark lines drawn about eyes and mouth as though to hold them in place. Hard to imagine her anywhere else. Where in the larger world could this vision possibly fit?

Susan tucked into the restaurant's signature appetizer of melon and prosciutto as I nursed a second espresso. Entrees of pasta with sausage and sauteed spinach, pasta with salmon and asparagus, were forthcoming. We'd brought our own wine.

"You're making another of your sudden turns, aren't you?"

I hadn't even to tell her. She knew.

"I suppose I am."

"That's okay."

Outside, rain broke, sweeping across the parking lot, left to right, like the edge of a hand brushing debris from a tabletop.

"I half expected it, you know," she said. "More than half, at first. But I still had hopes."

Remember the limbo? One dances beneath a pole set lower and lower. That's hope. Only every year the pole goes further up, not down.

"You'll still have them. I'm not taking those with me."

Brought to our table by the owner of the restaurant himself, our entrees arrived. Susan sat quietly as these were put before us, waited as another swing to kitchen and back cast a basket of bread on the shore.

"Yes," she said then. "You are."

Chapter Thirty-Three

"WE'RE HEADING HOME," Sarah Hazelwood said. "I need to get back to my job while I still have one. Dad's okay here, but he does best with people he knows, familiar surroundings. Doc Oldham says there's no problem having Carl's body shipped home. I wanted to stop by and thank you for all you've done."

Through the window I could see her father propped up in the van's back seat. The sliding door was open, and Adrienne, willowy, protecting, ranged alongside. Something of both shade tree and sentinel in the way she stood there.

"I'm sorry we haven't been able to clear this up."

"You will. And when you do, you can reach me here." Handing over a sheet of paper with multiple addresses, phone and fax numbers.

I'd been saying I'm sorry a lot of late.

"Why?" Susan had responded that night at Giuseppe's. "You've nothing to be sorry for. I made the choices that brought me here."

"You're not responsible for Jimmie's death, or for Brian's," a therapist I'd briefly engaged back in Memphis told me. "You know that as well as I do. So why are you apologizing? More to the point, why are you here?"

"*Then*'s ancient history," Lonnie said. "Might as well be the Peloponnesian Wars, Penelope's suitors. Sure they're important, sure they matter. Meanwhile your coffee's getting cold and the warm-blooded person you're supposed to be having dinner with is waiting for you."

Meanwhile, as well, two videocassettes had arrived via FedEx from a specialty store in California. I'd been alerted to their presence by a phone call from Mel Goldman. One purported to be a rough cut of *The Giving*, the other a weird documentary sort of thing put together by some precocious high-school kid in the Midwest, incorporating clips from BR's films and Sammy Cash's appearances elsewhere. The latter was heavy on science fiction, gangster and prison films, including episodes from a fourteen-part serial about a blind man who, "to bring the slate to balance," had been given supernatural powers by "the Queen of Morning." Since I didn't have credit cards, Lonnie let me use his to order copies. The vendor tacked on a healthy fee for express delivery.

I had to borrow a TV and VCR too, from Val this time, but once I had them, those tapes ran continuously. I'd wander out to the kitchen to make a sandwich or brew coffee, return in time to see the blind man lift his cane to halt a school bus as it skewed towards a cliff; step out onto the porch for air and back through the screen door to images of gigantic Sammy Cash, victim of an atomic blast, on a picnic with minuscule nurse-girlfriend Carla; take a brief turn through the woods and come back to that strange beginning of *The Giving*.

It's the crucifixion, the killing, everyone talks about, and the image is a strong one—even if it makes little sense in light of the rest of the movie. In fact, that salutary scene appears to have been added at the last moment. Perhaps when funds were exhausted? When the movie had to be brought to some kind of end, at any rate. By contrast, the early part of the film fairly drips with atmosphere, connection, portent. A man walks down the streets of a city. To either side, almost off camera, we glimpse what life is like for most of those who live here. Dark-eyed, ragged children stand in alley shadows waiting. Women in doorways open blouses to exhibit wilted breasts. Sleepers, or perhaps they are only bodies, lie alongside buildings and in ditches running with excrement. Dogs drink from the ditches and eat from the bodies. Carrion birds wheel above, waiting their turn.

The man sees or registers little of any of this. For him it's daily life. He has purpose, a destination, sweeps through it all. Farther along he passes the window of an apartment behind whose bars a couple sits having afternoon tea and watching TV. The sound track, which to this point has consisted solely of footsteps, growls and horrible slurpings, now echoes the TV inside.

In breaking news, the territory's governor vows to pursue reelection from his prison cell. "I did nothing wrong," he declaimed in today's press conference, shortly before asking reporters for cigarettes. . . .

. . . On the international front, fifty thousand ground troops were put ashore on Ayatollah Beach around noon today. The invasion force, which was supposed to have struck at dawn, had been given inaccurate coordinates.

The man is, as it turns out, a detective. He goes into a bar.

"What can I do for you, friend?" the guy behind the bar says. Hair missing from his head is made up for by that growing out of nose and ears.

"Scotch. Whatever's cheap."

The barkeep pours. "Then you've come to the right place. It's all cheap."

Friend grabs hold of the barkeep's wrist.

"Hey, no problem. I can leave the bottle."

"Ice Lady been in today?"

"Who?"

"Cowboy?"

There's a long hold, these two guys with eyes locked as the world, such as it's become, goes on behind and beyond. A young woman in jeans and T-shirt hacked off well above the navel dances alone. Sharp points of her breasts come into focus and the barkeep pours a new Scotch just as we cut to another, seemingly unrelated scene. Then another.

Did these disparate, disjunctive scenes comprise a movie, comprise even the bare outline of one? Were the abrupt cuts and sudden changes (as though the film had constantly to reinvent itself) in fact part of some inchoate aesthetic weave, ultimately unrealized—or simply what happened when some kid in Iowa fancifully patched together snippets and snatches of film?

Finally, the rough cut of *The Giving* and the documentary were birds of a feather. Neither made much sense narratively, both failed to provide much by way of vertical motion while attempting to camouflage this with horizontal busyness. They were jottings, notes, scrapbooks, diary entries, letters to the editor, casual conversation, junk sculpture.

Two things about them stuck, though.

In the documentary, from internal evidence of the films, much was made of twin theses that BR had to be a southerner, and that the films were in fact collaborations between the director and Sammy Cash.

Then the other.

I came back from the kitchen with new ice in a glass of freshly poured, very old Scotch. I'd started the cassette of *The Giving* again before I left; as I reentered the room, credits were running. Ordinarily I'd have paid no attention. Until the movie began in earnest, I wasn't really watching. But a glance brought me up short with the glass halfway to my face, staring at the screen.

Listed as producer was H. L. "Bubba" Sims.

Chapter Thirty-Four

"IT WAS MAYBE nine years back, driest season we'd had in a long time. You could sit out on the porch listening to limbs crack and fall, shingles on roofs curl in the heat. Fires had started up in the woods just east and started moving in. Oaks, elms, pines, they all went up like flares. Thought sure we were gonna have to evacuate the town.

"There was this kid over to the funeral home had been there seventy, eighty years, everyone'd taken to calling him Mojo. He'd fallen, jumped or got pushed from a train. Presented with a bill for $108, the family said, 'You all can keep him.' So he got kept, mummified, coffin leaning up in the corner of the back room. Funeral home was sold, Mojo went with it. Poker players'd drag him out each week for luck, prop him up by the table.

"But when it looked like the town was going under, they decided Mojo had to be given a proper burial. Been waiting since 1920, mind you. But they dragged him out, found a clear spot and put him under.

"The fire was maybe four miles outside town when the rains started up. They went on for a week or more. Everything was sodden. Afterwards they never could find where they'd put Mojo in the ground. Old Man Lanningham claimed he hadn't won a hand of poker since."

Lonnie grinned at me across the top of his coffee mug.

"Don't know why I'm remembering that now."

June called the night before, he'd told me. She was on her way home. That son of a bitch was history.

"So, what do we do about this?" Lonnie said.

"I was thinking the best thing'd be to go out to the house."

"Without calling ahead."

"Yes."

"Henry Lee won't much like that."

I shrugged.

"Here I thought no one could keep secrets in a town this size, and Henry Lee turns out to be a Hollywood wheel."

"A small one. Something on the order of a training wheel—if I'm right."

Lonnie levered the mug onto his desk and stood in a single motion, fishing out keys.

"No sense putting it off, then."

Mayor Sims answered the door in a bathrobe.

"Like to get an early start, do you, Henry Lee?"

"Why don't you give it a rest, Lonnie? Better yet, why don't you go do something worthwhile, like shining those damn boots of yours."

"Think they need it?"

"What I think they need is throwing out. Don't suppose you even had the decency to stop and get coffee on the way?"

"Sorry."

Sims ran a hand through thinning hair. "I was at the nursing home all night. Dorothy's taken a turn for the worse. Started having trouble breathing around ten o'clock."

"Sorry to hear that. She okay?"

"Stable—for the time being, anyway. She's on a breathing machine. Just for a day or two, they tell me, just to give her some temporary support. Doctor taking care of her looks to be about fourteen. Has a diamond stud in one ear, probably comes to work on a skateboard."

"Anything I can do?"

"Not very damn much, aside from telling me why the hell you're out here this time of day."

I don't figure Lonnie'd ever played tennis in his life, let alone doubles, but his instincts were good, and he fell back. This lob was mine.

"I asked you before if you'd come across a filmmaker known as BR."

"And I told you I hadn't."

"Even though you're listed as producer of his last film."

Mayor Sims sat gazing out the window. At porch's edge, by a red-and-yellow feeder looking like some child's crayoned notion of a flower, three hummingbirds did their version of a Mexican standoff.

"There aren't any copies of that movie," he said.

Should he have added: I saw to that? I didn't ask.

"There's a rough cut someone managed to patch together. It doesn't make much sense."

"Believe me, it never did."

Lonnie spoke up. "We need to know what's going on, Henry Lee. What this is all about."

"I understand."

We sat silently as the hummers outside the window went on squabbling. Ferocious little beasts. Fearless. To the east, above a stand of maples, pillowy white clouds, cumulonimbus, began gathering.

"You two feel up for a longish ride?"

"Whatever it takes," Lonnie said.

"Give me a minute. I need to call in to the nursing home, see about Dorothy. Then I'll grab some clothes and we can be on our way."

• • •

JUST SHORT OF TWO HOURS LATER, having traversed a patchwork of narrow-lane roads through thick stands of oak and evergreen, kudzu and honeysuckle at roadside everywhere, we reached our destination. Mayor Sims and Lonnie sat in front speaking of inconsequential things, how new kids were doing on the football team, rumors of a Kmart, shorter hours at the city dump. Hardly cabbages and kings. Either because he didn't care or from some design to look like trendy folk he saw on TV, Sims wore a sport coat over black T-shirt. I sat on the cramped, shelflike back seat. The radio was on low, a call-in show of some sort. Responding to an impassioned statement on world poverty, today's authority explained that the problem lay in those societies failing to "incentivize" people to go out and "live creatively." Listening to Authority's voice, I mused again that it's not so much accent as rhythm that gives us away. Where stresses fall, the momentum towards sentence's end, pauses on nouns or verbs.

"Take this next right," Sims said. We'd come onto an oasislike eruption of buildings. Service station, feed store, garage. All of them seemed to be still up and running. Maggie's Café, despite promises of $1.98 breakfasts and daily $2.95 specials painted on the windows, didn't.

"Now left." Bearing us into an unsuspected town.

The first house, built to quarter-scale on antebellum models and set back from the road, was now a real estate agency. Two chairs would be a tight fit on the gallery. Next to it sat Mercer Mortuary, inhabiting, to all appearances, what had once been a church. Across the street, a convenience store, Manny's, with a single gas pump out front. A grill made from a fifty-gallon drum cut in half and hinged, legs welded on, stood to one side under the overhang. Then came a long stretch of wooden houses set among trees, several with turrets or wraparound galleries.

We pulled into the shell driveway of a tan two-story with dark brown roof and trim whose elaborate gingerbread made me remember a trip to the Ozarks my family took when I was ten or so and the jigsaw with which, a year or so later, my father duplicated the boomerang I'd mail-ordered. On the first throw it had crashed against the garage and broken; I was devastated. My father fished a scrap of wood from a box of same, laid the broken pieces on top and made a new one. He used that same saw, and the band saw next to it, to make much of the furniture in the sprawling room we called the den. This was back before he turned into a piece of furniture himself—leaving my sister to take care of the family.

There was also the smell of figs. As a child, four years old maybe (couldn't have been much more, since Mom was gone the next year), I'd fallen from a fig tree in which I was climbing, had the breath knocked from me, and staggered onto the back porch where I lay gasping. Mom swept from the house, apron over print dress, hands white with flour, crying Help him! My father took one look and knew what had happened. He'll be all right, just give him a moment. Looks kinda like a fish, doesn't he?

The door was answered by a man wearing, I swear (I'd never seen one before, outside of movies), a smoking jacket. Dapper indeed, even if upon closer inspection the jacket's felt proved to be worn smooth, the tie beneath to be spotted with historic fluids and foodstuff. And while the glass in his hand held milk rather than a martini, the effect was much the same.

Actually, I later learned, it wasn't milk but something called a milk punch compounded of bourbon, milk and sugar. Easy on the ulcers, he'd tell me.

"Bubba!" this apparition said, blinking at the light. "What an absolutely marvelous surprise!" Heavy stress on *marvelous*, tiptoe pauses before and after. "And you've brought friends!"

"How's it going, Billy?"

"Please do come in. Come in, come in. All of you."

Ushered into a lavender living room, we stood there like de-bused campers uncertain what was expected of us. Purple vases, cobalt pitchers and violet-hued glasses sat about. Still-life paintings featuring bowls of fruit and fresh game, in the classical style but obviously new, hung on two walls. Above a mauve leather couch, the massive photograph of an erect penis, blown up to such point and such graininess as to become almost abstract, took pride of place above a mauve leather couch. On the opposite wall hung a poster of women's vaginas, like exotic fruit.

"We have *com*pany?" a voice piped from above.

"Henry Lee. And friends."

"Oh." Disappointment audible in the voice.

"What can I get you all? Perhaps some champagne? Always a couple bottles chilling in the fridge. One never knows who might drop by, what possibilities for celebration the day could bring. Or mimosas! We've a sack of some of the biggest, juiciest oranges you're likely to see. From last weekend's farmer's market on the square?"

"Billy, this is Sheriff Bates. Mr. Turner's a detective down from Memphis."

"Oh, I love Memphis."

"I know you do."

"Good to meet you, Billy," Lonnie said.

Our eyes met, Billy's and mine, and we shook hands. His was surprisingly warm, his grip firm.

"Coffee sounds good," Lonnie went on, "if it's not too much trouble. Little early for anything else, for me."

"We have that. Coffee. Out in the kitchen somewhere."

He'd set his milk punch on a polished ebony table just inside the door, African origin from the look of it, in order to embrace Sims. Now he looked longingly towards it. So far away. He went to the base of the stairs and called weakly upwards: "Help!"

"Be right down."

"Sit, sit," our host said. "We don't often get company."

Lonnie glanced at Sims, who nodded.

"Something I need to ask you, Mr. Sims."

"Actually it's Roark. Henry Lee and I had different fathers. But please call me Billy."

"Billy, then. You used to direct movies, right?"

"That was a long time ago. All the sweet silly birds of our youth, surely they've flown by now. Mine have, at any rate. Yours?"

Lonnie smiled. "Occasionally they still come home to roost. When they do, I try to make sure they get fed."

"Good for you. Speaking of which: I haven't served you all yet, have I? I really should attend to that." After gazing out the window for a moment, he went on. "It was a much smaller world back then. Everything was simpler. You had this feeling anything was possible—anything at all. I think I fancied myself a modern Shakespeare, half-owner of the Globe and running it, directing and acting in the very plays I wrote. I could do it all, create my *own* world. Create and inhabit it."

"He hasn't seen or thought of those movies in years. They have nothing to do with who he is now. You should not be bringing this in here, into our home. You know that, Henry."

All our heads turned to the source of the voice.

Sammy Cash stood at the foot of the stairs.

Chapter Thirty-Five

HE WORE LOOSE KHAKI SLACKS, a pink oxford-cloth shirt from which the left collar button was missing, oxblood loafers, possibly Italian, without socks.

"Billy's offered refreshments, I assume?"

"He did. But then he kind of got off track."

"He does that. I won't say it's good to see you, Henry, it never is. Who are these people you've brought?"

"I'm the sheriff who answers to Henry Lee," Lonnie said. "Mr. Turner here is a consultant, helping me with an investigation. No reason you'd know this, but someone's driven murder right up on our steps and parked it there."

"In which case you should be off doing your job."

Lonnie glanced down at sockless feet, up to the missing button.

"I appreciate the fact this is your home, sir," he said, "and that I'm an intruder here."

Cash nodded.

"What *you* have to appreciate is that this is a murder

investigation. Statutes give me a lot of latitude. Take me about eight seconds flat, for instance, to have you down on that polished wood floor in cuffs."

"Lonnie, surely—"

"You shut the fuck up too, Henry. Obstruction of justice's a big door. Don't make me open it."

"Oh dear," Billy said.

Lonnie sat beside him on the mauve couch. He'd snagged the milk punch on the way, and handed it to him. "I agree completely. Now." He looked from face to face. Mayor Sims, Billy Roark, the man we only knew as Sammy Cash. "Who's going to tell me what happened?"

*   *   *

BILLY ROARK was fourteen years older than Henry Lee, out of the house and gone by the time Henry Lee was coming up, but always a role model—for that very reason if for no other. Because he'd reached escape velocity, you see, escaped the drag of the town they'd both grown up in, left behind the broken, near-mute mother and the fathers, gentle but long absent in Billy's case, violent in Henry Lee's. Billy Roark had gone up to Memphis at age nineteen and bluffed his way into selling furniture at Lowenstein's. Third day on the job he sold a houseful of it, a whole goddamn houseful, prime quality all, to an older, balding man and a magnificently stacked young blond. A runner was sent to the bank with the check and came back to report it was good. "I could use a man like you," the customer told him. A week later Billy found himself in a bright red Fairlane, coursing between El Paso and Dallas, flogging movies to drive-ins and main-street theaters with names like Malco and Paramount. He was a natural, able to turn on a dime, become whatever the customer seemed to expect of him. Theatre owners loved him and took whatever he had to offer. Soon a Cadillac replaced the Fairlane—a used Cadillac, and one day in of all places Fate, Texas, Pop. 1400, it broke down. Not much to do in Fate. He had breakfast at Mindy's Diner, lunch there a few hours later. Then he found himself at the Palace watching a film about a woman's prison. Jesus, he thought, *this* is what I've been selling? It was awful. He sat there watching, running numbers in his head. Obviously he was at the wrong end of the business. By six P.M., when he drove out of Fate with a new distributor cap and fuel pump, into a blood-red sunset, he'd blocked out what he was going to do. He found a place he could rent cameras, lights, the whole works, then some kids at a local college who'd been doing stage plays and figured how different could it be. Talked his current girl-friend, Sally Ann of the dirigible, gravity-defying breasts, into starring. Then over a weekend in a motel in New Braunfels, cartons of cigarettes, bags of hamburgers and bottles of Scotch ever to hand, not to mention Sally Ann, he roughed out a script. *Devil Women of Mars.* And it had, by God, every-thing. Scenes of small-town American life. Long shots of empty Arizona sky. Suspense. A message. Cleavage. Butts pushed up intriguingly by high-heel silver boots. When Billy drove out of New Braunfels that Monday, hungover in a bor-rowed car since he'd sold the Cad to get money for equip-ment rental, Sally Ann snoozing beside him, he was a new man. Everyone on his route, El Paso, Las Cruces, Midland-

Odessa, Midlothian, Cockrel Hill, Duncanville, signed up for *Devil Women of Mars*. That next weekend, in an abandoned aircraft hangar outside Fort Worth, they shot the thing.

"It holds up, even now," Sammy Cash said. "I'm the guy who fills the gas tank when the kids pull into the Spur station. I see this thing in the back of the pickup and start backing away. Audience never sees it, all they have to go on is my reaction. The gas nozzle falls out. One of the kids goes to light a cigarette. I was in the first one he made, I was in the last one. He *is* a genius, you know."

Billy started cranking them out like no one had seen. He'd take a motel room for the weekend and emerge with a script, shoot the thing Monday through Wednesday, edit it that night and the next day, have it to the processors by late Thursday, out in the world the following week. Science fiction, horror, crime movies, prison films, teen exploitation. Sally Ann never appeared onscreen, nor remained long in Billy's life, after *Devil Women of Mars*. Most of the actors were amateurs, lured away from college and community-theatre productions or from porn films for a day or two, Sammy Cash (real name Gordie Ratliff) being the exception. He'd had small parts in several low-end Hollywood movies and proudly carried a Screen Actors Guild card. But when the guild found out he'd appeared in a nonunion film and busted him, he decided right then and there that their gentlemen's agreement was over. Never paid the fine, never looked back. And never again used any other name than Sammy Cash.

"It was as though the experience liberated him," Billy

Roark said. "Before, he'd been a good journeyman, always dependable, you knew he'd show up on time, stay however long he was needed, get the job done. But then Sammy just . . . flowered. Soon *everyone* wanted him. Film after film— all of my own, those of half a dozen other filmmakers as well—he was brilliant, stone brilliant. Whatever the part."

All but imperceptibly at first, though, things began changing. TV became a six-hundred-pound linebacker flattening the opposition, providing, free and in one's own home, what B and lesser movies could provide only cheaply. Locally owned movie houses disappeared or were bought up by chains who in turn found themselves forced to bid high on upcoming Hollywood product and then, scrambling to meet expenses, to block bookings in every possible theatre. Meanwhile, costs of film, equipment rental and essential facilities such as editing studios increased astronomically. A few filmmakers held on. Till the bitter end.

⁘ ⁘ ⁘

"AND BY OUR TOENAILS," Billy Roark said. "Those days won't ever come again." He looked up. "Did we ever get you drinks? No? We really should do that. I'm afraid we're a bit out of practice vis-à-vis entertaining."

"He doesn't like to talk about all that," Sammy Cash said. "Rarely thinks much about it anymore."

The sadness in his companion's eyes belied him even before Billy spoke.

"I hated them for taking it all away from me. Taking away my life, really."

"Billy. Please," Sammy Cash said.

"There was talk about *The Giving* being my swan song, some kind of ultimate homage to the great art of film. Piss on that. What I was *giving* them, all of them—Hollywood, the studios, newcomer merchants who went about buying up everything in sight—was the finger. Fuckers didn't even have enough sense to know it. Swallow this, I was telling them. Take this wad of crap and stuff it right back up where it came from."

"It's all right, Billy. All that's long in the past. We're fine now, aren't we? We have a good life." Sammy Cash looked from Lonnie's face to mine. "Don't you think you've upset him enough?"

"We never liked one another much, Gordie," Henry Lee said, "and you probably don't believe this, but I've always appreciated what you've done for my brother, your devotion to him."

Then, turning to Lonnie and me: "After Billy's troubles—"

"Troubles?" I said.

"A breakdown. He was in the hospital for almost a year. When he came out, I bought this house for him, set everything up so he'd be safe the rest of his life, never want for anything."

"Your brother cares for you a lot," the sheriff said. "So does Sammy."

Billy nodded.

"Did you ever meet a man by the name of Carl Hazelwood, Billy?" I asked.

No response this time. I thought of all those movies

about submarines cutting engines and playing dead, hoping to stay off sonar.

"He'd been trying to get in touch with you. Carl's a great fan of yours, Billy. Maybe your *top* fan. He understood what you were doing, what you'd accomplished. He wanted desperately to talk to you about the films you made, tell you how important they'd been to him."

"I—" Billy began. Even the drink was dry when he tried for refuge there. Foundering, lost, he looked about. At Sammy's face. Out the window. At these familiar walls.

"Others did everything they could to keep him away from you, Billy. But he wasn't going to be stopped. It was that important to him. *You* were that important to him."

Lonnie's gaze turned to Henry Lee.

"You knew about this all along."

He nodded. "Boy showed up at my door one night. Hadn't bathed for a month or two. Mumbling and twitching. Said he was looking for the man who'd made *The Giving*. What was I supposed to do? What would *you* do? I had to protect Billy. I told him—Carl Hazelwood, as we later learned—that I didn't know any such person. Told him to go away. Okay, sorry to have bothered you, sir, he said. But he didn't go away. Far from it. I'd catch glimpses of him scuttling behind the garage, slipping off into the woods."

"He'd seen more than enough movies to know about stakeouts," Lonnie said. "And despite your disavowals, he knew you were connected with Billy, if not precisely what the relationship was. Knew he had only to keep watch."

"And go through my mail."

"That's how he found his way to Billy."

"Enough," Sammy Cash said. "*Enough*, goddamn it."

"Did you talk to Carl Hazelwood, Billy?"

His eyes wandered about, settled on Sammy, who shook his head. Billy nodded. "Nice young man."

"Yes. Yes, he was."

"Told me people were still watching my films, still talking about them. I had no idea. He only came that one time. I asked him to dinner the next night, insisted on cooking, though Sammy usually does all that. Baked bass, a salad of couscous and goat cheese. Put out the good china, chilled two bottles of white. We waited almost two hours, but he never showed."

Billy's eyes came up and went from face to face.

"Sammy—"

"I'm sorry," Sammy Cash said. He held a handgun. "This has to be over now. Billy's suffered enough."

"What you have there's a twenty-two," Lonnie said. "Shoot someone with that, you're likely to make them mad." He stood and, hand extended, stepped forward. The gun barked. Bubbles of blood spotted his lips.

"Son of a *bitch*," Lonnie said.

Chapter Thirty-Six

THE SECOND SHOT had struck Billy square in the neck—transecting his trachea, though we didn't know that at the time. I don't think Sammy Cash even intended to fire. When he saw what he'd done, not knowing even the half of it, his hand fell onto his lap and he sat immobile, tears in his eyes like chandeliers in empty ballrooms. For the moment Lonnie seemed okay: down but not out. I'd pulled Billy from the chair onto the floor, felt for a carotid. Thinking with amazement how much blood a body holds, how much blood it gives up, and how quickly. Billy wasn't breathing. Pinching his nose, hyperextending his neck, I stacked in three quick breaths and checked again. Still no pulse, no respiration. I began compressions. When next I looked up, Lonnie had been there by me, counting. He'd do the breaths, turn aside to spit blood or cough as I did compressions. Three, four minutes in, he folded, gasping. That's when I put the mayor to work. *Need your help over here*, I said. *Now*.

A middle-aged man in badly faded purple scrubs walked through automatic doors into the waiting room and spoke briefly with the volunteer at the desk before coming towards me. "Mr. Turner?" Fatigue sat heavily in his eyes. "You're with Sheriff Bates, right?"

I nodded.

"He's going to be okay. The bullet barely nicked an upper lobe. Of his lung, that is. Simple enough to deal with. Blood loss, shock to the system, that's a different thing, that's what's on the boards now. Take some time for full recovery, I'm afraid."

"And Billy Roark?"

"The other GSW? What, you're with him, too?"

"I've been working with Sheriff Bates on a murder case. It's all connected."

"I see. . . ." He looked at the window, at a gurney being pushed along the hallway upon which lay an oxygen tank, electronic monitors, IV pumps and the deformed body of a young girl, then back at me. "Mr. Roark expired over an hour ago." He told me about the trachea, *just like you'd hack a garden hose in two*, how, despite our best efforts at the scene, Roark had gone too long without oxygen. His heart stopped twice in ER. The second time, they failed to restart it. "I'm sorry. We did everything we could."

* * *

"STRANGE AS IT MAY SEEM looking about that house, the way Bill and Sammy were together, they were only partners. Close partners, but never lovers. Sometimes it was almost as though they were a single being. For years. How can things come apart so quickly?"

"I'm sorry, Mayor."

"Lonnie's going to be all right, they say."

"He'll be out of commission for a while. Back on the job soon enough."

"Good. That's good. I should have spoken up. I didn't know. I suspected. Most of all—"

"Most of all you hoped your brother hadn't done it."

"I didn't want to lose him."

"I understand."

"Or for him to lose himself again—which is more or less what happened that other time. Before he went to the hospital, I mean. He seemed fine. A little quiet. Then he just . . . floated away. He'd always been a dynamo, five or six projects going at once. The breakdown, or the drugs, or the electroshock, they changed him. He came back. But he'd become this meek, sweet man—the one you met."

All that he said, about his movie giving them the finger, Sammy Cash told me. *That wasn't true. He was trying to make a good movie. In his mind, I think, a great movie. Something he'd be remembered for. After years of churning them out, ambition, real ambition, had overtaken him.*

Did he succeed?

Hard to say. All we know for sure is that he never made another one—because he did exactly what he wanted with that one, or because he realized that really was the best he could do? Ambition is a strange rider. Sometimes the horse it picks can't carry it.

Our house? he suddenly said.

Yes.

The decorating's mine. Everything else in our life is Billy. You have no idea how much I did for him. Everything. He was so sweet. . . . That man, Hazelwood, should never have come. After he left, Billy was agitated. There's nothing to stop me, he kept saying over and over, I could go back, I could work again. The look in his eye was a terrible thing. Hazelwood had told me where he was staying. I went there and tried to talk to him. Told him if he truly cared about Billy he'd leave him alone, but he wouldn't listen. What else could I do? I had to stop him. I couldn't let Billy be hurt again. And now . . . Now I've made Billy immortal, just a little, haven't I? No one will ever forget how Hazelwood died. And whenever they think of that, they'll remember Billy's movie.

He was quiet for a while.

It's harder than you think to kill a man.

I nodded, remembering.

They don't die easy. He looked up. *You have to keep on killing them.*

•   •   •

I REMEMBER lying on my bunk back in prison waiting to die. Definitely I wasn't one of the bad ol' boys. From the first there'd been verbal baiting, buckets of attitude, people stepping up to me, sudden explosions of violence, broken noses, broken limbs. Everyone inside knew I was a cop. So I just naturally expected the next footsteps I heard would be coming for me.

One night a few weeks in, I heard them slapping down

the tier, footsteps that is, figuring this was it. Nothing happened, though, and after a time I realized that what I was hearing, what I was waiting for, wasn't footsteps at all, it was only rain. I started laughing.

A voice came from the next cell. "New Meat?"

"Yeah."

"You lost it over there?"

Half an hour past lights out. From the darkness around us were delivered discrete packets of sound: snoring, farts, grunts clearly sexual in nature, toilets flushing. A single bulb burned at the end of each tier. Guards' steel-toed boots rang on metal stairs and catwalks.

"Damn if I don't think I have," I told him.

Chapter Thirty-Seven

LOSING IT'S THE KEY, the secret no one tells you. From the first day of your life, things start piling up around you: needs, desires, fears, dependencies, regrets, lost connections. They're always there. But you can decide what to do with them. Polish them and put them up on the shelf. Stack them out behind the house by the weeping willow. Haul them out on the front porch and sit on them.

The front porch is where Val and I were. She had on jeans, a pink T-shirt, hair tied up in a matching pink bandanna. I was thinking how it had all started with Lonnie Bates and myself out here on the porch just like this. Where Lonnie's Jeep had been then, Val's yellow Volvo sat. That seemed long ago now.

Val and I were both playing hooky. Somehow the world, our small corner of it, would survive such irresponsibility.

"All our conflicts, even the most physical of them, the most petty—at the center they're moral struggles," Val said.

"I don't know. We like to think that. It gives us comfort.

Just as we want to believe, need to believe, that our actions come from elevated motives. From principles. When in truth they only derive from what our characters, what our personal and collective histories, dictate. We're ridden by those histories, the same way voodoo spirits inhabit living bodies, which they call horses."

"People can change. Look at yourself."

There's change and there's change, of course. The city council had tried to hire me as acting sheriff and I'd said you fools have the wrong man. Now, *just till Lonnie returns, we all understand that, right?,* I was working as deputy under Don Lee. I'd come here to excuse myself, to further what I perceived as exemption, to withdraw from humanity. Instead I'd found myself rejoining it.

Val a case in point.

"I have something for you," I told her. I went in and brought it out. She opened the battered, worn case. The instrument inside by contrast in fine shape. Inlays of stars, a crescent moon, real ivory as pegheads.

"It's—"

"I know what it is. A Whyte Laydie. They're legendary. I've never actually seen one before, only pictures."

"It was my father's. His father's before him. I'd like you to have it."

She ticked a finger along the strings. "You never told me he played."

"He didn't, by the time I came along. But he had."

"You can't just up and give something like this away, Turner."

"It's my way of saying I hope you'll both stay close to me."

The banjo and Val, or my father and Val? She didn't ask. With immense care, she took the instrument from its case, placed it in her lap, began tuning. "This is amazing. I don't know what to say."

The fingernail of her second finger, striking down, sounded the third string, brushed across, then dropped to the fourth for a hammer-on. Between, in that weird syncopation heard nowhere else, her cocked thumb sounded the fifth.

Li'l Birdie, L'il Birdie,
Come sing to me a song.
I've a short while to be here
And a long time to be gone.

Val held the banjo out before her, looking at it. I had forgotten, or maybe I never fully understood until that very moment, what a magnificent thing it was: a work of art in itself, a tool, an alternate tongue, blank canvas, an entire waiting and long-past world. Lovingly, reverentially, Val set it back in its case. "I don't deserve this. I'm not sure anyone deserves this."

"Instruments should be played. Just as lives should be lived."

She nodded.

"Come with me."

"Where?"

"A special place."

Off the porch and fifty steps along, the woods closed around us, we'd left civilization behind. Trees towered above. Undergrowth teemed with bustling, unseen things. Even sunlight touched down gingerly here. We paced alongside a stream, came suddenly onto a small lake filled with cypress. There were perhaps two dozen trees. Hundreds of knees breaking from the surface. Steam drifted, an alternate, otherworldly atmosphere, on the water.

"I grew up next to a place just like this."

"You've never told me much about your childhood."

"No. But I will."

I reached for her hand.

"I spoke to my sister this morning. The one who raised me. I was thinking about going to see her, wondered if you might consider coming with me."

"Arizona? Be a little like visiting Oz. I've always been curious about Oz."

"My grandfather—the one who owned the banjo? His name was John Cleveland. He spent much of his life wading among cypress like this. Made things from the knees. Bookends, coffee tables, lamps. Most of my favorite books I first read in the shade of a lamp he'd made for me. He'd carved faces on the knees, like a miniature Mount Rushmore, even drilled out holes so I could keep pencils there. He'd come back from the lake and head straight for the workshop, stand there with his pants dripping wet because he'd come across a new knee that suggested something to him. Walk into that workshop, all you'd see was half an acre of cypress knees. Like being here, without the water."

"It's all but unbearably beautiful, isn't it?" Val said. "I feel as though I'm standing witness to creation." Her arm came around my waist, heat of her body mixing with my own. "Thank you."

Shot with sunlight, the mist was dispersing. A crane kited in over the trees, dipped to skim the water and went again aloft.

Speechless, we watched. Sunlight skipped bright disks of gold off the water.

"Guess we should get to work, huh?"

"Soon," Val said. "Soon."

CRIPPLE CREEK

To my brother John
and beloved sister Jerry—
in memory of our search for food
somewhere near where Turner lives

The blood was a-running
And I was running too. . . .

—*Charlie Poole*
and the North Carolina Ramblers

CHAPTER ONE

I'D BEEN UP TO MARVELL to deliver a prisoner, nothing special, just a guy I stopped for reckless driving who, when I ran his license, came back with a stack of outstandings up that way, and what with having both a taste for solitude and a preference for driving at night and nothing much on the cooker back home, I'd delayed my return. Now I was starved. All the way down County Road 51 I'd been thinking about the salt pork my mom used to fry up for dinner, squirrel with brown gravy, catfish rolled in cornmeal. As I pulled onto Cherry Street for the drag past Jay's Diner, the drugstore and Manny's Dollar $tore, A&P, Baptist church and Gulf station, I was remembering an old blues. Guy's singing about how hungry he is, how he can't think of anything but food: *I heard the voice of a pork chop say, Come unto me and rest.*

That pork chop, or its avatar, was whispering in my ear as I nosed into a parking space outside city hall. Don Lee's pickup and the Jeep were there. Our half of the building was lit. Save for forty-watts left on in stores for insurance purposes, these were the only lights on Main Street. I hadn't, in fact, expected to find the office open. Lot of nights, if one of us is gone or we've both worked some event, we leave it unattended. Calls get kicked over to home phones.

Inside, Don Lee sat at the desk in his usual pool of light.

"Anything going on?" I asked.

"Been quiet. Had to break up a beer party with some of the high school kids around eleven."

"Where'd they get the beer—Jimmy Ray?"

"Where else?"

Jimmy Ray was a retarded man who lived in a garage out back of old Miss Shaugnessy's. Kids knew he'd buy beer for them if they gave him a dollar or two. We'd asked local stores not to sell to him. Sometimes that worked, sometimes it didn't.

"You got my message?"

"Yeah, June passed it on. Good trip?"

"Not bad. Didn't expect to find you here."

"Wouldn't be, but we have a guest." Meaning one of our two holding cells was occupied. This happened seldom enough to merit surprise.

"It's nothing, really. Around midnight, after I broke up the kids' party, I did a quick swing through town and was heading for home when this red Mustang came barreling past me. Eighty-plus, I figure. So I pull a U. He's got the dome light on and he's in there driving with one hand, holding a map in the other, eyes going back and forth from road to map.

"I pull in close and hit the cherry, but it's like he doesn't even see it. By this time he's halfway through town. So I sound the siren—you have any idea when I last used the siren? Surprised I could even find it. Clear its throat more than once but it's just

2

like with the cherry, he's not even taking notice. That's when I go full tilt: cherry, siren, the whole nine yards.

"'There a problem, Officer?' he says. I'm probably imagining this, but his growl sounds a lot like the idling Mustang. I ask him to shut his engine off and he does. Hands over license and registration when I ask. 'Yeah, guess I did blow the limit. Somewhere I have to be—you know?'

"I call it in and State doesn't have anything on him. I figure I'll just write a ticket, why take it any further, I mean it's going to be chump change for someone in his collector's Mustang, dressed the way he is—right? But when I pass the ticket to him he starts to open the door. 'Please get back in your car, sir,' I tell him. But he doesn't. And now a stream of invective starts up.

"'There's no reason for this to go south, sir,' I tell him. 'Just get back in your car, please. It's only a traffic ticket.'

"He takes a step or two towards me. His eyes have the look of someone who's been awake far longer than nature ever intended. Drugs? I don't know. Alcohol, definitely—I can smell that. There's a friendly bottle of Jack Daniels on the floor.

"He takes another step towards me, all the time telling me I don't know who I'm messing with, and his hands are balled into fists. I tap him behind the knee with my baton. When he goes down, I cuff him."

"And you tell me it's been quiet."

"Nothing we haven't seen a hundred times before."

"True enough. . . . He get fed?"

Don Lee nodded. "Diner was closed, of course, the grill shut down. Gillie was still there cleaning up. He made some sandwiches, brought them over."

"And your guy got his phone call?"

3

"He did."

"Don't guess you'd have anything to eat, would you?"

"Matter of fact, I do. A sandwich Patty Ann packed up for me, what? ten, twelve hours ago? Yours if you want it. Patty Ann does the best meatloaf ever." Patty Ann being the new wife. Lisa, whom he'd married months before I came on the scene, was long gone. Lonnie always said Don Lee at a glance could pick out the one kid in a hundred that threw the cherry bomb in the toilet out at Hudson Field but he couldn't pick a good woman to save his life. Looked like maybe now he had, though.

Don Lee pulled the sandwich out of our half-size refrigerator and handed it to me, then put on fresh coffee. The sandwich was wrapped in wax paper, slice of sweet pickle nestled between the halves.

"How's work going on Val's house?" he asked.

"She's got three rooms done now. Give that woman a plane, a chisel and a hammer, she can restore anything. Yesterday we started sanding down the floor in one of the back rooms. Got through four or five coats of paint only to find linoleum under that. 'There's a floor here somewhere!' Val shouts, and starts peeling it away. Sometimes it's like we're on an archaeological dig, you know? Great sandwich."

"Always."

"Eldon Brown's come by some days to pitch in, says it relaxes him. Always brings his old Gibson. Thing's beat to hell. He and Val'll take breaks, sit on the porch playing fiddle tunes and old-time mountain songs."

Don Lee poured coffee for us both.

"Speaking of which," I said, "I was sitting out front noticing how *this* place could use a new coat of paint."

Don Lee shook his head in mock pity. "Late-night wisdom."

Early-morning, actually, but he had a point. Beat listening to what the pork chop had to tell me, anyway.

"We're way past due on servicing the Chariot, too."

The Chariot was the Jeep, which we both used but still thought of as belonging to Lonnie Bates. Lonnie'd been shot a while back, went on medical leave. When the city council came to ask me to take his place I told them they had the wrong man. *You fools have the wrong man,* was what I said. Graciously enough, they chose to overlook my ready wit and went ahead and appointed Don Lee as acting sheriff. He was a natural—just as I said. I'd never seen a man more cut out for law enforcement. I would agree to serve temporarily, I told city council members, as his deputy. Snag came when Lonnie found he liked his freedom, liked being home with his family, going fishing in the middle of the day if he had a mind to, taking hour-long naps, watching court shows and reruns of *Andy Griffith* or *Bonanza* on TV. Now we were a year into the arrangement and *temporarily* had taken on new meaning.

Headlights lashed the front windows.

"That'll be Sonny. He was at his mom's for her birthday earlier. Couldn't break loose to tow in the Mustang till now."

We went out to thank Sonny and sign the invoice. Probably he was going to wait a couple or three months for payment. We knew that. He did too. The city council and Mayor Sims forever dragged feet when it came to cutting checks. Just so she'd be able to meet whatever bills had to be paid to keep the city viable, payroll, electric and so on, the city clerk squirreled away money in secret accounts. No one talked about that either, though it was common knowledge.

"Could be a while before you get your fee," I told him as I passed the clipboard back.

"No problem," Sonny said. In the year I'd known him I'd never heard him say much of anything else. I just filled up, out front. No problem. Jeep's pulling to the right, think you can look at it? No problem.

Sonny's taillights faded as he headed back to the Gulf station to trade the tow truck for his Honda. Don Lee and I stood by the Mustang. Outside lights turned its red a sickly purple.

"You looked it over at the scene, right?" I said.

"Not really. Kind of had my hands full with Junior in there. Not like he or the car was going anywhere."

Don Lee pulled keys out of the pocket of his polyester-cum-khaki shirt.

Inside, whole thing smelling of patchouli aftershave and sweat, there was the half-bottle of Jack Daniel's, the crumpled map like a poorly erected tent on the passenger seat, an Elmore Leonard paperback with the cover ripped off on the floor, some spare shirts and slacks and a houndstooth sport coat hanging off the back-seat hook, an overnight bag with toiletries, four or five changes of underwear, a half-dozen pair of identical dark blue socks, a couple of rolled-up neckties.

A nylon sports bag in the trunk held two hundred thousand dollars and change.

CHAPTER TWO

TWO DAYS EARLIER, I'd been sitting on my porch with the dregs of a rabbit stew. Not that I hunted, but my neighbor Nathan did. Nathan had lived in a cabin up here for better than sixty years. Everyone said set foot on his land, expect buckshot, but right after I moved in he showed up with a bottle of homemade. We sat out here sharing it silently, and ever since, every few weeks, Nathan turns up. Always brings a bottle, sometimes a brace of squirrels so freshly killed they still have that earth-and-copper blood smell, a bundle of quail, a duck or rabbit.

I'd grown up with relatives much like Nathan. We'd see them once or twice a year maybe. On a Sunday, pack ourselves into the cream-over-green Dodge with green plastic shades above the windshield and forward of the wing windows, and drive along narrow highways that let onto blacktop roads flanked on either side by cotton fields, bolls white and surprising as popcorn, sometimes a biplane dipping to spew double barrels of insecticide; then down dirt roads to a rutted offload by Madden Bay where pickups and empty boat trailers sat waiting, and where

Louis or Monty would wave as he throttled down the outboard coming into shore, finally kill it and, paddle tucked under an armpit, tracing figure eights, ease the boat back to ground.

What freedom the boat gave up then.

Louis or Monty as well, I think.

I never knew quite what to say to them. They were kind men, tried their best to engage my brother and myself, to care about us and take care to show they did, but the simple truth is that they were as uncomfortable with us as with these towns sprung up all about them, this bevy of decision makers, garbage collectors, bills and liens. I suspect that Louis and Monty may have felt a greater kinship with the bass and bream they pulled mouths gaping from the bay than with Thomas or me. Deep at the center of themselves, my uncles longed for outposts, frontiers, forests, and badlands.

Your own penchant for living at the edge, could it have derived from them? my psychiatric training prompted—silent companion there beside me on the porch, though not as silent as I'd have wished. One of many things I had thought to leave behind when I came here.

The stew was delicious. I'd hacked up the rabbit, put it in a Dutch oven to brown with coarse salt and pepper rubbed in, then added a dash of the leftover from one of Nathan's bottles, carrots and celery and some fresh greens, covered the whole thing, and turned the flame low as I could.

Val had left around midnight. Not only was she uncannily attuned to my need for solitude, she shared that need. We'd been working on her house earlier, came back here afterwards, where I'd set the stew on to simmer as we porched ourselves and sat talking about nothing much at all, clocking the barometer-like

8

fall of whiskey in a bottle of Glenfiddich as the thrum of cicada and locust built towards twilight, then receded. Birds dipped low over the lake, rose against a sky like a basket of abstract fruit: peach, plum, grapefruit pink.

"Third session in court on a custody case," Val replied when I asked about her day. Legal counsel for the state barracks, she maintained a private practice in family law as well. "Mother's a member of the Church of the Old God."

"Some kind of cult?"

"Close enough. Claim to have returned to the church as it began, in biblical times. Think Baptists or Church of Christ in overdrive."

"I'd rather not."

"Right . . . The father's a teacher. Medieval history at university level."

"Given the era and perspective, those must be interesting classes."

"I suspect they are, yes."

"How old is the girl?"

"I didn't say it was a girl."

"My guess."

"She's thirteen. Sarah."

"What does *she* want?"

Val snagged the bottle, poured another inch and a half of single malt for both of us.

"What do we all want at that age? Everything."

Dark had fallen. Dead silent now—broken by the call of a frog from down on the lake.

"Smelling good in there." Val lifted her glass, sighting the moon through it as though the glass were a sextant. Find your position, plot your course. "She'll wind up with the mother, I suspect."

"You're representing the father?"

She nodded. "Even though Sarah's where my heart lies."

"Given the circumstances, she must have . . . what do you call it? a court-appointed advocate, a spokesman?"

"Guardian ad litem, but more a guardian pro forma, I'm afraid, in this case."

Taking my glass with its dreg of Glenfiddich along, I went in to check on our dinner. It would be better tomorrow, but it was ready now. I pulled out bowls and ladled rabbit stew with barley and thick-cut carrots into them, laid slices of bread atop.

Outside, Val and I sat scooping up steaming spoonfuls and blowing across them.

"It's a messy system," Val said after a blistering mouthful, sucking air. "All kinds of slippage built into it."

"Slippage you can use, though."

I was remembering Sally Gene, a social worker back in Memphis. The whole thing just kind of *grew*, Sally Gene told me, this whole system of child protection and the laws supporting it—the way people'll take a trailer and keep adding on to it, a porch here, a spare room. No real planning. So half of it's about to fall down around you, none of the doors close, stuff flies in and out of the windows at will. You can use that—but it can also use you. It can use you right up.

"Exactly," Val said. "And a lot of what I manage to accomplish has more to do with slippage than with law. You're standing there before a judge, you *think* you understand the situation, think you know the law and have made a case, but whatever that judge says decides it. Should one man or woman have that much power?

Finally you're just hoping the judge slept well, didn't get pissed off at his own kids over the breakfast table."

We ate, then Val, miming a beggar's plea for alms, held out her bowl. I refilled mine as well and came back onto the porch, screen door banging behind. Immediately Val began dunking the bread, letting it drip.

"Always so dainty. Such manners."

She stuck out her tongue. I pointed to the corner of my mouth to indicate she had food there. She didn't.

"So often there's just no right answer, no solution," she said. "We always insist there has to be. Need to believe that, I guess."

Neither of us spoke for a time then. Spooky cry of an owl from a nearby tree.

"You know, this may be the best thing I've ever eaten. We should have a moment of silence for the rabbit."

"Who gave his life . . ."

"I can't imagine it was voluntary. Though the image of Mr. Rabbit knocking at Nathan's back door and offering himself up for the better good is an intriguing one."

Finished, she set the bowl on the floor beside her chair.

"Sarah's lost," she said. "Nothing I can do about it. Life with her mother will warp her incontrovertibly. Her father is barely functional. Dresses in whatever's to the left in his closet and through the month moves steadily right, has his CDs numbered and plays them in order. Books on his shelves are arranged by size."

"Maybe she'll save herself."

"Maybe. Some of us do, don't we? It's just others that we can never save."

Within the hour I saw Val to her car. Knew she wouldn't stay but asked anyway. She pulled me close and we stood in silent embrace. That embrace and the warmth of her body, not to mention the silence, seemed answer enough just then to any questions the world might throw me. From the rooftop a barn owl, perhaps the one we'd heard earlier, looked on.

"Fabulous dinner," she said.

"Fabulous companion."

"Yes. You are."

Owl and I watched as the Volvo backed out to begin the long swing around the lake and away. Owl then swiveled his head right around, 180 degrees, like a gun turret. As the sound of Val's motor racketed off the water, I remembered listening to Lonnie's Jeep as it came around the lake that first time. I'd put a spray of iris in the trunk where Val kept her briefcase and enjoyed thinking of her finding the flowers there.

Bit of Glenfiddich left in the bottle, meanwhile.

I poured as the owl flew off to be about its business. This Scotch was mine, and I was going to be about it.

I'd been close to two years on the streets when I came awake in a white room, hearing beeps and a soughing as of pumps close by, garbled conversation further away, ringing phones. I tried to sit up and couldn't. A matronly face appeared above me.

"You've been shot, Officer. You're fine now. But you need to rest."

Her hand rose to the IV beside me and thumbed a tiny wheel there—as I sank.

When next I came around, a different face loomed above me, peering into my eyes from behind a conical light.

"Feeling better, I hope?"

Male this time, British or Australian accent.

Next he moved to the foot of my bed, prodded at my feet. Checking for pulses, as I later learned. He made some notations on a clipboard, set it aside, and reached towards the IV.

I grabbed hold of his hand, shook my head.

"Doctor's orders," he said.

"The doctor's here?"

"Not at the moment, mate."

"He's not, and we are. But he's still making decisions for both of us?'"

"You're refusing medication?"

"Do I need it?"

"You have to tell me."

"That I refuse?"

"Yes. So I can chart it."

"Okay, I refuse medication."

"Right you are, then." He picked up the clipboard, made another notation. "Surgeons here like to keep their patients snowed the first twenty-four to thirty-six hours. Some of the nurses question that, and rightly so. But who are we?"

"Besides the ones at bedside going through this shit with us, you mean."

"That's exactly what I mean."

"How long have I been here?"

"Came in around six, p.m. that is, not long before my shift started. That's to intensive care, mind you. You were in OR before, I'd guess an hour or so, started off in ER. They wouldn't have kept you down there long with a GSW, you being police and all."

"What's your name?"

"Ion."

13

Dawn nibbled at the window.

"Do you know what happened to me, Ion?"

"Shot on duty's what I got at report, just back from OR, standard ICU orders, no complications. Always anxious to get home to her young husband, Billie is. Hold on a sec. I'll get the chart, we can sort this out."

He was back in moments. Phones rang incessantly at the nurse's station outside my door. There must have been an elevator shaft close by. I kept hearing the deep-throated whine of the elevator's voyage, the thunk of it coming into port, the shift in hallway sounds when the doors opened.

Ion pulled a molded plastic visitor's chair up beside the bed, went rummaging through the chart.

"Looks as though you responded to a domestic dispute called in by neighbors. Got there and found a man beating his wife with a segment of garden hose. You took him down—"

"From behind, with a choke hold."

"Oh?"

"And the wife shot me."

"Coming back to you, is it?"

"Not really. But I know how these things usually go."

Perfunctory rap at the door, around the sill of which a face then leant. Young woman with something very close to a Marine buzz cut and a diamond stud in her nose.

"That time already?" Ion said. "Be right with you, C.C. Just give me a minute.

"Shift change," he told me, looking back down at the chart. "Here we go. . . . Bullet passed cleanly through your upper thigh, no major vessels involved. There'd have been a lot of blood, I imagine. A couple of major muscle groups got more or less dissected. All put back right, but muscles take an amazing time to forgive you."

"That why I can't move?"

"That would be the restraints. Sorry." Ion unlashed trailing nylon ties from sidebars of the bed, slipped padded cuffs off wrists and ankles. "Seems you reacted poorly to one of the sedatives, hardly uncommon. But all that lot should be well out of your system by now."

The stud-nosed face appeared again in the doorway.

"C.C. What is it, you've a bloody bus to catch? You're here for twelve hours. Go take some vitals, pretend you're a nurse. I'll be along straightaway, just as I said."

I thanked him.

Standing, he pulled up a trouser leg and rapped knuckles at the pinkish leg thereunder, which gave off a hollow sound. "I've been where you are, Officer, right enough. Compliments of Miss Thatcher."

He never showed up beside my bed again. When I asked, I was told that he'd been assigned to another unit, that all the nurses rotated through the various intensive cares.

"How many ICUs are there?"

"Seeks." Six.

"That's a lot of care."

"Is hard world."

Angie was, what, twenty-four? On the other hand, she was Korean—so maybe she did know, from direct experience, how hard the world could be.

I thought *I* knew, of course. Weeks of physical therapy, weeks of furiously sending messages down the spinal column to a leg that first ignored the signals then barely acknowledged them, weeks of watching those around me—MS patients, people with birth defects, victims of severe trauma or strokes—taught me different. My world was easy.

Four months later, back at work though still on desk duty, I had personally thanked everyone else involved in my medical care, but in trying to track down Ion found that he'd not merely been assigned to another ICU, as I'd been told, but had left the hospital's employ.

Two or three purportedly official calls from Officer Turner at MPD, and I was pulling into the parking lot of an apartment complex in south Memphis. No sign of air conditioning and the mercury pushing ninety degrees, so most of the apartments had doors and windows open, inviting in a nonexistent breeze. Parking lot filled with pickups drooling oil and boxy sedans well past expiration date. The one-time swimming pool had been filled in with cement, the cement painted blue.

I knocked at the door of 1-C. Had in hand a sack of goodies with a gift bow threaded through the paper handles—candy, cookies, cheese and water biscuits, thumb-sized salamis, and summer sausage.

"Whot?" he said as the door opened. Puffy face, sclera gone red. Wearing shorts and T-shirt. The foot on his good leg was bare; a shoe remained on the other. Van Morrison playing back in the depths. "Tupelo Honey."

"Whot?" he said again.

"You don't remember me, do you?"

"And I should?"

"Officer Turner. Came in with a GSW long about August. You took care of me."

"Sorry, mate. All a blur to me."

Motion behind him became a body moving towards us. Buzz-cut blond hair, diamond stud, not much else by way of disguise. Or of clothes, for that matter.

"I just wanted to thank you," I said, passing across the bag. "Forgive me for intruding."

He took the bag and pulled the handles apart to look in. The bow tore away, dropping to the floor.

"Hey! Thanks, man." He stared for a moment at the bow on the floor by my foot. "You take care, okay?"

None of us, I thought later at home, remembering his kindness and concern, thirty straight leg lifts into what amounted to an hour-long regimen, wall slides and step-ups to go, muscles beginning at last to forgive me, *none of us are exempt.*

CHAPTER THREE

THE MAN BACK IN our holding cell, Judd Kurtz, wasn't talking. When we asked him where the money came from, he grinned and gave us his best try at a jailyard stare. The stare just kind of hung there in no-man's-land between close-cropped brown hair and bullish neck.

We made the necessary calls to State. They'd pull down any arrest records or outstanding warrants on Kurtz, run the finger-prints Don Lee took through AFIS. They'd also check with the feds on recent robberies and reports of missing funds. Barracks commander Bailey said he'd get back to us soonest. We woke bank president Stew Daniels so he could put the money in his vault.

"Want me to stay around?" I asked Don Lee. By this time dawn was pecking at the windows.

"No need to. Go home. Get some sleep. Come back this af-ternoon."

"You're sure?"

"Get out of here, Turner."

Still cool out by the cabin when I reached it, early-morning sunlight skipping bright coins across the lake. Near and far, from ancient stands of oak and cypress, young doves called to one another. Mist clung to the water's surface. I didn't come here for beauty, but it keeps insisting upon pushing its way in. Val's yellow Volvo was under the pecan tree out front. Two squirrels sat on a low limb eyeing the car suspiciously and chattering away. As I climbed out, Val stepped onto the porch with twin mugs of coffee.

"Heard you were back in port, sailor."

"Aye, ma'am."

"And how's the Fairlane?"

"Not bad, once you discount crop dusters trying to land on the hood."

I'd finally broken down and bought a car, from the same old Miss Shaugnessy who rented out her garage to Jimmy Ray, who bought beer for minors. Thing was a tank: you looked out on a hood that touched down two counties over. Miss Shaugnessy'd bought it new almost forty years ago, paying cash, but never quite learned to drive. It had been up on blocks since, less than a hundred miles on the odometer. Lonnie was the one who talked her into selling it to me. Went over with a couple of plate lunches from Jay's covered in aluminum foil and a quart of beer and came back with the keys.

I don't remember too much more about that morning. Val and I sat side by side on the porch on kitchen chairs I'd fished out of the city dump up the road. I told her about Don Lee's latest catch. About the money in the nylon sports bag. Told her I was tired, bone tired, dead tired. Watched sparrows, cardinals, and woodpeckers alight in the trees and bluejays curse them all. A pair of quail ran, heads and shoulders down like soldiers, from brush to brush nearby. A squirrel came briefly onto the porch and sat on haunches regarding us. I think I told Val about the pork chop.

Next thing I know she's beside me on the bed and I'm suddenly awake. No direct sunlight through east or west windows, so most likely the sun's overhead.

"What, you didn't go in to work today?"

"New policy. State employees are encouraged to telecommute one day a week."

"What the hell for?"

"Clean air legislation."

"Someone's been trucking in the other kind?"

"Sorry. Thought you were awake, but obviously you're not quite. I did mention the government, right?"

"See your point."

"You said to wake you around noon. Coffee's almost fresh and Café Val's open for business. Need a menu?"

"Oatmeal."

"Oatmeal? Here I hook up with an older man, expecting to reap the benefits of his life experience—plumb the depths of wisdom and all that—and what I get is oatmeal?"

She did, and I did, and within the hour, following shower, shave, oatmeal breakfast, and a change of clothes, I pulled in by city hall. The Chariot and Don Lee's pickup were still there, along with June's Neon. Blinds were closed.

Those blinds never get closed except at night.

And the door was locked.

If I hadn't been fully awake before, I was now.

I had a key, of course. What I didn't have was any idea where

21

the key might be. Time to rely on my extensive experience as a law-enforcement professional: I kicked the door in. Luckily a decade's baking heat had done its work. On my third try the doorframe around the lock splintered.

Donna, one of two secretaries from the other half of city hall—mayor's office, city clerk, water and sewage departments, the administrative side of things—appeared beside me to say "We have a spare key, you know." Then she glanced inside.

June lay there, shamrock-shaped pool of blood beneath her head, purse still slung over her shoulder. She was breathing slowly and regularly. Bubbles of blood formed and broke in her right nostril with each breath. As on a movie screen I saw her arrive for her shift, surprising them in the act. She'd have keyed the door and come on in. One hand on the .22 that had spilled from her purse when she fell, I imagined. She'd have realized something wasn't right, same as I did.

Two smaller questions to add to the big one, then.

Why was June carrying a gun in her purse?

And was Don Lee already down when she arrived?

He lay on the floor by the door leading back to the storage room and holding cells. A goose egg the color and shape of an overripe Roma tomato hung off the left side of his head. Glancing through the open door I saw the holding cell was empty. Don Lee's eyes flickered as I knelt over him. He was trying to say something. I leaned closer.

"Gumballs?"

He shook his head.

"Goombahs," he said.

Donna meanwhile had put in a call for Doc Oldham, who, as usual, arrived complaining.

"Man can't even be left alone to have his goddamn lunch in peace nowadays. What the hell're you up to now, Turner? This used to be a nice quiet place to live, you know? Then you showed up."

He dropped to one knee beside June. For a moment I'd have sworn he was going to topple. Droplets of sweat, defying gravity, stood on his scalp. He felt for June's carotid, rested a hand briefly on her chest. Carefully supported her head with one hand while palpating it, checking pupils, ears.

"I'm assuming you've already done this?" he said.

"Pupils equal and reactive, so no sign of concussion. No fremitus or other indication of respiratory difficulty. No real evidence of struggle. Someone standing guard at the door's my guess. A single blow meant only to put her down."

Oldham's eyes met mine. We'd both been there too many times.

"Not bad for an amateur, I was about to say. But you're not, are you? So I was about to make myself an asshole. Not for the first time, mind. And, I sincerely hope, not for the last." Grabbing at a tabletop, he wobbled to his feet. "I need to look at the other one?"

"Pupils unequal but reactive. Unconscious now, but he spoke to me earlier and responds to pain. Doesn't look to be any major blood loss. Vitals are good. BP I'd estimate at ninety over sixty, thereabouts."

"Ambulance on the way?"

"Call's in."

"Could take some time. Rory ain't always easy to rouse, once he's got hisself bedded down for the day. Damn it all, we're looking at a major goddamn crime scene here."

"Afraid so."

"Ever tell you how much I hate court days?"

"Once or twice."

"There're those who'd be pleased to pay for your ticket back home, you know." He leaned heavily against the wall, reeling down breaths in stages, like a kite from the sky. "But you ain't going away, are you, boy?"

"No, sir."

"You sure 'bout that?"

"I am."

He pushed himself away from the wall.

"Good. Things been a hell of a lot more interesting around here since you came."

Doc Oldham and I packed the two of them off to the hospital up Little Rock way, then he had to demonstrate his new step. He'd recently taken up tap dancing, God help us all, and every time you saw him, he wanted to show off his latest moves. This from a man who could barely stand upright, mind you. It was like watching a half-rotted pecan tree go au point. But eventually he left to make another try at his goddamn lunch, and I went to work. I'd barely got started when Buster arrived. Buster filled in as relief cook at the diner, cleaned up there most nights, snagged whatever other work he could. I never could figure what it was about him, some kind of palsy or just plain old nerves, but some part of Buster always had to be moving.

"Doc says you could use help gettin' th'office cleaned up," he said, looking around. When his head stopped moving, a foot started. "'Pears to me he was right."

"You don't have to do that."

"Well, no sir, I don't," he said, grinning. Then the lips relaxed and his eyes met mine. A shaky hand rose between us. "Sure enough could use the work, though."

"Twenty sound okay?"

"Yessir. Sounds *right* good. Specially with my anniversary coming up and all."

"How many years does this make for you and Della?"

"Fifty-eight."

"Congratulations."

"She the one deserves congratulations, puttin' up with the likes of me all these years."

Buster went back to the storage room to find what he needed as I sank in again. Buster could clean the stairs at Grand Central Station during rush hour without getting in anyone's way. Someone once said of a Russian official who survived regime after regime that he'd learned to dodge raindrops and could make his way through a downpour without ever getting wet. That's Buster.

Don's desk tray held his report, with a photocopy of the original speeding ticket stapled to it. In the ledger he'd logged time of arrest, reason for same, time of arrival at the office, booking number. The column for PI (personal items) was checked, as was that for FP (fingerprinted) and PC (phone call).

Just out of curiosity, I paged back to see when we'd last fingerprinted or given a phone call. We rarely had sleepovers, and when we did they were guys who'd had a little too much to drink, bored high school kids caught out vandalizing, the occasional mild domestic dispute needing cool-off time.

Four months back, I'd answered a suspicious person call at the junior high. Dominic Ford had offered no resistance, but I'd brought him in and put his stats in the system on the off chance that he might be a pedophile or habitual offender. Turned out he was an estranged father just trying to get a glimpse of his twelve-year-old daughter, make sure she was okay.

Six months back, Don Lee responded to a call that a man "not from around here" was sitting on the only bench in the tiny park at the end of Main Street talking to himself. Thinking he could be a psychiatric patient, Don Lee printed him. What he was, was minister of a Pentecostal church in far south Memphis, out towards the state border where gambling casinos afloat on the river have turned Tunica into a second Atlantic City. He'd only wanted to get back to the kind of place he grew up, he said. Touch down there, *feel* it again. He'd been sitting on the bench working up his sermon.

The previous entry was for that time, a year ago, when Lonnie, Don Lee, and I discovered how Carl Hazelwood had been killed—the day the sheriff got shot.

All these years, I'd never seen anything remotely resembling a jailbreak and assumed they only happened in old Western or gangster movies. But it was obvious this crew had come here specifically to spring Judd Kurtz. Goombahs, Don Lee had said. Even among the most hardassed, there aren't many who'll step up to a law office, even a far-flung, homespun one like ours, with such impunity.

I sat looking at that tick underneath PC. Then I made my own call, to Mabel at Bell South.

"Don Lee and Miss June gonna be okay?" she said immediately upon hearing my voice.

"We hope so. Meanwhile, I need a favor."

"Whatever I can do."

"How much do you know about what went down over here?"

"Just someone stormed in and beat crap out of the two of them's all I heard."

"That someone came to town to break out a man Don Lee had detained on a traffic violation."

"Take safe driving seriously, do they?"

Known for her biting wit, Mabel was. Not to mention the choicest gossip in town.

"The man made a phone call from this office just after Don Lee booked him in, around one a.m. I know it's—"

"Sure it is. Now ask me if I care. Just give me five, ten minutes."

"Thanks, sweetheart."

"For what? I'm not doing this."

Never mind five or ten minutes, it was more like two.

She read out the number. "Placed at one-fourteen." A Memphis exchange.

"Any way you can check to see what that number is?"

"Like I haven't already? Nino's Restaurant. Two lines. One's the official listing, looks like it gets almost all the calls. The other—"

"Is probably an office or back booth."

"Must be a city thing," Mabel said in the verbal equivalent of a shrug. "That do it for you?"

"I owe you, Mabel."

"You just be sure to give Miss June and Don Lee my best when you see them."

"I will."

"'Scuse me, Mr. Turner?" Head bobbing, Buster stood in the doorway. "'Bout done here. S'posed to go wash the mayor's car now. One or two more besides, I s'pect." When his head went still, an arm rose. "Came upon this back in there."

A business card. I took it. Put a twenty and a ten in its place.

"Much obliged, sir."

"When's your anniversary, Buster?"

"Thursday to come."

"Maybe you could bring Della over to my place that night, let Val and me fix dinner for you both. We'd love to meet her."

"Well now, I'd surely like that, Mr. Turner. 'Preciate the asking. And forgive me for saying it, but Della'd be powerful uncomfortable with that."

"I understand. Maybe some other time."

"Maybe so."

"A shame, though."

"Yessir. It surely is."

CHAPTER FOUR

LATTER-DAY CITY CONSTABLES, we seldom know the outcome of our efforts. We take on the end runs and heavy lifting, fill in paperwork, testify at trials, move on. It's not *Gunsmoke*, not even *NYPD Blue*. Occasionally we hear on the grapevine that Shawn DeLee's been sent up for life, or, if we care to check computerized records and have time to do so, learn that Billyboy Davis has been re-renabbed by federal marshals on a fugitive warrant. To others our talk is forever of justice and community standards. Among ourselves it's considerably baser.

I'd been out of the life a long time now. But weeks back, Herb Danziger up in Memphis had somehow tracked me down and called to tell me that Lou Winter, having exhausted appeals, was scheduled for execution.

Danziger was pro bono lawyer for Lou Winter at his initial trial. He'd put in thirty-some years making certain that big rich corporations got bigger and richer, then one day ("No crisis of conscience, I was just bored out of my mind") he gave it up and started taking on, in both senses of the phrase, the hard cases.

Another six years of that before an unappeased client stepped out of the doorway of Danziger's apartment house one evening as he returned home. Damndest thing you ever saw, the paramedic who responded said. We get there and this guy is sitting on the sidewalk with his back against the wall and his legs out straight in front of him. There's the handle of a hunting knife sticking out of his head, like he has a horn, you know? And he's singing "Buffalo Gals Won't You Come Out Tonight."

He survived, but with extensive brain damage. His hands shook with palsy and one foot dragged, paving of his memory gone to potholes. He'd been in an assisted-living home ever since. But old cohorts showed up regularly to visit, bringing with them all the latest courthouse gossip.

"Early September is what they're saying. I'll keep you posted."

"Thanks, Herb. You doing okay?"

"Never better. Occupational therapist here would adopt me if she could. Who'd ever have suspected I had artistic talent? My lanyards and decoupage are the best. Others look upon them and weep."

"Anything you need?"

"I'm good, T. You get up this way, just come see me, that's all."

"I'll do that."

Lou Winter had killed four children, all males aged ten to thirteen. Unlike other juvenile predators, he never molested them or was in any way improper. He met them mostly at malls, befriended them, took them out for elaborate meals and often a movie, then killed them and buried them in his backyard. Each grave had a small garden plot above it: tomatoes above one, zucchini above another, Anaheim peppers above a third. From the ground of the most recent, only a short stem with two tiny leaves protruded.

It was my fourth, maybe fifth catch as detective, just a missing-persons case at the time. I'd been kicked upstairs arbitrarily and had little idea what I was doing or how to go about it. Everyone in the house knew that—watch commanders, other detectives, technicians in forensics, patrol, probably the cleaning lady. I was a week into the case with no land in sight when I knocked off around six one night and went out to find a note tucked under my windshield wiper. I never did find out who put it there. It had the name of the missing child on it, the one I was looking for, followed by the number four. It also had another name, and the address of a pet shop at Westwood Mall.

A buzzer sounded faintly as I walked in. Lou Winter came out of the back of the store and stood watching me, knowing even then, I think, who I was. When I told him, he just nodded, eyes still on mine. Something strange about those eyes, I thought even then.

"I have a mother cat giving birth back there," he said. "Can you give me a few minutes?"

I went with him and stood alongside as, cooing and petting, tugging gently with a finger to urge the first kitten out, the first of five, he helped ease her birth. No, not five: six. For, long after the others had dropped into our world, another head began showing.

The last kitten had only one front leg, something wrong with its skull as well. Holding it tenderly, Lou Winter said, "She'll reject it, but we have to try, don't we?" as he pushed the others aside and placed the new one closest to her.

"I'll get my things." A gray windbreaker. A gym bag containing,

I would learn later, toothbrush and toothpaste, a Red Chief notebook and a box of Number 2 pencils, several washcloths, six pair of white socks still in paper bands, a pocket-size paperback Bible. "I'll just lock up." Taking a cardboard sign off a hook alongside, "Back in a Jiff," he hung it on the door. "Marcie comes in after gym practice. Be here any minute now."

He never asked how I found him, never showed any surprise.

Once we'd left the store, I noticed, he began to seem awkward or uncertain, staying close to me, face bunched in concentration. Macular degeneration, I'd learn later. Like many whose faculties decay slowly, he had compensated, memorizing his surroundings, working out ways to function. But Lou Winter was more than half blind.

Outside the station house, a man in an expensive suit and shoes that cost about the same as the suit stepped up and introduced himself as Mr. Winter's lawyer. He and Winter regarded one another a moment, then Winter nodded.

And that was Herb Danziger.

Years later, after we'd got to be friends of a sort, I asked Herb how he happened to show up that day. "I was tipped off," he said. "An anonymous phone call." Then, smiling, added: "You don't think a man's own lawyer would turn him in, do you?"

Inside, waving aside Danziger's caution and counsel, Lou Winter told us everything. The four children, what they'd eaten together, movies they'd seen, the gravesites. Dr. Vandiver, a psychiatrist who did consulting work for the department, came over from Baptist there towards the end. "What do you think, Doctor?" Captain Adams asked. Vandiver went on staring out the window. "I've been trying to put it into words," he said after a moment. "The word I keep coming up with is *sadness*."

It took the jury less than thirty minutes to come back with a verdict and the judge all of two to sentence Lou Winter to death. Herb Danziger carried on appeal after appeal in Winter's name, right up to the day of his assault. He'd even tried to represent him once afterwards. But when his time came, Herb sat there watching the blades on the ceiling fan go round and round, intrigued by the shadows they made. The judge put off proceedings till the following week and appointed a new attorney.

I hung up the phone after talking to Herb. Clouds moved along the sky as though, having misspoken, they were in a hurry to get offstage. Across the street Terry Billings's legs stuck out from beneath his pickup as he worked on his transmission for the third time this month, trying to wring out yet another few hundred miles.

I was thinking about Herb, about Lou Winter, and remembering what Dr. Vandiver had so untypically said.

Sadness.

Not for himself, but for the others, the children. Or for all of us. In some strange manner, Lou Winter was connected to humanity as few of us are, but the connection had gone bad. Small wires were broken, sparks dribbled out at joins.

Once I had wanted nothing more than to see Lou Winter convicted, then executed. I understood why Herb held on: in a world all too rapidly emptying itself of Herb's presence, Lou was one of the few tangible links to his past, to what his life had stood for, what he had made of it.

Was it really any different for me?

Lou Winter had been a part of my life and world for as long. It was altogether possible that in losing him I would be losing some unexplored subcontinent of my self.

That same day, I remember, I stopped Gladys Tate for driving drunk. She was in husband Ed's '57 Chevy and almost fell twice getting out. She'd already run into something and smashed the headlight and half the grille. When I mentioned that Ed was going to be damned mad, she grinned with one side of her face, winked with the other, and said, "Ed won't care. He's got a new toy." His new toy was a woman he met at the bowling alley up by Poplar Grove, the one he'd left town with. Gladys looked off at the old church, now mostly jagged, gaping boards and yellowed white paint, though a skeletal steeple still stood. Then her eyes swam back to mine. "My clothes are in the dryer," she said, "can I go home soon?"

CHAPTER FIVE

THE BUSINESS CARD was for a financial consultant in offices just off Monroe in Memphis. That consultant thing had always eluded me, I could never understand it. As society progresses, we move further and further away from those who actually do the work. Consulting, I figured, was about as far as one could get before launching oneself into the void.

I came here with clear purpose. I'd be on my own, no attachments, no responsibility. Now I look around and find myself at the center of this community, so much so that freeing myself for a few days in Memphis took some doing.

First call was to Lonnie. Sure, he'd fill in, no problem. Be good to be back in harness, long as he knew it was short-term.

"I'll try to keep it down to a minimum," I said.

"You're going after them, aren't you?"

"You wouldn't?"

"They hurt my daughter, Turner. For no good reason save she was there."

"Figure they can do whatever they want out here on the edge, I'm thinking."

"That's what they're thinking too. Just don't forget to give the local force a courtesy call."

"I'm not sure MPD wants to hear from me."

"Call them anyway. You still have any contacts there?"

"Tell the truth, I don't know."

"Find out. And if you do, cash them in for whatever they're worth. Nickel, dime—whatever."

Next call was to barracks commander Bailey, who pledged to send down a couple of retired state troopers to rotate shifts as deputies. "Believe me, they'll appreciate the chance to get out of the house."

Then Val.

"Let me guess. You're going to be away for a while." She laughed. "Commander Bailey told me." She was counsel for the barracks, after all. "Have to admit it came as no surprise. Any idea when you'll be back?"

"I'll call, let you know."

"You better."

"I'll miss you."

Another rapid burst of the laughter I had come so to treasure. "It's pitiful," she said, "how much I hoped you might say something like that."

Forty minutes later I was heading up Highway 51 in the Chariot, Lonnie's Jeep, with an overnight bag of underwear and socks, two shirts, spare khaki pants just in case, basic toiletries. The gun I never carried, a .38 Police Special Don Lee insisted on providing me when I started working with him, lay swaddled in a hand towel, in a quart Glad bag, under the passenger seat. I imagined that I could feel it pulling at me from there, a gravity I was loath to give in to or admit.

I hadn't been back to Memphis in, what, close to two years? At some essential level it never seems to change much. More fast-food franchises and big-box stores pop up, the streets continue to crumble from center to sides, there are ever-longer stretches of abandoned shops, businesses, entire office buildings. When the economy goes bad, the first leaks spring at the weakest segments. The Delta's been hard hit for decades. You cruise the main street in small towns like Helena, just down the river a piece, or over by Rosedale, half the stores are empty as old shoes. The river's still impressive, but it ceased offering much by way of economic advantage long ago.

Just inside the city limits, I stopped at Momma's Café for coffee and a burger. Place was all but hidden behind a thicket of service trucks and hard-ridden pickups. Even here in the South, central cities become ever more homogeneous, one long stuttering chain of McDonald's and KFC and Denny's, while local cafés and restaurants cling to the outskirts as though thrown there by centrifugal force. Nowadays I find I have to lower myself into the city environment, any city environment, by degrees, like a diver with bends coming up—but I'm going down. And Momma's was just right for it. From there I drove on in and dragged for a couple of hours the streets I used to run as a cop, feeling the city slowly fall into place around me. Drove north on Poplar where East High School once stood, now a nest of cozy aluminum-sided single-family dwellings with tiny manicured lawns front and back. Drove by Overton Square. Cruised down Walnut, took the left at Vance and crossed Orleans. Hit Able and proceeded north past Beale and Union. Swung by 102-A Birch Street where I'd shot my partner Randy.

When I worked out of it, Central Precinct was on South Flicker, second floor of the old Armor Station. Now it was housed at 426 Tillman in the Binghamton section, for many years a hard and hard-bitten part of the city that looked to be, especially with the recent completion of Sam Cooper Boulevard just north, on its way back.

I pulled into a visitor space, went in and gave my name and credentials to a sergeant at the front desk, who said someone would be with me directly. *Directly,* I surmised, here meant something on the order of *any day now* back home. Eventually Sergeant Collins came out from behind his desk and escorted me through a reef of battered metal desks to an office at the rear.

Sam Hamill had been a rookie along with me. Now, heaven help him, he was Major Hamill, the watch commander. Forty pounds heavier than back in the day, a lot less hair, deltas of fat deposits around the eyes. Wearing a navy gabardine suit and a charcoal knit tie that would have been the bee's knees circa 1970.

"Turner. Good Lord."

"Never know who or what's likely to walk into a police station, do you?"

He came up from behind the desk to shake my hand. Took some effort. Definitely the coming up from behind the desk. Probably, too, in another way, shaking my hand.

"So how the hell've you been?"

"Away."

He eased himself back into his chair in a manner that brought hemorrhoids or getting shot in the butt to mind. "So I heard. Guys that told me, it was like, 'Hey, he's gone. Let's celebrate.'"

"Don't doubt it for a minute."

We sat regarding one another across the archipelago of his desk.

"You fucked up bad on the job, Turner."

"Not just on the job."

"What I heard." He stared, smiled and wheezed a bit before saying, "So where've you been?"

"Home, more or less."

"And now you're back."

"Briefly. Touching down. Here and gone before you know it."

"I was just on the phone with Lonnie Bates."

"Guess that explains why Sergeant Collins at the desk had me cooling my heels."

"Sheriff Bates speaks well of you. Seems a good man."

"He is. Would have made a great con artist. People tend to see him as just this hicktown officer, and he plays up to it, when the truth is, he's as smart and as capable as anyone I've ever worked with. Same goes for his deputy."

"Other deputy, you mean."

"Other deputy, right."

Sam nodded. When he did, cords of loose skin on his neck writhed. "Bates told me what happened."

He fiddled with a Webster cup. Clutch of ballpoint pens, letter opener, scissors, six-inch plastic ruler, couple of paper-sheathed soda straws, a cheap cigar in its wrapper.

"Deputy sheriff from another county won't hold much water here in Memphis."

"I know that. On the other hand, I do have a fugitive warrant."

"So Sheriff Bates informed me. So after I hung up from talking to him, I called over to our own sheriff's office and spoke with the fugitive squad there, people you'd ordinarily be expected to coordinate with. We help them out sometimes. Game of 'Mother May I?' is mostly what it is. You know how it works."

I nodded. "They give you permission to take one giant step?"

"So happens they did."

"Your town, Sam, and your call. Just I'd appreciate being there."

"Course, first we have to figure out where *there* is."

"Judd Kurtz doesn't ring any bells?"

"Not with me. Nino's we know. Also Semper Fi Investments. We keep an eye out. Hang on a minute."

He punched in an interoffice number, waited a couple of rings.

"Hamill. Any word on the street about a missing quarter-mill or so? . . . I see. . . . Say I was to whisper the name Judd Kurtz in your ear, would it get me a kiss? . . . Thanks, Stan."

He hung up.

"Stan heads up our task force on organized crime. Says a week or two back, a minor leaguer made his rounds—passed the collection plate, as Stan put it—then went missing. Rumor has it he's a nephew to one of the bosses. Stan also says someone's tried his best to put a lid on it."

"But even the best lids leak."

Sam nodded.

"Stan have any idea where we can find this supposed nephew?"

"You really been away that long, Turner? You think we're

gonna find this guy? What, he ripped off one of the bosses, then got himself arrested in the boondocks, made them send in the thick-necks? Those sound like career moves to you? Nephew or not, he's under Mud Island by now."

"In which case I need to find the thick-necks."

"How did I know?" Eyes went to the window looking out into the squad room. All the good stuff happened out there. He used to be out there himself. "You know your warrant doesn't cover them."

"I'm not asking you to help me, Sam. Just hoping you and your people won't get in my way."

"Oh, I think we can do a little better than that."

Again he punched in a number. "Tracy, you got a minute?"

Ten, twelve beats and the door opened.

Thirtyish, button jeans, dark T-shirt with a blazer over, up-turned nose, silver cuffs climbing the rim of one ear.

"Tracy Caulding, Deputy Sheriff Turner. Believe it or not, this man used to be one of ours. The two of us came on the job together, in fact."

"Wow. Now *there's* a recommendation."

"Back home, his sheriff got taken down by some of our local hardcases. Turner would like to meet them."

"Taken down?"

"He's alive. Badge is gonna spend some time in the drawer, though."

"That really blows."

"No argument from me. City rats gone country, Tracy. It's not their territory, what the fuck? They're in, they're out, they're gone."

"Where am I in this, Sam?"

"You ever said 'sir' or 'boss' your whole life?"

"Not as I recall. My mother—"

"Was a hardcore feminist, six books, whistle-blower on the evils of society. I do read personnel files, Tracy."

She smiled, quite possibly in that moment adding to global warming.

"Thing is, Turner here's been away a while. We don't want him getting lost. Show him around, help facilitate his reentry."

"Ride shotgun is what you mean," Tracy Caulding said.

"I don't need protection, Sam."

"I know you don't, old friend. What I'm thinking is, with you back, maybe *we* do."

CHAPTER SIX

HAD A WONDERFUL BARBEQUE dinner that night, Tracy Caulding and I, at Sonny Boy's #2 out on Lamar: indoor picnic benches, sweaty plastic pitchers of iced tea, roll of paper towels at each table. There was no Sonny Boy's #1, Tracy told me—not that, after a bite or two, anyone was likely to care. Amazing, blazing pork, creamy cool cole slaw, butterbeans and pinto beans baked together, biscuits. "Biscuits fresh ever hour," according to a hand-lettered sign.

For all its cultural razing, Memphis remains one of the great barbeque towns.

Tracy lowered a stand of ribs she'd sucked dry onto her plate and, tearing off a panel of paper towel, wiped her mouth as lustily as she'd taken to the barbeque. She picked up another segment of ribs, held it poised for launch, told me: "Stan Dimitri and I had coffee together this afternoon. From organized crime? He filled me in on the Aleché network."

"That what they're calling them now? Networks? To us they were just gangs."

"Then for a while it went to crews. Now it's networks. This one's responsible for much of the money that gets dry-cleaned through Semper Fi Investments. Run by, if you can believe it, a Native American who passes himself off as some sort of Mediterranean. Born Jimmy McCallum, been going by Jorge Aleché for years now."

"He the one with the nephew?"

"Stan thinks so."

"Stan thinks—that's the best you have?"

Shrugging. "What can I say?"

"Well . . . What *I* think is, it's time for a massive rattling of the cage."

The second portion of ribs dropped onto her plate. A third or fourth paper towel wiped away sins of the immediate past. Older sins took a bit longer.

"And here Sam thinks you're out of touch." She held up her beer, tipping its neck towards me. "I know who you are, Turner."

"I'd be surprised if you didn't. However big the city, the job's always a small town."

"I started hearing stories about you the day I first hit the streets."

"And I remember the first time I looked in a car's rearview mirror and saw the legend 'Objects May Be Closer Than They Appear.'"

"What the fuck's *that* mean?"

"That you can't trust stories."

"Yeah, but how many of us ever get to have stories told about us?" She drained her beer. "You notice how these bottles keep getting smaller?"

From the breast pocket of her blazer she took a narrow reporter's notebook. Found a free page, scribbled addresses and phone numbers, tore the page off and passed it me.

"Consider it part of your orientation package."

"You memorized all this?"

"Some people have trick joints, like their thumbs bend back to their forearms? I have a trick memory. I hear something, see something, I've got it forever."

"Buy you another beer before the bottles get too small? Alcohol kills brain cells, you know—could help wean you off that memory thing."

"Worth a try."

I got the waiter's attention, ordered another beer for Tracy, bourbon straight up for myself. He brought them and began clearing plates.

"Speaking of stories, I remember one I read years ago," Tracy said. "I was into science fiction then, and new to reading. Every book I opened was a marvel. One of the older writers—Kuttner, Kornbluth, those guys. People lived almost forever. But every hundred years or so they had to come back to this center where they'd plunge into this pool and swim across it. To rejuvenate them, I'm sure the story pointed out. Symbol of rebirth. But what *I* got from it was how the water of that miraculous pool would take away their memories, wipe them clean, let them go on."

I took a fond, measured sip of my bourbon. There was a time in my life when measured sips hadn't been called for. That whole measurement thing creeps up on us. Start off counting hairs in the bathtub drain, before we know it we're telling people we're only allowed a cup and a half of coffee a day, reading labels for saturated-fat content, trying to portion out our losses, like a double-entry accountant, to history and failing memory.

"I'm not sure I know how to respond," I told Tracy.

"Yeah. Me either. Exactly what I mean. Four hundred killed when the roof of a substandard apartment building collapses in Pakistan. A fifteen-year-old goes into his high school with an assault weapon and kills three teachers, the principal, twelve fellow students. Half the citizens of some country you never heard of go after the other half, kill or butcher them and bulldoze them into mass graves. There's a proper response to something like that? You get to wishing you could go for a swim, wipe it all away. But you can't."

We tossed off the remainder of our drinks in silence and called it a night. Enough of the world's eternal problems and our own.

"Check in tomorrow?" Tracy said.

"First thing."

"Where are you staying?"

Since I was here on my own dime, I'd taken the cheapest room I could find, at Nu-Way Motel on the city's outer rings. Each unit was painted a different pastel shade, mine what I could only think of as Pepto-Bismol pink. A stack of fifties magazines inside would not have surprised.

Walking Tracy Caulding to her blue Honda Civic, I gave her my location, room and phone number. "No need to write them down for you's my guess," I said, getting another glimpse of the smile that had lit up Sam's office back at the station. From habit I looked in to clear the car, saw a ziggurat of textbooks on the back seat.

"What's this? Not a dedicated law officer?"

She held up her hands, palm out, in mock surrender. "Got me dead to rights."

"Graduate school, from the look of it."

"I confess. M.A. in social work, six credits to go."

She leaned back against the rear door, tugging at the silver-cuffed ear.

"Cop was the last thing I thought I'd be. From the time I was eleven, twelve years old, I was going to be a teacher. Nose forever in a book and all that. But I grew up in a trailer park, no way my parents could afford even local colleges. I had grand ambitions, though, applied all over the mid-South, even places like Tulane and Duke. Memphis State came through with a full scholarship. I had a job teaching sixth grade promised before I'd even graduated. Five weeks in, I walked away from it."

She put her hand on my arm.

"Everything I'd taken for granted all those years was gone. I had no idea who I was, what I could do, and I had to work. Of a Sunday morning I was reading want ads when one at the very corner of the page caught my eye. Police badge to the left. Have a degree? it said. Want to make a difference?—or something equally lame. Another of the department's periodic thrusts to improve its image. Wanted people with degrees, offered an accelerated training program for those who qualified. So here I am. Telling you way more than you wanted to know. Sorry."

"Don't be."

She was in the car now, looking out.

"We should talk about counseling and social work sometime," I said.

"Did a bit of it yourself, from what I hear."

"More like I muddied the water."

"So we should. Just don't tell me I'm wrong, okay?" Hauling her seat belt across. "See you tomorrow, Turner." Face in the rearview mirror as she drove away. Objects may be closer than they appear.

Back at the motel I punched my way through a thicket of numbers, 9 for an outside line, 1 for long distance, area code, credit-card number, personal code. Quite the modern lawman.

"Sheriff's office."

"Who's speaking?"

"Rob Olson."

"Trooper?"

"You bet. Who's this?"

"Turner, up in Memphis."

"The deputy, right?"

"Right. Don't guess Lonnie'd be around this late, would he?"

"He's always around. Though it might be best if you didn't tell him I said that." Miles and miles away, coffee got slurped. "Be here right this minute save he's out to an accident. Told him I'd go but he wouldn't hear of it. You hold a minute, Turner? Got someone on the other line."

Then he was back.

"That's Bates on line two. He's at the hospital with an accident victim, wants to speak with you. Hold on, I'll try to transfer you."

Some time went by.

"Turner. You there? I can't get this damn thing to work. And I think I just hung up on the sheriff. He's still over to the hospital. You wanta call him there?"

He gave me the number, and I did.

"Those boys at the barracks are the best you'll see at paper-work," Lonnie said when I told him what happened. "Other things . . ."

Someone was there by him, complaining. I'd probably called in to the ER nurse's station, which might be the only line functioning this time of night. The local hospital wasn't a hell of a lot larger or more complicated than our office.

"Official police work," he said. "Chill, Gladys." Then to me: "So you're still in Memphis. Any action?"

I filled him in on my visit. Connecting with Sam Hamill, meeting Tracy. Think I may have found out where to go to get what I'm looking for, I told him.

"That's good. Quick."

"I followed your advice."

"Hamill put you and Tracy together knowing she'd give up the contact, he wouldn't have to." As always, Lonnie was a move ahead.

"Way I saw it, too."

"So why the fancy footwork?"

"Maybe they figure I can take care of a problem they haven't been able to."

Lonnie was silent for a moment.

"In which case, since Hamill laid out the official face of the thing for you, even assigned an officer, the MPD can in no way be held responsible. Either you handle it and you're home before anyone knows better—"

"Or I get, as our British friends say, nicked for the deed, in which case Sam and the MPD disclaim to their heart's content."

"Clean."

"More than one way to get the job done."

"Always. Damn! Now the goddamned beeper's going off. Hang on."

I heard voices behind, just out of range of intelligibility.

"Shirley checking in," Lonnie said moments later.

"You've got a beeper now."

"Simon has a band concert tomorrow, some kind of solo. Wife wanted to be sure I would make it, gave me hers." Simon in buzz-cut and baggies was the older of two sons. The younger, Billy, despite the flag of multiple piercings, had no direction any of us could discern but was a sweetheart, maybe the closest thing to an innocent human being I've known.

"How's June?"

"Cleared by her doctors and home with us. Mostly herself, but sometimes it's like she's not really there, she's gone off someplace else."

"Not surprising, with what she's just been through."

"I hope."

"Give it time. Don Lee?"

"Stable, they keep telling me—though he hasn't come round yet. Wait and see, they say, we just have to wait and see."

Gladys was back, loudly demanding return of the phone he'd taken hostage. Lonnie ignored her.

"Trooper said you wanted to talk to me. What's up?"

"May be nothing to it, but the accident I answered the call to?"

"Yes?"

"It got called in as a collision, but what happened was, Madge Gunderson passed out at the wheel and ran into a tree."

"Madge okay?" Madge had been a not-so-secret drinker most of her life. Her husband Karel died last year, and since then, maybe from grief, maybe from the fact that she didn't have to hide it anymore, the drinking had kind of got out of control.

"She will be. Just some gashes and the like. Looked worse than it is. This happened out on State Road 419. Woman driving behind her saw the whole thing, called it in on a cell phone."

"Okay."

"Woman's from up Seattle way, just passing through. I thanked her, naturally, took her statement. Then she says, 'You're the sheriff?' and when I say, 'Right now I am,' she asks does a man named Turner work with me."

"Say what she wanted?"

"Not a word. Sat there smiling at her and waiting, all she did was smile back."

"What's she look like?"

"Late twenties, early thirties, light brown hair cut short, five-eight, one-thirty. Easy on the eye, as my old man would of said. Jeans and sweatshirt, kind with a hood, ankle-high black Reeboks."

"Name?"

"J. T. Burke. That's Burke with an *e,* and just the initials."

No one I knew. Maybe a patient from my days as a counselor, was my first thought. Though it was doubtful any patient could have traced me here, or would have reason to.

"Don't suppose she said where she was headed."

"Gave me that same smile when I asked."

"That it, then?"

"Pretty much."

"So give Gladys back her phone already."

In exchange I gave him the name and location of my motel and my phone number, told him to call if he had any updates on Don Lee or happened to hear again from Ms. Burke.

CHAPTER SEVEN

COULDN'T SLEEP.

Out on the streets at 2 a.m. looking for an open restaurant. Back to city habits that quickly. Had my book, just needed light, coffee, maybe a sandwich. Do the Edward Hopper thing.

Dino's Diner, half a mile in towards the city proper. "Open 24 hours" painted on the glass in foot-high blue letters. Also "Daily Specials" and "Hearty Breakfasts." These in yellow.

"Getchu?" the waitress, Jaynie, said, handing over a much-splattered menu. "T'drink?"

Coffee. Definitely.

And received a reasonable facsimile of same, though it took some time. Peak hour, after all. Had to be three or four other patrons at least.

"Two scrambled, bacon, grits, biscuit," I told Jaynie when my coffee came.

Eggs were rubber—no surprise there—bacon greasy and underdone, biscuit from a can. Here I am in the Deep South and I get a canned biscuit? On the other hand, the grits were amazing.

The book also disappointed. Three refills and I was done with it, wide margins, large type, pages read almost as quickly as I turned them. Novels tend to be short these days. Probably most of them should be even shorter. This one was about a doctor, child of the sixties and long a peace activist, who goes after the men who raped and killed his wife and disposes of them one by one. Title: *Elective Surgery*.

I took out my wallet, unfolded the notebook page Tracy Caulding had given me. Three addresses, none of which meant much to me. A lot of Lanes and Places, bird names the rage. Meadowlark Drive, Oriole Circle, like that. But just then a cab pulled up out front and the driver came in. Jaynie slapped a cup of coffee down before him without being asked. He was two stools away. One of those in-betweens you find all over the South, darkish skin, could be of Italian descent, Mediterranean, Caribbean, Creole. Fine features, a broad nose, gold eyes—like a cat's. Wearing pleated khakis with enough starch to have held on to their crease though now well crumpled about the crotch, navy blue polo shirt, corduroy sport coat.

I caught his eye, asked "How's it going?"

"Been better. Been worse, too."

"And will be again."

"Believe it."

He pulled out a pack of Winstons, shook one loose and got it going. Then as an afterthought glanced my way, took the pack out again and offered me one. When I declined, he put the cigarettes back, held out his hand. We shook.

"Danel. Like Daniel without the *i*."

"Turner. . . . Any chance you could help me with these?"

I slid the paper across. After a moment he looked up.

"From out of town, are you."

I pled guilty.

"But you have business here." He tapped at the paper.

Yes.

"Well, sir, this here ain't part of Memphis at all, it's another country. Birdland, some of us call it. Bunch of whitebread castles's what it is. Some Johnny-come-lately builds him a house, next Johnny comes along and has to outdo him, build a bigger one. Kind of business that gets transacted out there, most people'd do best to stay away from. I'm guessing you're not most people."

"Can you give me directions?"

"Yeah, sure, I could do that. Or—" He threw back his coffee. "What the hell, it's a slow night, I'll run you out there."

We struck a deal, I picked up the Chariot as he sat idling in the Nu-Way Motel parking lot, then pulled in behind and followed him to city's edge. Here be dragons. We'd been cruising for close to thirty minutes, I figured, six or seven classics on whatever station I'd found by stabbing the Seek button—Buffalo Springfield ("There's some-thing hap-pen-ing here . . ."), Bob Seger's "Night Moves"—when Danel pulled his Checker cab onto the shoulder, a wide spot intended for rest stops, repairs, tire changes. I came alongside and we wound down windows.

"Here's where I bail," he said. "Place you're looking for's just around that bend. Don't be lookin' for the welcome mat to be out. Ain't the kind to be expecting company up in there."

I hoped not.

"Good luck, man."

"Thanks for your help." I'd paid him back at the diner. He had a good night.

"You're welcome. Prob'ly ain't done you no favor, though."

I pulled back onto the road, along the curve, cut the engine to coast into a driveway inhabited by a black BMW and a gussied-up red Ford pickup, chrome pipes, calligraphic squiggle running from front fender to rear wheel well, driver's-side spotlight. Backed out then and parked the Jeep a quarter-mile up the road, at another of those pull-offs.

The house was a castle, all right—like something imagined by Dr. Seuss. Classic middle-American tacky. Once in El Paso I'd seen a huge bedroom unit that looked to be marble but, when you touched it, turned out to be thin plastic. It was like that.

In the front room just off the entryway (as I peered through what I could only think of as eight-foot-tall wing windows) a large-screen TV was on, but there was no evidence of anyone in attendance. Action appeared to be centered in the kitchen—I'd come around to the back by then—where a card game and considerable beer consumption were taking place. Many longnecks had given their all. Bottles of bourbon and Scotch. One guy in a designer suit, two others in department-store distant cousins.

Newly awakened from its slumber in Glad bag and hand towel, the .38 Police Special felt strangely familiar to my hand.

One of the cheap-suit players was raking in chips as I came through the door. Undistracted, his counterpart pushed to his feet, gun halfway out as I shot. He fell back into his chair, which went over, as though its rear legs were a hinge, onto the floor. I'd tried for a shoulder, but it had been a while, and I hit further in on his chest. There was more blood than I'd have liked, too, but he'd be okay.

Thinking it over for a half-minute or so, the second cheap suit held up both hands, removed his Glock with finger and thumb and laid it on the table, just another poker chip.

Dean Atkison in his designer suit looked at his flunky with histrionic disgust and took a pull off his drink.

"Who the hell are you?" he said.

I was supposed to be watching *him* at that point, of course—cheap suit's cue. He almost had the Glock in hand when I shot. His arm jerked, knocking the Glock to the floor, then went limp. He stood looking down at the arm that would no longer do what he willed it to do. His fingers kept on scrabbling, the way cat paws will when the cat's asleep and dreaming of prey.

It was all coming back.

Atkison's eyes went from his fallen soldiers to me.

"Be okay if I call for help for my boys here?"

"Go ahead."

I stood by as he punched 911 into a cell phone, asked for paramedics, gave his address, and threatened the dispatcher. Thing about cell phones is you can't slam the receiver down.

"Think we might attend to business now?"

"We don't have any business."

I whacked his knee with the gun, feeling skin tear and hearing something crunch. Blood welled through the expensive fabric. None of that should have happened.

"I live in a small town far away from here," I said. "Not far enough, apparently. A few days ago you brought your garbage to it."

He'd grabbed a hand towel off the table, was wrapping it around his knee.

"Paid some goddamn arrogant surgeon nine thousand to have that thing fixed, not six weeks ago. Now look at it."

"A man named Judd Kurtz came through. He didn't get through fast enough and wound up in jail. Then a couple of others came in his wake. None of them stayed."

"And I should care what happened in Bumfuck?"

I walked to him, helped wrap the towel.

"I need to know who Judd Kurtz is. I need to know if he's alive. And I need to know who the goons were who thought they could come into my town and tear it up."

"That's a lot of need."

Pulling hard at the ends of the towel, I knotted them.

"I was in a state prison for seven years," I told him. "I managed okay in there. There's not much I won't do."

He looked down at his shattered knee. Blood seeped steadily into the towel.

"Looks like a fucking Kotex," he said. "I'm a mess." He shook his head. "I'm a mess—right?"

"It could be worse."

He pulled a napkin towards him. Started to reach under his coat and stopped himself. "I'm just getting a pen, okay?"

I nodded, and he took a bright yellow Mont Blanc out of his coat pocket, wrote, passed the napkin across. Classic penmanship, the kind you don't see anymore, all beautifully formed loops and curls—confounded by the absorbent napkin that blurred and feathered each fine, practiced stroke.

"My life's not all that much, mind you," he said, "but I'd like to know it doesn't end here."

I shook my head. Sirens of fire truck and ambulance were close by now.

Nodding towards the napkin, Atkison said, "You'll find what you need there."

What I needed right then was to go out the back door, and I did.

When first I held it, the gun had felt so familiar. The body has a memory all its own. I started the car, pulled the seat belt across and clicked it home. Slipped into gear. The body remembers where we've been even as the mind turns away. I eased off the clutch and pulled out, hot wires burning again within me, incandescent. Blinding.

CHAPTER EIGHT

MY FATHER'S UNIFORM hung in the back of a closet at the front of our house, in an unused bedroom. I found it there one rainy Saturday afternoon. It smelled of mothballs—camphor, as I'd later learn. Again and again I ran my fingers over its scratchy, stiff material. Dad never talked about his army time, what he'd done. In my child's mind I had him traversing deserts in Sherman tanks or diving fighter planes that looked much like Sopwith Camels through air thick with gunfire, smoke, and disintegrating aircraft. Much later, after his death, Mother told me he'd been a supply clerk.

I was, I don't know, twelve or so then. It was a couple of years after that that Al showed up in town.

He'd been in the service, people said, some place called Korea. Before, they added, he'd been the best fiddler in the county, but he'd given that up. He worked at the ice house, swinging fifty-pound blocks of ice off the ramp with huge tongs and all the time looking around, at the sky, at broken windows in the old power plant across the street, as though he wasn't really there, only his body was, doing these same things over and over, like a machine. He always had this half-smile on his face. He rented a room over the ice house but went there only to sleep. The rest of the time he was out walking the streets or sitting on the bench at the end of Main Street. He'd sit there looking off into the woods for hours. Pretty soon after I met him, when the ice house shut down, he lost his job. They let him stay on in the room, but then they tore the building down and he lost that too, so he lived out in the open, sleeping where he could. Later I'd get to know a lot of people like Al, people damaged deep inside, people whom life had abandoned but wouldn't quite let go of.

How did we meet? I honestly can't remember. I just remember everyone at school talking about him, then there's a skip, like on a record, and we're together throwing rocks into the Blue Hole, which everyone said had no bottom and half the world's catfish, or walking through Big Billy Simon's pasture with cows eyeing us, or sitting under a crabapple tree passing a Nehi back and forth.

It wasn't long before my folks heard about it and told me to stay away from him. When I asked why, Mother said: He's just not right, son, that war did something to him.

But I went on seeing him, after school most every day. That was the first time I openly defied my parents, and things got tense for a while before they gave up. Many subsequent defiances took place in stone silence.

I was fourteen when Al and I met; a couple of years later I was getting ready to go off to college, first in New Orleans then in Chicago, little suspecting that but a few years down the line I'd be crawling through trees not unlike the ones Al stared into every day. In the time I'd known him, I'd grown two feet taller and Al had aged twenty years.

I was sitting outside the tent one day taping up my boots when mail came around. I was on my third pair. In that climate, leather rotted fast. The French had tried to tell us, but as usual we didn't listen. They'd tried to tell us a lot of things. Anyway, it was five or six in the morning—you never could sleep much after that, what with all the bird chatter—and Bud chucked a beer my way, giving out the standard call, "Breakfast of champions," as I settled in to read my letter. Mom had written two pages about what was going on back home, who'd just married who, how so many of the stores downtown were boarded up these days, that the old Methodist church burned down. Newsreels from another world. Then there at the end she'd written: I'm sorry to have to tell you this, but Al died last week.

I grabbed another warm beer and went out to forest's edge, remembering that final summer.

For as long as I could remember, there'd been an old fiddle tucked away in the back of a closet no one used, in a cracked wood case shaped like a coffin. It had been my grandfather's, who played it along with banjo. I asked Dad if I could have it and after looking oddly at me, since I'd never shown much interest in music before, he shrugged and said he didn't see why not. This was late in his life, after the sawmill shut down, when he mostly just sat at the kitchen table all day.

I put some rubber bands around the case to hold it together and took it to Mr. Cohen, the school band director, who played violin in church some Sundays. Looked to him like a German-made fiddle from the 1800s, he said. He put on new strings and got the old bridge to stand up under them and gave me an extra bow he had. Not a full-size bow, only three-quarters, he said, but it'll do.

That afternoon I walked up to Al with the fiddle behind my back.

He eyed me suspiciously. "Whatchu got there, boy?"

I laid the case down on the bench and opened it. To this day I don't know what to call the expression that came over his face. I think maybe it's one of those things there's no word for.

"It's for you," I told him.

His eyes held mine for some time. He took the bow from under its clip. Al's hands always shook, but when he touched that bow they stopped. He weighed the bow in one hand, felt along its length, tightened the hair and bounced it against his palm, tightened it a little more.

Then he reached out with his left hand for the fiddle.

"It's all tuned up," I said.

He nodded, tucked the fiddle under his chin and sat there a moment with his eyes closed.

I don't remember what he played. Something I'd heard before, from my father or grandfather, one of the old fiddle tunes, "Sally Goodin" or "Blackberry Blossom," maybe. Next he tried a waltz.

He took the fiddle out from under his chin and held it against one leg, looking off at nothing in particular, smiling that half-present smile of his.

"It's just an old, cheap instrument," I said.

"No. The fiddle's fine," he said, putting it back in the case, clipping in the bow, carefully fastening the hooks. His hands were shaking again. "The music's in there. It just ain't in me no more."

We sat a while, hearing cars and trucks pass behind us, looking out into the trees. Towards sundown when I was getting ready to head home, he said, "Reckon we won't be seeing much of each other for a time."

I nodded, too desperately young—soon enough, that would change—to understand good-byes.

After a moment he added: "Appreciate what you did, boy."

I picked up the case. I'd put on a new coat of paint, shiny black. In lowering light it looked like a puddle of ink, a pool of darkness. "Sure you don't want this?"

He shook his head. "Didn't mean about the fiddle, but I appreciate that too." Holding out his hand, he said, "Like you to have something. Got this when I was overseas, what they call in country, and it's been with me ever since. Want you should take it with you. Be your good luck charm."

A tiny cat carved out of sandalwood.

CHAPTER NINE

DAWN BEAT ITS PROUD pink breast as I and Chariot chugged to a stop. International news on the radio, a couple of ads for car dealers, now suddenly Jeremiah was a bullfrog, joy to the world.

Another mansion on the hill. Two cars, Mercedes, Lincoln, in a garage remarkably free of clutter. Ancient weeping willow like a bad sixties haircut outside, smell of fresh-brewed coffee from within. Older man in a terrycloth robe sitting at a table just inside glass doors from the patio. Wineglass of orange juice, possibly a mimosa, before him. Basket of bread, bowl of fruit. Scatter of woven rugs on what looked to be Saltillo tile and spotless. Mexican furniture in the room beyond. Lawn sprinklers went off behind me as I peered in.

Snooping about, I found a breachable window in the utility room and took advantage. Stood just inside listening, then slipped the door and listened some more before stepping through. No footsteps or other sounds of movement. Soft ersatz jazz from a radio out in the room by the patio.

He was tearing the horn from a croissant as I came up behind him and put thumbs to his neck.

"Compress carotids," I said, "and you shut off blood supply to the brain." I told him what I wanted to know. "We can talk when you come back around," I added, adding pressure as well, as his hands fell onto his lap and the others entered the room like silk. One of them facing me, the other one, the one that mattered, behind. Where they were before, I've no idea. I would have sworn he was alone.

Catching a glance from the one in front, I managed a half turn before the one behind closed on me and I joined the older man in darkness.

I came awake with a woman's face above me. The guy who had been standing behind me was male, no doubt about it. Not much doubt, either, that I was on the floor. Turning my head to the right, I saw swollen pink feet rising towards bare legs topped with a hem of terrycloth robe that in my confused state put me in mind of Elizabethan ruffled collars. Turned my head to the left and saw a body desperately attempting to drag itself out of harm's way, though at this point most of the harm it was likely to withstand had already befallen it.

"You're okay," the woman above me said. Not a question. Shortish dark hair pulled back. Hazel eyes in which glints of green surfaced and sank. She sounded pretty certain. I'd have to take her word for it.

"Mr. Aleché has agreed to call off his dogs. That right, Mr. Aleché?"

From high above terrycloth and tabletop, out of the clear blue sky up there, came a "Yes."

"One of his dogs seems to have taken bad," I said, glancing left again.

"Other one's a bit the worse for wear, too."

"Terrible shame."

Her face broke into a smile. Before, I'd always believed that to be merely a figure of speech.

"And lest you wonder, Mr. Aleché says these are the two men you're looking for. He seems to be under the impression that I know what's going on and that I am somehow your partner in this enterprise."

She held out her arm at a ninety-degree angle, inviting me to take it and lever myself to a sitting position. We grasped hands thumbs-over and, leaning hard into strong forearm and biceps, I pulled myself up.

"Mr. Aleché has also been kind enough to agree that by way of reparation he'll cover all medical expenses for your fellow officer and dispatcher. And he hopes you'll accept his apologies for his employees' misguided enthusiasm."

It's over, then, is what most people would think. But, even as she helped me up, I saw that she knew better, saw her clearly: the stance, feet planted squarely, center of gravity kept low, eyes taking it all in even as they appeared not to.

"You're a cop."

"That obvious, huh?" Again the smile. "I'm also your daughter." She held out a hand. "J. T. Burke."

. . .

Lots of scatlike noise and harrumphing from Sam Hamill back at the station, words to the effect that here was another fine mess I'd gotten him and MPD into, one shouldn't lie down with dogs, and it would be best if I were out of town by sundown.

"No sign of Judd Kurtz, huh?" Tracy Caulding asked. She'd stayed behind for her own counsel once Sam was done with me, then followed me out to the parking lot.

"Doubt there will be. Hope it didn't go too bad for you in there."

"About as you'd expect. What the hell was I thinking, tuck in the corners, it better not come back to bite his butt. Then he said, 'You need any help with this—stitches show up in the works, anyone whosoever tries giving you grief—you call me, you hear?'"

"Don't guess he added he'd be happy to have me back on the job any time?"

"I don't believe that came up. Take care, Turner."

We surrendered J. T.'s rental Buick at a drop-off on Lamar, grabbing coffee to go at a Greek diner next door. The cups were shaped like Shriner's hats and, inexplicably, had rabbits on them. Not cuddly little bunnies, but huge kangaroo-thighed jackrabbits.

"Obviously they think a lot of you back at the station house," J. T. said as we pulled into traffic.

"I'm a legend here on the frontier."

"Must be nice." She stared silently out the window. "It all starts looking the same after a while, doesn't it? Same streets, same victims, same impossible stories and apologies."

We passed a car with the hood up, driver leaning into it. As we came abreast, he hiked his middle over the rim and slid in further. It looked as though the car were swallowing him piecemeal.

"If that's what you're looking for, an apology, I don't have one."

"Good. I've had enough of those, plenty to last me. And I'm not looking for anything—well, I *was* looking for you. But I found you, didn't I? So now I'm not."

"And how, exactly, did that come about, the finding me?"

"I talked to some people in town, learned about the cabin, and went out there. There was a woman sitting on the porch."

"Val."

"I'd figured just to look around, maybe wait till you showed up. But I introduced myself, told her who I was, and we got to talking. She told me what's been going on, and that you were up here. I was waiting to turn in at the motel when I saw the Jeep pulling out."

"So you followed. Keeping well back, from the look of it."

She shrugged. "Old habit. Check exits before you go in, try to figure what's going down before you step in it. Like that."

"Cop thinking."

"You know how it is. Kind of takes over after a while."

Later, after one last stop in the city, well out of it and coming abreast of a long line of tarpaper shacks bordered by a service station and a church whose white paint had long ago gone to glory, we'd pick up the conversation. J. T.'s head turned to read the sign that told us we were entering the town of Sweetwater.

"So this is the South."

"Part of it, anyway. Disappointed?"

"Not really, just trying to get the lay of the land. Disappointment requires expectations. Like people have these scripts running in their heads about how life is supposed to go?"

"And you don't?"

"Mostly, no."

"Just take things as they come."

"I try." After a moment she added: "Seems to have worked for you."

We rode on past Sweetwater, through Magnolia and Rice-town, into mile after mile of cotton and soybean fields, plumes of dust on far horizons where pickups and farm machinery stalked the land.

"How's your mom?"

"Speaking of expectations." She laughed. "Somewhere in Mexico, last I heard. One of those gringo artist enclaves. That was over a year ago."

"She's an artist now?"

"I think she applied for the Grande Dame position. I'm sure they needed one, whether they knew it or not. Actually, she's mellowed."

"Some of us do. Others just wear down. . . . And your brother?"

An ancient, battered lime green Volkswagen bus with lace curtains in the windows came up behind. Pointing to the VW's bumper sticker, J. T. said, "Kind of like that."

GOD WAS MY CO-PILOT
BUT WE CRASHED IN THE MOUNTAINS
AND I HAD TO EAT HIM

When I looked at her, she said, "You don't know, do you?"

I shook my head.

"Don died last year. Had a little more fun than he planned one Saturday night, got deeper than he thought, and flew off forever on his magic carpet of crack." Her eyes came to mine. "I'm sorry, I don't mean to be crude. Or cruel."

"It's okay."

Problems had lay coiled up beside Don in the crib from the day of his birth. Even then he wore a tense, fretful frown, as though he knew bad things were coming, as though he knew he had to be constantly on guard—though it probably wouldn't help much. Everything was a challenge, even the simple routines of daily life, getting up, getting dressed, leaving the apartment, shopping, a succession of near-insurmountable Everests. When things were going well, he managed to kind of plod along. But things didn't go well very often, or for very long. Choosing between breakfast cereals paralyzed him. On the phone, back when he used to call, he'd talk for hours about all these plans he had, never manage to carry through on the first half-step of any of them.

"I thought you knew. I'm sorry."

"Don't be. It's not as though we couldn't see it coming. The surprising thing is that he held out as long as he did. Were the two of you close?"

"Not for a long time. I tried. I'd go over to wherever he was crashing and check on him, try to be sure he ate something, got some rest."

"But you can't . . ."

"No," she said. "You can't. Like you said: we wear down. Or wear out."

CHAPTER TEN

"I'M SORRY, I don't remember you. Should I?" His eyes moved aimlessly about the room. Guards had told me he was almost completely blind now. When I spoke, the eyes would come momentarily to me. Then they'd move away again.

Because of the blindness, Lou Winter had been kept out of the general population. But they'd got to him a time or two anyway, as the wing-shaped scar splitting the side of his face attested. Cons totally lacking in conscience, people who'd slit throats over a supposed insult and murder a grandmother for busfare, can get themselves worked into a moral frenzy over child molesters.

I told him who I was.

"I'm sorry. I'm afraid I don't remember much these days." Guards also told me that he'd had a series of small strokes over the years. "Everyone says that may be a good thing. I don't know what they mean by that. But thank you for coming."

After a pause he added, "Is there something I can do for you?"

"I just stopped by to say hello."

For a moment then I sensed the effort, the force of will. If he could just get hold of it, could just concentrate hard enough . . . But his eyes moved away, the curtains stayed shut, the play was over.

"I brought you this."

His hand reached out and found by sound the box I pushed across the table.

"It's not much. Some of the peppermints and circus peanuts the guards say you like, toiletries, a few other things."

But he had found the totem, the tiny cat carved out of sandalwood that Al had given me all those years ago, and was not listening. He held it close to his face, smelled it, rubbed it against his cheek where the scar ran down. I told him what it was. That a friend gave it to me.

"And now you've given it to me?"

I nodded, then said yes.

"Thank you." He shifted the totem from hand to hand. "Were we friends, then? Are we, I mean?"

"Not really. But we've known one another a long time."

"I'm sorry . . . so sorry I don't, can't, remember."

He held up the totem. "It's beautiful, isn't it? Small and beautiful. I can tell."

"Do you need anything, Lou? Is there anything I can do for you?"

"Good of you, son. But no." For that moment I would have sworn he was looking directly at me, that he saw me. Then his eyes went away. He closed his hand over the sandalwood cat. "I'm pretty well set up here." He nodded. "Yessir. Pretty well set up."

J. T. asked no questions when I got back to the car. But for some reason as we drove out of Memphis I started telling her about Lou Winter, about my first months on the force, about how hard it had been, going through those prison gates and doors. We sat together quietly then for a while until, looking out at the sign welcoming us to Sweetwater and the tarpaper shacks beyond, she said, "So this is the South."

Getting in towards town, I pointed out the Church of the Ark, a local landmark. It had once been just another First Baptist Church, but in 1921 during a major flood that wiped out most of the area, the building had miraculously lifted off its moorings and floated free, pastor and family taking aboard other survivors clinging to trees and housetops. It was renamed shortly thereafter.

CHAPTER ELEVEN

SHE'D GROWN UP wherever her mother lit in her never-ending pursuit of best job, best house, best climate, best schools, best place to live. Took the name of her first stepfather, then resolutely refused to change it when others came along. That was the Burke. Just after she turned twenty-one she started calling herself J. T. Never felt like a Sandra, she said. It didn't stand for anything, "just your initials."

She'd graduated high school at seventeen, done two years of prelaw in Iowa City, where Stepfather of the Month, a teacher of religion, had moved to study the Amish, then when that household broke up (and the marriage shortly thereafter—"in a roadside diner on the way to their new home's the way I always imagine it, him hugging his Bible as Mom steps out to flag a ride with some trucker"), she stayed behind, crashing with friends, hanging out in college bars. Got all that essential youth experience behind me in record time, she said, couple, three months, and was done with it. Never could get the knack of small talk, parties, hobbies, that kind of thing.

She'd driven to Chicago with a friend one weekend and stayed behind when the friend headed back. Worked as a corrections officer, which led to process serving, which led to a stint as a federal marshal. Now she worked up in Seattle, detective first grade. Knew she'd hit it right the first day on the job, went home glowing.

Then she hit the second day.

A sixteen-year-old had come in late one night and quietly murdered his whole family. Drowned his baby sister in the kitchen sink so she wouldn't have to see the rest, then with a Spiderman pillow smothered the six-year-old brother with whom he shared a room. Got the father's ancient service revolver from a box in the garage, loaded it with three bullets he'd bought on the schoolyard (just chance that they proved the right caliber) and shot both parents to death in their bed. Before shooting himself, he sat down at their bedside and painstakingly wrote out in block letters, vaguely Gothic, a note, just one word: ENOUGH.

But it wasn't, because the boy survived. Brian was his name. The round had gone through the roof of his mouth, wiping out any higher brain functions but leaving the brain stem untouched. He was still breathing, after all these years. And his heart went on beating. And one could only hope that his mind truly was gone, that he wasn't trapped in place somewhere in there going through all this again and again.

J. T. and her new partner, who had about two weeks more experience than she, were first call, right after patrol responded. Nothing can prepare you for a sight like that, she said. Or for what happens afterwards. It gets in your head like some kind of parasite and won't turn loose, it just keeps biting you, feeding on you.

She was quiet for a time then.

My partner quit the force not long after, she said. Why did I stick with it? Why do any of us?

So I told her a few stories of my own.

CHAPTER TWELVE

WORST THING I'VE ever seen?

Not something I brought home from jungles halfway across the world. Not a body dead ten days of a long hot summer, not a black man hanging from the streetlamp of a strip mall in the New South. Or a gentle old blind man waiting to be strapped to a table in the name of justice and injected with poisons that will stop his lungs and heart.

I got the call one Friday night a year or so back, 11 p.m. or so. We'd had three or four quiet days, just the way we liked them. Traffic accident out on the highway, troopers would meet me there. I chalked code and destination on the board on my way out.

Four teenagers had taken a Buick for a joyride. Doug Glazer, the high-school principal's son; his girlfriend Jennie; local bad boy Dan Taylor; and multi-pierced Patricia Pope. They'd left a high school football game and seen the Buick there, keys in the slot, motor running. Why not. Drove it through town a couple of times, then out onto the interstate where they ran up under a semi at eighty-plus mph. I seen them comin', the driver said, I just couldn't get out of their way fast enough, I just couldn't get out of the way, not fast enough.

Most of Jennie's head was on the dashboard, mouth still smiling, lipstick bright. Dan Taylor and Pat Pope were a jumble of blood and body parts out of which one silver-studded ear protruded to catch light from the patrol car's bubble light. Glazer, the driver, had been thrown clear, not a mark on him. He looked quite peaceful.

We never know, do we? The hammer's hanging there as we go on about all the small things we do, paying bills, scouring sinks, restringing banjos, neglecting yet again to tell the one beside us how much he or she is loved.

Troopers had beat me to the site. The younger of them was throwing up at roadside. The senior one approached me.

"You'd be the sheriff."

"Deputy." We exchanged names, shook hands.

"Just a bunch of kids. Don't make any sense at all. . . . Yo, Roy! you done over there?" Then to me: "Boy's first week on the job."

Since it was the interstate, they'd do the paperwork. I'd be left to notify the families.

"Gonna be a long hard night," Trooper Stanton said.

"Looks like."

"That yours?" he said, nodding towards the fire truck that had just pulled up. Benny waved from within. All we had was a volunteer department. Benny in real life worked at the auto parts store just down from city hall. He'd been through EMT training up at the capital.

"Sure is."

Took us better than two hours to clear the scene. Almost 3 a.m. when I knocked on Principal Glazer's door. I was there just under a half hour, then passed on to Jennie's parents, to Dan Taylor's father, Pat Pope's mother.

Sheila Pope lived in a trailer park outside town. She came to the screen door in a threadbare chenille robe, wearing one of those mesh sleep bonnets. It was pink. When I told her, there was no response, no reaction.

"You do understand—right, Mrs. Pope? Patricia's dead."

"Well . . . She was never a good girl, you know. I think I'll miss her, though."

That night I got back to the office not long before Don Lee showed up to take day shift. I made coffee, filled him in on the MVA, and headed home. In the rearview mirror I saw June pull into the spot I left.

A lazy, roiling fog lay on the water as I came around it to the cabin. One of the sisal-bound kitchen chairs on the porch had finally come apart. I suspected that the possum sitting close by may have had something to do with that. Maybe as a trained officer I should check for traces of twine in its teeth. I went in, poured milk into a bowl, and set it out on the porch.

She was never a good girl, you know. I think I'll miss her, though.

That's what a life came to.

Years ago, back when I had such arrogance as to think I could help anyone, I had as a patient a young woman who'd been raped and severely beaten while jogging. It happened near a reservoir. Every time she lifted a glass of water to drink, she said, it was there again. Of the attack she remembered nothing at all. What she remembered was being in ER just after, hearing caretakers above her talking about brain damage, saying: She'll only come back so far. I'd help her up from the chair at session's end. A well-mannered young man, her fiance Terry, always waited for her in the outer room.

Restless, turning as on a spit, I sensed a shadow fall across me and opened my eyes to see a possum crouched in the window. Possums are wild, they are resolutely not pets. But this one wanted in. I opened the window. The possum came in, sniffed its way down the bed, eventually fell asleep beside me. Not long after, I fell asleep myself.

I think I'll miss her, though.

CHAPTER THIRTEEN

OUTSIDE, inches away, a face leaned in close to the plateglass. Soon it loomed above our table.

"Trooper Rob Olson," he said without preamble. "We spoke earlier."

"Right."

"Okay if I turn the town over to you? Sheriff's been pulling more weight than he should, I don't really want to buzz him on this. When I signed on, I never counted on clocking this much time. Now the wife's threatening to change the locks."

Trooper Olson slid something across the table.

"What's this?"

"The beeper."

"We have a beeper now?"

"*You* do, anyway," J. T. said.

"Wear it in good health," Trooper Olson said.

By this time we were sitting in Jay's Diner over scrambled eggs, sliced tomatoes, and toast, complete with the little rack of bottled vinegar and oil, ketchup, steak sauce, and pepper sauce. Neither of us had been in the mood for dinner-type food.

"More coffee?" Thelma asked. Near as I could tell, she was here any time the diner was open. Hard to imagine what the rest of her life might be like. Which was odd, the fact that I didn't know, given what I knew about so many other lives hereabouts.

Both sides of the booth, we nodded.

"So you're on vacation."

"Only because they made me take it."

"And with nothing better to do, you figured What the hell, I'll track down the old man."

"Like I say, never got the knack of normal pastimes. I'd been thinking for some time about looking you up. Wasn't sure how you'd feel about that."

Nor was I.

"No one back there?"

"A guy, you mean?"

"Anyone."

"Not really. Handful of friends, mostly from the job." She glanced up to watch a new arrival, eyes following him from door to booth. Not from around here, you could tell that from the way he looked, way he moved. She saw it too. "I'm good at what I do, very good. I put most of myself into the work. Until recently that seemed enough."

"And now it's not?"

"I don't know. And most of all I hate not knowing."

"Maybe you just inherited a little of your mother's restlessness."

"Or yours."

Come home to roost, as they say around here. Probably didn't bear too much thinking, what other prodigal chickens might have shown up, for J. T. or for her brother Donald.

I set my cup down and waved off Thelma's query, via raised eyebrows, as to another refill.

"I have to thank you for what happened back there, J. T. But I also have to ask why you're here."

There was this strange energy to her, this sense of contained intensity in everything she did. It was in her eyes now, in the way she canted forward in the booth.

"I wanted to meet my father," she said. "It really is that simple. I think."

"Fair enough. How much vacation's left?"

"I'm still in the first week."

"Any plans?"

She shook pepper sauce onto her last piece of toast and made it disappear. Good eater.

"Tell the truth, I've started thinking maybe I could hang out here. With you. If you don't mind."

"I think I might like that."

"Done, then." She reached across to spear my last piece of tomato with her fork.

J. T. was half asleep as we drove to the cabin. When we came to the lake, she opened her eyes and looked out the window, at the water shimmering with light. "It's like the moon's come down to live with us," she said. Despite protests I got her settled in, insisting she take the bedroom, and to the sound of her regular breathing called Val. I hadn't had a phone at first or wanted one. Working with Don Lee pretty much demanded it, though. So I

89

had one now. And I had a pet, Miss Emily the possum, gender no longer in doubt since she'd recently given birth to four tiny naked Miss Emilies living in a shoebox near the kitchen stove.

And I had a daughter.

"Apologies for calling so late," I said when Val answered. "Keep on the Sunny Side" by the Carter Family in the background.

"Any apologies you might conceivably owe me would be for *not* calling. How'd it go up there?"

I told her everything.

"Wow. You really cowboyed it."

"You okay with that, counselor?"

"As long as no warrants followed you home. Hope you didn't mind my telling J. T. where you were staying. She's there with you?"

"Asleep."

Strains of "The Ballad of Amelia Earhart" behind. *There's a beautiful, beautiful field, far away in a land that is fair.*

"So . . . Suddenly you have a family. Just like Miss Emily."

"I've had a family for a while now."

"Kind of."

"How's work been going?"

"Let's see. Yesterday the judge sent home a preteen whose older sister, eight years out of the house, submitted a deposition alleging long-term sexual abuse from the father. Fourteen-year-old firesetter Bobby Boyd's gone up to the state juvenile facility, where he'll be flavor of the month and learn a whole new set of survival skills."

"Business as usual."

"Always."

"Still, you stay in there batting."

"Never a home run. But sometimes we get a walk."

I stood listening to Val's breath on the line. From the kitchen came a squeal. One of the kids as Miss Emily rolled onto it? Or Miss Emily herself, one of them having bitten down too hard on a teat?

"When am I going to see you?" Val asked.

"What do you have on for tomorrow?"

"Tomorrow's Wednesday, always heavy. Three, maybe four court dates, have to meet with a couple troopers at the barracks on upcomings."

"Any chance you could break away for dinner up this way?"

"I'd be late."

"We could meet you somewhere—that be better?"

"*We,* huh? I like that. No, I'll manage. Look for me by seven, a little after."

Moments passed.

"Racking my brain here," I said, "but I can't recall the Carter Family's ever having banjo on their recordings."

"You caught me. I've got you on the speaker—"

"Hence that marvelous fifties echo-chamber sound."

"—and I'm playing along with Sara, Maybelle, and A.P. Some days this is the only thing that relaxes me. Going back to a simpler time."

"Simpler only because we had no idea what was going on. Not even in our own country. Certainly nowhere else. We just didn't know."

"Whereas now we know too much."

"We do. And it can paralyze us, but it doesn't have to." Silence and breath braided on the line. "See you tomorrow, then?"

"Sevenish, right. . . . Did you really say *hence*?"

"I admit to it. Makes up for your *whereas*."

She left the line open. I heard the stroke, brush, and syncopated fifth string of her mountain-style banjo, heard the Carters asserting that the storm and its fury broke today.

CHAPTER FOURTEEN

WE WERE SITTING to dinner the next night when the beeper went off and I went Shit! I'd forgotten I had the thing. Dropped it on the little table inside the door when I got home the night be-fore and hadn't thought of it since. There it sat as I'd gone in to pull the day shift. There it still sat.

One of Miss Emily's babies was doing poorly when I got home. Seemed to be having difficulty breathing, muscle tone not good, floppy head, dark muzzle. Miss Emily kept carrying it away from the shoebox and leaving it on the floor. I'd pick it up and put it back, she'd carry it off again. Val came in and immediately scooped it up, rummaged through the medicine cabinet until she found an old eyedropper, cleaned out its mouth and throat, blew gently into its nose. Then she put it in her shirt pocket "to warm." When she pulled it out a half hour later, it looked ready to take over the shoebox and take on all comers.

"What *can't* you do?" I asked her.

"Hmmm. Well, world peace for one. And I'm still working on bringing justice to the Justice Department." She smiled. "Possums are easy. They're what I had for pets when I was growing up. You named these guys yet?"

It hadn't even occurred to me.

"Okay, then. That's Lonnie, that one's Bo, that one's Sam."

"The Chatmons."

"You have any idea how few people there are alive on this earth who would know that?"

"And the fourth one, odd man out, has to be Walter Vinson."

"Right again."

Wearing one of my T-shirts, J. T. emerged from the back room. "There's the problem with all you old folks," she said, "forever going on about the great used-to-be."

"Old folks, huh?" Val said.

"Well, you have to admit he weighs down the demographics." The two of them hugged. "Good to see you again."

"Me too. Glad you found him—and in the nick of time, from what he tells me."

"Pure chance. Seems I'm always blundering into things without knowing what's going on."

"May be a family trait."

J. T. laughed. "We were just talking about that. . . . Came out all right in the end, anyway."

We'd assembled, quite naturally, in the kitchen, where Miss Emily watched us warily from her shoebox. Southerners are known to dine sumptuously on possum.

I pulled a dish of cornbread out of the oven, along with a casserole of grits, cheese, and sausage. Turned the fire off under a pot of greens after dropping in a dollop of bacon fat. Miss Emily and her brood were safe, for the moment.

"This food looks, I don't know," J. T. said, "weird?"

Val took the challenge. "This? This is nothing! Wait till he does the pig tails for you, or squirrels fried whole, with hollow eye sockets staring up at you."

"Maybe I'll just have a beer."

But after a while her fork found its way into the mound of grits on her plate, then into the greens, just reconnoitering mind you. Next thing you know, she's at the stove spooning up seconds.

"Must be in my blood," she said as she rejoined us. "Strange to be eating this time of night, like a normal person. Normal except for the food, I mean." She had a forkful or two before going on. "I usually work nights. Prefer them, really. The department has rotating shifts, like most, but I always swap when I can. The city's different at night. *You're* different."

"Plus most of chain-of-command is home asleep."

"There's that too. You're really *out there*."

On the edge, yes. "And night's when the cockroaches come out." It was an old homily among lawmen, probably been around since the praetorian guards. Hail Caesar, they say behind their lanterns. And here come the cockroaches.

"Right. So, like them, that's when I usually eat. Great steaming mounds of indigestible food at two in the morning. Rib-eye steaks like shoe soles, potatoes with chemical gravy, caramelized burgers, vulcanized eggs."

"Food that sticks to your ribs," Val said, invoking a homily every bit as ancient.

"Nothing like *this,* of course."

My daughter had kept her sense of humor. Kind of work we do, what we see day after day, so many don't. Never trust a man (or woman) without a sense of humor. That's the first rule. The *other* first rule, of course, is never trust anyone who tells you who to trust.

"Rest of the night and day's mostly coffee," J. T. went on, "maybe a bowl of oatmeal once the paperwork's done. Then home to movies I picked out over the weekend and, two to four hours later, sleep, if I'm lucky. By three in the afternoon, mind that I've got home at like nine, ten in the morning, I'm up again and marking time. Put a pot of coffee on and drink the whole thing while watching *Cops*, *Judge Judy*, and the rest. Still have Mother's old Corningware percolator and use it every day."

"Blue flowers on the side?"

"That's the one."

"And it still turns out drinkable coffee?"

"Following a few rounds of bleach and baking soda, yeah—it was in storage a long time."

That's when the beeper went off.

Most phone service these days is automated, but in small towns like ours, operators are still in the thick of it. They dial for the elderly or disadvantaged, do directory work, take emergency calls.

The number from the beeper was answered on the first ring.

"Sorry to disturb you, Deputy."

"That you, Mabel? It's what? eleven o'clock at night? You don't ever get off?"

"We don't have anyone on the switchboard after six, no money for it, they say. So emergency calls get routed to my home phone. I tried the office first, just in case. No one there."

There wouldn't be. With my return, the retired boys from the barracks had flown. Lonnie and I were doing broken runs down the field of days, passing the ball back and forth.

"It's Miss June. Called in saying there was trouble out to her place."

"I thought she was living with her parents."

"Nope. Moved into a little house out on Oriole, belonged to Steve and Dolly Warwick when they were alive. Now it's rented out by their son."

"What kind of trouble are we talking, Mabel?"

"Break-in, I'd say, from the sound of it."

"Why didn't June call her father? He's still the sheriff."

"Can't say. They've had problems in the past—everyone knows that. But she specifically asked for you."

I took down the address such as it was, offered apologies to Val and J. T., Miss Emily and her progeny. I reminded J. T. that, if a strange man showed up at the door, one who looked like he belonged here, then it was probably just my neighbor Nathan.

"You mean like one of the trees trying to fake its way inside?"

"He won't come inside, but yeah, that's Nathan."

June was sitting on the porch, bare feet hanging over and almost touching ground, as I pulled in. House was built in the thirties. Floods being a regular part of life back then, houses were built high.

I climbed down from the Chariot but didn't advance, eyes from old habit sweeping windows, porch, and nearby trees, looking for anything that didn't fit.

"You okay, June?"

"Fine." She dropped the few inches to the ground and stood. "Thanks for coming."

"You're welcome."

"Permission to come aboard."

"What?"

"That's what they're always saying in old movies, old books. Permission to come aboard."

As I started towards her she turned, went up the steps through the door and into the house. I found her just inside, surveying the wreckage. Every drawer had been pulled and up-ended, cushions sliced into, chairs and tables and shelves broken apart, lamps and appliances overturned.

"Funny thing about violation," she said. "Once it happens, somehow you expect it to keep on happening, you know? Like that's how the world's going to work from now on." She turned to me. "Of course you know. Would you like a drink? I keep a bottle of Scotch here for Dad."

I said sure, and she went off to the kitchen to get it.

"Mind if we go back outside?"

Nothing had changed out there. I sat beside her at the edge of the porch.

"When you were injured," I said after a while. "You were carrying a handgun."

"And you never asked why."

"Not till now."

Before, I'd never seen much of Lonnie in her. Now, as she ducked her head and looked off into the distance, I did.

"I had a teacher back in twelfth grade. Mr. Sacher. He'd lost both arms in the Korean war. He'd pick up the textbook between the heels of the hands of stiff prosthetic arms and place it gently on the desk. We're all good at one thing, he told us over and over. The problem lies in finding out what that one thing is.

"Mr. Sacher's thing was comedy. He'd get a bunch of us in the car and, eyes rolling in mock terror, throw up his hands. But he'd be steering with his knees on the wheel. He'd bring in a guitar and make terrible efforts to play it.

"Mr. Sacher may have been right. The one thing *I* seem to be good at is picking bad men."

"This," I said, remembering the black eye she had tried to conceal, "wouldn't be the work of the guy you were with a year or so back, would it?"

"No way. But there've been others."

"Any of them likely to have done this?"

"I don't think so."

"So maybe it was random."

We sat silently.

"Maybe you should give some thought to coming back to work."

"I don't . . ." I saw the change in her eyes. "You're right. Give me tomorrow to clean up this mess. I'll be in the day after. Do me good to have something else to concentrate on."

"Great." Finishing my Scotch, I set the glass on the warped boards of the porch. Those boards looked as old and as untamed as the trees about us. "Mabel said you asked for me."

"I did."

"How do you want to handle this?"

"There's not much to handle, is there?"

"There's Lonnie."

She nodded. "I thought you could talk to him, tell him what happened. I go to him with this, it'll be my fault. The losers I hang out with. When am I going to learn. My misspent life."

"I'll talk to him, first thing in the morning."

"I appreciate it."

"Be good to have you back, June."

J. T. was sitting out on the porch when I got home. I settled beside her. Frogs called to one another down in the cypress grove.

"Val gone?"

"Hour or so back."

"Feel up to helping a friend clean house?" I asked.

CHAPTER FIFTEEN

BACK WHEN I WORKED as a therapist, having acquired something of a reputation around Memphis, I tended to get the hard cases, the ones no one else wanted. Referrals, they're called, like what Ambrose Bierce said about good advice—best thing you can do is give it to someone else, quick. And for the most part these referrals proved a surly, deeply damaged lot, none of them with much skill at or inclination towards communication, all of them leaning hard into the adaptive mechanisms that had kept them going for so long but that were now, often in rather spectacular fashion, breaking down.

I was therefore somewhat surprised at Stan Bellison's calm demeanor. I knew little of him. He was, or had been, a prison guard, and had suffered severe job-related trauma. The appointment came from the state authority.

Why are you here? is the usual, hoary first question, but this time I needn't ask it. Stan entered, sat in the chair across from me, and, after introducing himself, said: "I'm here because I was held hostage."

Two inmates had, during workshop, dislodged a saw blade from its housing and, holding it against one guard's throat, taken another—Stan, who tried to come to his fellow guard's aid—hostage. Sending everyone else away, the inmates had blockaded themselves in the workshop and, when contacted, announced they would only speak to the governor. The first guard they released as a gesture of goodwill. Stan, whom they referred to as Mr. Good Boy, they kept.

"You were a cop," Bellison said. Once again I remarked his ease.

"Not a very good one, I'm afraid."

"Then let's hope you're better as a therapist," he said, and laughed. "I don't want to be here, you know."

"Few do."

His eyes, meeting mine, were clear and steady.

Each day the inmates cut off a finger. The crisis went on eight days.

On the last, the lead inmate, one Billy Basil, stepped through the door to pick up a pizza left just outside, only to meet a sniper's bullet. The governor hadn't come down from the capitol to parlay, but he had sent instructions.

"So then it was over, at least," I said. "The trauma, what they did to you, that'll be with you for a long time, of course."

"You don't understand," Stan Bellison told me. "The other inmate? His name was Kyle Beck. That last day, as he stood staring at Billy's body in the open door, I came up behind him and gouged out his eyes with my thumbs."

He held up his hands. I saw the ragged stumps of what had been fingers. And the thumbs that remained.

CHAPTER SIXTEEN

"SHE'LL NEVER LEARN, will she?"

"That's what she said you'd say."

We were sitting on the bench outside Manny's Dollar $tore, where almost exactly a year ago Sarah Hazelwood and I had sat, when her brother was murdered. Lonnie took a sip of coffee. A car passed down Main Street. Another car. A truck. He sipped again. A light breeze stirred, nosing plastic bags, leaves, and food wrappers against our feet. "You still have that possum you told me about?"

"Miss Emily. Yeah. Got a family now. Ugliest little things you can imagine."

Brett Davis came out of the store buttoning a new flannel shirt, deeply creased from being folded, over the one he already wore.

"Lonnie. Mr. Turner."

"First purchase of the millennium, Brett?"

"Last one just plumb fell apart when Betty washed it. Says to me, Brett, you better come on out here, and she's holding up a tangle of wet rags. Damn shame."

"For sure." Lonnie touched forefinger to forehead by way of saying good-bye. Brett climbed into his truck that always looked to me like something that had been smashed flat and pumped back out, maybe with powerful magnets.

"June's right," Lonnie said after a while. "I've always blamed her, always turned things around in my mind so that they got to be her fault. I don't know why."

"Disappointment, maybe. You expect as much from her as you do from yourself—and expect much the same things. We construct these scenarios in our minds, how we want the world to be, then we kick at the traces when the world's not like that. We're all different, Lonnie. Different strengths, different weaknesses."

"Don't know as I ever told you this before, but there's times I feel flat-out stupid around you. We talk, and you tell me what I already know. Which has got to be the worst kind of stupid."

"It's all the training I've had."

"The hell it is."

Lonnie took June to dinner that night, just the two of them. She'd spent the day, with J. T.'s help, getting her house back in order. He put on his best shirt and a tie and the jacket of a leisure suit that had been hanging in the back of his closet for close on to thirty years and met her at her door with a spray of carnations and drove all the way over to Poplar Crossing, to the best steakhouse in the county. "Everybody must of thought this was just some poor foolish old man romancing a young woman," June said when she came in to work the next morning.

With her there to hold down the fort, I decided to go visit

Don Lee. He'd been transferred to the county hospital an hour or so away.

He was off the respirator now. An oxygen cannula snaked across the bed to his nose. Water bubbled in the humidifier. IV bags, some bloated, others near collapse, hung from poles. One of the poles held a barometer-like gadget that did double duty, registering intercranial pressure and draining off fluid.

"He's intermittently conscious," a nurse told me, "about what we'd expect at this point. He's family? A friend?"

"My boss, actually." There was no reason to show her the badge but I did anyway. She said she was sorry, she'd be right outside the door catching up on her charting, and left us alone.

I put my hand against Don Lee's there on the bed. His eyes opened, staring up at the ceiling's blankness.

"Turner?"

"I'm here, Don Lee."

"This is hard."

"I know."

"No. This is *hard*."

I told him what went down in Memphis.

"Kind of let the beast out of the cage there, didn't you?"

"Guess I did, at that."

"You okay?"

"Yeah."

"Good. I'm tired, really tired. . . . Why did someone stick an icepick in my head, Turner?"

"It's a monitor."

"Man-eater?"

"No, monitor."

"Big lizard you mean."

"Not really."

He seemed to be thinking that over.

"They keep telling me and I keep forgetting: June's okay, right?"

"She's fine. Back at work as of today."

I thought he'd fallen off again when he suddenly said, "You sure you don't want to be sheriff?"

"I'm sure."

"Smart move," he said.

I was backing the Chariot out of a visitor's space when the beeper went off. I sat looking at the number while a car and an SUV roughly the size of a tank blared horns at me.

June.

I pulled back into the space, earning a middle-finger salute from the tank driver, and went to use the phone in the hospital lobby.

"How's Don Lee?" June asked.

"Looking good. Still gonna be a while. So what's up?"

"Maybe nothing. Thelma called. From the diner? Said some guy was in there early this morning. Waiting in his car when they came in to open, actually. Just ordered coffee. Then a little later—she and Gillie and Jay were setting up, of course, but she swung by a time or two to check on him—he asked after you. Said he was an old friend."

Any old friends I was supposed to have, I probably didn't want to see.

"When Thelma said he should check in at the sheriff's office, he said well, he was just passing through, pressed for time. Maybe he'd come back."

"Thelma say what he looked like?"

"Slight, dark skin and hair, wearing a suit, that was dark too, over a yellow knit shirt buttoned all the way up. Good shoes. Thing was, Thelma said, he didn't ask the kind of questions you'd expect. Where you lived, what you did for a living, all that. What he wanted to know was did you have a family, who your friends were."

"Thanks, June. He still around?"

"Got back in his car, Thelma said—a dark blue Mustang, I have the license number for you—and drove off in the direction of the interstate."

"I'm on my way in. See you soon."

Half an hour later I pulled off the road onto the bluff just above Val's house. The old Ames place, as everyone still called it. Val was up at the state police barracks doing her job, of course, but a dark blue Mustang sat in her drive.

I went down through stands of oak and pecan trees trellised with honeysuckle, through ankle-deep tides of kudzu, to the back door opening onto the kitchen. No one locked doors here, and the kitchen would have no interest for him.

I also had the advantage of knowing the house and its wood floors. Focusing on creaks above, I followed his progress: master bedroom, hallway, second and third bedrooms, bath. Then the tiny tucked-wing room probably meant for servants, and the hallway again.

"You'd be Turner," he said from the top of the stairs.

One cool guy. Sure of himself and waiting to see which way the wind blew.

I put a round through one knee. He came tumbling down the stairs with left hand and drawn weapon bumping behind him, to the base, where my foot pinned his wrist.

"Apologies first," I said. "You're obviously not one of the thick-neck boys. They wouldn't know subtlety if it ran over them, then backed up and had another go."

"Contract," he said.

"Who's paying?"

"You know how it works. I can't tell you that."

I moved the snout of the Police Special vaguely in his direction, a sweeping motion. "Ankle or knee?"

I used Val's phone to call and tell June I was going to be a little later than I'd thought. Then I drove back to the hospital, one of Val's sheets wrapped tight around my passenger's leg. There wasn't much vessel damage, but joints do get bloody. Ask any orthopedic surgeon.

I was doing just that ("Case like this, we can rebuild the joint from the fragments, adding a bit of plastic here and there—sometimes that's best, staying with the original—or we can replace the whole thing. The newest titanium appliances are remarkable") when Val walked through the double doors.

"June called me."

I thanked the doctor and said I'd get back to him about cost, responsibility, and so on.

"Not a problem," he said. "Mr. Millikin had proof of insurance with him. He's fully covered. Says he wants to be the man of steel. I've got to go finish a procedure up in OR—got interrupted to check him out. Then we'll have him brought up." Nodding his leave-taking: "Sheriff. Ma'am."

"What the hell is going on?" Val asked. "This guy was in my house? Why was this guy in my house? Who the hell *is* this guy?"

In the basement we found a place to get coffee, not really a cafeteria, more a kind of commissary, and I walked her through what had happened.

"So, what? He was going to hold me hostage?"

"Or worse. Beyond saying it's a contract, he won't talk."

"This ties in with what went down in Memphis."

I nodded.

"Going back in turn to Don Lee's arrest of what's-his-name—Judd Kurtz?"

"Right again."

"From what little I know about it, farming out enforcement work's not the way these people usually handle things."

"True enough. What I'm thinking is, given how it went down last time, they've elected for a low profile. Set it up so nothing can be traced back to them."

Blowing across her coffee cup—absolutely superfluous, since the coffee was at best lukewarm—Val tracked a young woman's progress down the line. An elaborate tattoo scored the nape of her neck. She wore studded boots and sniffed at everything she took from narrow, glass-shuttered shelves. Most of it, she set back.

"These guys have the longest memories of all," Val said. "They've got wars that have been going on for centuries. Sooner or later, they don't hear from their scout, they'll figure out it went wrong."

"We could send them his head."

Having reached the register, the tattooed young woman stood

beaming at the cashier as he spoke, waited, and spoke again. Then the smile went away and she came back into motion.

"Just kidding," I said. "You're right. They'll wait a while, but they'll be back. Someone will."

CHAPTER SEVENTEEN

THAT NIGHT AROUND ELEVEN I got a call. Mabel had routed it through to me at home. I could barely hear the speaker over the jukebox and roar of voices behind.

"This the sheriff?"

"Deputy."

"Good enough. Reckon you better get on out here."

"Where's here?"

"The Shack. State Road Forty-one, mile past the old cotton gin."

I told him I was on my way and hung up.

"Where's Eldon playing these days?" I asked Val.

"Place called The Shack. Why?"

"Thought so. They've got trouble."

"He okay?"

"I don't know. You be here when I get back?"

"I have a home day tomorrow, and some briefs I need to get started on tonight. Call me?"

I said I would, and asked her to leave a note for J. T. in case

111

she woke while I was gone. Clipped the holster on my belt and headed for the Chariot.

The Shack was surprisingly well constructed, built of wood and recently repainted, dark green with lighter highlights. Shells paved the parking lot, crunching as I walked across. Specimens of every insect native to the county swarmed in dense clouds around the yellow lights at the door.

The bar took up the wall just inside and to the right, allowing the bartender to keep an eye on everything. The ceiling was low, bar lit by a single overhead light that filled the shelves with shadows.

The bandstand, little more than a pallet extending a foot or so above the floor, occupied the corner opposite the bar. Most of the patrons were gathered there. Upon hearing the heavy door, they looked around. How they heard it, I don't know, what with the war sounds coming from the jukebox.

"Turn that thing off."

The bartender reached under the bar. A saxophone solo died in mid-honk, like a shot goose.

The crowd drew back as I approached. Eldon sat on the edge of the bandstand. One eye was swollen almost shut; blood, black in the half-light, black like his face, blotched the front of his shirt. His guitar lay in pieces before him. The bass player stood backed against the wall, hugging his Fender. The drummer, still seated, twirled a stick in each hand.

"Come *on*, you son'va'bitch! Stand up and fight like a goddamn man!" This from a stocky guy with his back to me.

I put a hand gently on his shoulder and he came around swinging, then grunted as I tucked one fist in his armpit, grabbed his wrist with the other, pulled hard against the latter and leaned hard into the former. When he brought the other hand around to strike, I gave his wrist a twist. What must have been a buddy of his started towards me, saying "Hey man, you can't—" only to have a drumstick strike him squarely between the eyes. He staggered back. The drummer, who'd thrown the stick like a knife, wagged a finger in warning.

"You okay, Eldon?"

"Yeah."

"How about you?" I asked the stocky guy. "You cooled down?"

He nodded, and I let go, backing off. Watching his eyes. I saw it there first, then in the shift of his feet. Stamped hard on his instep, and when that knee buckled, I kicked the other foot out from under him.

"Don't get up till you're ready to behave." Then to Eldon: "What's this all about?"

"Who knows? Guy starts hanging around the bandstand, has something to say every minute or two, I just smile and nod and ignore him. So he starts getting louder. Tries to get up onstage at one point and spills a beer on my amp. So then he stumbles getting down and starts yelling that I pushed him. Next thing I know, he's grabbed my guitar and smashed it."

"You want me to take him in?"

"Hell no, Turner. Not like I ain't been through this before. Just get his buddy there to take him the fuck home and let him sleep it off."

I helped the man up.

"Your lucky day," I told him. "Give me your billfold." I took the driver's license out. "You come pick this up tomorrow and we'll have a talk. Now get the hell out of here."

I waited at the bar while Eldon borrowed a towel from the

bartender and went in the bathroom to clean up. He came back looking not much better.

"Shirt kinda makes me homesick for tie-dye. Buy you a drink?"

"Tomato juice."

"And a draft for me," I told the bartender.

The jukebox came back on. I looked hard at the bartender and the volume went down about half.

"He wanted you to fight him."

"Sure did."

"But you didn't."

Eldon looked off at the bandstand, where drummer and bassist were packing up.

"Must be about six, seven years ago now. Club down in Beaumont. I's out back on a break and this guy comes up talkin' 'bout You shore can play that thing, boy. Gets up in my face like a gnat and won't go away."

He finished off his juice.

"I damn near killed him. Vowed that day I'd never take another drink and I'd never fight another man. You ever killed anyone, Turner?"

"Yeah. Yeah, I have."

"Then you know."

I nodded.

The bass player had scooped up what was left of Eldon's guitar and put it in the case. He brought the case over and set it at Eldon's feet.

"Talk to you tomorrow," Eldon said.

"Don't call too early." An old joke: they both grinned.

Out on the floor, four or five couples were boot-scooting to Merle Haggard's "Lonesome Fugitive."

"Back when I played R&B, I always had half a dozen or more electric guitars," Eldon said. "Have me a Gibson solid-body, a Gretsch, one of those Nationals shaped like a map, a Telecaster or a Strat. Ain't had but this old Guild Starfire for years now. When I bought it, place called Charlie's Guitars in Dallas, it had the finish torn off right above the pickup, where this bluesman had had his initials glued on. Guess he slapped it on his next guitar. And guess *I'll* be heading up to Memphis in the morning to do some shopping."

Val hadn't gone home after all. She lay on the couch with one bent leg balanced across the other forming a perfect figure 4. Miss Emily was asleep on the armrest by her head. I tucked a quilt around Val, then went out to the kitchen and poured myself a solid dose of bourbon.

I'd made pasta earlier, and the kitchen still smelled of garlic. The back door was open. A moth with a body the size of my thumb kept worrying at the screen door. Frogs and night birds called from the lake.

J. T. had all but fallen asleep at the dinner table. Used to being busy, she said. Not being wears me out, plus there's the shift thing. She insisted on cleaning up, then the minute it was done went off to bed. That the bed was hers was something *I'd* insisted on, despite voluble protests, when she came to stay with me. I'd taken the couch. And now the couch had been retaken, by Val. And Emily. The house was filling up fast.

"Is Eldon okay?"

Wrapped in the quilt, Val stood in the doorway. Miss Emily bustled around her to go check on the kids.

"A little the worse for wear—but aren't we all." I told her what had happened. "Thought you were going home."

She sat across from me, reached for my glass and helped herself to a healthy swallow.

"So did I. But the more I thought . . ."

I nodded. There are few things like home invasion to rearrange the furniture in your head. "Give it time."

She yawned. "That's it, enough of the good life. I'm going back to bed."

"To couch, you mean."

"There's room for both of us."

"There's barely room for you."

"So where will you sleep?"

"Hey, eleven years in prison, remember? I can sleep anywhere. I'll grab a blanket or two, take the floor in here."

"You sure?"

"Go to couch, Val."

"Don't stay up too long."

"I won't, but I'm still a little wired. I'll just sit here a while with Miss Emily and family."

"Night."

I poured another drink and sat wondering why Miss Emily had chosen to live among people, and what she thought about them. Hell, I wondered what I thought about them.

Satisfied the kids were all right, Miss Emily had climbed to the window above the sink, one of her favorite spots. Glancing up at her, I saw her head suddenly duck low, ears forward.

Then I saw the shadow crossing the yard.

I was out the door before I'd thought about it, taking care not to let the screen door bang. A bright moon hung above the trees. My eyes fell to their base, seeking movement, changes in texture, further shadows. Birds and frogs had stopped calling.

Never thought they'd show up this soon.

I eased across the porch and onto the top step, looking, listening. Stood like that for what seemed endless minutes before the floorboards creaked behind me. I turned and he was there, one sinewy arm held up to engage my own.

"Nathan!"

His grip on my wrist loosened.

"Someone been up in them woods," he said, "going on the better part of a month now."

"You know who?"

He shook his head. "But early on this evening, one of them came in a little too close to the cabin, then made the mistake of running. Dog took out after him, naturally, came back looking pleased with hisself. So I tracked him down this way. Blood made it some easy."

We found him minutes later by the lake, lying facedown. Early twenties, wearing cheap jeans and a short denim jacket over a black T-shirt, plastic western boots. Blood drained rather than pumped from his thigh when I turned him over.

Nathan shook his head.

Dogs hereabouts aren't pets, they're functional, workers, brought up to help provide food and protect territory. Nathan's had gone at the young man straight on, taking out an apple-sized chunk of upper thigh and, to all appearances, a divot from the femoral artery.

"Damn young fool," Nathan said. "Reckon we ought to call someone."

"No reason to hurry." I took my fingers away from the young man's carotid. When I did, something on his forearm caught light. I pushed back his sleeve. "What's that look like to you?"

Nathan bent over me.

"Numbers."

CHAPTER EIGHTEEN

I REMEMBERED THEM from childhood. I was six years old. They were everywhere. Covering the trees, climbing the outside walls of the house and barbecue pit, swarming up telephone and electric poles, making their way along the chicken wire around dog runs. There they erupted from the back of their shells and unfurled wings. Hadn't been there at all the night before. Then suddenly thousands of them: black bodies the size of shrimp and maybe an inch long, transparent wings, red eyes. The males commenced to beat out tunes on their undersides, thrumming on hollow, drumlike bellies. As the sun warmed, they played louder and harder. Dogs, the wild cat that lived under the garage, chickens, mockingbirds, and bluejays ate their fill. People did too, some places, Dad told me.

People thereabouts still called them locusts. My friend Billy and I collected their husks off trees and the house and lined them up in neat rows on the walls of our bedrooms. Later I'd learn their real name: cicadas. I'd learn that they emerge in thirteen- or seventeen-year cycles, coming out in May, all dead by June. The male dies not long after coupling, whereupon the female takes to a tree, cuts as many as fifty slits in one of the branches, and deposits 400 to 600 eggs. Once her egg supply is gone, she dies too. Six to eight weeks later the nymphs hatch and fall to the ground, burrowing in a foot or so and living off sap sucked from tree roots until it's their turn to emerge, climb, shed skins, unfurl wings.

Most of this I learned forty-odd years later.

Not a title—my name, Bishop Holden told me at our first meeting. He and I were of an age. When, after my childhood experience of them, the cicadas came again, I was in a jungle half a world away and Bishop was in line at the local draft where, told to turn his head and cough, he instead grabbed the doctor's head in both hands and planted a hard, wet kiss on his lips. He was carried away, discoursing incoherently of conspiracies and government-funded coups, and remanded by courts to the local psychiatric hospital. He'd been in and out of one or another of them most of his life. At the last, during convulsions caused by a bad drug reaction, he'd bitten off the finger of an orderly trying to help him and developed something of a taste for flesh. He'd bagged another finger, half an ear, and a big toe before (as he said) putting himself on a strict diet.

He had skin like a scrubbed red potato, pouchlike, leathery cheeks. In khakis, cardigan, and canvas shoes, he reminded me of Mr. Rogers.

"Ready for them?" he asked. Our chairs stood at a right angle, a small shellacked table pushed close in to the apex. I turned my head to him. His turned to the window.

Ready for what exactly, I asked.

"The cicadas. It's time. I've called them."

Called them up from the depths of the earth itself, he said; and while I was never to learn much about Bishop Holden, over the next hour and in later sessions (until one bright morning he bit through the chain of a charm bracelet on the wrist of a teenage girl passing his breakfast sandwich through a carryout window) I learned quite a lot about cicadas.

Now, so many years later and a bit further south, it was time for them again.

Two abandoned shells, spurs hooked into mesh, hung on the screen of the window above the sink when I got up the next morning. It sounded as though a fleet of miniature farm machinery, tiny tractors and combines and threshers, had invaded the yard.

Thanks to Bishop, I knew that three distinct species always surface at the same time, and that each has not only its own specific sound but a favored time of day as well. Someone once said that the three sounded in turn like the word *pharaoh,* a sizzling skillet, and a rotary lawn sprinkler. The morning cicadas, the sizzlers, were hard at their work.

"What the hell *is* that racket?" J. T. asked from the doorway. I told her.

She came up close behind me and stood watching as they swarmed.

"Jesus. This happen often?"

"Every seventeen years, like clockwork. No one understands why. Or how, for that matter."

I filled her in on cicadas as I pulled eggs and cheese from the icebox and poured coffee for a reasonable facsimile of Val that wandered in—what a writer might be tempted to call a working draft. I dropped a tablespoon of bacon grease from the canister on the stove into a skillet, laid out bread in the toaster oven I really needed to remember to clean. Dump the crumbs, at least.

"Did I hear cars?" Val asked as I poured her second cup. The rewrite was coming along nicely.

"Doc Bly and his boy."

"Not a delivery, I assume." Doc ran the mortuary. He was also coroner.

Putting breakfast on the table, I told them about the young man who'd died out by the lake.

"He'd been living in the woods?"

"According to Nathan. More than one of them."

"Have any idea what's with the numbers?"

"Not really."

"They were permanent?"

"Looked to be."

"Not just inked in, like kids used to do back in school?"

"Not that crude. Not professional, either, but carefully done. In prison there were guys who'd do tattoos for cigarette money. They used the end of a guitar string and indelible ink, took their time. Some of them got damned good at it. That's what this reminded me of, that level of skill."

"Nathan have any idea what these people are doing up there?"

"None."

"But now you're going to have to find out."

"Guess I am."

"I'll come along," J. T. said.

Half an hour later we were scraping cicadas off the Chariot's windshield as Val pulled out on her way to work. J. T. went in to get the thermos of coffee we'd forgotten and came back out saying the beeper had gone off while she was inside.

"On the table," she said.

Of course it was.

And of course it was the bugs. Raising hell everywhere, June told me, getting in houses that left their windows open, in water troughs and switch boxes and attics, reminded her of that movie *Gremlins*. She'd already logged over a dozen calls. Though what anyone thought *we* could do about any of it was beyond her. Was I on my way in?

Sure, I said.

New plan was (I told J. T.) we'd go in for an hour, two at the most, and sand down the rough spots.

It took Lonnie, J. T., and me well into the afternoon to get everyone calmed down and the town more or less back on track. House calls included the local retirement home, where one of the cicadas had somehow got down a resident's mouth and choked her to death; a little girl terrified that the bugs were going to eat her newborn kittens; and a Mr. Murphy living alone in an old house I'd thought long abandoned. Neighbors having heard screams, J. T. and I arrived to find that Mr. Murphy had intimate knowledge of insects: when we lifted him from his wheelchair, maggots writhed in ulcers the size of saucers on his buttocks, some of them dropping to the floor, and more could be seen at work in the cushions and open framework of the chair. "Don't much mind the littluns," he said, looking from J. T.'s face to mine. "Them big ones is a different story altogether."

So the *new* new plan was to get a late lunch, then head up into the hills. And since chances were good we might not be out of there by nightfall, I'd look up Nathan first. No way I was going to be in those hills after dark without someone who knew them.

CHAPTER NINETEEN

WE PARKED BY THE DERELICT cotton gin and came up the line of humps and hollows that form the mountain's side, an easier but much longer ascent. By the time we reached the cabin, it was going on four o'clock. The owner didn't take too much to yard work. Every couple of years he'd clear a space around the cabin. The rest of the time pine trees, shrubs, and bushes, along with a variety of grasses and wildflowers, had their way. We were well along into the rest of the time.

Nathan stepped out from behind an oak, twelve-gauge in the crook of an elbow. His dog came out from beneath the cabin growling, then, at Nathan's almost silent whistle, went back under.

"Defending the realm?" I asked.

"Been out."

"Hunting?"

"After a fashion."

Meeting J. T.'s eye, he said, "Miss." I introduced them. "Found the camp," he went on, "maybe three miles in, 'bout forty degrees off north-northeast. Ain't much to it, mostly the hind end of a cabin they done put some lean-tos up against."

"How many are there?"

"If you mean lean-tos, there's three. If you're asking after people, which I expect you are, then my guess'd be close on to a dozen. Youngsters was all I saw. You headin' up that way?"

I nodded. "Talk you into coming along?"

"Figured to."

Instinctively tilting the shotgun barrel maybe ten degrees to clear a low branch, Nathan stepped back into the trees.

It took us almost two hours to get there. By the time we did, the sun had put in its papers and was marking time. The lean-tos were saplings lashed together with heavy twine, a spool of which I later saw inside what was left of the original cabin. The cabin hadn't been much to start with. Now it came down to half a room, five-sixths of a chimney, and a smatter of roof. A smatter of people sat on a bench out front—more saplings, these set into notches in two sections of log.

One of the homesteaders, a woman like all of them in her early to late twenties, sat beside a pile of sassafras root, cleaning with a damp cloth what was to be a new addition to the pile. Another was picking through field greens. They watched us silently as we approached. A man emerging from one of the lean-tos paused, then straightened and stepped towards us. Another, that I'd not seen and damn well should have, swung down off the low branch of a maple at the edge of the clearing. Scraps of plank from the cabin were nailed to the trunk at intervals to make a ladder.

Boards had also been nailed up over the cabin's gaping front, three of them, bridging the void. Crude block letters in white paint: "All the Whys Are Here."

"Tell me you're not the trouble you look to be," the man from the lean-to said, holding out his hand, which I shook. Older than the rest, pushing thirty from the far side, dark eyes, beetle brow, bad skin.

"Deputy sheriff," I said, "but not trouble. Not the kind you're thinking, at any rate."

"Always good to hear. Isaiah Stillman." Nodding towards Nathan, who stood apart at clearing's edge, he said, "Your friend's welcome, too."

"My friend's not much for company."

"Um-hmm. He the one lives down the mountain?"

"The same."

"So what can we do for you, Deputy? If we're—" He stopped, eyes meeting mine. "Our understanding is that this is free land."

"Close as it gets these days, anyhow."

I described the young man who'd died by the lake last night, told Stillman how it happened.

"I'm truly sorry to hear that."

"You knew him, then?"

"Of course. Kevin. We wondered where he'd got off to this time. Never could stay in place too long. He'd go off, be gone a day or two, a week. But he'd always come back."

The woman cleaning sassafras had put rag and roots down and walked up behind Stillman, touching him on the shoulder. When he turned, her mouth moved, but no sound came. Taking her hand and placing it against his throat, he said: "It's Kevin, Martha. Kevin's dead." Her mouth opened and went round in a silent *no*. After a moment she returned to the bench and her work. The other woman there put a hand briefly to her cheek.

"We'll be having our dinner soon," Stillman said. "Will you join us?"

We did, settling into a meal of lukewarm sassafras tea, greens, rice cooked with black-eyed peas—

"Our take on hopping John," Stillman said.

"Interesting."

"Flavored with roots instead of salt pork or bacon, since we're vegetarians."

—and something that must have been hoecake, which, like hopping John, I'd read and heard about but never seen.

"Delicious."

J. T. cocked eyebrows at me at that. Nathan, having got over his standoffishness, was busy sopping up juice from the greens with crumbly bits of hoecake.

"We plan to grind our own cornmeal eventually," Stillman said. Of course they did.

"I should notify your friend's family," I said. Helped myself to another spoonful of the hopping John. Stuff kind of grew on you.

"We *are* his family, Mr. Turner."

"No direct relatives?"

"His father threw him out of the house when he was fourteen. 'The old man was an engineer,' Kevin always said. 'He knew how things were supposed to work.' For a year or two he stayed around town. His mother would meet him, give him money. When she died, Kevin left for good."

"What about the rest of you?"

"Have family, you mean."

"Yes."

"Some of us do, some don't. For us, family is—"

Leaning over the makeshift table, the young woman I assumed to be deaf and dumb moved her hands in dismissive, sweep-it-away gestures.

"Moira's right," Stillman said.

"You always *think* she is," one of the others said.

He ignored that. "This isn't the time to be talking about such. . . Besides, night's closing in. I imagine you'll be wanting to get back."

"We should, yes."

"You and your friends are always welcome here. . . . Can you see to Kevin's burial, or should we?"

"We can do that."

"We'd expect to pay for it, of course."

"The county—"

"It's our responsibility. We do have money."

We both looked about the camp, then realized what we were doing, looked at one another, and smiled.

"Really," he said. "It's not a problem—despite appearances. So we'll be expecting an invoice. Meanwhile, you have our gratitude."

Moira raised a hand in farewell. Nathan, J. T., and I stepped out to the accompaniment of a half moon and the calls of whippoorwills, down hills and across them, right and left legs lengthening alternately like those of cartoon figures to meet the challenge, or so it seemed, returning to a world gone strange in our absence.

CHAPTER TWENTY

"I KNOW ALMOST NOTHING about you."

Her eyes went from my eyes to my mouth and back, ever steady.

"Why should you?"

Outside, rain slammed down, turning lawns and walkways to patches of mud. A mockingbird crouched in the window, soaked feathers drawn tightly about.

"I come here every week for—what? a year now?—and we talk. Most of my relationships haven't lasted near that long."

I let that go by.

"I know almost nothing about you. And you know so much about me."

"Only what you've agreed to have me know, or what you've told me yourself."

"Here's something you don't know. When I was a child, ten or so . . ." For a moment she drifted away. "I had this friend, Gerry. And I had this T-shirt I'd sent away for, off some cereal box or out of a comic book. Nothing special, now that I think about it, just this thin, cheap shirt, blue, with 'Wonder Girl' stenciled on it in yellow letters. But I loved that T-shirt. I'd waited by the mailbox every day till it came. My mother had to take it out of my room at night while I was sleeping, just to wash it. . . . It was summer, and all day there'd been a rain, like this one. Then late afternoon it slowed, still coming down, but more a shower now. Gerry starts running down the drive and sliding into this huge mud puddle at its end. This is back in Georgia, we didn't have paving, just a dirt drive cut in from the street. At first I didn't want to, but I tried it, then . . . just gave myself to the simple joy of it. Gerry and I went on sliding and diving for most of the rest of the afternoon. My shirt was ruined, of course. Mother tried everything to get it clean. The last I saw of it, it was in with the rags."

She looked back from the window.

"Poor thing."

"The bird?"

She nodded. Muffled conversation came from the hall, indecipherable, rhythmic. It sounded much like the rain outside.

"You must have to turn in some sort of reports," she said.

"I do."

"In which case, it has to be coming up on time for one."

After a moment I said, "They're not going to give your license back, Miss Blake."

She looked at the watch, which from old habit she still wore pinned to her shirt pocket. "I know. I do know that. . . . And I've asked you to call me Cheryl." She smiled. "Recently I've taken up reading again. Do you know the science fiction writer Philip K. Dick?"

"A little."

"Late in life, while visiting in Canada, he underwent some

kind of crisis, something like Poe's last days, maybe. He came to in a fleabag hotel and had himself committed to a detox center. Another patient there told a story that promptly became Dick's favorite slogan. This junkie goes to see his old friend Leon, and once he gets to his friend's house he asks the people there if he can see Leon. 'I'm very sorry to have to tell you this,' one of them says, 'but Leon is dead.' 'No problem,' the junkie responds, 'I'll just come back on Thursday.'"

She stood.

"See you on Thursday."

Long after she was gone—my next client had canceled—I sat quietly. Eventually the rain lightened and, with a vigorous shake of feathers, the mockingbird launched itself from the window.

As an RN on a cancer ward, Cheryl Blake, who now worked as a cosmetics salesperson, had drawn up morphine and injected it through the IV ports of at least three patients. At trial, asked if the patients had told her they wished to die, her response was: "They didn't need to. I knew." She served six years. Two days before Christmas last year, the state had paroled her. I saw her first on New Year's Eve.

Memory opens on small hinges. A prized T-shirt long ago lost. The pale green chenille bedspread, its knots worn to nubbins, I'd had as a child and sat night after night in my cell remembering. I'd gone in, in fact, on New Year's Eve.

In prison, trees are always far away. From the yard you could look across to a line of them like a mirage on the horizon, so distant and unreal that they might as well have been on another planet. They were bare then, of course, just gray smudges of trunk and limb against the lighter gray of sky. When springtime came, their green was a wound.

In a corner of the yard that spring, Danny Lillo planted seeds from an apple his daughter brought him. Each day he'd dip the ladle into the tank that provided our drinking water on the yard, fill his mouth, and take it over to that corner. Week after week we watched. Saw that first long oval of a leaf ease from the ground, watched as the third set of leaves developed pointy tips. Then we went out one afternoon and someone had pulled it up. Maybe four inches long, it lay there on its side, trailing roots. Danny stood looking down a long time. All of us who had given up so much already, the one who put it in the ground, those who simply watched and waited, the one who pulled it up—all of us had lost something we couldn't even define, all of us felt something that, like so much else in that gray place, had no name.

CHAPTER TWENTY-ONE

BACK HERE IN THE WORLD, so strange and so familiar at the same time, this was my life. No sign of insight or epiphany peeking through floorboards, sound track of my days innocent of all but the din of memories going round and round. One longs for the three chords of a Hank Williams song to nose it all into place.

The short list was this: an old cabin I had every intention of fixing up, a job I'd blundered into, a clutch of friends likewise unintended. And Val. She was intended. Maybe not at first, but later on.

And always, the simple fact that I'd survived.

Miss Emily was happy to have me back, I'm pretty sure. The young ones were now getting around all too well on their own, straying into every corner of the cabin, not that the house had many corners, or that we could ever fail to locate them by their squeals. Val, in underpants and a faded Riley Puckett T-shirt, was asleep on the couch. When I kissed her she looked up at me blankly, focused for a moment to tell me "J. T. had a call," then plunged back asleep. Her briefcase was on the kitchen table.

Labels of folders peeked above the edge. The Whyte Laydie banjo case sat on the floor beside the table.

"They want me back," J. T. said, coming in off the porch after returning the call. "Couple of federal marshals paid a call to a gentleman at a motel out on St. Louis Avenue and got themselves blown away for their trouble. All hell's broke loose."

She took a glass off the drying rack and poured from the bottle before me, sat down at the table. Emily strode in again to check on us, snout worrying the air. Pesky offspring are bad enough. She's expected to keep track of us as well?

"I told them no way."

"You sure about that?"

"I'm sure. You mind?"

"Not in the least. It's good to have you around."

"Same here."

I poured again for both of us. "Listen."

The outside door was open and she looked that way, through the screen. "To what?"

Exactly. Too quiet. Not even frogs. Of course, it was altogether possible that I'd just grown paranoid.

At any rate, we sat there, had another drink, and nothing came of it. When J. T. went off to bed, I got the Whyte Laydie from its case and took it outside, to the back porch. Touched fingers gently to strings, remembering the songs my father played and his father before him, "Pretty Polly," "Mississippi Sawyer," "Napoleon Crossing the Rhine," remembering, too, my father's touch. The strings went on ringing long after I'd raked a finger across them.

"I had," Isaiah Stillman would tell me on my second visit, as

J. T. and Moira sat getting silently acquainted on the bench, "the overwhelming sense that my life was a book I'd only skimmed—one that deserved, for all its apparent insignificance, actually to be read. Meanwhile, my grandmother was dying. We'd moved away and I never had the chance to know her. I went there, moved in with her—rural Iowa, a farmhouse in a place called Sharon Center, four houses and a garage, few besides Amish anywhere around—and saw her through her final days."

Holding the Whyte Laydie close, I sat remembering my own grandmother who in my shallow youth had refused to acknowledge the cancer that all too soon took her, commanding Grandfather to walk behind so he could tell her if her dresses showed traces of blood. What did I have of her? A few brief memories, blurred by time. Grandfather I got to know when he came to live with us afterwards. Neither of my parents showed much interest in anything he had to say. I on the other hand was fascinated by his stories, in thrall to them.

"At the end, she went into a hospital in Iowa City," Stillman said. "Not what she wanted, but there were other considerations. Standing there by her bed, I watched the tracings of the EKG monitor, the hillocks it made one after another, and I saw them as ripples, ripples going out into the world, becoming waves, waves that would go on and on and in a way would never end."

My grandparents had a country store. Ancient butcher block in the back, cooler full of salt pork, bacon, and other such cheap cuts of meat, an array of candy bars in one glass-front cabinet, another of toiletries and the like, worn wooden shelves of canned goods stacked in pyramids, the inevitable soft-drink machine with the caps of Coke, Pepsi, Nehi grape, and chocolate drink bottles peering up at you. You slid the desired drink along steel slats where it hung from its neck, into the gate, and dropped in your dime. Summers, when I spent a week or two with them, they let me work in the store. I'd hand over Baby Ruths, loaves of white bread, tubes of toothpaste, and squat jars of Arid deodorant, collect money, hit the key that so satisfyingly opened the register, make change. Most of our customers were black folk working on farms nearby. Afternoons, the white owners would come in, help themselves to a soft drink, and sit gossiping with my grandfather.

"You mentioned other considerations," I said to Stillman.

"Local family members. Despite her mode of life, they were convinced—a longtime family legend—that Gram had squirreled away huge sums of money."

Seeing me glance towards her, Moira lifted her hand in a sketchy wave. Moments later J. T. did the same.

"Funny thing is, she had, literally," Stillman said. "Almost a million. By then she'd given a lot of it away. Imagine how pissed they were."

I did and, petty human being that I am, rather enjoyed doing so.

"What was left went into a foundation that I still oversee."

"Without electricity or phone service?"

"Batteries. Satellites. A laptop."

"What a world it's become."

"Same way I went about finding others like myself. It took a great while. Whereas, before, it would have been hit-and-miss at best." He stood and walked to clearing's edge, after a moment turned back. "My grandmother was twelve when she got off the train at Auschwitz. A child, though she would not be a child much longer. She survived. Her parents and two siblings didn't."

Folding back the sleeve of his shirt, he revealed the numbers that stood out on the muscles of his forearm. "It's as exact a reproduction as I could manage. Many of us have them."

CHAPTER TWENTY-TWO

THE CICADAS WERE GONE. Val lost two cases, won another, went on the Internet to pull down tablatures of "Eighth of January" and "Cluck Old Hen." The reek of magnolia was everywhere, and single-winged maple seeds coptered down on our heads—or was that earlier? Lonnie resigned. "Thing is, Turner, I don't do it now, I'm never going to." Eldon had a new guitar, a Stella with a pearloid fingerboard from the thirties in which someone had installed a pickup. "Not collectible anymore, but it still has that great old sound." J. T. sat on the porch tapping feet, drinking ice tea, and saying maybe this time-off thing wasn't so bad after all. Don Lee was out of the hospital, making the two-hour drive to Bentonville three days a week for rehab. He'd tried coming back to work a few hours a day. Second week of it, June pulled me aside. He and I had a talk that afternoon. I told him he was one of the best I'd ever worked with. But you don't have to do this anymore, I said. You know that, right? He sat looking out the window, shaking his head. It's not that I don't want to, Turner, he said. With all that's happened, I want to more than ever. I just don't know if I can.

No further foul winds came blowing down out of Memphis.

Patently, I was an alarmist.

Town life went on. Brother Tripp from First Baptist was seen peering into cars at one of the local parking spots popular among teenagers. Barry and Barb shut down the hardware store after almost twenty years. Customers routinely made the forty-mile drive to WalMart now, they said, and, anyway, they were tired. Thelma quit the diner. Sally Johnson, last year's prom queen, promptly took her spot. Slow afternoons, I'd give a try to imagining Thelma's existence away from waitressing. What would her house or apartment look like, and what would she do there all day? Did she wear that same sweater distorted by so many years of tips weighing down one pocket? Robert Poole from the feed store left his wife and four children. Melinda found the note on the kitchen table when she came home from a late shift at Mitty's, the town's beauty shop. *Took the truck. The rest is yours. Love, Rob.*

Everyone in town knew what happened up there in the hills, of course, and reactions were mixed, long-bred suspicion of outsiders, youth, and those demonstrably different tripping tight on the heels of declarations of What a shame about that boy! When the funeral came round, Isaiah Stillman and his group filed down from their camp, sat quietly through the ceremony, then got up quietly and left. More than a dozen townspeople also attended.

When Val told me she was thinking about quitting her job, I said she was too damned young for a midlife crisis.

"Eldon's asked me to go on the road with him."

"What, covering the latest pap out of Nashville? How proud I am to be a redneck, God bless the U.S.A.?"

"Quite the opposite, actually. He's bought a trailer, plans on living in it, travelling from one folk or bluegrass festival to the next, playing traditional music."

Buy an eighty-year-old guitar, that's the sort of thing that can happen to you, I guess. Suddenly you're no longer satisfied working roadhouses for a living.

"You've no idea how many there are," Val said. "I know I didn't. Hundreds of them, all across the country. We'd be doing old-time. Ballads, mountain music, Carter Family songs."

No doubt they'd be an arresting act. Black R&B man out of the inner city, white banjo player with a law degree from Tulane. Joined to remind America of its heritage.

"I wouldn't expect to take the Whyte Laydie, of course."

"You should, it's yours. My grandfather would be pleased to know that it's still being played."

"And how very much it's revered?"

"He might have some trouble getting his head around that. Back then, he most likely ordered it from the local general store, paid a dollar or two a week on it. Instruments were tools, like spades or frying pans. Something to help people get by."

We were out on the porch, me leaning against the wall, Val with feet hanging off the side. Bright white moon above. Insects beating away at screens and exposed skin.

Val said, "I'd never have come to this place in my life without you, you know."

"Right."

143

"I mean it."

I sat beside her. She took my hand.

"You have no idea how well you fit in here, do you? Or how many people love you?"

I knew *she* did, and the thought of losing her drove pitons through my heart. Climbers scrambled for purchase.

"This is not just something you're thinking about, then."

She shook her head.

"I'll miss you."

Leaning against me there in the moonlight, she asked, "Do I really need to say anything about that?"

No.

She stood. "I'm going to spend the last few days at the house shutting it down. Who knows, maybe someday I'll actually complete the restoration."

I saw her to the Volvo and returned to my vigil on the porch, soon became aware of a presence close by. The screen door banged gently shut behind her as J. T. stepped out.

"She told you, huh?"

"A heads-up would have been good."

"Val asked me not to say anything. I don't think she was sure, herself, right up till now. Amazing moon." She had a bottle of Corona and passed it to me. I took a swig. "Talked to my lieutenant today."

Hardly a surprise. The department was calling daily in its effort to lure her back. Demands had given way to entreaty, appeals to her loyalty, barely disguised bribes, promises of promotion.

"Be leaving soon, then?"

"Not exactly." She finished the beer and set the bottle on the floorboards. "You didn't want the sheriff's position, right?"

"Lonnie's job? No way."

"Good. Because I met with Mayor Sims today, and I took it."

CHAPTER TWENTY-THREE

OBVIOUSLY IT WAS MY TIME for surprises. And for mixed feelings. Wounded at the thought of Val's departure, nonetheless I was pleased that she'd be doing what she most loved. The two emotions rode a teeter-totter, one rising, the other touching feet to earth—before they reversed.

And J. T.? As my boss? Well . . .

I gave some thought to how she, city-bred and a city-trained officer, would fit in here. But then I remembered the way she and Moira had sat together up in the hills and decided she'd do okay. It goes without saying how pleased I was that she'd be around.

I was considerably less pleased when Miss Emily chewed a hole in the screen above the sink and took her brood out through it.

Because I considered it a betrayal? Because it was yet another loss? Or simply because I would miss them?

I was standing in the kitchen, staring at the hole in the screen, when J. T. swung by to see if I wanted to grab some dinner. She had moved into a house on Mulberry, or, more precisely, into one room. The house had been empty a long time, and the rest would take a while. But the price was right. Her monthly rent was about what a couple in the city might spend on a good dinner out.

"They're wild animals, Dad, not pets. What, you expected her to leave a note?"

"You think she moved in just to be sure her offspring would be safe? Knowing all along she'd leave afterwards?"

"Somehow I doubt possums very often overplan things."

"I thought . . ." Shaking myself out of it: "I don't know what I thought."

"So. Dinner?"

"Not tonight. You mind?"

"Of course not."

Some time after she left, second bourbon slammed down and coffee brewing, the perfect response came to me: But we slept together, you know, Miss Emily and I.

Rooting through stacks of CDs and tapes on shelves in the front room, I found what I was looking for.

It had been one of those drawling, seemingly endless Sunday afternoons in May. We'd grilled chicken and burgers earlier and were dipping liberally, ad lib as Val kept insisting, into the cooler for beers, bolstering such excursions with chips, dip, carrot sticks, and potato salad scooped finger-style from the bowl. Eldon sprang open the case on his Gibson, Val went inside to get the Whyte Laydie, and they started playing. I'd recently had the cassette recorder out for something or another and set it up on the windowsill in the kitchen. Just about where Miss Emily and crew went through.

148

"Keep on the Sunny Side," "White House Blues," "Frankie and Albert." No matter that lyrics got scrambled, faked, or lost completely, the music kept its power.

"We should do this more often," Val said as they took a break. I'd left the recorder running.

"We should do this all the time." Eldon held up his jelly glass, half cranberry juice, half club soda, in salute. Only Val and I were dipping into the cooler.

Soon enough they were back at it.

"Banks of the Ohio," "Soldier's Joy," "It Wasn't God Who Made Honky-Tonk Angels."

I left the tape going and went back out onto the porch. Just days ago I'd been thinking how full the house was. Now suddenly everyone was gone. Even Miss Emily. Val and Eldon shifted into "Home on the Range," Eldon, playing slide on standard guitar, doing the best he could to approximate Bob Kaai's Hawaiian steel.

"What the hell *is* that you're listening to?" a voice said. "No wonder someone wants you dead, you pitiful fuck."

Diving forward, I kicked the legs out from under the chair and he, positioned behind with the steel-wire garrote not quite in place yet, went along, splayed across the chair's back. An awkward position. Before he had the chance to correct it, I pivoted over and had an arm locked around his neck, alert to any further sound or signs of intrusion. The garrote, piano wire with tape-wound wood handles, sat at porch's edge looking like a garden implement.

"Simple asphyxiation," Doc Oldham said an hour later.

I do remember pulling the arm in hard, asking if he was alone, getting no answer and asking again. Was he contract? Who sent him? No response to those questions either. Then the awareness of his body limp beneath me.

"Man obviously didn't care to carry on a conversation with you," Doc Oldham said, grabbing hold of the windowsill to pull himself erect with difficulty, tottering all the way up and tottering still once there. "'S that coffee I smell?"

"Used to be, anyway. Near dead as this guy by now's my guess."

"Hey, it's late at night and I'm a doctor. You think I'm so old I forgot my intern days? Bad burned coffee's diesel fuel for us—what I love most. Next to a healthy slug of bourbon."

Meanwhile J. T. waited, coming to the realization that further black-and-whites would not be barreling up, that there were no fingerprint people or crime lab investigators to call in, no watch commander to pass things off to. It was all on her.

She sat at the kitchen table. Doc nodded to her and said "Asphyxiation," poured his coffee and took the glass of bourbon I handed him.

"Tough first day," I said.

"Technically I haven't even started."

"Hope you had a good dinner at least."

"Smothered chicken special."

"Guess homemaking only goes so far."

"Give me a break, I'm still trying to find the kitchen. Speaking of which, this coffee really sucks."

"Don't pay her any mind, Turner," Doc Oldham said, helping himself to a second cup. "It's delicious."

"I'm assuming there's no identification," J. T. said.

"These guys don't exactly carry passports. There's better than a thousand dollars in a money clip in his left pants pocket, an-other thousand under a false insole in his shoe. A driver's license that looks like it was made yesterday."

"Which it probably was. So, we have no way to track where he might have been staying because there isn't any place to stay. And with no bus terminals or airports—"

"No airports? What about Stanley Municipal? Crop duster to the stars."

"—there's no paper trail." She sipped coffee and made a face. "Nothing I know is of any help here."

"What you *know* is rarely important. The rest is what matters— all those hours of working the job, interviews, people you've met, the instincts nurtured by all of it. That's what you use."

"Something you learned in psychology classes?"

"From Eldon, actually. Spend hours practicing scales and learning songs, he said, then you get up there to play and none of it matters. Where you begin and where you wind up have little to do with one another. Meanwhile we," I said, passing it over, "do have this."

I gave her a moment.

"Thing you have to ask is, this is a pro, right? First to last he covers his tracks. That's what he does, how he lives. No wallet, false ID if any at all, he's a ghost, a glimmer. So why does a stub from an airline ticket show up in his inside coat pocket?"

"Carelessness?"

"Possible, sure. But how likely?"

I was, after all, patently an alarmist, possibly paranoid, a man known to have accused a possum of overplanning.

It was only the torn-off stub of a boarding pass and easily enough could have been overlooked. You glance at aisle and seat number, stick it in your pocket just in case, find it there the next time you wear that coat.

But I wasn't running scales, I was up there on stage, playing. And judging from the light in J. T.'s eyes, she was too.

CHAPTER TWENTY-FOUR

HIS NAME, or at least one of his names, was Marc Bruhn, and he'd come in on the redeye, nonstop, from Newark to Little Rock. Ticket paid in cash, round trip, no flags, whistles, or bells. These guys play everything close to the vest. Extrapolating arrival to service-desk time, despite false identification and despite Oxford, Mississippi, having been given as destination, J. T. was able to track a car rental.

"That's the ringer, what got me onto him. Who the hell, if he's heading for Oxford, would fly into Little Rock rather than Memphis?"

"Hey, he's from New Jersey, remember?"

We'd found the car under a copse of trees across the lake. There was a half-depleted six-pack of bottled water on the floorboard, an untouched carton of Little Debbie cakes on the passenger seat, and a self-improvement tape in the player.

June was able to pull out previous transactions in the name of Marc Bruhn, Mark Brown, Matt Browen, and other likely cognates. Newark International, JFK, and La Guardia; Gary, Indiana, and nearby Detroit; Oklahoma City, Dallas, Phoenix; Seattle, St. Louis, L.A.

"That's it, that's as far as my reach goes."

But good as J. T. and June proved to be, Isaiah Stillman was better.

"You told me you managed a conservatorship via the Internet," I said on a visit that evening. "And that's how you put all this together."

"Yes, sir." I'd asked him to stop the *sir* business, but it did no good. "I grew up limping, one leg snared forever in a modem. The Internet's the other place I live."

I told him about Bruhn, about the killings. We were dancing in place, I said, painting by numbers, since we were pretty sure who sent him. But we hadn't been able to get past a handful of basic facts and suspicions.

"We take the individual's right to privacy and autonomy very seriously, Mr. Turner."

"I know."

"On the other hand, we're in your debt. And however we insist upon holding ourselves apart from it, this community is one we've chosen to live in, which implies certain responsibilities."

Our eyes held, then his went to the trees about us: the rough ladder, the treehouse built for children to come.

"Excuse me."

Entering one of the lean-tos, he emerged with a laptop.

"Moira tells me Miss Emily left," he said.

"And Val."

"Val will be back. Miss Emily won't. Marc, right? With a *c* or a *k*? B-R-U-H-N?" Fingers rippling on keys. "Commercial history—which you have already. List of Bruhns by geographical distribution, including alternate spellings . . . Here it is, narrowed down to the New Jersey–New York area. . . . You want copies of any of this, let me know."

"I don't see a printer."

"No problem, I can just zap it to your office, right?"

Could he? I had no idea.

"Now for the real fun. I'm putting in the name . . . commercial transactions we know about . . . the Jersey–New York list . . . and a bunch of question marks. Like fishhooks." His fingers stopped. "Let's see what we catch."

Lines of what I assumed to be code snaked steadily down the screen. Nothing I could make any sense of.

"Here we go." Stillman hit a few more keys. "Looks as though your man advertises in a number of niche publications. Gun magazines, adventure publications and the like. Not too smart of him."

"The smart criminals are all CEOs."

"No Internet presence that I can—" Stillman's hands flashed to the keyboard. "There's a watcher."

I shook my head.

"A sentinel, a special kind of firewall. The question marks I put in, the fishhooks—that was like opening up a gallery of doors. We were entering one when the alarm triggered. I hit the panic button pretty quickly, so chances are good the watcher never got a fix on me. Probably be best if I stayed offline a while, all the same." He shut the computer off and lowered the lid. "Sorry. Have a cup of tea before you go?"

We sat on the bench, everyone else gone to bed by this time. I held the mug up close, breathing in the rich aroma, loving the feel of the steam on my face. Stillman touched me on the shoulder and pointed to the sky as a shooting star arced above the trees.

Big star fallin', mama ain't long fore day . . . Maybe the sunshine'll drive my blues away. My eyes dropped to the boards nailed up over the cabin and the legend thereon. Stillman's eyes followed.

"I've been meaning to ask you about that."

"It went up the moment we moved in." He sipped his tea with that strange intensity he gave most everything—as though this might be the last cup of tea he'd ever drink. "From my grandmother's life, like so much else."

Bending to lift the teapot off the ground (ceramic, thrown by Moira, lavender-glazed), he refilled our mugs.

"*Hier ist kein Warum.* A guard told her that on her first morning at the camp as he brought her a piece of stale bread. There is no *why* here. In his own way, she said, he was being kind."

Mind tumbling with thoughts of kindness and cruelty and the ravage of ideas, I struck out for my newly empty house, fully confident of finding the way without a guide now, though once I could have sworn I saw Nathan off in the trees watching to be sure I made it out all right. Imagined, of course. That same night I also thought I saw Miss Emily in the yard, which could have been only the shadow of a limb: wind and moonlight in uneasy alliance to take on substance.

CHAPTER TWENTY-FIVE

HERB DANZIGER CALLED that morning to tell me the execution had been carried out and Lou Winter was dead. I thanked him. Herb said come see him sometime before he and his nurse ran away together. I asked how long that would be and he said it probably better be soon. I hung up, and had no idea what I felt.

I sat thinking about a patient I had back in Memphis. He'd come in that first time wearing a five-hundred-dollar suit, silk tie, and cordovan shoes so highly polished it looked as though he were walking on two violins. "Harris. Just the one name. Don't use any others." He shook hands, sat in the chair, and said, "Ammonia."

"I'm sorry?"

"Ammonia."

I looked around.

"Not here. Well, yes: here. Everywhere, actually. That's the problem."

Light from the window behind bled away his features. I got up to draw the blinds.

"Everywhere," he said again as I took my seat. His eyes were like twin perched crows.

Eight and a half weeks before, as he rummaged about in stacks of file boxes in the basement looking through old papers, the smell of ammonia had come suddenly upon him. There was no apparent source for it; he'd checked. But the smell had been with him ever since. He'd seen his personal physician, then by referral an internist, an allergist, and an endocrinologist. Now he was here.

I asked the obvious question, which is mostly what therapists do: What papers had he been looking for? He brushed that aside in the manner of a man long accustomed to ignoring prattle and attending to practicalities, and went on talking about the stench, how sometimes it was overpowering, how other times he could almost pretend that it had left him.

From session to session over a matter of weeks, as in stop-motion, I watched dress and demeanor steadily deteriorate. That first appointment had been set by a secretary. When, a couple of months in, with an emergency on my hands, I tried to call to cancel a session, I learned that Harris's phone had been disconnected. The poise and punctuality of early visits gave way to tardiness and to disjunctive dialogue that more and more resembled a single, ongoing monologue. When he paused, he was not listening for my response but for something from within himself. Trains of thought left the station without him. He began to (as a bunkmate back in country had said of the company latrines) not smell so good.

The last time I saw him he peered wildly around the corner of the open door, came in and took his seat, and said, "I've been shot by the soldiers of Chance."

I waited.

"Not to death, I think—not quite. Casualties are grave, though."

He smiled.

"I'm bleeding, Captain. Don't know if I can make it back to camp." As he smiled again, I recalled his eyes that first time, the alertness in them, the resolve. "It was a report card," he said.

Not understanding, I shook my head.

"What I was looking for in the basement. It was a report card from the eighth grade, last one before graduation. Three years in junior high and I had all A's, but some of the teachers put their busy heads together and decided that wasn't such a good idea. I got my report card in its little brown envelope, opened it, and there were two B-pluses, history and math. Just like that."

"I'm sorry."

"Sorry. Yeah . . . You know what I did? I laughed. I'd always suspected the world wasn't screwed down so well. Now I had proof."

After he left, I sat thinking. The world's an awfully big presence to carry a grudge against, but so many people do just that. Back in prison, the air was thick with such grudges, so thick you could barely breathe, barely make your way through the corridors, men's lives crushed to powder under the weight. On the other hand, maybe that was a part of what had motivated Harris all these years. But it gave out, quit working, the way things do.

Just over a week later, I was notified that Harris had been picked up by police and remanded by the courts to the state hospital. Declaring that he had no family, he'd given my name. I had the best intentions of going to see him, but before I could, he broke into the janitor's supply room and drank most of a can of Drano.

"You okay, Deputy?"

I pushed back from the desk and swiveled my chair around. J. T. had taken to calling me that of late. What began as a passing joke, stuck. I told her about Lou Winter. She came over and put her hand on my arm.

"I'm sorry, Dad."

Her other hand held a sheaf of printouts.

"So Stillman *was* able to zap it here."

"It's not magic, you know."

To this day I remain unconvinced of that. But I spent most of two hours bent over those sheets, trying to find something in them that Stillman had missed, some corner or edge sticking out a quarter-inch, any possible snag, and remembering what one of my teachers back in college used as an all-purpose rejoinder. You'd come in with some grand theory you'd sewn together and she'd listen carefully. Then when you were done, she'd say, "Random points of light, Mr. Turner. Random points of light."

Around eleven I took my random points of light and the butt that usually went along with them down to the diner. The raging controversy of the day seemed to be whether or not the big superstore out on the highway to Poplar Bluff was ever really going to open. The lot had been paved and the foundation laid months ago, walls like massive jigsaw parts started going up, then it all slammed to a stop—because the intricate webwork of county payoffs and state kickbacks had somehow broken down, most believed. I sat over my coffee listening to the buzz around me and noticing how everything outside the window looked bleached out, as though composed of only two colors, both of them pale. But that was me, not the light.

Where had I read *the broken bottles our lives are?*

"You hear about Sissy Coopersmith yet?"

Sy Butts slid into the booth across from me. He'd been wearing that old canvas hunting jacket since he was a kid, everyone said. Now Sy was pushing hard at sixty. Pockets meant to hold small game were long gone; daylight showed here and there like numerous tiny doorways.

I shook my head.

Sally brought his coffee and refilled my cup for the third or fourth time.

"You know as how she was working as a nurse's aide, going from house to house taking care of the elderly? Had a gift for it, some said. Well, she'd been saving up her money for this seminar down West Memphis way. Last week's when it was. Got on the bus Friday morning and no one's heard a word since . . . Kind of surprised Lon and Sandra ain't been in to see you."

"She's, what, twenty-five, twenty-six? Short of filing a missing-persons report, there's not a lot they can do."

"Never was much they could do, with that girl. Sweet as fresh apple cider, but she had a mind of her own."

"Some would say that's a good thing."

"Some'll say just about any damn thing comes to 'em."

Doc Oldham passed by outside the window and, catching my eye, did a quick dance step by way of greeting. Then, inexplicably, he leveled one finger at me, sighting along it.

Sy looked at Doc, then at me. I shrugged. Sy told me more about Sissy's having a mind of her own.

Doc Oldham walked in the door of the cabin that night half an hour after I did. No knock, and for some reason I'd failed to hear

161

him coming, which was quite a surprise considering the old banger Ford pickup he'd been driving since Nixon and McCarthy were bosom buddies.

"Man works up a thirst on the road," he said.

I poured whiskey into a jelly glass and handed it to him. The glasses, with their rims and bellies, had been under the sink when I bought the place. I hadn't seen jelly glasses since leaving home.

"So what brings you all the way out here?"

He downed the bourbon in a single swallow, peered into the glass at the drop, like a lens, left behind.

"Here to do your physical."

"You're joking."

"Nope. Regulations say twice a year. When'd we do your last one?"

"We didn't."

"Exactly."

I'd learned long ago that, for all his seeming insouciance, once Doc got something in his mind it stayed there. So as he pulled various instruments from the old carpetbag ("A real one, from right after the war. Some good ol' boys shot the original owner down in Hattiesburg") I pulled myself, per instruction, out of most of my clothes.

Somehow, as he poked and prodded at me and mumbled to himself, we both got through it, me with the help of well-practiced fortitude, Doc with the help of my bourbon. "Not bad," he said afterwards, "for a man of . . . oh, whatever the hell age you are. Watch what you eat, drink less"—this, as he dumped what was left of the bottle into his jelly glass—"and you might think about taking up a hobby, something that requires physical exertion. Like dancing."

"Dancing, huh?"

"Yep."

"Would carrying an old man outside and throwing him in the lake count?"

He considered. "Well, of course, for it to be of benefit, you'd have to do it repetitively." He threw the stethoscope and reflex hammer into the bag, then, noticing that the blood-pressure cuff was still on my arm, unwrapped that and threw it in too. "Day or two, I'll fetch a copy of my report round to the office. Take a little longer for the lab work, have to send that over to the hospital at Greer's Bay. Used to run the blood myself, but just don't have the patience for it anymore."

Doc started for the door, light on his feet as ever: the cabin walls shook.

"This had to be done today, right?"

He turned. "Fit things in when I can."

"Sure you do."

Our eyes met. Neither of us said anything for a moment.

"I heard Val might be pulling up stakes."

"Guess there's no 'might' to it. Just do me a favor, Doc: don't ask me what I feel about this, okay?"

"Wouldn't think of it. Sorry, though."

The walls shook a little more. I looked through the screen door and saw him sitting motionless in the truck. Then I heard the old Ford cough and gasp its way into life. I listened as it wound down the road and around the lake.

The phone rang not too long after. I took my time getting in off the porch. Thing quit about the time I got to it, then started up again as I was pouring a drink to carry back out.

"You forgot the beeper," J. T. said when I answered.

"Hope you don't—"

"Never mind. Meet me at the camp."

"Stillman's, you mean."

"Right. We just got a call. A little confusing—but I think it was Moira."

CHAPTER TWENTY-SIX

BACK BEFORE I CAME HERE, for reasons that still escape me—one of those random, pointless notions that sometimes overtake us, especially, it seems, in middle age—I went home. I suppose I shouldn't say home. Where I grew up, rather.

It had never been much of a town. Now it wasn't much of anything. Many of the stores along Main Street were boarded up. Outside others, owners sat in lawn chairs, heads moving slowly to follow as I made my way down the cracked WPA sidewalk opposite. Every second or third tie was missing from the railroad tracks, rails themselves overgrown. A spike lay nearby, alongside the dried-out, mummified skin of a lizard, and I bent to pick it up. Its weight, the solidity of it, seemed strangely out of place here in this fading, forsaken landscape. Only stumps of walls, like broken bottom teeth, remained of the Blue Moon Café, whose porch and mysterious inner reaches for the whole of my childhood had been inhabited by black men eating sandwiches red with barbeque sauce and drinking from squat bottles of soft drinks. Outside town, the country store in which my grandparents spent eighteen hours every day of their adult life had become, with a crude white cross nailed to the front, the Abyssinian Holy God Church.

I walked along the levee thinking of all the times I'd sat here with Al, the two of us silhouetted against the sky as the town carried on its business behind and below. Old folks still talked about the great flood of 1908, but the river had begun drying up long before the town did, and now a man, if he watched his footing, could pretty much walk across and never wet his belt.

Like myself, the town was falling slowly towards the center of the earth.

Why is it that so often we begin to define a thing—come to that desire, and to the realization of its uniqueness—only at the very moment it is irrevocably changing and passing from us?

My life at the cabin and in the town, for instance. My family.

J. T.

Val.

I wasn't thinking about it that day back by the river, naturally, since none of it had happened then, but I was definitely thinking about it the morning I stood on a hill looking down at Stillman's camp.

Another thing I was thinking about, both times, was that all my life, with my time in the jungle, my years on the street as a cop, prison days, psychiatric work, even the place I grew up—all my life I'd lived out of step and synch with the larger world, forever tottering on borders and fault lines. It wasn't that I chose to do so; that's simply where I wound up.

As a counselor, of course, I'd have been quick to point out that we *always* make our choices, and that not choosing was as much a choice as any other. Such homilies are, as much as anything else, the reason I'd quit. It's too easy once you learn the tricks. You start off believing that you're discovering a way of seeing the world clearly, but you're really only learning a language—a dangerous language whose very narrowness fools you into believing you understand why people do the things they do.

But we don't. We understand so little of anything.

Such as why anyone would want to cause the rack and wreckage I saw below me in bright moonlight.

J. T. came trodding up the hill, sliding a bit on the wet grass. I curbed my impulse to make smart remarks about city folk.

"What do you think?"

Pretty much what she did, at that point.

The kids were down below, sifting through the rubble. For all my best intentions I couldn't help but think of them that way. Smoke curled from the remains of the cabin and crossed the moon. They'd come straggling in not long after we arrived—all but Stillman, who after sending the rest off into the woods had stayed behind to confront the interlopers.

We didn't hear Nathan until he was almost beside us.

"Missing someone?"

He carried his shotgun in the crook of an arm, barrel broken. My father and grandfather always did the same.

"Boy's back in about a mile."

"He okay?"

Nathan looked down at what was left of the camp. "Will be. Have to splint that leg 'fore we move him."

J. T. and I exchanged glances. "You saw who did this?" she said.

Nathan nodded.

"Three of 'em. Watched the others head off and knew they'd

be all right. The boy, one that sorta runs things—"

"Isaiah."

"Him and the ones did this, I followed them. Figured, push came to shove . . ." He lifted a shoulder, raising the gunstock an inch or two, then, without saying more, turned and stepped off into trees. We followed.

"No way you're out hunting in the middle of the night."

"Not usually."

I stopped, putting a hand on Nathan's shoulder. I doubt anyone had touched him for years. He looked down at my hand, probably as surprised as I was, but none of it showing on his face.

"I been watching out for them," he said. "One way or the other, you knew they'd be having some trouble."

"Watching them, huh." We went on up a steep slope and down into a hollow. I saw Isaiah Stillman ahead, propped against a fallen maple. Another body lay a few paces away. "Because of your dog. Killing that boy."

"Just started me thinking, all the trouble could come their way up here."

"Like this," J. T. said.

"Or worse. Yes, ma'am."

"Sheriff," Stillman said as we approached. "Are the rest okay?" I nodded.

"That old fucker shot me," the other one said. It looked bad, but it wasn't. Nathan knew his distance and how much buckshot would disperse. The boy's pants were shredded and his lower body well bloodied and someone at the ER was going to be picking out shot with tweezers for a couple of hours, but the boy'd be back on his feet soon enough.

"Shut up," J. T. told him.

"There was three of them," Nathan said, "all of them youngsters. Figure his friends'll be on the way to hiding under their beds by now."

J. T. looked at me. "Not another message from Memphis, then." Which is what we'd both been thinking, though neither of us had said it.

"Guess not."

"They tried to make me fight them," Stillman said. "When I wouldn't, that enraged them."

"Took to beatin' on the boy some fierce. Mainly that one there."

As Nathan nodded his direction, the boy started to say something. J. T. kicked his foot.

"So you stopped them," I said.

Nathan nodded. Pulling his knife, he peeled a thick slice of bark from the fallen tree, then hacked some vines from a bush nearby. Three minutes later he had Isaiah's leg splinted. "Other one, I figure we just throw him in the truck."

"Or in one of the ravines," J. T. said.

Girl was definitely catching on.

CHAPTER TWENTY-SEVEN

WE TOOK ISAIAH and the boy called Sammy to Cahoma County Hospital, then picked up the other two and put them away in the cells for the night. Tomorrow they'd either be headed to Cahoma County detention themselves, or up to Memphis, depending on what Judge Gray decided. Both of them stank of old beer and a kind of fear they'd never known before. One set of parents came in, listened to what we told them, shook their heads, and left. The other, a single mother, asked what she needed to do. You could tell by the way she said it that she'd been asking herself the same question for a long time.

From over by Jefferson, the boys said. Been drinking at the game and after, just having fun, you know? You remember what that was like. Someone had told them about these weirdos playing Tarzan up in the hills and they decided to go check it out.

"Be a long time before they get their lives unbent again," J. T. said.

Maybe. Always amazing, though, how resilient human beings can be.

It was Moira who, as they all quit camp, grabbed the laptop and took it along. She sent an e-mail, "an IM" as J. T. explained to me, to an old friend back in Boston, who then placed a "land-line" call to the office.

I was thinking about that later in the morning, about Moira and about people's resilience, when Eldon stopped by and asked me if I felt like taking a walk. J. T. was home trying to get some sleep. June was off at lunch with Lonnie, their lunches having gotten to be a regular weekly thing. I signed out on the board and grabbed the beeper. We headed crosstown, out past the old Methodist church into what used to be the Meador family's rich pastureland and was now mostly scrub.

"You okay with this?" Eldon said after a while.

"Val and you, you mean."

"What we're doing, yeah."

"I think it's great."

"Most people think we're crazy."

"That's because you are."

"Well . . ."

We stopped to watch a woodpecker worrying away at a sapling the size of a broomstick.

"No way there's anything in there worth all that work," Eldon said. "We'll be back, you know."

"Sure you will. But it will never be the same."

"No. It won't."

He bent down and pulled a blade of grass, held it between his thumbs and blew across it. Making music even with that.

"Hard to pick up and go, harder than I thought. Never would have suspected it. All these years, all these places, this is the only place that's ever felt like home."

"Like you say, you'll be back."

"What about those others—think they'll be back?"

"Memphis?"

He nodded.

"Not much doubt about it."

At wood's edge a young bird staggered about, flapping its wings.

"Trying them on for size," Eldon said. "Like he has this feeling, he's capable of something amazing, even if he doesn't know what it is yet."

We started back towards town.

"Good you're okay with it, then."

"You and Val? Sure. The other . . ."

"That's the way of it. Violence is a lonesome thing, it gets inside you and sits in there calling out for more. But they had no right bringing it here."

"And there should be an end to it. A natural end, an unnatural one—*some* kind of end. How long does it have to go on?"

"You're asking a black man?"

"Good point."

As we walked back, he talked about his and Val's plans, such as they were. An old-time music festival up around Hot Springs, this big campout that got thrown every year down in Texas, a solid string of bluegrass and folk festivals running from California up to Seattle.

"That's where all the VW microbuses go to die," Eldon told me. "Regular elephant's graveyard of them, all along the coast. VW buses, plaid shirts, and old guys with straggly gray ponytails everywhere you look."

We stopped outside the office. June waved from inside. Eldon looked in.

"She doing okay?"

I nodded.

"And Don Lee?"

"Not quite so good."

"Yeah." He started away, then turned. "All that stuff about giving something back? I always thought that was crap."

"Mostly it is."

"Yeah. Well . . . Mostly, everything is."

Lonnie had come back to the office with June. The two of them plus Don Lee were all sitting with coffee. Don Lee nodded. Lonnie raised his cup in invitation.

"Who made it?" I asked.

June smiled.

Safe, then.

"Don't worry, Turner," Lonnie said. "Happens to all of us as we grow older, that getting cautious thing. Starts off with the coffee, say, then before you know it you're wearing double shirts on a windy day and stuffing newspapers around your door."

"Maybe even have a silly little hat you wear to bed when you take your afternoon naps," June said, Lonnie giving his best "Who, me?" look in response.

They'd heard about most of what had taken place out at the camp. The rest, I filled them in on.

"So why the hell'd they trash the place?" Lonnie asked.

"Who knows? But it's pretty much destroyed."

"We should get a bunch of people together," June said. "Go up there and help them rebuild."

We all looked at her. She was right. Sympathy had been gathering in the town for some time, since the day of the funeral for the boy Nathan's dog had killed. The camp's destruction, along with June's urging, put that sympathy over the top. In ensuing months, furniture, lumber, clothing, household goods, and a lot of time and effort would go up into those hills, all of us the better for it.

Lonnie shook his head. "Just kids."

"Just kids."

"You must have thought . . ."

"Of course we did."

"Anything further on that?"

"Nothing substantial, no. Eldon and I were just talking about it, wondering how long this has to go on."

"Once it starts . . ." Lonnie got up and poured himself another cup of coffee. "Some of these families have grudges reaching back to the day the first caveman said 'Hey look at me, I can walk upright!' They don't know any other way."

"You have to cut the head off," Don Lee said, speaking for the first time. "You cut the head off, it dies."

CHAPTER TWENTY-EIGHT

I'M GOING TO SKIP ahead here, past Monday and Tuesday, to the aftermath.

The call from Memphis came on a bright morning, Wednesday.

Unable to sleep, I'd been shuffling papers and creating unnecessary files since 3 a.m. I was looking out the window, watching Bill from the Gulf station teaching his kid to ride a bike down the middle of Cherry Street, when the phone rang. A spider had built a spectacular web in the corner of the window. The web and bright-colored joints of the spider's legs caught morning sunlight like prisms.

"Sheriff's office."

"Turner?"

"You got him."

"Sam Hamill here."

"Always a pleasure."

"Sure it is."

"I assume you're not calling just to say hello."

"Not hardly." He held his hand over the receiver for a

moment—to speak offstage, as it were. Then he was back. "Thing is, something strange has just happened up this way."

"It usually does."

"I've got a body."

I waited.

"Two, actually. But only the one that matters. Man goes by the name of Jorge Aleché?"

"When?"

"Some time between noon and four yesterday, him and the bodyguard. Why do you ask?"

"Curiosity. What is it exactly that I can do for you, Sam?"

"I don't suppose there's any chance you'd have been back in town, right?"

"None at all. Been a little busy down this way, too."

"So I heard." After a moment he added: "I spoke to Sheriff Bates. Sorry about the shooting. He said you got the one who did it, though."

"The one who pulled the trigger, anyway."

"Well, it looks like someone may have gone a little deeper in country, if you know what I mean. 'Bout as far in as you *can* go, matter of fact. You think that's what happened, Turner?"

"Possible."

"I tried calling the current sheriff, one J.T. Burke, and was told by . . . just a minute . . . Mabel? Do I have that right?"

"Mabel. Right."

"Told me the sheriff was off on official business and would return my call as soon as possible. Little before that, I tried someone named Don Lee—"

"Acting sheriff."

"What I was told. So there's this Mabel person, secretary by the name of June, two or three sheriffs that I know of. You got one hell of a staff for a town that size."

"We take turns. Monday's my day as crossing guard."

"Sure it is. Anyway, the wife said this Don Lee was under the weather—recently sustained some injuries, I understand?—and was resting, and unless it was really important she didn't want to disturb him."

"Is there a message I can give Sheriff Burke for you, Sam?"

"What it comes down to is, since no one else seems to be available, here I am talking to you."

"Likewise."

"In an official capacity."

"Hold on then, let me get my badge and gun."

What sounded suspiciously like a snort came over the line. "Never change, do you?"

"All the time."

"Given the possibility of a connection between the series of attacks you've suffered and the shootings here—"

"Not much gets past you boys, does it?"

"—MPD believes it important to extend our investigation. I have instructions to request a full local investigation, and to hand off responsibility for that investigation to your office. I'm doing so with this call."

"But suh, we don't know—"

"Shut up, Turner. Just be glad the FBI's not on its way down there."

He was right, of course.

"Turner . . ."

"Yeah?"

"I'm sorry for the way this went down. All of it."

"Thanks, Sam."

"We'll be expecting your reports, then. In due time. No particular hurry-up, we've got our hands full."

"Business as usual."

"God's truth. And Turner . . ."

"Yeah?"

"You do get up this way again, you should think about giving Tracy Caulding a call. For some twisted reason, the woman likes you."

"I know you find it hard to believe, Sam, but people do."

"Go figure. . . . One hell of a world, ain't it?"

CHAPTER TWENTY-NINE

IT SURE AS HELL IS.

I didn't know exactly what it was that MPD expected us to investigate, but over the next several days I made gestures in that direction. J. T. had taken time off to head back up to Seattle—"thing or two I need to take care of." She'd left right before it happened, so I was pretty much running things.

I swung by Don Lee's that afternoon to see if he might be up to coming in to help. Patty Ann answered the door and told me how sorry she was. She said Don Lee was sleeping. The yeasty, rich smell of baking came from inside.

"He doing okay?" I asked.

"Just fine."

"Heard he'd been feeling bad."

She looked at me a moment before saying, "It comes and goes. Kind of like Donald." She ducked her eyes, then added: "I can get him up for you."

"No, no. He needs his rest. Have him call me?"

"I'll do that. Time for a piece of pie before you go? I was just about to take it out of the oven."

"Best be going, but thanks."

Her gaze held mine. Something was pushing from inside, something that wanted to be said (about what had happened? about Don?) but never made it to the surface.

I stopped to help Sally Miller, whose car had stalled outside town, and pulled in at Lonnie's just behind Himself. He wore the usual khakis, which he must buy by the dozen, and a blue shirt. He had a sport coat tossed over one shoulder, his book bag over the other. The bag, he'd liberated from June years ago when she graduated high school, and now he took it everywhere. God knows what all's in there.

"Been on a jaunt, have we?"

"Little business I had to take care of, couldn't put it off any longer. How're you holding up?"

"I'm all right."

"Figuring I'd grab some late lunch and head down to the office, see what I could do to help."

Shirley opened the door as we stepped onto the porch. She gave me a hug, then hugged Lonnie. Inside she had a plate of sandwiches already made, fresh coffee in one of those pots that look like small urns.

"Call ahead and place an order?" I said.

He shrugged. Shirley smiled, said she was praying for us, and excused herself.

As he ate and I drank coffee, I told him about the call from Memphis.

"Full local investigation my ass," Lonnie said when I finished.

Picking a divot of celery from between his teeth, he asked, "Those kids on the mountain doing okay?"

"Isaiah's back with them, cast and all. With everyone pitching in like they have, it's beginning to look good up there."

He got up, unplugged the pot and brought it over, poured more coffee for both of us.

"Is there anything you need, Turner? Anything I can do?"

"Just time . . ."

"Time, right. Worst enemy, best friend, all rolled into one. If there is anything—"

"I will, Lonnie."

"Like to think I don't need to say that."

"You don't."

"Good."

"This business of yours that came up . . ."

"Nothing much to it. Some old loose ends. It's done." He snagged another half sandwich, crusts cut off. This one was pimento cheese, which Shirley ground in an old hand-cranked processor heavy as an anvil. "We were worried about you, all alone up there at the cabin. Time like this, a man needs—"

"I was where I needed to be, Lonnie. Doing what I needed to do."

"Right. Who else would know, huh?"

"I'm fine."

Out in the living room, the TV was on and our current president, one of a cadre of archconservatives who had seized this country to wring its neck in the name of liberty, a man with a to-do list to whom everything was crystal clear, was speaking about "recent troubles in the old world." Yet again I marveled at how we always manage to persuade ourselves that our actions are justified, righteous, for the good.

"Thing is, you have to admire what those kids are doing up there," Lonnie said, "foolish as it is. They have an idea, a star to guide by, and they're willing to put everything they are behind it. How many of us can say that?"

J. T. got back to town not long after. I saw her pickup coming down the street, met her out front of the office. She looked exhausted—exhausted and wired—as she hauled a gym bag out of the cab and held it high to show this was the whole of it. Travel always does that, she said, stomps her flat, jacks her up. I filled her in on the call from Memphis. She listened carefully, shook her head and said nothing.

"So how'd it go?"

"Okay. How are you?"

"I've been worse. Get things taken care of?"

"Did my best, anyway."

"They still trying to get you back?"

"No. No, that's over. That's over, the flight's over, the drive's over—and I'm starved."

"Come on home with me, then. I'll cook."

She hesitated. "I don't think I want to be at the cabin just now, Dad."

"Fair enough, we'll go out. What are you up for?"

"Anything—as long as it's not the diner. No, I take that back. Meat. Serious meat."

And since Eldon was playing at the steakhouse an hour and spare change away, what better choice?

So we chose, and drove, only to find Eldon MIA. Said he had

to be out of town a day or two, our waitress told us, her expression and inflection suggesting that she'd give damn near anything to be the same.

We'd made the drive with windows down, on deserted roads, through tide pools of moonlight and the smell of tomorrow's rain. It was at times like this, sitting together at the kitchen table or in a car, suspended for moments from causality and process, that the natural barriers between J. T. and myself receded. Not that they went down, just that they ceased for those suspended moments to matter.

"I've been thinking about my brother, about Don, a lot," she said. "Thinking how so many people I know have these lives that seem impossible to them. People who do really stupid things over and over. Stupid things, violent things—either to themselves or to others."

"Pain as the fulcrum, loss as the lever, to keep their worlds aloft. After a while that can get to be all they feel, all that reassures them they're alive."

"Exactly. You worked with them, Dad. You must understand."

"No. You always think you will. Every time you learn something new, develop a new passion, you think that's where you're heading. Like that song Eldon and Val used to sing. *Farther along we'll know all about it.* . . . But you don't. You wind up holding the same blank cards—just more of them."

Despite Eldon's absence, we made the most of it, and of three or four pounds of steak between us, then drove back. It was not hard to imagine ghosts just off the road among the trees, riders out of a hundred Sleepy Hollows, fading echoes of great notions, fond hopes, and longed-for lives.

That night I heard, or dreamt I heard, a scratching at the screen on the window by my bed. I went out on the porch, but nothing was there. Only the old chair held together by twine, the stains on the floorboards.

Nothing.

CHAPTER THIRTY

MONDAY NOW. Before the call from Memphis, before my half-assed investigation. Or just *before*. Val and I are sitting on the porch.

"We're leaving in the morning, first light."

Instruments laid away in the back seat of the yellow Volvo, trailer hitched behind, road unfurling ahead. Westward ho.

Before.

"Like hunters."

"Exactly."

"I'll—"

"I know you will. . . . I've already shut the house down. Thought I'd stay here tonight, if that's okay with you."

"Of course it is. Still planning on Texas as first stop?"

"As much as we're planning on anything. We'll get in, point the car in that direction, see what happens."

I went in and got a bottle of wine I'd chilled the way she liked, rejoined her on the porch. I remember that the bottle had a colorful old-world label, red, yellow, purple, green, with a wooden gate or door on it; afterwards, when everyone was gone, I'd sit staring at it.

"You're okay as far as funds, right?"

"Jesus, you sound like a father sending his daughter off to school. But yeah, I'm good."

She picked up the glass, smelled the wine and smiled, put the glass down. Chill it, then let it sit to warm before drinking. There was this perfect moment in there somewhere.

"All these years, paycheck from the state, billings on clients, the only thing I ever spent money on's the house, and that was just for materials, since I—we—did the work. The rest I put away or, God help me, but I do drive a Volvo after all, invested. So I've got a raft that'll keep me afloat through the whitewater."

A ladybug lit on her glass, closing its wing case. Val watched as it traversed the rim.

"There's so much I'll miss," she said. "About the job, I mean—the rest goes without saying."

"Giving something back, making a difference, being a force for good . . ."

"Winning. Being right."

Neither of us said anything for a time. I sipped at my wine. She anticipated hers.

"It scares me that so often that's what it comes down to. Which is as much as anything else why I need to stop. For now, anyway. Everything I've done, I start just trying to figure out how to get by. Not make a mess of it. Then before I know it, I've gotten serious about it, whatever it is—marble collecting, fence-mending, it doesn't matter—and I'm trying to connect all the dots, trying to change things, make those marbles and fence slats *matter.* Turn those damn stupid marbles into whole round worlds."

She looked back at the ladybug, now on its third or fourth pass.

"The French call them *bêtes à bon dieu*," she said. "What a sweet, beautiful name."

"For so small and insignificant a thing."

"Exactly." She looked off to the trees. "The music will be the same. I know that."

Then: "The mythmakers had it wrong, Turner. It's not a clash of good and evil. It's a recondite war between the blueprinters, all those people who know just how things need to be and how to get that done, and the visionaries, who see something else entirely, and I've never been able to decide—"

"'Which side are you on, boys, which side are you on?'" Another old song.

"Right."

"We're all caught in the middle, Val."

"Which is why it's the stuff of myth."

Putting one leg up on the chair arm, she turned to me. The chair's joints went seriously knock-kneed, the twine that held them together at the point of letting go.

"There's a story I love, that I don't think I ever told you. Once, years ago, Itzhak Perlman was giving a concert at Carnegie Hall, some huge venue like that, and of course the house is packed. He hobbles onstage, puts aside his crutches, takes his seat. The orchestra begins, fades for his entrance, and when he hits the second or third note, a string breaks. Goes off like a shot. And everyone's figuring, Well, that's it. But very quietly Perlman signals the conductor to begin again—and he plays the entire concerto on three strings. You can all but see him rethinking the part in his head as he plays, rearranging it, recasting it, remaking it. And he does so faultlessly. 'You know,' he says afterwards, 'sometimes it is the artist's task to find out how much music you can still make with what you have left.'"

Smiling, she picked up her glass and lifted it to her mouth. I glanced away as the wings of a bird taking flight caught sunlight.

After the shot, I realized it had been quiet for some time. Night birds, frogs, none of them were calling. And I had missed it.

The sound of the glass shattering came close upon the shot. Val sat straight in the chair, her mouth opening twice as if to speak, then slumped. I went to her, expecting at any moment a second shot. As I held her, she pointed at the wine running slowly along the floorboards. The second shot came then—but from a shotgun, not a rifle.

Nathan stepped into the clearing, from lifelong habit extracting the shell casings and replacing them even as he moved forward. In moments he was there and had Val on the floor. We'd both seen our share of shootings, we knew what had to be done.

Later I'd learn that the kids up at the camp weren't the only ones Nathan had been keeping an eye on. He'd arrived after the man had taken his first shot and was preparing for the second. Must of heard the click of the safety release, Nathan said, 'cause he for damn sure didn't hear me, and looked round just in time to see both barrels coming at him.

No identification on the body, of course. Keys for a Camry that turned out not to be a rental but stolen, thick fold of hundreds and twenties in a money clip, full whiskey flask snugged in one rear pocket of his jeans. In the other they found a Congressional Medal of Honor.

J. T. came back to the cabin to tell me this.

"We might be able to trace him by it," she said, "assuming of course that it's his."

But tracing him was dancing in place. We all knew that. We all knew where he came from. One dead soldier more or less, named or nameless, mattered little in the scheme of things.

"Dad?"

Only then did I realize I'd made no response.

"Are you going to be okay?"

Of course I would be, in time.

"You shouldn't be out here by yourself. Come on into town and stay with me, just for tonight."

But I declined, insisting that being by myself was exactly what I needed right now.

Again and again people say everything's a blur at these times, but it's not. For all that it happens fast, each single moment takes forever to uncoil in your mind, each image is clear and separate and rimed with light. Somewhere in my memory Val will always be sitting there slumped forward in the chair with a surprised expression on her face pointing to the spilled wine.

Lonnie showed up not long after, then Don Lee with Doc Oldham in tow. At one point Lonnie threatened to slap cuffs on me and haul my ass back to town if he had to. He didn't carry through on it, though. Most of us don't carry through; that's one of the things you can usually count on.

Eldon was the last to turn up, after the rest had gone, even Nathan—though for all I knew, Nathan was still out there skulking. Eldon sat on the edge of the porch.

"I'm sorry, man," he said.

"We all are."

"You have no idea."

I didn't have much of anything.

"Rain heading this way."

"Good."

After a moment he said, "I loved her, John."

After a moment I said, "I know you did."

"What the hell are we gonna do now, man?"

"You're going to go on, to Texas and all those places you two had talked about, and you're going to play and sing the songs you and Val always did together."

I went in and got the banjo.

"She told me you were learning to play."

"I don't think you can call what the banjo and I do together *play*. It's more of an adversary relationship."

When I handed it to him, he said, "I can't take this."

"Sure you can. It needs to be played, it needs to be allowed to do what it was made for."

We argued about it some more, and finally he agreed. "Okay, I'll take it, I'll even learn to play the thing. But it's not mine."

"That's what Val always said: that instruments don't belong to people, we just borrow them for a while."

"What about you? What are *you* going to do?"

I'm going to sit here on this porch, I told him. And once he was gone that's what I did, sat there on the porch looking out into the trees and back at the label on the wine bottle and thinking about the ragged edges of my life. About daybreak I saw Miss Emily walking at wood's edge with young ones in a line behind her. "Val," I said aloud, and as her name came back to me in echo from the trees it sounded very much like a prayer.

Somewhere deep inside myself I'm still sitting there, waiting.

SALT RIVER

To Odie Piker
and Ant Bee—
for putting on The Dog

CHAPTER ONE

SOMETIMES YOU JUST HAVE to see how much music you can make with what you have left. Val told me that, seconds before I heard the crash of her wineglass against the porch floor, looked up, and only then became aware of the shot that preceded it, two years ago now.

The town doesn't have much left. I've watched it wither away until some days you'd think the first strong wind could take it. I'm not sure how much I have left either. With the town, it's all economics. As for me, I think maybe I've seen a few too many people die, witnessed too much unbearable sadness that still had somehow to be borne. I remember Tracy Caulding up in Memphis telling me about a science fiction story where these immortals would every century or so swim across a pool that relieved them of their memories, then they could go on. I wanted a swim in that pool.

Doc Oldham and I were sitting on the bench outside Manny's Dollar $tore. Doc had stopped by to show off his new dance step and, worn out from the thirty-second performance, had staggered outside to rest up a spell, so I was resting up with him.

"Used to be Democrats in these parts," Doc said. "Strange creatures, but they bred well. 'Bout any direction you looked, that's all you'd see."

Doc had retired, and his place had been taken by a new doctor, Bill Wilford, who looked all of nineteen years old. Doc now spent most of his time sitting outside. He spent a lot of it, too, saying things like that.

"Where'd they all get to, Turner?" He looked at me, pulling his head back, turtlelike, to focus. I had to wonder what portion of the world outside actually made it through those cataracts, how much of it got caught up in there forever. "Town's dried up, same as a riverbed. What the hell you stayin' here for?"

He grabbed at a knee to stop the twitching from the exercise minutes ago. His hands looked like faded pink rubber gloves. All the pigment got burned out a long time back, he said, when he was a chemist, before medical school.

"Yeah, I know," he went on, "what the hell are any of us staying here for? Granted, the town wasn't much to start with. Never was meant to be. Just grew up here, like a weed. Farms all about, back then. People start thinking about going to town of a weekend, pick up flour and the like, there has to *be* a town. So they made one. Drew straws, for all I know. See who had to move into the damn thing."

A thumb-size grasshopper came kiting across the street and landed on Doc's sleeve. The two of them regarded one another.

"Youngsters used to be all around, too, like them Democrats. Nowadays the ones that don't just get *born* old and stay that way, they up and leave soon's they can." Looking down, he told the grasshopper: "You should, too."

Doc liked people but was never much for social amenities, one of those who came and went as he pleased and said pretty much what he thought. Now that he didn't have anything to do, sometimes you got the feeling that the second cup of coffee you'd offered might stretch to meet your newborn's graduation. He knew it, too, duly noting and relishing every sign of unease, every darting eye, every shuffled foot. "Wonder is, I'm here at all," he'd tell you. "My own goddamn miracle of medical science. Got more wrong with me than a hospital full of leftovers. Asthma, diabetes, heart trouble. Enough metal in me to sink a good-size fishing boat."

"What you are," I'd tell him, "is a miracle of stubbornness."

"Just hugging the good earth, Turner. Just hugging the good earth."

The grasshopper stepped down to his knee, sat there a moment, then took off, with a thrill of wings, back out over the street.

"Least *somebody* listens," Doc said. "Back when I was an intern . . ."

Apparently a page had been turned in the chronicle playing inside his head. I waited for his coughing fit to subside.

"Back when I was an intern—it was like high school machine shop, those days. Learn to use the hacksaw, pliers, clamps, the whatsits. More like *Jeopardy* now—how much obscure stuff can you remember? Anyway, I was working with all these kids, all in a ward together. A lot of cystic fibrosis—not that we knew what it was. Kids who'd got the butt end of everything.

"There was this one, ugliest little thing you ever saw, body all used up, with this barrel chest, skin like leather, fingers like baseball bats. But she had this pretty name, Leilani. Made you think of flowers and perfume and music. An attending told us one day that the truth was, Leilani didn't exist anymore, hadn't really been alive for years, it was just the infection, the pseudomonas in her, that went on living—moving her body around, breathing, responding."

He looked off in the direction the grasshopper had taken.

"That's how I feel some days."

"Doc, I just want you to know, any time you feel like dropping by to cheer me up, don't hesitate."

"Never have. Spread it around."

"You do that, all right."

He waited a moment before asking, "And how are *you* doing?"

"I'm here."

"That's what it comes down to, Turner. That's what it comes down to."

"One might hope for more."

"One does. Always. So one gets off one's beloved butt and goes looking. Then, next thing you know, the sticks you used to knock fruit out of a tree have got sharpened up to spears and the spears have turned to guns, and there you are: countries, politicians, TV, designer clothes. Descartes said all our ills come from a man being unable to sit alone, quietly, in a room."

"I did that a lot."

"Ain't sure a prison cell counts."

"Before. And after. The ills found me anyway."

"Yeah. They'll do that, won't they? Like a dog that gets the taste for blood. Can't break him of it."

Odie Piker drove by in his truck, cylinders banging. Thing had started out life as a Dodge. Over the years so many parts had been replaced—galvanized steel welded on as fenders, rust spots filled and painted over in whatever color came to hand, four or five rebuilt clutches and a motor or two dropped in—that there was probably nothing left of the original. Nor, I think, had it at any time in all those years ever been washed or cleaned out. Dust from the fallout of bombs tested in the fifties lurked in its seams, and back under the seat you'd find wrappers for food products long since extinct.

Doors eased shut on pneumatics as Donna and Sally Ann left City Hall for lunch at Jay's Diner. Minutes later, Mayor Sims stepped out the side door and stood brushing at his sport coat. When he saw us, his hand shifted into a sketchy wave.

"Frangible," Doc proclaimed, his mind on yet another track.

"Okay."

"Frangible. What we all are—what life is. Fragile. Easily broken. Mean the same. But neither gets it near the way *frangible* does."

He looked off at the mayor, who had gotten in his car and was just sitting there.

"Two schools of thought. One has it we're best off using simple words, plain words. That fancier ones only serve to obscure meaning—wrap it in swaddling clothes. Other side says that takes everything down to the lowest common denominator, that thought is complex and if you want to get close to what's really meant you have to choose words carefully, words that catch up gradations, nuances . . . You know this shit, Turner."

"A version of it."

"Versions are what we have. Of truth, our histories, ourselves. Hell, you know that, too."

I smiled.

"Frangible Henry over there's trying to talk himself out of going to see his lady friend up by Elaine." He gave the town's name a hard accent. *E*laine. "But it's Thursday. And whichever side of the argument you pick to look at it from, he'll lose."

"You never cease to amaze me, Doc."

"I'm common as horseflies, Turner. We all are, however much we go on making out that it's otherwise . . . Guess we should both be about our work. If we had some, that is. Anything you need to be doing?"

"Always paperwork."

"Accounts for eighty percent of the workforce, people just moving papers from one place to another. Though nowadays I guess there ain't much actual paper involved. Half the *rest* of the workforce spends its time trying to find papers that got put in the wrong place. Well," he said, "there goes Henry off to Elaine."

We sat watching as the mayor's butt-sprung old Buick waddled down the street. A huge crow paced it, sweeping figure eights above, then darted away. Thought it was some lumbering beast about to drop in its tracks, maybe.

Doc pushed to his feet and stood rocking. "They say when you stare into the abyss, the abyss stares back. I think they're wrong, Turner. I think it only winks."

With that sage remark Doc left, to be about his business and leave me to mine, as he put it, and once he was gone I sat there alone still resting up, wondering what my business might be.

Alone was exactly what I'd thought my business was when I came here. Now I found myself at the center of this tired old town, part of a community, even of a family of sorts. Never had considered myself much of a talker either. But with Val conversation had just gone on and on, past weary late afternoons into bleary early mornings, and I was forever remembering things she'd said to me.

Sometimes you just have to see how much music you can make with what you have left.

Or the time we were talking about my prison years and the years after, as a therapist, and she told me: "You're a matchbook, Turner. You keep on setting fire to yourself. But somehow at the same time you always manage to kindle fires in others."

Did I?

All I knew for certain was that for too much of my life people around me wound up dying. I wanted that to stop. I wanted a lot of things to stop.

The car Billy Bates was in, for instance. I wanted it to stop—can't begin to tell you how very much I wish it had stopped—when it came plowing headlong down the street in front of me, before it crashed through the front wall of City Hall.

CHAPTER TWO

A WONDER, always, to watch Doc work. You'd swear he was giving things no more attention than tying a shoelace, but he was well and surely *in there,* and nothing got by him. By the time I'd crossed the street he had Billy out of the car, one hand clutching the back of his shirt, the other cradling his head. Man can barely stand, and here he is hauling someone out of a car. Had Billy on the sidewalk in no time flat, feeling for pulses, prodding and poking.

Donna and Sally Ann came out of the diner, Donna with half a BLT in her hand. Three steps past the door, a slice of pickle fell out and she looked down at it, vacantly, the way others stood staring at the hole in the wall plugged by Billy's Buick Regal. Country music, or what passes for country music these days, played on the radio. Someone reached into the car and turned it off.

"Pupils look okay," Doc said. "Not blown, anyway. You want to go on back in the office there and bring me out some tape, Turner? Any kind should do her, long as it's heavy. Duct tape be perfect. I assume," he said at the same volume, but to the gathering crowd, "that one of you has had sense enough to call Rory?"

"Mabel's tracking him down," Sally Ann told him. Mabel, who'd been at it long enough to have been (some said) ordained by Alexander Graham Bell himself, was our local telephone operator, unofficial historian, and town crier. "She's also trying to find Milly."

As I came out, Doc pulled a loose-leaf binder from the backseat of the car and slid it under Billy's head and shoulders. He tore off a length of tape and turned the ends in, so that it stuck to itself, to make a cradle for Billy's head. Then he started taping, back and forth, around and down, till head and notebook were a piece. That done, he splinted the left wrist, where a bone protruded, with tape and a paperback book also from the car. He sat with his legs straight out in front of him, picking glass out of Billy's face with finger and thumb, wiping them on his pants.

Everyone wanted to know where the mayor was, but Doc never batted an eye.

"Damn," he said afterward, as we waited, "that felt gooood," dropping a couple extra *o*'s in there. "I'm of half a mind to kick that boy doctor out and take back my office." After a moment he added, "He's good, though. I made sure of that."

"You miss it, don't you?"

"Hell, Turner, my age, I miss damn near everything."

Heads turned as Rory's ambulance came up the middle of Main Street. Once a delivery van for the local builders' supply, the old Pontiac now doubled as hearse, and letters from the store's name still showed beneath new paint when light fell just right. Rory had taken time to pull back the curtains inside. He got out, wearing hip boots and the smell of the river, leaving the door open. Lonnie climbed out the other side, in knee boots, and stood looking down at his younger son without saying anything.

Doc's wrappings made it look as though a mummy's head had taken over Billy's body. Of course, in Lonnie's view something had taken over Billy long ago.

I remembered when I first met Billy, how I thought he might be the closest thing to an innocent human being I'd ever known. He was dressed all in black back then, with multiple piercings and no discernible sense of direction any of us could make out, parents included, just a sweet kid kind of happily adrift. He'd dropped out of school not long after, not dropped out so much as just, well, drifted out. Missed a few days, then a week, and never went back. Worked at the hardware store a while, but that didn't last either. Then he was playing drums with a band that worked a lot outside town in the bars along Old Highway, but for some reason, the way he looked, his quietness, he was a magnet for trouble. People kept stepping up to him and he wouldn't back down. Don Lee and I'd answered our share of call-outs only to find Billy at the other end. Bar brawls, traffic incidents, domestic disturbances. Then, a year ago, he'd got married, gone back to the hardware store, and things were looking good for him. Few months later, he disappeared. We found his truck out on the Hill Road Bypass where he'd pulled it over and flagged down the bus headed toward Little Rock. Milly, his wife, said she'd often go looking for him and find him sitting in the basement sawing wood up into smaller and smaller pieces.

I helped Rory load Billy into the ambulance, then went over and stood by Lonnie.

Two guys off fishing, looking forward to a quiet, easy day. Sandwiches, maybe a beer or two, bait bucket standing by, drowsy sun in the sky. Now this. *Frangible,* like Doc said. How brittle our lives are, how tentative, every day of them, every moment.

Once I'd been up at the camp while Isaiah Stillman was, as he put it, "doing laundry"—balancing the books on the family funds he managed. That evening he was cleaning out old folders and files, had them all lined up in the recycle bin. "We're never more than a keystroke away from oblivion, you know," he said, and hit the key to delete the contents.

So one minute Lonnie's off fishing, the next he's standing on Main Street looking down at his bloody, broken son.

Or you're together on the porch then suddenly she's gone and you have to start finding out how much music you can make with what you have left.

"You're not going to tell me everything's going to be okay, are you, Turner."

I shook my head.

"Or start with 'If there's anything I can do,' then trail off."

"No."

"Course you're not."

Lonnie stepped over to the Regal and shut the door. One of Billy's shoes was just outside it.

"You ever read a story called 'Thus I Refute Beelzy'?" Lonnie asked.

I said I hadn't.

"About a boy whose father forces him to admit that his imaginary friend isn't real. Kid holds out a long time, but he finally gives in. At the end of the story, all they find of the old man on the stairs is a shoe with the foot still in it."

He walked around to the car's rear. "That the right license plate, you think?"

"I'll run it." The nuts had the same grime as the plate itself. No signs of abrasion around them. "Doesn't look to have been changed, though."

"First thing we have to find out is whose car this is."

"Absolutely. I'll get right on it. Oh, and . . ."

"Yeah?"

"Good to have you back, Sheriff."

CHAPTER THREE

THIS TIME IT WAS the sound of a motorcycle, not a Jeep. It came up around the lake in late sunlight, echo racketing off the water and the cabin wall behind me as I stood thinking about Lonnie, that first time. I'd been here a few months then. The sheriff had come to pay a visit, and to ask me to help with a murder.

The banjo case was slung on the bike behind him, neck sticking up so that, at the distance, for a moment there seemed to be a second head peering over his shoulder. He dismounted, stood, and nodded. He'd gone wiry, body and hair alike, but his grin hadn't changed at all.

"Things about the same, I see. Still a nice quiet place to live."

"That *was* you in town, then." He'd been standing off from the rest, in the closest thing we had to an alley, a space by the boarded-up feed store that caught runoff from adjacent roofs and where, following each rain, crops of mushrooms sprang up.

"You didn't say anything."

"I figure a man doesn't declare himself, he has reasons."

Eldon followed me onto the porch. I hadn't sat out on it much since that day, but the chairs I'd strung together with twine were still in place.

"What *was* all that commotion?" he said, settling into one and tucking the banjo case between his feet.

I told him about Billy.

"Lonnie's boy, right?"

I nodded.

"He gonna be okay?"

"We'll know more tomorrow."

Eldon peered off into the trees. A mild wind was starting up, the way it does most nights. "It really is peaceful here. I forget."

"Long as you don't look too closely."

"Right. What was it someone said, Peace is only the time it takes to reload? . . . I wasn't sure I wanted to come out here, you know."

"But you did."

"Looks like."

"And you rode in on a horse. Where's the wagon?"

"Val's Volvo? Sucker down in Texas took it out. Coming out of a rest stop, never looked. Had to be going eighty or better by the time he hit the highway. And by the time I saw him it was too late, I was bouncing back and forth between a semi and the guardrail doing my best not to crash into someone else. You'll be glad to know the Volvo's rep holds up. Safest car around. There it is, pretty much demolished, but Homer and I don't have a scratch."

"Homer?"

"Val told me she sometimes thought of the Whyte Laydie as Homer."

"Blind poet?"

He shrugged. "You get my letters?"

"Got them. And would have answered them, if I'd had any kind of address." In the months following Val's death, those letters, telling me where Eldon had been, where he was headed next, rambling on about what he was thinking and the people he'd met, had become important to me. "When they stopped, I had to figure either they'd served whatever purpose you had in writing them, or that the purpose didn't matter anymore."

"Everything have to have a purpose?"

"Purpose, reason, motivation. Pick your word. Not that we ever actually understand our motives—but we seldom act arbitrarily."

"Sounds suspiciously like you believe it all has a meaning."

"Not the way we think, locked as we are into cause and effect. Some grand design? No. But patterns are everywhere."

"Maybe it's all just messages in a bottle."

"As you recall, I spent a few years of my life decoding

those. Messages in a bottle generally come in two flavors. SAVE ME! Or FUCK YOU ALL."

He glanced back at me before the trees regained his interest. Fault lines at eyes and mouth, hair chopped almost to his scalp and going a stately gray. Two years. And he looked to have aged ten.

"Don't know as I'd ever written a letter before. I can remember at the time thinking: Man plays a hundred-year-old banjo, he might do well to put his hand to a letter now and again, seems only right. Which sounds like something *she*'d say, doesn't it?"

"She's in us all, Eldon. Part of who we are, the way we see the world."

"You ever think maybe people should be allowed to just pass on, that we shouldn't have to carry them around inside us forever?"

"Of course. But we do, right alongside what we've done with our own lives."

"Or haven't. Yeah."

None of us, Lonnie, Don Lee, J. T., Eldon, or myself, had ever openly spoken of what happened up in Memphis the day after Val's death. Each had been out of pocket then: Don Lee under the weather, Lonnie returning from a business trip, J. T. checking in back home in Seattle, Eldon absent from his gig.

"So I'd be sitting there, in Bumfuck, Texas, or Grasslimb, Iowa, writing on motel stationery when some was to be had, on tablets from the 7-Eleven when it wasn't, and I'd be remembering how you told me that so much of what you'd been taught about counseling—that it's imperative to talk things out, drag feelings into daylight—how so much of that was dead wrong."

"Humankind has a purblind passion to find some single idea that will explain *everything*. Religion, alien visitation, Marxism, string theory. Psychology."

"And I'd remember your saying that people don't change."

"What I said was, we adapt. Everything that was there before is still there, always will be. The trick's in how we come to terms with it."

"I'd think about all that, and I'd go on writing. Then one day I stopped. For no particular reason—same as I'd started."

Dark was coming on. Out in the near border of trees a pair of eyes, a hawk's or owl's, caught light. From deep in the woods came a bobcat's scream.

"*I've* changed," Eldon said.

I waited and, when nothing else was forthcoming, went in and poured half a jelly glass of the homemade mash Nathan brought 'round on a regular basis. *Designer,* he'd taken to calling it, having picked up the modish epithet somewhere. God only knows where that might have been, since he never left the woods, had no radio, hadn't set eyes on a newspaper since around V-day, and met with a shotgun anyone who set foot on his land. But he loved the word and used it every chance he got, grinning through teeth like cypress stumps.

By the time I came back out, that quickly, dark had claimed everything at ground level; only a narrow band of light above the trees remained. Eldon was sitting with his head on the back of the chair, eyes closed. He spoke without opening them.

"When I was twelve—I remember, because I'd just started playing guitar, after giving up on school band and a cheap trumpet that kept falling apart on me. Anyway, I was twelve, sitting out on the porch practicing, it was one of those Silvertones with the amp in the case, only the amp didn't work so I'd bought it for next to nothing, and this mockingbird staggers up to me. Can't fly, and looks better than half dead already. Dehydrated, weak, wasted. It's like he's chosen me, I'm his last chance.

"I got a dish of water for him, some dry cat food, lashed sticks together with twine to make a cage. Too many dogs and cats around to leave him out.

"Whatever was wrong—broken wing, most likely—he never got over it. Spent the last eight months of his life on that back porch looking out at a world he was no longer part of."

Eldon reached over and snagged the glass from me, took a long swallow. I remembered our sitting together in The Shack out on State Road 41 after someone had smashed his guitar and tried to start a fight, remembered his telling me that night why he never drank.

"I'm sitting there trying to keep a bird alive, and all around me people are dying and there's two or three wars going on. What kind of sense does that make?"

He handed the glass back.

"They think I killed someone, John."

"Did you?"

"I don't know."

We sat watching the moon coast through high branches.

"Been a hell of a ride," he said after a while, "this life."

"Always. If you just pay attention."

CHAPTER FOUR

LONNIE WAS SETTING a coffee mug down by June's computer when I walked in. She handed me a call slip. Since when did we have call slips? The name Sgt. Haskell, with a tiny smiley face for the period in *Sgt.*, and a number in Hazelwood, which was a couple of counties over, tucked into the state's upper corner like hair into an armpit. I looked at Lonnie. He couldn't have taken this?

He ambled over with a mug for me. Fresh pot, from the smell of it. "The sergeant would only talk to the sheriff, thank you very much."

And that was me, since I'd failed to step backward fast enough. I'd stepped back sure enough, resolutely refusing the job again and again, but when I stepped back that last time and looked around, there was no one else left. Lonnie had retired. After a little over a year in the catbird seat, my daughter J. T. had found she missed the barely restrained chaos (though that was not the way she put it) and headed back to Seattle. Don Lee stayed on as deputy, but he was a little like Eldon's mockingbird, he'd never quite got over what happened to him.

Haskell answered on the second ring and said he'd call right back. I could have been anyone, naturally, but I had a feeling this had less to do with precaution or procedure than it did with things being kinda slow over in Hazelwood.

"You had a vehicle up on LETS," he said once we'd exchanged pleasantries concerning families (I had none, he had six maiden aunts), weather ("not so bad of a morning"), and a fishing update. "Buick Regal, '81." He read off the VIN. "MVA?"

"Right."

"Nothing too bad, I hope."

"We'll know more soon."

"Sorry to hear that. If this is any help, the car's from over our way. Belonged to Miss Augusta Chorley, but seeing as the lady is pushing eighty, from the *far* side, some say, the vehicle's been out of circulation awhile."

"Chances are good it's going to be out of circulation permanently now." Now that it had taken out half of City Hall. I told him what had happened. "We'll have to hold it for a few days, naturally, but please let Miss Chorley know that we'll get it back to her as soon as possible. And if you can give me the NIC number and fax a copy of the report—"

"Would have done that already if I'd had one. Car wasn't stolen, Sheriff."

I waited. Sergeant Haskell there in his cubbyhole of an office next to Liberty Bank over in Hazelwood, me looking out at Main Street through spaces between sheets of plywood Eddie Wilson had nailed in place: two cool, experienced law enforcement officials going about our daily business.

"Driver a young man, early twenties? Slight build, dark hair, flannel-shirt-and-jeans type?"

"That's him. Billy Bates."

"One of yours?"

"Grew up here. Been gone awhile."

"I see." Over there in Hazelwood, Sergeant Haskell cleared his throat. I tried the coffee. "Boy'd been doing some work for old Miss Chorley is what I'm hearing. Lady lives in this house, all that's left of what used to be the biggest plantation hereabouts, down to two barely usable rooms now, nothing but scrub and dead soil all around. House itself's been going to ground for fifty or sixty years now. No family that anyone knows of. Old lady's all alone out there, wouldn't answer the door if someone *did* show up, but no one does. Your boy—Billy, right?"

"Right."

"He'd moved into an old hunter's shack out by the lake here. Started fixing it up, making a good job of it, some say. Kind of living on air, though. Picked up part-time work delivering groceries for Carl Sanderson, which has to be how he met Miss Chorley. Next thing anyone knows, the porch is back up where it's supposed to be, house has old wood coming off, new paint going on."

"And the car?"

"Rumor is that no one in the family ever had much use for banks and the old lady has a fortune out there. Under the floorboards, buried out by the willow tree in a false grave—you know how people talk. If money ever changed hands, it never showed. Boy had one pair of pants and a couple of mismatched socks to his name. But Miss Chorley up and gave him the car. Maybe as payment, maybe because she had no use for it. Maybe just because she liked him. Had to be some lonely, all by herself out there all these years."

"And you know this how?"

"Week or so back, Seth's out by the old mining road making his usual rounds and recognizes the Buick, pulls it over. Boy had the title right there, signed over to him by the old lady."

"Doesn't sound as though he'd done enough work to earn it. Jacked up the porch, patched some walls—"

"I don't think he was done here. Stopped by the grocery store, on the way out of town from the look of it, to tell Carl Sanderson he'd be away a few days, back early in the week."

"Thanks, Sergeant."

"No problem. Anything else, you let me know. Hope things turn out for the boy."

26

"We all do."

While I was talking to Sergeant Haskell, a man had come into the office, standing just inside the door staring at the plywood sheets Eddie had nailed up. Fiftyish, wearing a powder blue sport coat over maroon slacks with a permanent crease gone a few shades lighter than the rest. A mustache ran out in two wings from his nostrils, as though he had sneezed it into being.

He'd been talking to Lonnie. Now, as I hung up, Lonnie pointed a finger in my direction and the man started over. Most of the hair on top was gone. Most of the sole was gone on the outside of his shoes, too. Not a heavy man, yet he had the appearance of one.

"Sheriff Turner? Jed Baxter."

June brought a chair over, and he sat, putting him a head or so below my eye level. Just as he gave the appearance of being a heavy man, he had also seemed on first impression taller. Attitude.

"What can I do for you?"

He was going for the wallet and badge, but I waved it off as obvious. He nodded. "PD in Fort Worth, Texas."

"Then you're a long way from home."

"Tell the truth, things up this way don't look a hell of a lot different from back home. Just smaller."

"Again: What can I do for you?"

"Right. You know an Eldon Brown, I believe." When I said nothing, he continued. "He went missing on us. And we have some questions for him. Man hasn't left much of a footprint in his life. We started looking into it, this is one of the places that came up."

"He lived here a while. As Lonnie no doubt told you."

"That he did. Gone, what, two years now?"

"About that."

"No contact since then?"

"Handful of letters, at first. Then those stopped."

"Something happen that caused him to leave?"

He smiled, eyes never leaving mine. Like many cops, Baxter had rudimentary interviewing skills, equal parts bluster, attempted ingratiation, and silence. Eldon used to talk about bass players he'd worked with, guys who had two patterns they just moved up or down the neck. It was like that. I smiled back, waited, and said "Nothing."

"Don't suppose you'd have any idea where he was heading when he left."

Texas, I said, and told him about the festivals.

"Musician. Yeah, that's most of what we do know."

Again the smile. Hair that had migrated from the mother country of skull had colonized the ears, from which it sprouted like sheaves of wheat. I sat imagining them waving gently in the current from the revolving fan across the room.

"Who would he be likely to contact, if he was back?"

"It's a small town, Detective. Everyone here knows everyone else."

Baxter took his time peering about the room, then at Lonnie and June, who obviously had been listening. June looked down. Lonnie didn't.

"You don't say a lot, do you, Sheriff? Odd, that you haven't even asked why I'm looking for Brown."

"Not really."

His eyebrows lifted.

"You may have reason for not telling me. And if you *are* going to tell me, you will, in your own time. Meanwhile, I can't help but notice there's been no mention of a CAPIS warrant."

Baxter made a sound, kind of the bastard offspring of *harrumph* and a snort. "I see . . . That how you live 'round here?"

"We try, some of us."

"Well, then." He stood, tugging at his maroon slacks. The lighter-shaded crease jumped like a guide wire, seemingly independent of the rest. "Thank you for your time, Sheriff."

With a nod to the others, he left. Through the window we watched him stop just outside the door and look up and down the street. Fresh from the saloon, checking out the action.

"Shark," Lonnie said.

June looked up at him.

"What we used to call lawmen who'd get a wild hair up their butt, go off on some crusade of their own."

"Has that feeling to it, doesn't it?" I said.

"I'll be checking in with the Fort Worth PD, naturally," Lonnie said.

"Naturally."

Back in prison, when I was working on my degree, an instructor by the name of Cyril Fullerton took an interest in me, no idea why. It started off slowly, an extra comment on a paper I'd written, a note scribbled at the end of a test, but over time developed into a separate, parallel correspondence that went on through those last years, threading them together. Once I was out, we met, at a downtown diner rich with the smell of pancake syrup, hot grease, and aftershave. Cy had helped me set up a practice of sorts, referring an overflow patient or two to me and coercing colleagues to do the same, but, for all the times we'd made plans on getting together, something always came up.

We talked about that as a waitress named Bea with improbably red hair refilled our coffee cups again and again, how transparent it was that we'd both been finding a multitude of reasons not to get together, and later about how we were both bound to be disappointed, since over time we'd built up these images of the other and the puzzle piece before us didn't fit the place we'd cut out for it. At the time, new convert that I was, I thought we were speaking heart to heart, two people who understood the ways of the world and how it worked, their own shifts and feints included. Now I recognize the shoptalk for what it was: a blind, safe refuge, something we could hide behind.

We never met again. He was too busy, I was too busy. Gradually our feeble efforts to remain in touch faded away. But as it turned out, everything wasn't bluster, blinds, and baffles that day; Cy said something that has stayed with me.

"The past," he said, resting three fingers across the mouth of his cup to keep Bea from pouring yet another refill, "is a gravity. It holds you to the earth, but it also keeps pulling you down, trying, like the earth itself, to reclaim you. And the future, always looking that direction, planning, anticipating—that's a kind of freefall, your feet have left the ground, you're just floating there, floating where there *is* no there."

CHAPTER FIVE

I'D LEFT ELDON plucking disconsolately at his banjo and humming tunelessly, the occasional word—*shadow, shawl, willow*—breaking to the surface. Breaking, too, onto disturbing memories of Val doing much the same. Pull the bike around back, I'd told him, and don't leave the place.

He'd been playing a coffeehouse in Arlington, Texas, near the university campus. After the gig, this guy came up to him to say how much he liked the way he played. They went out for a beer—Eldon was drinking by then—and, after that beer and an uncertain number of others were downed, to breakfast at a local late-night spot specializing in Swedish pancakes the waitress assembled at tableside. ("She folded them so gentle and easy, it looked like she was diapering a baby.") The guy, whose name was Steve Butler, told Eldon he was welcome to crash at his house, that there was plenty of room and no one would be getting in anyone else's way. I'd been on the road for months, Eldon said, sleeping where I could, in parks and pullovers, behind unoccupied houses and stores; that sounded good.

First morning, he woke up with a young woman, Johanna, "like in the Bob Dylan song," beside him. Pretty much had her life story by the time I got my pants on, Eldon said. Butler, he discovered, was a lawyer who liked artistic types. People came and went in the house all day and night, some sleeping there, others just passing through. Johanna had staggered in around daylight, found space in a bed, and claimed it.

Second morning, Eldon woke to find his guitar, the old Stella he'd bought up in Memphis before he left, gone. Luckily he had the banjo stashed. Butler first insisted on paying for the guitar, then decided instead to buy him a new Santa Cruz as replacement, but Eldon never got it.

That was because on the third morning, Eldon woke up to find an empty house. He'd played at a bar that evening and remembered thinking how quiet the house was when he got back, but it had been past three in the morning and he was dead. Dead tired—not dead like the body he found in the kitchen when he dragged himself out there around ten a.m. hoping for coffee.

It was over by the refrigerator, where it had clawed a trench in the shingled layers of postcards, shopping lists, clipped cartoons, photographs, playbills, and magnets on its way down. The handle of a knife, not a kitchen knife but an oversize pocketknife or a hunting knife from the look, protruded from its back. There was blood beneath, but surprisingly little.

It was no one he'd seen before.

Eldon was pretty sure.

He'd been in the bar, playing country music, and he was in the right town for it, no doubt about that, all night. People kept buying him drinks. Figured he'd sung "Milk Cow Blues" four or five times. Maybe more—he didn't remember much of the last set.

He'd called 911, patiently answered and reanswered the police's questions for hours even though he had precious little to tell them, and while there was no evidence aside from Eldon's presence there, the fit—musician, itinerant, obvious freeloader, alcohol on his breath and squeezing out his pores ("Not to mention black," I added)—was too good for the cops to pass up.

Next morning, Steve Butler, who had been out of town at a family-law conference, showed up to arrange bail and release. Still couldn't get back in his house, he said. Eldon had shaken hands with him outside the police station, walked to his bike, and skedaddled. "Not a word I've used before," he said, "but given the circumstances, Texas, lawmen on my trail, out of town by sundown, it does seem appropriate."

Once Officer Baxter had left, as well as Lonnie, saying he'd make the calls to Texas from home, I sat thinking about the previous night as I dialed Cahoma County

Hospital and waited for a report on Billy, a wait lengthy enough that I replayed our conversation, Eldon's and mine, twice in my head. The nurse who eventually came on snapped "Yes?" then immediately apologized, explaining that they were, as usual, understaffed and, *un*usually, near capacity with critical and near-critical patients.

"I'm calling about one of those," I said, giving her Billy's name and identifying myself.

He was doing well, I was told, all things considered. He'd gone through surgery without incident, remained in ICU. Still a possibility of cervical fracture, though X-rays hadn't been conclusive and the nearest CAT scan was up in Memphis. They were keeping him down—sedated, she explained—for the time being, give the body time to rebound from trauma.

I thanked her and asked that the office be called if there were any change. She said she'd make a note of it on the front of the chart.

And I sat there thinking—as June asked if it would be all right with me if she went out for a while, as Daryl Cooper's glass-packed '48 Ford blatted by outside, as a face and cupped hand came close to the single window that was left. Frangible, Doc had said. And who would know better? He'd seen one generation and much of another come and go. Delivered most of the latter himself.

What I was thinking about was death, how long it can take someone to die.

Back in prison, there was this kid, Danny Boy everyone

called him, who, his third or fourth month, became intent upon killing himself. Tried a flyer off the second tier but only managed to fracture one hip and the other leg so that he Igor-walked the brief rest of his life. Tore into his wrist with a whittled-down toothbrush handle, but like so many others went cross- instead of lengthwise and succeeded only in winning himself a week at the county hospital cuffed to the bed and in adding another layer to a decade of stains on the mattress in his cell.

Next six months, Danny Boy got it together, or so everyone thought. Stayed out of the way of the bulls and badgers, which is ninety percent of doing good time, spent days in the library, volunteered for work details. Worked his way up from KP to library cart to cleaning crew. Then just after dawn one Saturday morning Danny Boy drank a quart or so of stuff he'd mixed up: cleaners, solvents, bleach, who knows what else.

The caustic chemicals ate through his esophagus then on into his trachea before burning out most of his stomach; what they didn't get on the first pass, they got a second chance at on the reflux.

He spent eight days dying. They didn't bother to export him this time, since the prison doctor said there was nothing anyone could do, they might as well keep him in the infirmary. He'd be gone within twenty-four hours, the doctor said. Then stood there shaking his head all week saying, The young ones, the healthy ones, they always go the hardest.

They had him on a breathing machine that, with its two pressure gauges and flattened, triangular shape, looked like an insect's head. And he was pumped full of painkillers, of course. A lot of us went up there to see him. Some because it was different, it was a new thing, and anything that broke through the crust of our days was desirable; some to be relieved it wasn't them; probably others to wish, in some poorly lit corner of their heart, that it were. I went because I didn't understand how someone could want to die. I'd been through a lot by then, the war, the streets, nineteen months of prison, but that, someone wanting to die, was unimaginable to me. I wanted to understand. And I guess I must have thought that looking down at what was left of Danny Boy somehow would help me understand.

That was the beginning. Fast forward, zero to sixty in, oh, about six years, and I'm sitting in an office in Memphis listening to Charley Call-Me-CC Cooper. The curtains at the open window are not moving, and it's an early fall day so humid that you could wring water out of them. Even the walls seem to be sweating.

"Before I was dead, before I came here," CC is saying, "I was an enthusiast, a supporter. I voted. I mowed, and kept the grass trimmed away from the curb at streetside. I kept my appointments. My garbage went out on the morning the truck came. My coffeemaker was cleaned daily." He pauses, as though to replay it in his mind. "You, the living, are so endlessly fascinating. Your habits, about which you never think, your cattle calls as you crowd together for warmth, the way you stare into darkness all your lives and never see it."

CC believed himself to be a machine. Not the first of my patients with such a belief—I'd had two or three others—but the first to verbalize it. This was in the days before they became clients, back when we still called them patients, back before everything, the news, education, art of every sort, got turned into mere consumer goods. And truth to tell (though it would be some time before I realized this), the therapeutic tools we were given to treat them more or less took the patients as machines as well, simple mechanisms to be repaired: install the right switch, talk out a bad connection, find the proper solvent, and they'd take off across the floor again, bells and whistles fully functional.

I never knew what became of CC. He was a referral from a friend of Cy's who was giving up his practice to teach, and among the earliest of the deeply troubled patients who would become my mainstay. We had half a dozen sessions, he called to cancel the next one, pulled a no-show two weeks running, and that was it. Nothing unusual there; the attrition rate is understandably high. You always wonder if and how you could have done more, of course. But if you're to survive you learn to let it go. Couple of months after, I got a card from him, a tourist's postcard for some place in Kansas. Wheat fields, a barn, windmill, an ancient truck. He'd drawn in the Tin Man sitting astride the barn roof and written on the back, *Whichever way the wind blows!* Still later, around year's end, I got another. This one was plain, no location, just a photo of a white rabbit almost invisible against a snow-covered hillside. On the back he'd written, *I'm thinking seriously about coming back*, and underlined it. To Memphis? To sessions? To the living? I never knew.

The face at the window and the hand belonging to it, as it turned out, were those of Isaiah Stillman, on one of his rare forays into town. And looking uncomfortable for it, I first thought, but then, I don't believe Isaiah has ever looked uncomfortable anywhere. It was something else.

"Well . . ." I said.

"As well as can be expected." He smiled. "And you? It's been too long, Sheriff."

"Not for much longer." I gave him a second, then told him what had happened with Billy, and that Lonnie was back.

"Meaning that you'll be getting out from under."

"Right."

"Assuming that you *want* to get out from under."

He sat—not in a chair, but on the edge of Don Lee's desk next to mine. He was wearing jeans, a white shirt tucked in, the fabric-and-rubber sandals he wore all the time, summer, winter, in between.

"The boy going to be okay?" he said. Isaiah had maybe twelve, fourteen years on "the boy."

"We're waiting to see."

"We always are, aren't we? That's what we do."

"Meanwhile, what brings you to town?"

"Oh, the usual. Flour, salt, coffee. Get a new wheel on the buckboard."

"Miss Kitty'll be glad to see you."

"Always."

Isaiah and his group had arrived quietly, moved into an old hunting cabin up in the hills a couple hours from town, all of them refugees of a sort, he'd said. When I asked him refugees from what, he laughed and quoted Marlon Brando in *The Wild Ones*: "What do you have?" Some local kids had got themselves tanked up and destroyed the camp. Rape and pillage—without the rape, as Isaiah put it. Spearheaded by June, the town had pulled together and built a replacement camp, a compound, really: two thirty-foot cabins, a storage shed, a common hall for cooking and eating.

"Saw June down the street. She's looking good."

I nodded.

"You too."

"You know, Isaiah, in three years plus, I don't believe you've ever been in this office before."

"True."

"So what can I do for you?"

He started as someone banged hard on the plywood outside, once, twice, then a third time. We both looked to the window, where half a head with almost white hair showed above the sill. Les Taylor's son Leon. Deaf, he was always beating on walls, cars, tree trunks, school desks, his rib cage. Because the vibrations, we figured, were as close as he could get to the sound the rest of us all swam in.

"You understand," Isaiah said, "that it is very difficult for me to ask for help."

I did.

"Back not long after we first came here, one of us—"

It had been only a few years; even my aging, battered memory was good for the trip. "Kevin," I said. He'd been killed by my neighbor Nathan's hunting dog. That was when we first found out about the colony.

Isaiah nodded. "For some, like Kevin, the fit's not good. They drift away, leave and come back. Or you just get up one morning and they're not there. Not that they are necessarily any more troubled than the rest. It's . . ." He glanced at the window, where Leon was up on tiptoe looking in, and waved. "It's like specific hunger—pregnant women who eat plaster off the walls because their body needs calcium and tells them so, even when they've no idea why they're doing it. Whatever it is these people need when they find their way to us, we don't seem to have it, and eventually, on some level or another, they come to that realization. Usually that's it. But not always."

Pulling Don Lee's rolling chair close with his foot, he sank into it.

"This, what we have here, is . . . kind of the second edition? My first go at something like it was wholly unintentional. I was living with a friend, a critical-care nurse, in an old house out in the country, this was back in Iowa, and weekends we'd have other friends string in from all around, Cedar Rapids, Des Moines, Moline, even Chicago. Sometimes they wouldn't leave when Sunday night came, they'd stay over a day or two. Some of the stays got longer and, with the house an old farmhouse, there was plenty of room. One day Merle and I looked around and the thought hit both of us at the same time: We've got something here. By then, anywhere from half a dozen to a dozen people were resident or next door to being so.

"But things change, things that just happen, once you begin paying attention to them. People who've always been perfectly happy cooking up pots of spaghetti aren't around when dinnertime comes, Joanie's bread goes stale and gets fed to birds, people stay in their rooms, wander off into town . . . It was all over the space of six months or so. Toward the end, Merle and I were sitting outside in the sun one afternoon. He asked if I'd like a refill on iced tea, poured it, and handed it to me. 'Not working out quite the way we hoped, the way we saw it, is it?' he said. It was going to take a while, I said. He was quiet for moments, then told me he had a job over in Indiana, at the university hospital there, and would be leaving soon.

"Thing is, I wasn't so much upset that he was leaving as I was that he'd done it all, the planning, applying, without telling me. You've kept yourself pretty damn busy, he replied when I voiced that. And I'd already started to say, 'Yes, building the . . .' when I realized that, first, I wasn't building anything, and second, I didn't even know what it was I'd thought I was building."

This wasn't quite the same story I'd heard a couple of years back, but storytellers do that. We all do, memories shifting and scrunching up to fit the story we want to tell, the story we want to believe. And maybe it's enough that the teller believes the story as he tells it.

"That's the long of it," Isaiah said just as the phone rang. Red Wilson, complaining about his neighbor's barking dog. Red had recently moved into town after seventy-odd years on the farm. City life, he wanted me to know, was gettin' on the one nerve he had left.

"And the short?" I asked Isaiah after assuring Red I'd be out his way later that afternoon and hanging up the phone.

"There was a period when we didn't, but following that, Merle and I kept up over the years. He knew what we were doing here and kept saying he wanted to come see it for himself. Three months ago he set a date. When he didn't show up as planned, I thought, Well, something's come up at the hospital. Or, he was always driving these junker cars that gave out on him at the worst possible moment—maybe that was it. No response to my

44

e-mails. I even tried calling, home and hospital both, but he wasn't either place.

"Yesterday, I finally found him," Isaiah said. "He was killed two weeks ago on his way here. In Memphis."

CHAPTER SIX

SOME NIGHTS the wind comes up slowly and begins to catch in the trees, first here, then there, such that you'd swear invisible birds were flitting among them.

The dreams began not long after Val's death. I was in a city, always a city, walking. Sometimes it looked like Memphis, other times Chicago or Dallas. There was never any sense of danger, and I never seemed to have any particular destination to reach or any timetable for doing so, but I was lost nonetheless. Street signs made no sense to me, it was the dead of night, and no one else was around, not even cars, though I would see their lights in the distance, lashing about like the antennae of dark-shrouded insects.

I'd wake to the trees moving gently outside my windows and often as not go stand out among them.

As I was now.

Watching a bat's shadow dart across a moonlit patch of

ground and thinking of Val and of something else she'd told me, something Robert Frost had said, I think: "We get truth like a man trying to drink at a hydrant."

My to-do list just went on getting longer. Go see Red Wilson about the barking dog. Get up to Hazelwood to interview Miss Chorley, former owner of Billy's Buick, to try to figure out what had been going on with him. Check in with MPD about Isaiah's friend Merle. Do whatever it was I was going to do to help Eldon.

I'd told Isaiah I would see what I could find out about his friend, and asked for a favor in return. "Absolutely," he said. "Anything."

So Eldon was up there in the hills with Isaiah and the others, where he should be safe until I figured out what to do.

Of course, I'd been waiting all my life to figure out what to do.

Back in prison it was never quiet. Always the sounds of toilets flushing, twittery transistor radios, coughs and farts and muffled crying, the screech of metal on metal. You learned to shut it out, didn't hear it most times, then suddenly one night it would break in on you anew and you'd lie there listening, waiting—not waiting *for* something, simply waiting. Just as I'd sat out on this porch night after night once Val was gone.

Like nations, individuals come to be ruled by their self-narratives, narratives that accrue from failures as much as from success, and that harden over time into images the individual believes unassailable. Identity and symbology fuse. And threats when they come aren't merely physical, they're ontological, challenging the narrative itself, suggesting that it may be false. They strike at the individual's very identity. The narrative has become an objective in its own right—one that must be reclaimed at all costs.

I thought about the radical shifts in my own self-narratives over the years. And I had to wonder what scripts might be unscrolling in Eldon's head now.

Or in Jed Baxter's, to fuel his pursuit of Eldon.

Whether by heritage, choice, or pure chance, we find something that works for us—amassing money, playing jazz piano, or helping others, it doesn't much matter what—and we hang on, we ride that thing for all it's worth. The problem is that at some point, for many of us, it stops working. Those who notice that it's stopped working have a window, a way out. The others, who fail to notice, who go on trying to ride—it closes around them, like a wing casing. It wears them.

I sat on the edge of the porch floor. A sphinx moth had landed in a swath of moonlight on the beam beside me.

Back in country, some of the guys would keep insects in these cages they lashed together out of splinters of bamboo. Scorpions, a few of them, but mostly it was insects. Cockroaches, grasshoppers, and the like. They'd feed them, rattle them hard against the sides of their cages, jab them with thorns, talk to them. One kid had a sphinx moth he'd stuffed—with what, we never knew, but it was a raunchily amateur job, and the thing looked like one of the creatures-gone-wrong out of a bad horror movie. "Just think," he'd say, "it'll never leave me, never die, never break my heart." But the kid died, snipered while out on a routine patrol near the closest friendly village. Later that day Bailey brought the cage into the mess tent. He was sergeant, but no one called him that, and he had maybe a year or two on the kid. He set the cage on the table and stared at it as he slowly drank two cups of coffee. Then he picked up the cage, put it on the ground, and stomped it flat. His boots were rotting, like all of ours were (just as the French had tried to tell us), and like the feet inside them. A chunk of blackish leather fell off and stayed there beside the remains of the kid's cage as Bailey took his cup over to the bin.

CHAPTER SEVEN

TWO DAYS LATER, a cloud-enshrouded, bitter-cold Thursday, I was sitting in a Memphis squad room being lectured, basically, on what cat could piss on what doorstep.

I looked around, at the corkboard with its neat rows of Post-it notes, the ceramic-framed photo of a family from some fifties TV show, and the diploma awarded by Southwestern, as Sergeant Van Zandt wound down from his sermon on jurisdiction and proper channels. His wasn't all that different in kind from the sermons with which I'd grown up courtesy of Brother Douglas and successors back home among First Baptist's stained-glass windows, polished hardwood pews, and book-thick red carpeting. As kids, strung out by an hour of Sunday school followed by another hour or more of church service, my brother and I staged our own versions of such sermons over Sunday dinner, Woody preaching, me by turns amen-ing, egging him on, and falling out with rapture. Pressed by our mother, Dad would eventually succumb and send us from the table.

"Nice cubicle," I said when Van Zandt stopped to refill his lungs and drink the coffee that had gone lukewarm during his hearty polemic. "What is it, MPD's finally got so top-heavy with management that they've run out of offices?"

Sometimes you just can't help yourself.

Tracy Caulding's glance toward me and half smile said the rest: Always more generals, never enough soldiers.

Tracy, mind you, was no longer on the force, she was now, God help her, a clinical psychologist, but she'd kept her hand in. She was one of the ones the department called on to counsel officers and evaluate suspects. And she was the one I called when I first hit Memphis.

The M.A. in social work she'd been working on when we met turned out not to be a good fit. She'd figuratively gone in the front door of her first job, she said, and right out the back one, back to school. To me she seemed one of those people who skip across the surface of their lives, never touching down for long, forever changing, a bright stone surging up into air and sunlight again and again.

We'd met for breakfast at a place called Tony Weezil's to catch up over plates of greasy eggs and watery grits before breaching the cop house to submit to further abuse. Tony Weezil's served only breakfast, opening at six and shutting down at eleven. After all, Tracy said, lifting a wedge of egg with her fork to let equal measures of uncooked egg white and brown grease find their way back to the plate, you've got one thing down perfectly, why mess with it.

She was telling me about a conference she'd attended, "What Is Normal?" with authorities from all over delivering talks on Identity and Individuation, The Social Con Tract, Passing as Human, The Man Who Fell to Earth and Got Right Back Up. Some seriously weird people hanging around the hotel, she said—some of the weirdest of them giving the lectures.

"You miss it?" she said as the waitress, an anemic-looking thirtyish woman dressed all in pink, refilled our coffee cups.

"Why would I?"

"Not the professional stuff, the trappings. But the patients. Talking to so many different kinds of people, getting to know them on that level."

"I'm not sure I did, in any real sense. There's this kind of call-and-response involved—"

"You hear what you listen for."

"Right. And they figure out their side of it, what *they're* supposed to say. The good ones catch on right away, the others take a while. But sooner or later they all get there."

She poured milk into her coffee, which she had not done with the first two cups, and absentmindedly watched it curdle. I signaled the waitress, who brought another of the small stainless steel pitchers, the same ones they used for pancake syrup.

"Maybe I'll reach that point," Tracy said. "You did try to warn me about social work, after all."

"And like most warnings—"

"Exactly. But for now I like what I'm doing. I believe in it."

What she was doing, aside from the consultations, was working with disturbed children. "Troubled teens," she had said. "Put it that way, it sounds like something out of Andy Griffith, they'd meet in the church basement, have cupcakes, and talk about how no one likes them. When what *we're* talking about is kids who torture and kill the family pet, lock parents in basements, set fire to the house. I had one last month. Thirteen. A cutter. Couldn't get her to say a thing the whole hour—not that that's a big surprise. But then when she gets up to leave she says, 'What's the big deal? It's just another cunt, that's all. I'm just opening it for them.'"

Tracy had a warning of her own for me, about the gauntlet I'd be running. It would start with Sergeant Christopher Van Zandt, a man so devoutly incompetent that a new position had been created expressly to keep him—

"Out of harm's way?" I ventured.

"Out of the department's way."

He was, she said, continuing education and informations officer.

"And whose nephew?"

"We're not quite sure. But he is a man in love with the sound of his voice, and no subject has yet been broached, be it deciduous trees or Polynesian dances, about which he did not know everything there was to know."

"I believe we've met."

"I'm sure you have." She smiled. "Many times."

As I said, sometimes you just can't help yourself. With my remark about management, Van Zandt's locution ratcheted up a notch or two, tiny *b*'s exploding in the air directly before his lips, *t*'s clipped as though by shears. Complex sentences, dependent clauses, dramatic pauses—the whole nine yards.

Finally, having survived the sally, not to mention those *b*'s, we were passed along to someone who actually knew something. About the situation, that is.

"I suspect we won't be seeing one another again," Sergeant Van Zandt said in the last moments, to make it clear we were done. He stood and extended his hand. "It's been a pleasure."

I looked at him closely. There were two people shut away in there, each with only a nodding acquaintance of the other.

We found George Gibbs in the break room staring into a cup of coffee as though everything might become clear once he reached the bottom. Periodically sweaty officers walked through from the workout room adjacent. Gibbs's mug was flecked with tiny paste-on flags and read WORLD'S BEST DAD. A gift from his kids, he told us—two weeks before his wife packed up and moved them all off to Gary-fucking-Indiana.

George, it seems, played bass with country bands, which had become increasingly a cornerstone for the friction between them, standing in for all the other things that went wrong and unspoken. "Ain't no self-respecting black man alive that would play that shitkicker music," his wife kept telling him. At least he didn't have to listen to that anymore, he said. Hell, country music was what he *liked*.

George Gibbs had sixteen years in, Tracy had told me. He was solid, looked up to by almost everyone, a man no one on the force would hesitate to trust with his or her life.

I told him about Eldon and his music, and he laughed. "Banjo! Now that does beat all."

George had responded to the call about Isaiah's friend Merle. Owner of a used-furniture store was unlocking his store that morning, caught a glimpse in the window glass alongside, went across the street to look. A body. Smack in front of the old paint store and half a block or so down from a bar, The Roundup, that was about the only thing open around there at night.

"Near as we can tell," Gibbs said, "he stopped to ask

directions. Easy to get lost that side of town. Get caught up in there, everything looks the same—and there was a map half folded on the passenger-side seat . . . You know how it is: Maybe someone'll get wasted in The Roundup and start talking and that'll get back to us, but probably not. And maybe it didn't have anything to do with The Roundup. I could pull the report for you."

"Taken care of," Tracy told him.

"You read it?"

"Not yet," I said. "Wanted to hear you out first."

Gibbs nodded. Approvingly, I thought. "He was stabbed three, four times. With a small knife, probably just a ordinary pocketknife. ME thinks the first one was in the neck, of all places. Then the chest twice, maybe three times."

"Wallet?"

"Gone. Got to us a day or so later, some kids who'd found it in a doorway, brought it in thinking there might be a reward. No money. Didn't look like anything else was taken."

"But they left the car."

"And the keys, right there by him. Thing is, he was a while dying. Small knife, like I said, and done quickly, more like punches than stabs. Shouldn't have killed him. But somehow or another, with one of the chest wounds, a major vessel got snagged. Blood wasn't pouring out, but it was coming strong. We found him, he was slumped against the side of the building with shoelaces tied around his thighs. He'd strapped his coat to his chest, by the wound, with his belt."

"He was a nurse, he knew what was happening to him. Trying to keep himself alive until help arrived."

"What the ME figured." Gibbs finished his coffee and glanced into the empty cup. The answer wasn't there. Just like the help Merle had waited for.

"That it?" Tracy said once we'd thanked Gibbs and stepped back into the hallway. Its walls were paved with bulletin boards. "You heading back home?"

I'd filled her in on the situation with Eldon; she knew I was.

"Then maybe you could do the department a favor," she said.

Outside the property and evidence room in the basement, she spoke briefly to the officer in charge, who handed a clipboard across the half door. She signed and passed it to me, along with her pen. Officer Wakoski looked at the signatures, walked away into the maze of ceiling-high shelves, and returned with a package about six inches by nine.

"I'm pretty sure this isn't what Van Zandt had in mind," I said.

"Probably not. But Sam Hamill did." My old friend, now an MPD watch commander. He'd have sent the release through earlier.

The package was wrapped in plain white paper and heavy twine. Originally the knot on the twine had been sealed with wax, as on old letters, but the seal had been broken—when MPD opened it to check contents, I assumed. The front, in arching, thick cursive reminiscent of overdrawn eyebrows, read: FOR ISAIAH.

CHAPTER EIGHT

AS I RODE BACK toward home, along the river for a time before swinging inland, I watched a sky like old-time saddle shoes: horizon bright right up to the curving border where all went suddenly dark. It had been a season for storms. I remembered my grandfather's storm cellar, bare earthen walls, doors thick as tables with brackets into which you'd swing a two-by-four to close them, wood shelves sagging beneath the weight of water jugs, canned food, lanterns, and fuel. We'd all go down in there as the winds began, sit listening to them howl. As a kid I always expected the world to be new, fresh, changed all for the better, when we came back up. By the time I was ten or so we had stopped joining Grandad and his new family in the cellar, rode out the winds like modern folk.

Only the insurance lights were on, one on Municipal's side, one on ours, when I pulled in at City Hall. I put

Isaiah's package on my desk by a note from June asking me to call her. The *J* of her signature was drawn leaning to the right, toward the other letters, its crosspiece sheltering them. The exclamation point after *Call me* was a fat, balloonlike shape with a smiley face below.

"Billy's taken a turn for the worse," she said without preamble upon hearing my voice. "Something about a blood clot, and hemorrhage. Dad's on his way up to Memphis. Doc Oldham went with him. Milly's up there already."

"I'm sorry, June. Are you okay?"

"I guess. Better get off the phone, though. In case Dad or the hospital calls? But one more thing—"

"Okay."

"That detective from Fort Worth? He's still around, asking questions. Did a swing through town first, hit all the stores. Then he drove out to the bars and roadhouses. Dad thought maybe you might want to look into it. 'Since Eldon is nowhere about,' as he said. He left a note for you, top drawer of your desk."

I locked Isaiah's package in our possessions safe, which just about anyone could open with determination and a state-of-the-art nail file, and read the note from Lonnie, which told me, among other things, that Officer Jed Baxter was staying at the Inn-a-While out by the highway. So I got back in the Jeep and made the longish drive.

It's a habit you never quite get rid of. You pull in and sit for a time, watching closely, sizing up activity and positions, before getting out.

Three cars ranging from three to a dozen years old, an SUV with Montana plates, and a beat-to-hell pickup, half Ford, half spare parts, occupied the parking lot, making it a landmark business day for the motel. The number was missing from the door on room 8, but with 7 to the left and 9 to the right, and a Camry with Texas plates out front, I managed to figure it out. The Camry was gold-colored and well used, with stains on the carpet and seats, but all of it clean, none of the usual detritus of fast-food wrappers, sacks, paper cups. Even the boxes in the back-seat were neatly stacked.

Jed Baxter didn't look all that surprised when he answered the door in his boxer shorts and T-shirt.

"Sheriff." He backed out of the door to give me room.

A bottle of bourbon stood on the bedside table. From the look of things, the two of them had been keeping close company. The TV was on, one car in pursuit of another against what was all too obviously a back-projected city, volume turned so low it could have been sound from the next room. Baxter had been ironing his pants atop a damp towel on the dresser surface. One leg was folded back on itself, like a cripple's. He unplugged the travel iron and, since he was there by it, snagged his drink.

"You've been rooting around town, asking questions." I'd settled in on the wide window ledge. He sat on the bed. We were maybe a yard apart.

"What we do—right, Sheriff?" He shrugged. "I wasn't trying to hide anything. News in a town this size, it's not likely to gather flies."

"And I'm thinking you knew that; it was part of the plan. Maybe it *was* the plan."

"Ah. The plan." Baxter held up his empty glass and motioned with its toward the bottle, offering. Why not? Been a long day. He found another plastic cup in the bathroom, half filled it, and brought it over.

"We spoke with your people back in Fort Worth. Seems—"

"I'm on a leave of absence, Sheriff."

"Okay. Not quite the way they put it, but close enough. Explains the lack of a warrant or any other paperwork. You're here, they were careful to point out—a number of times—in no official capacity."

Baxter smiled.

"So," I said.

"So?"

"So it begins to look personal."

He took a long sip of his bourbon before responding. "It is, but not the way you think. Back in town I definitely got the feeling that you weren't eager to help."

"I had no information for you."

"Come on, Sheriff. You were just shining me on, didn't even want to talk to me."

"In which case, you acted in a manner that assured I would."

"Yeah, well. I've been doing this a long time. Whatever works."

"What do you have against Eldon Brown?"

Baxter shook his head. "Not him. My concern is Ron Nabors, the detective who nailed him for it and wouldn't hear otherwise. Still won't, for that matter."

"You have reason to believe this Nabors was involved?"

"Laziness and habit, more like."

"But you're looking to what? Take him down?"

"Not going to happen. And not that I'd want to. But your friend had nothing to do with the murder, and Big Ron's gotten away with too much for too long. Hell, we all have."

I was not only a psychologist of sorts, I was a cop who had seen some of the worst mankind had to offer and an ex-con who had been privy to society's best, gnarled efforts at greatheartedness and manipulation. Altruism gets handed to me, I'm automatically peeling back the label, looking to see what's underneath. But I didn't say anything.

Baxter held the bottle up and, when I shook my head, poured what remained into his cup.

"I just want this set right, Sheriff. Came here hoping I might persuade Eldon Brown to go back with me, turn himself in. Nothing more to it. This point, I'm not expecting a lot more from life. Small wins. Small rewards. And most of those for someone else."

CHAPTER NINE

"A MAN IS SLUMPED against a tree trunk in the jungle," Cy, my old mentor, said that one time we met, "or the side of an overpass, or a building smack in the heart of ritzy downtown—and he's dying. What he's thinking is, I'll never be able to tell Gladys how much I loved her, now I won't even get to try. What do you say?"

"I'm there?"

"For the benefit of the exercise, you are."

"I'm not your student anymore, Cy."

"Habit. So tell me: What do you, as a trained professional, say?"

"I say . . ." I began, and foundered.

"Exactly. You don't say anything. You listen." Cy got up to leave. "And that's the most important thing I can ever tell you. A small, simple thing—like most great secrets. You just listen."

Strange how, as we age, our lives turn to metaphor. Memories flood in often and with little provocation, to the point that everything starts to remind us of something else. We, our actions, our lives, become representational. We imagine that the world is deeper, richer; in fact, it is simply more abstract. We tell ourselves that now we pay attention only to what's important. But sadly, what's important turns out to be keeping our routine.

Much like the town back there behind us.

Billy, it turned out, was going to be okay. He'd thrown a major clot, but it lodged in a leg vein and they managed to excise it surgically before it hit lungs or heart. Lonnie's description of the procedure when I spoke to him on the phone just before we left made it sound a lot like pulling a worm out of its skin. Except for all the fancy tools, equipment, and degrees, of course.

And now Jed Baxter and I were hiking up-country through the heaviest growth, four or five hollows and a long hill or two away from Isaiah's colony. Morning sunlight fell at a slant through the trees, struck the ground, and slid away into undergrowth without much purchase. Bird calls everywhere, growing silent as we approached, starting up again behind us. The barky, lisping chatter of squirrels.

The colony was looking good. The townspeople did a great job rebuilding, and the kids had done an equally great follow-up. Kids—I still thought of them as that, though none of them were, and most hadn't been for some time. The old sign—HIER IST KEIN WARUM—was back up, over the common hall now. They'd left the scorched edges and glued the ragged crack running lengthwise down its middle. At the far end of the compound, they'd built a playground worthy of the swankest inner-city park: animal-shaped swings, treehouse, wooden jungle gym, tunnels made from crates, pint-size barn and corral. One of the colony's newer members had been a woodworker, custom stairways, door casings, and the like for a builder back in San Francisco. The swing in the shape of a horse bore an elaborate swirl of hand-carved mane; delicate whorls ran into its ears.

The group was having its morning meal outside at one of the tables. Moira spotted us first, lifting a hand high in what served as both alert and greeting. The others turned, Isaiah came to meet us just inside the clearing, and nothing would do, of course, but that we eat with them. Fresh-baked bread, elderberry preserves, a kind of farmer's cheese made (Moira signed, with one of the children interpreting) by curdling milk with lemon juice.

I'd told Baxter what to expect, but you could tell it was a reach for him, taking all this in, accepting it for what it was. After we'd finished eating, he and Eldon stood nearby playing horseshoes (horseshoes! how long had it been since I'd seen horseshoes?) and talking. We had helped clear the table and attempted to help more, but Moira and the others held up hands and pushed us away in pantomime, mugging in mock terror as though we were an invading army.

Isaiah and I sat beneath a pecan tree at a table splattered with dried bird shit. Isaiah wiped what he could of it away with his hand, then bent down to wipe his hand on grass. He'd come a long way for a city boy.

"It's his brother's diary, from the last days," Isaiah said of the package I'd brought him. "The only other person, besides me, that Merle was ever close to. Thomas was dying from cancer, this weird kind that doesn't metastasize but recurs. First time, they pulled a tumor out of his stomach that weighed eleven pounds. Called it Gertrude—and Merle sent a birth announcement instead of a get-well card. Everything fine, then a little over a year later it was back, bigger this time, with more organ involvement. With the fourth one, Thomas refused further surgery."

Isaiah leaned back against the tree.

"Remember when I told you about my grandmother, how she was the start of all this? How I was with her there at the end? Well, it wasn't like that with Thomas and Merle. Merle wasn't there with him, he was three states away, trying to save a marriage that had been too far gone for far too long. He was at work when the call came. A patient was going bad, a transplant that came in an hour or so before. They insisted the call was urgent, so Merle took it. It was the hospice telling him that Thomas had died that morning. Merle thanked them for letting him know and went back to work just as a code was called on the transplant patient. He was in charge that day, and ran it."

You just listen.

"Merle was never one to show emotion much. Part of that was what he did, part of it simply who he was. But Thomas's death hit him hard. He'd call some nights and we'd exchange three or four sentences the whole time, he'd just be there on the phone, six, eight hundred miles away."

I had to ask; old habits die hard. "How long ago was this?"

"Little over a year."

"So he was still depressed?"

"Why do you ask?"

I hesitated. "To all appearances he was coming here to give you the diary."

"You think he was suicidal."

"Why would he want you to have it now? Something that was so important to him. It's the sort of action that people take—"

"Yes. It is." Isaiah pulled off the tree and sat straight again, his hand flat on the diary. "But I don't know. We'll never know, will we?"

"Could he have been ill, like his brother? A premonition of some kind?"

Isaiah was silent. He picked up the diary and stood.

"Does it matter?" he said.

CHAPTER TEN

I HAD FAILED again to listen.

Eldon wanted to think it over, this turning-himself-in thing.

Jed Baxter was back in unmarked room 8 at the Inn-a-While.

And the dog that Red Wilson complained about had, as it turned out, good reason to be barking.

Late afternoon, I drove out that way. By the time I came around the curve, Red was standing at the mailbox waiting for me. Jerry Langston, who runs the rural mail route, told me that Red was there every day waiting to collect his mail in person, adding that "Heard you coming" was all he ever said. Which is what Red said to me.

My questions about the dog didn't fare a lot better. If I'd been collecting syllables, I'd never have made my quota. The barking had been going on for three, four days now, I managed to discover, but as of yesterday it got worse. Old man over there had taken to beating the dog for it, he was pretty sure.

Old man. Though still hard and lean, Wilson himself was well along in his seventies. He pointed across the dirt road to a house that gave the impression of having begun as a porch, developed a middling ambition, and undergone mitosis.

I drove over. It hit me the minute I stepped out of the Jeep, but the smell's common enough in the country that I didn't pay undue attention. The property owner, Bob Vander, stood inside the screen door peering out. He'd probably been watching me across the way at Red's. We'd never met, but I knew of him. Around to the side of the house, tethered on a ragged length of clothesline wrapped several times around its legs, the dog barked away.

"You want to step out here a minute, Bob?" I asked, though evidently that was about the last thing he wanted to do. As for me, I was tired and damned irritable and had, I thought, far more important things to attend to. Phrases like "Or I can come in there and get you" drifted unbidden to the surface of my mind.

He emerged, finally, standing with one hand still on the screen-door handle. In a kind of travesty of Sunday dress, he wore a pair of pants that had once been the lower portion of a navy blue suit, and a white shirt with areas gone so thin they looked like windows onto a pale pink world. A small woman or a girl stood inside, just back

74

from the door, peering out as Bob had done. I told him I was here in response to a complaint, and what the complaint was.

"I know, I know." Here, his expression insisted, was yet another instance of everything in life being out to confound him. "I done what I could," he said. "Dog just suddenly took hard to barking. Barking's what dogs do."

The dog snarled and bared teeth when I approached, but settled as I put my hand on its head. No more barking. It had a goodly portion of short-haired pointer mixed in with goodlier portions of other things, and was malnourished and severely dehydrated; you could make out each individual rib.

I cut the clothesline with my pocketknife. The dog looked up at me and went to the back of the house, where the stench was strongest. It reared up, put its front paws on the rotting wood, and began barking again. Nearby, an ax leaned against a tree. I took it, urged the dog aside, and sank the ax into the side of the house.

I was remembering stories my father told me, stories passed down from *his* father, about old-time fiddlers who got religion and put away their devil's instruments in the walls of their houses, where people found them a hundred years later.

"You can't—" Bob said, then, with the second blow, the smell hit us full on and a small arm fell out of the gap in the planking.

The child was around six years old. He'd crawled

through one of the broken boards inside the house, got stuck inside the wall, and died there. He'd been in the wall about a week, the coroner judged.

"And you didn't notice? That he was missing?" I asked Bob at the time. We were standing by the Jeep, him in cuffs I'd managed to find in the glove compartment, waiting for the troopers who would run him up to County.

"Well, it did get kinda quiet there for a while." He raised an eyebrow, which pulled the rest of his face into what may have been meant to register some emotion, though what emotion, I have no idea. "Before the damn dog commenced barking."

That night the storm that had been threatening finally hit. I stayed in town, no way I was going to try to get out to the cabin, even in the Jeep. Standing outside the office beneath the overhang, I listened to the rain pound down, so loud that it obliterated all other sound, so heavy that I couldn't see across the street. Periodically gusts of wind would blast down Main, sudden and forceful as cannon shot, lifting the rain momentarily to horizontal as they passed.

We never found out who the woman was. Around twenty years old, Doc Oldham estimated, and mute. That last caused the coroner to take a second look. The child's vocal cords, he decided, were undeveloped. Perhaps he had been mute too, or had simply grown up without learning to speak. The woman's child? Or younger brother? She went to the state home. Bob Vander went from county lockup to prison, where, weeks later, his body was found among a hundred pounds or so of bedding in one of the cement-mixer-like dryers in the prison laundry.

Eldon, I'd left surrounded by the compound's children, plunking on his banjo and singing, of all things, old minstrel songs. I had to wonder what the kids could possibly make of "That's Why They Call Me Shine." And I had to wonder, too, how they were making out up there, in all this rain. Fierce as it was here, they'd be getting it far worse. Rain could come down off those hills and through those hollows like a mile-long hammer, all at once.

I went back in to brew my second pot of coffee. Earlier I'd dialed up the Internet connection, thinking I'd e-mail J. T. and see how she was doing back in Seattle since I hadn't heard from her lately, but I kept getting kicked off. So we weren't the only ones getting slammed. And now even the phone itself was out.

When I heard the door, I wondered who could possibly be out in this and why; and when, disentangling myself from memories, I turned, for a moment I couldn't speak or think, because for just that moment I had the impression— I was certain—that it was Val standing there.

Then June threw back the hood of her coat.

"I—" And that was as far as she got. As though simply making her way here had used up whatever small reserves she had remaining. She went down all at once, the way kids do, onto the floor, and sat. I pulled her up out of the water and into a chair with a cup of hot tea in front of her and, as wind roared down Main and rain beat at the roof, learned that Billy was dead.

CHAPTER ELEVEN

"I DIDN'T KNOW where to go," June told me. "I thought you—someone—might be here."

She had barely pulled in the driveway after the trip home from Memphis, the last hour of it through the storm, when the call came. Everyone else was still up there. Her home phone was down, but she had service on her cell. A tree limb had gone through the window of her living room and rain was blowing in like a fury and—well, she couldn't stay there alone, she just couldn't. She didn't know exactly what happened. They were taking him for tests or treatments, something like that, and things went wrong.

He was being transported to X-ray for a scan, I learned from Lonnie two days later, and in the elevator, with a nurse and aide in attendance, began to have trouble breathing. The ambu bag didn't work properly when they tore it out of its packaging, and the nurse, a recent graduate, had failed to bring emergency drugs. By the time they reached the basement and the doors opened, with them shouting for help, Billy was in full arrest.

Lonnie and I were sitting at the diner, interrupted regularly by well-wishers offering sympathy, mumbled homilies, parables drawn from their own lives. At one point Mayor Sims came over, started to say something and teared up, then wordlessly picked up the check on the table there by us and took it to the register.

"People're always talking about closure," Lonnie said, "about putting things to rest, dealing with the past, moving on." He looked out the window, where Jody Ragsdale's rebuilt Ford Galaxie had broken down yet again. Car looked great, but it also was beginning to look as though Jody should have put in a little more time on the engine rebuild and a little less on bodywork. "Billy was gone a long time ago," Lonnie said.

"I know."

"You ever have the chance to get up that way and talk to the car's owner?"

"Yesterday."

I'd driven up late morning, after helping with the basic digging-out. Though there was a lot of standing water, loads of debris all around, and a few downed trees, the storm hadn't hit near as bad outside town. No cows in trees, no porcupine quills driven into stop signs.

The house was much as described, one of those you still find here and there in the Deep South, looming up suddenly like foundered ships from behind banks of black locust, maple, and pecan trees. You could see where Billy'd been at work—sanded patches, raw timber, braces made of two-by-fours—but it was still a mess. When I stepped onto the porch, the boards sagged alarmingly.

No sign of a doorbell. I knocked hard, then, getting no response, sidestepped to one of the tall, narrow windows flanking the door. Sheer curtains obscured the view, reminding me of scenes in old Hollywood movies shot through a lens smeared with Vaseline to soften the focus. But inside I could see objects scattered about the floor, an overturned table, a chair on its side.

The door was unlocked, and Miss Chorley lay breathing, but shallowly, against a back wall, where the baseboard showed remnants of at least three colors and the hash marks of being repeatedly chewed by a dog or other small animal. She'd caught the flocked wallpaper with her fingernails as she went down, ripping a long thin swatch that now curled around her arm like ribbon on a gift.

Her eyes opened when I knelt to take her pulse and speak to her. She wasn't really there, but she was stable. No wounds, as far as I could tell, other than a few bruises, and no blood. I found the phone, dialed the operator, and had her route me to the locals. Explaining what had happened, I asked for an ambulance and a squad. Then I asked for Sergeant Haskell.

He was on duty, I was told, but out on a call. They'd radio and send him right over.

I spent the wait checking the scene and checking back on her in equal parts.

They had come in through the back door, which looked to have been locked since about the time Roosevelt took office, but whose frame was so rotten that a child could have pushed the door in with one finger. Whether they had just started tearing the place up, then been interrupted by her, or whether they'd gone about it as she lay there, was impossible to say, but they'd done a thorough job. Walls had been kicked in, upholstered furniture sliced open, floorboards pried loose. If I read the signs right, they'd started here and, growing progressively frustrated at not finding what they were looking for, moved into the other of the two habitable rooms, which served as her bedroom, then about the house at random. The damage got less focused, more savage, as it went on.

Haskell was there inside of thirty minutes, trailing the ambulance by ten, a small, compact, muscular man dressed in trim-looking khakis and seersucker sport coat and so soft-spoken that listeners instinctively leaned toward him. I told him about Billy and we walked the scene together as the ambulance personnel packed up equipment, paperwork, and Miss Chorley.

"Yeah," Haskell said at the back door. "That's pretty much it. Then they went out the way they came in."

"There have to be tire tracks back there." If not the brunt of the storm, Hazelwood had got its fair share of rain.

Haskell nodded. "We'll get impressions. Most likely this was kids. And most likely the tracks—"

"Will match half the vehicles in the county."

"Not our first rodeo, is it?" He went through to the porch to light a cigarette. Much of the floor had rotted through out here; each step was an act of faith. From beneath, three newborn kittens looked up at the huge bodies crossing their sky. "Woman lives here all these years, no bother to anyone, you'd think she could at least be left alone. Sort of thing seems to be happening more and more."

He shook his head.

"And it's just starting. Towns like ours get closer to the bone, less and less money around, jobs hard to come by—no way it's going to stop."

We stood there as the ambulance pulled out. I looked down at the kittens, hoping their mother was not the cat I had seen dead and swollen doublesize beside the road on my way in.

"You figure they were looking for money?" Haskell said.

"Looking, anyway."

He stepped off the porch to grind his cigarette out on bare ground. "Kids . . ."

"Maybe not."

I don't know why I said that. There was no reason to believe it was anything other. Just a feeling that came over me. Maybe I had some sense—with Billy's being up that way and coming back to town after so long, with his accident, with my finding the old lady like this—that we had ducks lining up, or as my grandfather would have said, one too many hogs at the trough.

Or maybe it was only that I wanted so badly for the things that happen to us to have meaning.

CHAPTER TWELVE

MOST OF THE TOWN, what was left of the town, came to Billy's funeral. Mayor Sims gave a eulogy that had to have set a record for the most clichés delivered in any three-minute period, Brother Davis prayed, preached, and strode about with one or both hands raised, and toward the end Doc Oldham let out a fart that made people jump in the pews; when they turned to look, he himself turned, staring in disapproval at widow Trachtenburg there beside him.

Throughout, Lonnie sat quietly inside his dark brown suit as though it might be holding him upright and in place. June kept looking up, to the ceiling, and down, at the floor—anywhere but into her father's or other eyes.

There had been another hard rain, though this time without the dramatics, and the cemetery outside town had gone to bog, pallbearers slipping on wet grass, mud halfway up shoes and over the top of some, folding chairs sinking leg by leg into the ground.

I spent the afternoon with Lonnie and the family. Greeted visitors, poured gallons of lemonade and iced tea, helped with the cleanup once the last stragglers strayed onto the front porch and away.

Afterward, Lonnie and I sat together on the porch. He'd brought out a bottle of bourbon, but neither of us had much of a taste for it. He was looking at the tongue-and-groove floor we'd spent most of a week putting down the summer before.

"Hell of a mess out here," he said.

"In there, too." So much mud had been tracked from the cemetery, the porch floor could have been of dirt rather than wood. Lonnie was still wearing his suit. It didn't look any fresher than he did.

He asked if I'd heard any more on the old lady, Miss Chorley, who was recovering but, from the look of things, headed for a nursing home.

"Lived on that land, in that house, all her life," he said, "and now she gets shipped off some place where they'll prop her up in front of the TV, dole out crackers or cookies every day at two o'clock, and cluck their tongues when she complains. No family, so the county will end up taking the house."

He looked down again.

"Nothing right about it, Turner. Person gets through even an average life here on this earth, never mind a long one—they deserve better. Sitting in some brightly lit place with powdered egg or applesauce running down your front, can't even decide for yourself when you're going to pee."

I had nothing to say to that. He scuffed at the crust of dried mud there by his chair and after a moment asked, "Staying in town again tonight?"

"Thought I'd head back home, see if it's still there."

"Might want to take food, water, emergency supplies. A native guide."

"Hey, I've got the Jeep. Which, now that I mention it, since you're back on the job, you should reclaim."

"I'm *not* on the job, Turner. I don't want to be sheriff anymore. I'm not sure I want to be much of anything anymore. Other than left alone."

After a moment I said, "It will pass, Lonnie."

"Will it? Does it?"

We had one quick hit off the bourbon there at the end. As at the accident scene, I didn't make the usual noises— Everything's going to be all right, If there's anything I can do—because it wasn't like that between Lonnie and me. Instead we just said good night. Lonnie stood on the porch, all but motionless, and watched as I drove away. The lights were already off inside the house.

My slog back up to the cabin proved worthy of a brief PBS documentary, complete with process shots of looming black hills closing in on the Jeep's tiny headlights and time-lapse photography of the hapless vehicle negotiating treacherous mudslides, but I made it. The whole time, I was thinking about settlers carving their way into this country for the first time, how hard, how damned near impossible, it had been. Even in my grandfather's time, most people were like birds that never strayed far from their birth tree; a trip of a hundred miles was a major undertaking.

As I came around the bend in the lake, I saw the shadowy figure sitting on my porch.

"You walked here?" I asked minutes later, metal popping behind me as the Jeep's engine cooled. My night, apparently, for conversations on porches.

"Waded is more like it."

"And it looks like you brought about half the mountain with you."

Eldon took off his shoes, stomped his feet hard against the porch floor, and we went inside. I motioned for the shoes and, when he handed them over, tossed them in the sink. Poured a shot for me from the bottle there on the counter, looked up at him. He nodded, so I got another glass. I heard a moan, starting low and rising in pitch, and glanced outside to see tree limbs on the move: Wind was building again.

"How are things at the camp?" I asked.

"Could have been worse. Minor injuries, some broken windows. About half the storage building got taken out by a tree. Lot of the stores, bulk flour and so on, are likely ruined."

"But everyone's okay."

"They're a tough bunch up there. Take more than a storm to throw them."

I hauled myself bodily out of my thoughts, how I'd got to know the group, what they'd already been through both individually and collectively, to ask: "Been waiting around long?"

"Not too long. Easy to lose track of time here. Few hours, I guess."

"Then you have to be hungry."

I pulled bread, sliced ham, pickles, mustard, and horseradish out of the refrigerator, put together a couple of sandwiches for us. Eldon had his down in about three bites. Then he grabbed the bottle off the counter and poured for us.

"I came here—"

"I know."

He looked at me, utterly calm and not unduly surprised, but wondering.

"No other reason you'd be here."

He nodded. "I can't go back, John. My mind tells me I should, I know that's the smart thing to do, the only real solution. But something inside me, something as strong as all that logic and good sense, screams *No!* at the very notion."

It struck me again, as it had so often in my time as a therapist and in years since, how few of us actually make choices in our lives, how few of us *have* choices to make. So much is mapped out: in our DNA, our class and temperaments, the way we're raised, the influence of those we meet. And so much of the rest is sheer chance—where the currents take us. However much we believe or feign to believe that we're free agents, however we dress it up with debates on nature, nurture, socialization or destiny, that's what it comes down to.

"Where will you go?" I asked.

"Hey, the invisible man, right? *Dans la nuit tous les chats* and all that."

"Or as Chandler said, 'Be missing.'"

"Exactly."

"It won't be easy."

"Not as easy as it used to be, for sure. Too many electronic fingers in too many pots now. But I've been half off the grid my whole life. This is just about pushing it a little further—a matter of degree."

"They won't stop looking."

"For the most part, they already have. The documents are out there—warrants, arrest record, and all that. They'll stay. But only as history, and just as immaterial."

"You'll be out there as well, Eldon. A ghost. Nothing you can hold on to."

"I know." He smiled. "I feel lighter already."

"You should at least talk to—"

"Isaiah, yes. I had the same thought. Get the advice of an expert on the cracks and crawlspaces of society."

"And?"

"We talked. I've been well advised. He's a remarkable

person, John. They all are." I had fetched a couple of blankets from the closet and thrown them to him; he'd settled under them on the couch. "As, my friend, are you." He peered out, Kilroy-like. "There is no way I can ever say how much your friendship has meant to me."

"There's no way you'd ever need to."

When I got up the next morning, Eldon and bike were gone. The banjo case lay on the kitchen table. Eldon had scribbled a note on the back of a magazine I'd been intending to read for about a year now: *She always said that instruments don't belong to people, we just borrow them for a while.* I sat over coffee, thinking about when Eldon and I first met, about that time in the roadhouse out on State Road 41 when he'd refused to fight the drunk who'd smashed his guitar, about the music he and Val used to play together. About how much a man can lose and how much music he can make with what he has left.

I drove in to work to the accompaniment of a wide range of static on the radio, low bands to high, weather playing havoc with that the same as it was with everything else. Black and charcoal clouds hung just over the treetops. It was nine but in the half-light looked more like five, and as I scrabbled and slid along, gearing down, gearing up, momentarily I had the sensation of being underground.

CHAPTER THIRTEEN

THE DRIVE WAS FOLLOWED by an ordinary day in which, beginning the moment my feet hit the town's asphalt a little past ten, I dealt with:

Jed Baxter, who wanted to know where the hell Eldon had gone to;

Mayor Sims, who came bearing go-cups of coffee then casually got around to asking if it might be possible for "the office" to do a background check on Miss Susan Craft up Elaine way;

Dolly Grunwald from the nursing home, brought in by one of her nurses, with the complaint that they were poisoning her out there;

and Leland Luckett, who parked his shiny new Honda out front of City Hall with the butt of the buzzard who'd flown into the windshield pointed to the door of our office. He'd just been driving along when the thing flew straight at him, right into the windshield. Like a damn missile, he said. It was quite a sight. Thing was the size of a turkey, and stuck in there so firmly that it took the two of us to pull it loose. I'm still not sure what else Leland thought I could do for him. In exasperation I finally asked if he thought my arresting the damn bird, dead as it was, would be a deterrent.

Afterward I walked across the street to the diner for coffee and a slice of What-the-hell pie. Most places would just call it Pie of the Day, something like that, but Jay and wife Margie took notice of how many people said "Just a cup of coffee" only to add "What the hell—a piece of pie, too." Not surprisingly, since everyone had been watching out the front windows, most of the conversation was about Leland and his buzzard.

Margie came out from behind the counter to take my order and ask if I'd heard about Milly Bates. Everybody'd noticed how shaky she looked at Billy's funeral. Not just in pain or overwhelmed, Margie said; it was like you could see through her. Then this morning her folks'd gone over to check on her and she was gone. House wide open, no note, nothing.

"What about the car?" I asked.

"In the driveway. But it hadn't been running for weeks, someone said. The sheriff—" She stopped, realizing her blunder, embarrassed by it, but for me, not herself. "Lonnie, I mean—is checking on it. Coffee?"

"Coffee."

"And . . . ?"

"Just coffee. To go."

I drove out that way with the coffee in the cup holder on my dash. At some point the lid slipped and coffee sloshed over the dash and floorboard, and I barely noticed. I was busily trying to put things together in my head, things that in all likelihood didn't even belong together, a confused young man's death, an old woman who'd lost everything, now Milly.

Lonnie's car stood by the house with the driver's door open and its owner nowhere to be seen. It was his wife's car really, but after giving up the job and Jeep he'd "taken to borrowing it," and after close to a year of that, Shirley had gone out without saying a word to him and bought a new one just like it. The door to the house was open, too. Inside, flies shot back and forth like tiny buzz bombs, and I followed them to the kitchen where a table full of food brought around by neighbors and friends—a roasted chicken, casseroles, slices of ham, dinner rolls, cakes— sat mostly untouched. The coffeemaker was still on, with a few inches of coffee that looked like an oil spill; I turned it off. On the refrigerator alongside were a shopping list, discount coupons, a magnetic doll surrounded by clothing and accessories, also magnetic, and an old Valentine's Day card.

Lonnie spoke from behind me. "Milly and me, we never saw much of each other."

One thing about living in a town this size is, you pretty

much know what goes on between people without it's ever being said. One thing about living these fifty-plus years and having a friend like Lonnie is that when it does get said, you know to keep quiet.

"Boy had a hard life," Lonnie went on. "Not making apologies, and I know he brought a lot of it on himself. But there wasn't much that was easy for him, such that you had to wonder what kept him going."

I had been wondering that, ever since I could remember, about all of us.

"Milly married him, she took that trouble, Billy's trouble, to herself. And now . . ." He stared at flies buzzing into covers and containers, bouncing off, hitting again. "Now, what?"

"You sure you want to be out here, Lonnie? Shouldn't you be home with Shirley?"

"Too much silence in that house, Turner. Too much . . ." He shook his head. "Just too much."

In my life I've known hundreds paralyzed, some by high expectations, others by grief or grievous wounds; finally there's little difference. That's where Lonnie was headed. But he wasn't quite there.

"Footprints out back," he said. "Two, three men. Cigarette stubs mashed into the mud."

"Like they were there for a while."

"Could just be friends . . . Whatever tracks there were out front are mostly gone, from the rain. Took a look around back, though. Old soybean fields out that way. And someone's been in there recently, with what looks to have been a van, maybe a pickup."

"No signs of a search, I guess."

"Hard to say. Milly wasn't much of a housekeeper. Picking up Cheetos bags and wiping off counters with a damp rag being about the extent of it. Drawers and closet doors open, clothes left where they fell—all business as usual."

"Speaking of which—"

"Clothes? No way to know. And no one close enough to be able to tell us."

"So except for some tire tracks and a few cigarette butts that for all we know could have been a friend's, we have no indication that anything's amiss here. She could just have packed up and left."

"Without warning, and with her entire family here."

"People in stress don't plan ahead, Lonnie. They panic, they bottom out. They run."

"Like Billy did."

"As we all have, at some point."

"True enough." Stepping up to the kitchen table, he removed the clear plastic cover of a cake with white frosting. Flies began buzzing toward it—from the entire house, it seemed. "In the bathroom. There's a bottle of antidepressants, recently refilled, and a diaphragm on the counter in there. How likely is it that she'd leave those behind?"

We went through the house room by room. No sign of purse or wallet. There were two suitcases, bought as a set and unused, smaller one still nestled inside the larger, in a closet. In the bedside table we found the checkbook, never balanced, and beside it, nestled among a Bible, old ballpoints and chewed-up pencils, Q-tips and hairpins, we found a cardboard box in which, until recently, a handgun had made its home.

CHAPTER FOURTEEN

I NEVER SAW Eldon again.

So many people come into our lives, become important, then are gone.

Back in college, back before the government jacked me out of my shoes to drop me in jungle boots that started rotting from day one, I had an astronomy professor who compared human relationships to binary stars endlessly circling one another, ever apart yet exchanging matter. Dr. Rob Penny was given to fanciful explanations of the sort, amusing and embarrassing a classroom filled with freshmen there only because astronomy was the easy science credit. Planetary orbits, fractals and star systems, eclipses—all met with his signature version of the pathetic fallacy. Incipient meddler in others' lives that I was even then, I often wondered about Dr. Penny's own relationships.

Lonnie was at State headquarters co-opting their resources to do what he could about finding Milly, June was up at the colony with a handful of townspeople (including, to everyone's astonishment, Brother Davis) helping them rebuild, and I was answering the phone.

Jed Baxter had been in earlier, spitting and chewing scenery and saying over and over that I just didn't get it, did I, telling me how he had come all this way expressly to give Eldon a chance, then telling me he was heading back to Fort Worth. For a moment—something in his eyes—I actually thought he was about to say "back to God's country."

So I was answering the phone, and everybody in town or nearby was on the other end. Wanting to know

what was going on with the sheriff's daughter-in-law,

if someone could come out and talk to the senior class about careers in law enforcement,

why people were up there in the hills helping those weirdos when their own town could use a good cleanup,

what we were going to do about daughter Sherri Anne who kept going off with that no 'count Strump boy,

what the old military base out by the county line was being used for, because they'd been seein' strange blue lights over that way late some nights,

whether there was an ordinance against someone keeping pet snakes,

and again, off and on the whole day, what was going on with Milly, had we found her yet, they heard there was blood at the scene, we should check with her cousin in

Hot Springs, did we know she'd been seen in the company of that Joseph Miller person who'd recently up and moved here from Ill-uh-noise.

Between calls I did some of the things I most dislike doing: checked invoices and bills, marking the ones June should pay; organized the papers on my desk into four piles every bit as confusing as the single pile had been; and read through our voluminous backlog of arrest records (there were two). When I looked up, Burl Stanton was about a yard away from my desk, standing quietly. I hadn't heard him come in. But then, I wouldn't.

Burl is our local career vet. Most every town has one or two of them. He reminded me of Al, the ex-soldier, ex–fiddle player I'd befriended as a child. Al worked in the icehouse until it closed, then lived mostly on the street. Burl hadn't lost near as much as Al, but after six years as a ranger, after all he'd seen, he had no further use for society. He just damn well wanted to be left alone, and this was one of the few places left in the country that, if you damn well wanted to be left alone, people damn well did. He had a shack out by the old gravel pit, but spent most of his time ranging through the hills.

"Two men," Burl said. I waited. He wouldn't be here, in town, still less in this office, without good cause. And he had his own manner of talking, words alternately squeezed out and spurting, like water from old pipes. "Tracked them."

One of the men had been carrying the other— something Burl had seen a lot back in country, and what must have got his interest in the first place. He'd caught sight of them down one of the hollows, pulled back as they came up the hill, then fell in behind. The carried man was hurt bad, blood coming off him hard, and after a mile or so of stumbling along, barely staying afoot, the other one gave up, dumped him there. "Kin show you," Burl said. He'd lost interest at that point and backtracked the two men to where they'd started. They'd come a piece on that one man's two legs. All the way from the chrome-bedecked van where Burl found an unconscious woman. The van was lying on its side. "Looked like it done played pinball with more than one tree," Burl said. The woman was trapped partway beneath. He'd had to snap off a sapling, lever the van up with one hand, and reach in and get hold of her with the other. "Don't think I hurt her much extra."

Then Burl had fashioned a travois from saplings and vines and brought her all the way to town on it. Dropped her at the hospital, but they kept asking him questions, so he came here. He didn't have no answers for them.

Doc Oldham and Dr. Bill Wilford were standing alongside the gurney when I got there, each doing his level best to defer to the other. Finally, with a shrug, Doc went to work, Wilford assisting. The small ER reeked of fresh blood, alcohol, and disinfectant. One of the exam lights overhead flickered, as though the bulb were going bad. I remembered how field hospitals would be filled with the stench of feet shut up in boots for weeks, a smell so strong that it overpowered those of blood, sweat, chemicals, piss, and cooked flesh.

It was Milly. And it would be some time, Doc told me as he worked, before he'd know much of anything. Looked like a crushed chest, fractured hip, multiple compound fractures—for starts. Spine seemed intact, though. Lungs and heart good. Pressure down, but they were pumping fluids in as fast as they could. I might as well go about my business.

Outside, the day was bright, the air clear, giving no hint of devastations recently wrought, or of those to come.

I was able to get the Jeep within sight of the crash site. Burl sat beside me looking grim the whole time. He didn't care for motorized vehicles much more than he did for towns. Had too many of them shot out from under him back in the desert, he said.

The road was dirt, naturally, one of hundreds that crisscross these hills, and barely the width of the vehicle, with layer upon layer of deep-cut ruts and damn near as many recent washouts. Now, it was primarily mud. Their being up here, on a road like this, made no sense at all. And how they'd got as far as they did in that lame tank of theirs was anyone's guess.

The van was a glitz-and-glory Dodge, with enough chrome on it to look as though it might have escaped from some celebrity chef's TV kitchen. The sapling Burl used to free Milly was still there, half under the vehicle. Ants and other shoppers had found the blood. There were banners of duct tape on the front passenger seat. Doc had said much the same of Milly's clothing.

Most of the windshield was gone, the remains scattered about. I kicked at them, bent over, and picked up a floppy piece with a puncture surrounded by starring. So the shot had come from behind. Blood-and-meat splatter on the windshield fragments and on the dash where the insects were chowing down. I found the handgun eight or nine yards off, plunged into the ground muzzle-first as if planted there and just starting to grow.

The driver had been shot as the three of them slithered and slid along. With Milly taped into the passenger seat, apparently. Why? Why did they have her in the first place, why were they on this road that led essentially nowhere? And who made the shot? The half-buried handgun was a .38, same as the one that came out of Milly's bedside table. But Milly was in the passenger seat, and the shot had come from behind. What possible reason would the second man have had to shoot his driver partner? And if he did, why then would he sling the man across his back and try to carry him out?

Way, way too many questions.

Not to mention who the hell were these guys in the first place.

I looked around some more—as J. T. had discovered, it

wasn't like city work, with crime-scene officers, an ME, half the police force, and maybe a coffee runner or two at your beck and call—and figured I'd best give State a call, have them come down and get a fix on this. With some reluctance Burl got back in the Jeep and directed me to the dead man. There were snails all over his face. Something, a dog most likely, had eaten four fingers.

Burl helped me roll the man in a tarp and load him in the back of the Jeep, then said he'd be heading out if I didn't need him for anything else. I thanked him for being a good citizen, and at that he laughed. Stood peering closely at me in that way he had, not blinking.

"Don't know what went down here," he said. "Don't much care. But a man dies, it needs to be marked."

Simple sentiments divested of qualification or abstraction, plainly spoken—just as the speaker was out here attempting to lead an unabstracted life. It was foolishness, but it was a damned near heroic strain of foolishness.

Driving back I thought how, as Americans, there are mountain men or cowboys inside us all, Henry David Thoreau and Clint Eastwood riding double in our bloodstreams and our dreams.

Always slow off the block, I didn't have my first tree house till I was fifteen. Just past the backyard, a hill swelled, partly cut away and thick with trees, a remnant of wilderness tucked into one far corner of our property, jutting out above the chicken-wire run where my father kept his bird dogs. I had his permission, and a stack of lumber from a feed shed he'd torn down a while back. Just watch for nails, he said.

For weeks I prepared. Took graph paper I hadn't used since fifth grade and drew up plans. Dad had passed along a number of his old tools; I put them, along with a tape measure heavy as an anvil, in the shoeshine box he'd built me when I was ten or so. Struggled up the hill with two or three planks or two-by-fours at the time and left them there in piles roughly sorted by length. Had the wheelbarrow up there too, complete with jelly jars of nails and brackets, a bunch of rags, a carpenter's level, and a spot for a pitcher of red Kool-Aid. I was ready.

I went up the hill Saturday morning at eight after scarfing down the oatmeal my mother insisted upon. In turn I insisted upon taking lunch, peanut butter and apple-jelly sandwiches, with me. Dad came up around noon to see how I was doing, then a few hours later to tell me I should think about coming on down, then finally to fetch me back to the house.

I was at it again, not long after daybreak, on Sunday. And for the next two weeks I was obsessed. Up there after school until dark, one night even talked Mom and Dad into letting me take along an old kerosene lantern and hang it from a limb. Put the frame and floor down three times before I got it plumb, planed and whittled at boards till they fit together for walls, corners had to be aligned just so. I pulled old nails and filled the holes, sawed off ends, sanded out rough spots.

The tree house was completed late Saturday afternoon. I'd even built in benches along two sides, and a tiny porch out front. I sat on that porch most of the rest of Saturday and Sunday.

After that I rarely went back. From time to time I'd idly climb the hill and check, watching as it slowly came apart. Years later, back from jungles half across the world and on a rare visit, I wandered up there after dinner and came upon it, surprised. I'd forgotten my tree house. Little was left, a few floorboards and fragments of wall, rusted nails in the trees. On one of the remaining boards a mockingbird had built its nest.

CHAPTER FIFTEEN

THEY'D STABILIZED MILLY, sent her on up to Memphis, Doc said. Out of our hands now. He'd been sitting on the bench outside the office when I returned. We watched as lights went off and stores got locked up and cars pulled out toward home. Except for the diner now, everything was deserted. Framed in its front windows, anonymous heads bent over burgers, steak platters, pie and coffee.

"But *damn,* that felt good. Can't tell you how I miss it, Turner."

"Saving lives?"

Mind caught in memories, he was quiet a moment.

"Not really. It's more about knowing exactly what to do—the branching decisions you make, the way each decision, each change, calls up a sequence of actions—and doing it almost without conscious thought. Not much in the world that compares."

Doc would have gone on, possibly for hours, but it was right about then that Jed Baxter pulled up in his Camry. I met him at the street.

"Back so soon? And please tell me that the passenger in your backseat is merely sleeping."

"Damnedest thing," Baxter said. "Got a late start, so I figure what the hell, I'll grab lunch before heading out. And I stop at this mom-and-pop-looking place—out there right before you hit the highway?"

"Ko-Z Inn."

"Right. Nasty food."

"But filling."

"Ought to be their motto . . . So, after five or six coffees at the café and half an hour on the road, naturally I gotta pee, so I pull over. Do my thing, and when I look up, this guy's come out of the trees and is climbing in my car. Time I get there, he's got his head down under the dash poking around at wires." Baxter opened the back door. "Figured I'd bring him to you."

"Kind of a going-away present."

"For the one that's staying, right. Hope he's okay. Had to thump the sucker twice to put him down."

"Cuffs, huh?" Plastic, but police issue.

"Always carry some with me. Hey, you never know."

"That right arm's not looking too good."

"What can I say? Man didn't care to be cuffed. Laying there on the ground with his lights out, but he's still fighting at me."

"And you had to thump him again."

"Maybe. A little. You want the sonofabitch or not?"

Baxter and I hauled him in and laid him on the bunk in one of the cells. Doc sauntered in complaining that this didn't look to be much of a challenge, checked reflexes and pupils and the like, and said that in his hardly-ever-humble opinion the man was fit to be jailed.

Which left a couple of things hanging.

First off, since we had a prisoner, someone was going to have to hold down the fort tonight, which probably meant me.

Then there was the fact that this guy matched the description I'd got from Burl: medium height but looking taller because of being so thin, maybe 150, and what there was, muscle; hair light brown, long on the sides and back, not much left on top; blue-green Hawaiian shirt, heavy oxfords, khaki slacks.

So in all likelihood I had one of Milly's kidnappers (if that's what they were) and a killer (assuming that he shot his partner), all dressed up nice with his lights out, back in my cell. An enforcer of some kind? Runner? Or just hired help? I couldn't help but think how it turned out the last time something like this came along. I'd walked into the office to find June and Don on the floor unconscious, our prisoner gone. The fallout from that had rung in the air for some time, leaving behind a number of bodies, Val's included.

I called Don Lee to tell him what was going on, and that I'd take the night watch if he'd come in first thing in the morning. I sat there all night in the dead quiet drinking pot after pot of coffee, staring at the black window, and thinking about prison, how it was never quiet, how, surrounded by hundreds of others, you were as alone as it was possible to be.

But before that, I said good-bye again to Jed Baxter and rejoined Doc Oldham on the bench outside. The diner was closing for the night, Jay and Margie and Cook (the only name he'd admit to) making their final runs to the trash barrels in back. Pale rainbows shelled the few lights along the street, cyclones of flying insects pouring inexhaustibly into them.

"Sit here some days," Doc said, "and I half expect tumbleweed to come rolling down that street. Audie Murphy to ride in on his goddamn white horse. You know who Audie Murphy was?"

I did. Some of the first movies I remember seeing. Audie Murphy mugging and mumbling, Sergeant York doing turkey calls. All those grand films about war from a much younger, far more innocent nation, innocent not in the sense of guiltlessness but in that of immaturity, of callowness.

"We want so badly to believe things are simple, Turner. That good and evil are in constant battle and by Tuesday of next week one or the other will win. You've said the same yourself."

"Many times."

"And still—" He laughed, and had to catch his breath. "And still we are not exempt."

"No."

We sat there quietly, beset by mosquitoes and the occasional errant moth. Cook emerged from the alley with his bicycle, mounted it, and rode off into darkness. Jay's truck pulled out and turned in the other direction. Once-bright red and yellow flames on the bicycle were mostly shadow. The truck's patches and layers of paint resembled, more than anything, fish scales; some were thick as artichoke leaves.

After a time, Doc said, "You haven't told anyone, have you, Turner?"

"No."

"Maybe you should."

I was silent. Who would I tell? And why?

"Yeah," Doc said, "you're right. It's none of their damned business."

Two months back, on the routine physical he'd been hounding me about for ages, Doc found something he didn't like. Probably nothing to it, he said, just those damn fool kids up at the lab with their *e*-pods. But we'd best repeat it. Then he showed up at the cabin late one night with a bottle of single malt. As usual, I'd heard his banger coming three miles down the road.

"Greeks bearing gifts—" I began.

"Are as nothing compared to an old man with a bottle of old whiskey. The old man is tired. The whiskey isn't. So we'll put it to work."

We didn't talk much more for a while after that. Then,

along about the third pour, Doc told me, just flat out and plain, like he'd mention the weather or a dog he used to have. We drank some more, and as he was leaving he started to say something, then just looked into my eyes and shook his head.

I remember how warm and quiet it was that night, and how bright the stars.

CHAPTER SIXTEEN

SOME YEARS BACK I attended a wedding, one of the guys I was in the service with, and the last contact I had, I think, with any of them. We'd been through a lot together, and his take on it was close to my own: *getting through* meant we were now somewhere else. But his wife-to-be insisted that he have one of his "army buddies" there, so I became token grunt.

And it wasn't bad. He was marrying up, with a high-pay job awaiting him at the family firm. Even the house they'd be living in had been prepaid, so clean and white it looked as though it had been dipped in Clorox. The food was good and ample, the champagne excellent, the people, especially the women, attractive.

Barely into the ceremony, the preacher took a detour, leaving behind such commonalities as marriage vows and the couple standing there at the altar patiently waiting, to head off, instead, in praise of "the most important union of their lives," i.e., when they accepted Jesus Christ—a commercial announcement that went on for some time. But wind had been rising steadily, and as the preacher continued in his diversion, a powerful gust came up. It snapped the tableclothes, blew leaves sideways on the trees, and raised a twenty-foot dust devil into the air directly behind him.

A great moment.

Not that I have ever believed in portents, a belief that can only follow from the belief that there's direction at work behind the randomness of our world and lives. There are only patterns, and we make of them what we will. But sometimes, as with the preacher and the dust devil, events come together in a crazy, wonderful order.

I was thinking about that the following morning as I watched the storm build. Clouds with heavy bellies moved sluggishly about; far off I could see black pillars of rain, stabs of lightning.

Those were not the only storms building.

The guy back in the cell roused from his Van Winkle but had nothing to say, about the fake New Jersey driver's license we found on him, for instance, or about anything else except that he'd like his phone call now, thank you. He did accept a cup of coffee as he made the call, his end of the conversation consisting of *Mr. Herman, please,* the name of the town, and the word *sheriff.*

Within the hour Marty was in my office.

Before retiring here, Martin Baumann had been a big-city lawyer in Chicago, corporate accounts, three-hour lunches, the works. To this day he only smiled when asked how or why, of all places, he picked this town, but once here, he soon discovered how desperately unsuited he was for leisure time and started taking the odd case. He and Val had worked together on more than one occasion, going from colleagues to friends in short order.

Marty just kind of *appeared* in the office, without fanfare, in that way he has. As though he'd been there for hours and was just now speaking up. "You have a guest, I understand, here at the B and B. Who has, of course, been advised of his rights, blah, blah."

Marty poured a coffee for himself and settled into Don's chair. Don was out on patrol. I'd been expecting to head to the cabin once he got back but now wondered if I might want to wait out the storm.

"What'd he do, anyway?"

I filled Marty in, and he shook his head. Took a slug or two of coffee. "Suckers wired money, you believe that? Right into my account, damn near by the time we got off the phone."

"Whatever's going on, these people do seem to be used to getting their way."

"Don't seem to be much up on how things work in small towns though, do they?"

"Neither were you, as I recall."

He shrugged. "Fast learner. What do we know about your sleepover?"

"That he's connected to someone who can wire money—"

"A lot of money."

"—fast."

"That's it? Okay. Guy I spoke to was an attorney—"

"Honor among thieves?"

"An associate out of Crafft and Bailey, in St. Louis. Basically a messenger boy, but with a hardball firm."

"Not to mention confidentiality."

"What confidentiality? I haven't even spoken with my client. How could confidentiality possibly apply?"

"Point taken."

"I'll ask, if I need it back." Marty did a quick rim shot on the desk edge. "I went looking. Amazing what you can find out these days with a sidelong glance. Crafft & Bailey takes up a full two floors in a downtown high-rise, one of those places full of hardwood panels and polished mahogany rails that serve no purpose. You go in, and there'll be this huge room full of desks and cabinetry and down at the far end of it, on the horizon, a single human being."

"You've been there."

"More times than I care to think about. Cities are full of them. Places you could put up four or five extended families and most of the city's homeless. Empty—except, of course, for the fine appointments."

Unsure whether or not that was a pun, I remained silent.

"Good old C&B's what the boys in the club like to call a full-service firm. One thumb in the insurance pie, defending corporations, another in plaintiff's litigation, raking it in on contingency fees. List of clients as long as the building is tall. That's the public face, and one wing of the thing. The other wing has maybe five, six clients."

"One of them being Mr. Herman."

He tilted his head in question.

"That's the name our . . . guest, as you call him . . . brought up when he made his call."

"Of course." Marty refilled his cup, tasted, then poured the coffee out and set to making a fresh pot. "Not one of them—all of them. In some guise or another. And not Herman, but Harmon. Larry, born Lorenzo, Harmon. Owns huge portions of St. Louis, Chicago, and points between."

"We talking Monopoly?"

"We're talking numbers, off-book gambling, unsecured loans, escort services, strong-arm security. Anything on the borderline between legal and otherwise, he runs it. Or his crew does. Man himself doesn't go near the action. Golfs, drinks coffee, visits his mother every morning. Two children, son about thirty, owns a ring of low-end apartments, furniture-rental stores, and the like—a very *big* ring. Named Harm, if you can believe it. Hard to say if the man's got a weird sense of humor or if he's just plain stupid oblivious. Daughter's—get this—Harmony. Word is she's so ugly everyone calls her Hominy."

"That's who the man in my cell tracks back to."

"Looks like."

"And you got all this off the Internet."

"Well, I may have made a call or two."

"We're a long way from St. Louis or Chicago. What's the connection?"

Marty poured fresh coffee for us both, set mine down on the desk. "Why don't I go talk to my client and find out?"

CHAPTER SEVENTEEN

ETHICS BE DAMNED, as Doc would say. As he did say, in fact, when he arrived that morning to check on our guest. I had a presumed kidnapping, a presumed murder, a presumed assault or two. Doc: "What you have is a mess." Nothing presumptive about that.

The man's name was Troy Geldin and he hailed from Brooklyn, the old Italian section right across the river from Manhattan, now well in thrall to gentrification but resisting. State called about the time Marty emerged, an hour or so before Doc showed. They'd run prints for us. No sheet, which meant Geldin was smart, lucky, or both, but he'd done time eating sand in the elder Bush's war and we had his prints as mementos.

To this day I've no idea what Marty said to the man. I was little more than halfway into the initial sentence of my spiel when Geldin spoke over me. "My lawyer has advised me to cooperate. After due thought and with promise of immunity, I am prepared to do so."

Prepositional phrases and "I am prepared" didn't sound much like Geldin's native language, but then, neither did much of what followed. At first I assumed that he'd been coached, by Marty, or by his contact during the phone call when he'd said so little. Later I came to think that, whatever the reason, something vital had shifted inside him. He had changed elementally, and something that he himself may not have suspected was there, something deep within, had begun moving to the surface. I'd seen it happen before, both in the jungle and in prison. A prickly, nervous man turns suddenly calm. The one who was always talking sits silent, smiling.

Thus it fell to me to wake Judge Ray Pitoski out of a sound sleep (albeit now almost noon), assure myself that he was sober enough to remember, and have him, as our factotum district attorney, agree to grant Geldin immunity in exchange for testimony.

That testimony came measured out in drams, like a seaman's ration. Every few sentences Geldin would pause and look from Marty to me, whether to gauge the value and effect of his testimony or to allow his next phrases to settle into place before he spoke, I couldn't tell.

Irregardless of what we thought, he was not, well, not . . . what we thought. In fact, he'd never done anything like this before. Sure, he'd lost his job a while back, after twelve years—but so had a lot of others, these days.

And when his wife left, well, unlike the other, he'd seen that coming.

Hollis and he went way back, to grade school. He'd been the geeky kid back then, good grades, scrawny, out of step, always reading. Hollis was anything but, but he'd stepped in one day when the top bully, guy looked like a pug dog, had been beating on him. Not because Hollis had any feelings for him, mind you, or any sense of its being wrong, but because Hollis'd had his eye on this bully, figuring he was the one to take down. And here was his chance. Teachers came, it looked like Hollis was a hero, taking up for him. Not finessed—but sometimes finesse just happens, you know?

Anyway, that changed things for him. Year later, he was linebacker on the team. Still not fitting in, but he was good enough that they moved over to make room for him. Meanwhile Hollis went on getting into trouble, tiptoeing around this huge crater, shouting down into it. He was getting bigger, Hollis was shrinking. Took to cigarettes, got behind some serious drinking. Didn't see much of each other for a long time then, but he heard things from time to time: Hollis was boosting cars, was on the run, was doing time.

Not long after he lost his job, they met up again, neighborhood bar on Atlantic that he liked because they had no music or TV and, late morning, early afternoon, there'd be a lot of women coming through, usually in groups. They didn't recognize each other at first. Guy on the next stool looked up like him to watch three young women in gym

clothes enter and said, "Lesbo bar is what I'm thinking."
They took a closer look at each other then and realized.

Wasn't much catching up done, not a lot of talking either, after the first hour or two, but it was good to have a
friend, someone to sit with, drink a few beers, someone
with free time like him. And yeah, he had been wondering
what Hollis did to get by, what gave him all that free time,
but it's not the kind of thing you ask, once the first hints
get ignored, right?

They got pretty tight over the next month or six weeks.

One afternoon, almost night really, they'd had five, six
beers by then, he guessed, and the after-work crowd had
started drifting in, Hollis's phone went off. He laughed at
all of them reaching for their phones, then realized it was
his and skipped outside to answer. Came back in time to
buy the next round, and along about the third sip maybe,
Hollis asked if by any chance he might be free the next
couple days and up to picking up a nice chunk of change.
Naturally he asked for doing what. His man had just canceled on him, Hollis said. He had a pickup to make, and
sure could use the company. Nothing to it. And it paid
three hundred clear.

So he said yes and found himself in this godforsaken
place, no offense intended.

Things started going wrong from the first. Their flight
was delayed, the woman across the aisle puked in her
plastic tray of beef tips, some kid kept kicking the back of
his seat. The first rental car stalled out two miles from the

airport in Memphis. They had to call, wait over an hour, then take whatever was available, which turned out to be this clunky van that pulled hard to the right.

He didn't know what Hollis's intentions were, he was looking for someone, he knew that—then for something he couldn't find. By the time they got to the first house, where the old lady was, he was getting crazy, tearing up everything, hitting her—just once, but it didn't take much. It was like you could see that kid on the playground coming out of him all over again, you know? And it kept on getting worse. At the second place, he watched the woman while Hollis went through the house getting angrier all the time. It was when he realized Hollis planned on taking the woman that he got . . . not scared, but . . . sick. Physically ill. Heart pounding, skin crawling. Like he was going out of his body, leaving it behind.

He was in the backseat and he kept asking Hollis to stop this, take her back, this was just flat-out crazy, and Hollis kept telling him to shut up. At one point, scooting forward in the seat, he kicked the woman's purse, which was on the floor by him. Something heavy in there. He took it out, told Hollis to stop the car, and when Hollis laughed, he shot him.

He figured there had to be a farmhouse or something somewhere, he'd carry him there and get help if he was still alive, but there wasn't. And he couldn't. He was going to call, get help for the woman too, but when Hollis died, he just got scared, really scared.

Hollis had made him memorize that phone number and name, in case anything happened to him. To Hollis, that is. He was just supposed to call, say where they were, nothing more.

And that was it. He stopped talking and sat looking down at the table, lost in thoughts of Brooklyn and the past, maybe thinking how far away that past seemed now, or maybe just used up, empty. I stopped the tape. The light outside was muted, tentative. I could hear wind coming down Main Street, the shake of roofs, the shudder of doors and windows. I smelled dust, and rain. And I felt all about me the sadness of endings.

CHAPTER EIGHTEEN

MUCH OF THE REST of the story, we got from Milly two days later up in Memphis, what she'd pieced together from Troy's and Hollis's jagged conversation. She was propped up in bed, leg in traction, tubes running out of her chest into a Pleurovac, right arm in a cast. One or another caretaker, a nurse, an aide, had brushed her hair on the right, the left side having been shaved and stitched, and (at Milly's request?) put on blush and lipstick, unsettling against the bruises and wormy scars. She looked half little girl's doll, half ghoul.

It was all about something Billy'd got messed up in. Something he'd stolen, or found, or was holding, she still didn't know. Didn't know where either, if it was here before he left, or up in Hazelwood, but she thought Hazelwood.

The driver kept saying he had a job to do and his ass was dirt if he didn't get it done and these hicks were getting seriously in his way and on his nerves. First time he said that, she thought he said "ticks." The other one kept patting her on the shoulder, telling her it was going to be all right, and asking the driver, What are you going to do with the woman, Hollis, she can't help you. Telling him to pull over, stop. She remembered the driver laughing and not much after that.

Someone had been in the house, she was sure of that when she got home. Just didn't *feel* right. She never drank Cokes, and if she did she would never leave a can on the sink but there was one there, that had probably been in the icebox since Billy left. He was the Coke drinker. Then she noticed a few other things. Kitchen drawers weren't pushed shut, the door to the basement had been opened—you could tell because it was right next to the water heater and the paint kind of half-melted so the door stuck in the frame, then tore loose when it was opened. Things like that. She didn't know why, she hadn't even thought about the gun, all but forgot it was there, but before she knew it she'd gone in the bedroom and got it, shoved it in her purse. Then she kept the purse with her as she went through the house turning on lights. They were standing outside, behind the house, when she snapped on the lights back there. And she just stood there as they came in.

"One of them's dead," she said. "A nurse told me that." Her eyes were fixed not on mine but on the wall over my shoulder. When I took a step closer, she looked away.

"And we have the other one."

She reached up to readjust the NG tube, nostril reddened and crusty around it. "He tried to help me."

"Yes."

"His friend's dead."

I nodded.

"I was almost dead," she said.

"You're going to be okay."

"And Billy's dead."

"Yes. Yes, he is."

Before leaving we spoke with Milly's doctor, a thin, gangly woman of indeterminate nationality wearing a black T-shirt, scrub pants, and cheap white sneakers without socks. Physically, she said, there was every expectation that Milly would make a full recovery. She was showing signs of traumatic amnesia, remembering things then forgetting them, but with luck, and obviously she was due some, that should pass as well. It's similar to a short circuit, Dr. Paul said. The spark gets sent, there's power in the wires, sometimes the bulb lights, sometimes it doesn't. Or it flickers and goes out.

Lonnie was silent most of the way back to town, looking out the side window. Many fields remained partially under water; trees and the occasional power or telephone line were down. Here and there, blackbirds and crows crowded together at water's edge, covens of diminutive priests.

"You look back much, Turner? How things were?"

"Sure I do."

"Lot back there."

"At least, if we're lucky, it's not gaining on us."

"But it rears up and grabs us sooner or later, doesn't it?"

Does it? Patterns. You make of them what you will.

"She's going to be okay, Lonnie. She'll get over it."

"Of course. And so will Shirley, from our losing Billy. That's what we do." He turned from the window to look straight ahead. "I'm just damn tired of getting over things, Turner."

To our right, westward, over past Kansas and Oklahoma, the sun was sinking. As delta, cropland, and congregations of crows rolled by beside us, I told Lonnie what Doc had told me that night at the cabin, and when I was through he didn't say anything about miracles or prayers or remission, as I knew he wouldn't, he just sat there a moment, looked over at me and said, "That sucks too."

CHAPTER NINETEEN

"NOT THE BEST DECISION you ever made," I told Lonnie three days later. We were back in Memphis, waiting at the airport. Lonnie was flying to St. Louis and I'd driven him up. At check-in he'd flashed his badge to account for the handgun in his luggage. That was another argument I'd lost, just as I—not to mention Shirley, Doc and Don Lee—had lost the one about his going in the first place.

"Could be one of the worst," he said. "But I want to look at him face-to-face and tell him what he's done."

"He knows what he's done, Lonnie. He doesn't care. And he's not the kind of man it's easy to get face-to-face with."

"I'll manage."

Doubtless he would. There was no one for whom I had more respect than I had for Lonnie Bates, no one I thought smarter or more capable. I didn't know what he was feeling about Billy's death. We can never know how others feel, however much we pretend. I hoped it wasn't guilt. Guilt is a treacherous motivator.

Should you ever want a cross-section of America's minions, airports like this are where you'll find it. Students in torn jeans and T-shirts or in goth black and rattling when they walk; businessmen with one ear flattened from chronic cell phone use; families with groaning luggage carts topped by a stuffed bear; shell-shocked travelers who keep pulling tickets and itineraries out of pockets or purses and going back up to the check-in desk to ask questions; solitary men and women who sit staring ahead hardly moving until their flight is called; fidgeters and tap dancers and sub voce singers whose tonsils you see jumping in their cage; faces lit by faint hope that where they are going will be a happier, a better, a more tolerant, or at least a less painful place than the one they're leaving.

I remembered part of a poem Cy put in a letter: *The way your life is ruined here, in this small corner of the world, is the way it's ruined everywhere.* I had that quote on my cell wall for months. Strange, what can give you solace.

Lonnie was drinking coffee out of a plastic cup large enough to be used as a bucket to extinguish small fires. It had boxes to be checked on the side, showing all the choices available to us out here in the free world, and, at the top, vents vaguely reminiscent of gills.

Besides the quote, I was also remembering Cy's story about a client of his, one of those he called cyclers, people who come for a while, fade out, return. Guy'd been away most of a year and was so changed that Cy barely recognized him. Like looking at a mask, trying to make out the features beneath, Cy said. In the course of conversation Cy asked where he was living these days. The man looked around, as though he were trying the room on for size (again, Cy's analogy), and said "Mostly in the past." He was at work, he explained, on a major project, The Museum of Real America. What he was doing was collecting signs people held up at the side of the road. He'd give them a dollar or two. STRANDED. WILL WORK FOR FOOD. HOMELESS GOD BLESS. VETERAN—TWICE. Had over thirty of them now. Quite a display.

Lonnie spoke beside me. "I can remember rushing through the airport at the last minute, jumping on the plane just as they pulled up the gangway. Now you have to arrive two hours ahead, bring a note from your mother, walk through hoops, have dogs sniff you. Take off your goddamn shoes."

"Anyone tell you you're beginning to sound like Doc?"

His eyes moved to watch parents greet a young man coming down the corridor from the plane he'd be taking, then shifted back. "Things just get harder and harder, Turner."

He was right, of course. Things get harder, and we get soft. Or, some of us, we harden too, less and less of the world making it through to us.

"June tell you she was getting married?"

She hadn't.

"Her so-called gardener," Lonnie went on. "Man mows yards for a living, is what he does. This August. She wanted to ask you . . . But I guess I'd best leave that between the two of you."

Lonnie hadn't said anything more after our conversation in the Jeep coming home from Memphis three days back, but the awareness was there in his eyes, and for that moment I could feel it moving about in the narrow space between us. The world is so very full of words. And yet so much that's important goes forever unsaid.

Minutes later Lonnie's flight was called. I stood watching his plane taxi out, wait its turn, and begin its plunge, thinking about power, gravity's pride, about that magic moment when the ground lets go and you're weightless, free.

I had no idea what awaited my friend.

On the drive back, I rummaged in the glove compartment and found the tape I'd made of Eldon and Val playing together years back on a slow Sunday afternoon of potato salad, grilled chicken and burgers, beer and iced tea. At first the tape spun without purchase and I was afraid it had broken or snagged, then Val's banjo came in, Eldon's guitar sifting quiet chords and bass runs behind her as she began singing.

> The engine whistled down the line
> A-blowing every station: McKinley's dying
> From Buffalo to Washington

The sky was eerily clear and bright as I coursed along listening to the two of them. After all I've seen in this life, I'm not an emotional man, but I could feel tears building, trying to push through. Two good friends gone.

I'd done my best to dissuade Lonnie right up to the end. Finally, knowing that was not going to happen, having known it from the first but dead set on trying, I handed him the package. We had just taken seats in the terminal. A line of German tourists wearing identical sweaters debarked from a plane painted with snowcaps, icy streams, and blue-white skies, as though it were its own small, mobile country.

"What the hell is this?"

"A sled, as far as I can tell."

Ignoring or innocent of my reference, he waited.

"I started thinking, and went back to the car, the Buick that Billy was driving. I called and found out it was still in Hazelwood while the city tried to figure out what to do with it, so I took Sonny and went up there. Anyone knows cars, it's Sonny. Sergeant Haskell arranged for us to use the garage that does all the work for the police department and city. Sonny kept asking me, What are you looking for? Hell if I knew.

"He started tearing the Buick down, poking around. Before long, the mechanic who owns the garage came over and started talking shop with Sonny. Next thing I know he's under the car working away too.

"After a while, Sonny finds me outside. 'Well, we know

what caused it,' he tells me. The wreck, he means, why Billy plowed into City Hall. Looks like a tie rod disconnect, he said. Car'd been sitting up unused, then gets driven hard—not that surprising.

"He goes back inside. Maybe a half hour, a little more, passes. Then he brings out this package, wrapped in what looks like canvas or oilcloth—turned out to be an old chamois—with twine around it in a crisscross. The knot on the twine is a perfect bow. Inside the chamois there's a box with a faded silk scarf, another crisscross, this one of ribbon, and a tiny ball, like a Christmas-tree ornament. Thing had been under the seat, jammed into the springs.

"It's a necklace," I told Lonnie. "Silver, underneath a few decades of tarnish. Engraved inside with two small hearts, one with the initials LH, the other with AC."

"LH . . ."

"Could well be Lorenzo Harmon. AC is Augusta Chorley."

"The old lady."

"She wasn't always old, Lonnie. And it appears that her life may not have been as empty as everyone thought. She really did have a treasure out there, albeit it a personal one."

He held the package up, weighing it, thinking, I'm sure, of the damage that had accrued around it. "And Billy?"

"A messenger, maybe, delivering the necklace to someone here in town, or up in Memphis—with or without

Miss Chorley's knowledge. Or it could only be that the necklace has been in the car all these years, forgotten."

"Here we've been thinking this whole thing had to do with money, drugs—"

"The usual suspects, yes. And it still may have. The necklace could be coincidence."

"That's a lot of maybes."

I spread my hands in mock resignation. "Go have your face-to-face with Harmon. If you choose to, give the necklace to him. For good or bad—I've no idea. See what happens."

"I'd be finishing Billy's job."

Again I spread my hands at the world's uncertainties, its unreadability.

As afterwards, driving home alone in the Jeep, listening to Eldon and Val, I shrugged at the same. Briefly Val retuned to one of the old mountain tunings, sawmill or double C, then came the hard stutter of clawhammer, and her voice.

> Li'l birdie, li'l birdie
> Come sing to me a song
> I've a short while to be here
> And a long time to be gone

CHAPTER TWENTY

SO MANY STORIES LEAVE YOU standing at the altar. The crisis has been met, the many obstacles averted or overcome, most everything's back to the way it was before or has righted itself to some new still point. You always wonder what happened to these people. Because they had pasts, they had lives, before you began reading. And they have futures, some of them, once you stop.

I remember a story I read years ago, hanging at a news-stand on Lamar waiting for the bar across the street to open for the day. Must have been the early seventies. I wasn't long out of Nam. On the first page this young guy stands on a hill looking down into the valley where the worms that tried to take over the world are dead and dying. He did that. He saved the world. Then for the next ten pages and the rest of his life he's living in a trailer park drinking beer for breakfast and bouncing off bad relationships.

That's pretty much how it goes, for most of us. We don't stub our toes on streets of gold and lead rich lives, we don't tell the people we love how much we love them when it matters, we never quite inhabit the shadows we cast as we cross this world. We just go on.

And some of us, a self-chosen few, go about finding how much music we can make with what we have left.

In my dream that night I couldn't find the town I live in. Friends and family awaited me, I knew, and I had started out for home hours before but somehow kept losing my way. Parts of the town, certain streets and buildings, looked familiar, others didn't, and I was always close, always *almost* home, but could never make it there. Occasionally in the distance I would catch glimpses of the sea, of high-rise buildings, of missile silos and grain elevators, of clouds and darkening sky.

I didn't go home or to the office that day upon returning from Memphis. Instead I did something I'd been putting off a long time.

The house had sat empty since the day Val died. I kept telling myself I should go over there, and thinking about it, but there was always a swing through the town in the Jeep that needed doing, or paperwork to attend to, or one more cup of coffee to drink at the diner, and I never did.

It didn't look greatly different from the outside, simply abandoned. I thought of faces—I'd seen a lot of them, in prison, and in my practice—that showed no emotion. Weather had had its way with roof and windows, and a tree nearby had split down the length of its trunk, taking out half a room at the back. Runners had advanced (the word *politely* came to mind) onto porch and sides.

I don't know what I expected to find, save memories. But I certainly didn't expect to find what I did. I used the key Val had given me when she planned to go on the road with Eldon, stepped in, and stopped just inside the door. As handy with a hammer or saw as with a banjo (her words), Val had been at work restoring the old house since before we met. Three rooms had been pretty much done, as far as basics go—framework, floors, walls.

Now it was all but finished.

I went from room to room: smooth hardwood banisters, coving expertly fitted at juncture of floor and wall, inlays of tile at thresholds, crown molding curved like bird wings overhead, two-tone paint in most rooms, what looked like period wallpaper in a couple of them. It was stunning.

Someone had spent a lot of time in here. Someone with amazing skill. And with motivations I couldn't even begin to guess at.

In this small town where we all know one another's business, or think we do. 'Round here you sneeze, Doc says, and the people four houses down yell Bless you.

Ever the lawyer, Val, as we found out following her death, had a will on file. The house was mine. I stood wondering, trying to imagine who might be moved to come here day after day, month after month, to do all this work, and what that person's reasons could possibly be.

Maybe, like so much in life, reason had little to do with it.

Then puzzlement turned to laughter at the sheer, wonderful craziness of this. You get to be my age, you figure life doesn't have many surprises left for you. And here I was, in my dead girlfriend's house that time and weather had done its best to destroy and that someone had gone hell-bent on bringing back to life.

I sat there most of the afternoon, on the floor, out on the porch, out under one of the trees, marveling.

CHAPTER TWENTY-ONE

BACK TO STORIES, then. Here's where we are. Here's what happened.

Next day, a little after noon but decidedly dark for that hour, I'm sitting outside the office in an all-but-deserted downtown. Lonnie is in St. Louis doing what he feels he has to do. Milly lies slowly fitting the pieces of her world back together in a Memphis hospital room. Val's house, my house, having withstood well over a hundred years of ravage and neglect, stands waiting for the blows that finally will bring it down. The weather service has announced a major storm heading directly toward us, torrential rains, sixty-mile-an-hour winds, funnel clouds. We can see it already in this plum-dark sky, smell it on the breeze beginning to assert itself, as lights go on in houses at town's edge. Birds have taken to, then deserted, the wires. Dogs bay in the distance.

The storm is coming in. And the town, in its last hour, is waiting.

My daughter sits beside me.

An hour ago the door opened, right beside the new window we at last got installed, and there she was. Longer hair, but looking much the same. Except for fresh stitches over one eye.

"Nice scar."

"Important thing is, he came around to my way of thinking."

"I'll bet he did."

After a moment she said, "Doc Oldham called."

"Man's a public nuisance."

We made coffee and sat around catching up, like so many times before. As though nothing were different. Her department had put in a computer system no one could figure out, there was a new drug on the street, last month they'd had a murder in, of all places, the Wal-Mart parking lot. I filled her in on Billy, Eldon, and the rest. Told her about Val's house. And how not long before she arrived, Isaiah Stillman and a group from the colony had come walking down Main Street, saying they were here to do what they could to help.

At her suggestion we took the last of the coffee outside and sat on the bench polished by a generation or so of butts.

"Good seat for the show," she said.

"Best in the house."

So here we are. The air is charged, electric. I think back to Lonnie's plane, that moment just before the ground lets go. That's what it feels like.

Takeoffs. Landings. And the lives that happen in between.

"Thought I might stick around a while, if that's all right," J. T. says.

"Probably ought to be my line." We both laugh. "Though from the look of things . . ."

"Who knows. Could be I'll spot my first airborne cow."

"There you go, Miss City Dweller. Having your fun at the poor rural folks' expense."

Cabbages and kings don't come into it, as I recall, but, sitting there on the bench, we touch on close to everything else: J. T.'s childhood, my old partner on the MPD and my prison time, genealogy, where the country is headed politically, a novel she'd recently read about small-town life, the day Kennedy died, beer for breakfast back in Nam, third-strike offenders, Val.

Then we sit quietly, for an hour, maybe more, as black thunderheads roll in. Initially we see the jags of lightning and hear the muffled rumbling only through the dark screen of clouds. Then it breaks through. The rain, when it comes, is sweet and stinging.

A heavy metal trash can rolls down the street, driven by wind. "City tumbleweed," J. T. says, and when I look at her there are tears in her eyes. I reach and touch her face, gently.

"I'm not crying because I'm sad," my daughter says. "I'm crying because we're here, together, watching this, I'm crying because of friends like Doc Oldham, because I have had the chance to get to know you. I am crying because the world is so beautiful."

As should we all.